BASED ON THE *NEW YORK TIMES* BESTSELLING SERIES

Five Nights at Freddy's™

FAZBEAR FRIGHTS

GRAPHIC NOVEL COLLECTION VOL. 3

BY SCOTT CAWTHON,

KELLY PARRA, AND ANDREA WAGGENER

ADAPTED BY CHRISTOPHER HASTINGS

STEP CLOSER
ILLUSTRATED BY DIDI ESMERALDA
COLORS BY BEN SAWYER

BUNNY CALL
ILLUSTRATED BY CORYN MacPHERSON
COLORS BY GONZALO DUARTE

HIDE-AND-SEEK
ILLUSTRATED BY DIANA CAMERO
COLORS BY JUDY LAI

LETTERS BY TAYLOR ESPOSITO

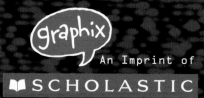
graphix
An Imprint of
■SCHOLASTIC

All rights reserved. Published by Graphix, an imprint of Scholastic Inc.,
Publishers since 1920. SCHOLASTIC, GRAPHIX, and associated logos are
trademarks and/or registered trademarks of Scholastic Inc.

The publisher does not have any control over and does not assume any
responsibility for author or third-party websites or their content.

ISBN 978-1-338-86046-7 (hardcover)

ISBN 978-1-338-86042-9 (paperback)

10 9 8 7 6 5 4 3 2 1   23 24 25 26 27

Printed in China   62

First edition, September 2023

Edited by Michael Petranek

Book Design by Jeff Shake

Inks by Didi Esmeralda, Coryn MacPherson, and Diana Camero

Colors by Ben Sawyer, Gonzalo Duarte, and Judy Lai

Letters by Taylor Esposito

Layout Compositor: Dawn Guzzo

STEP CLOSER

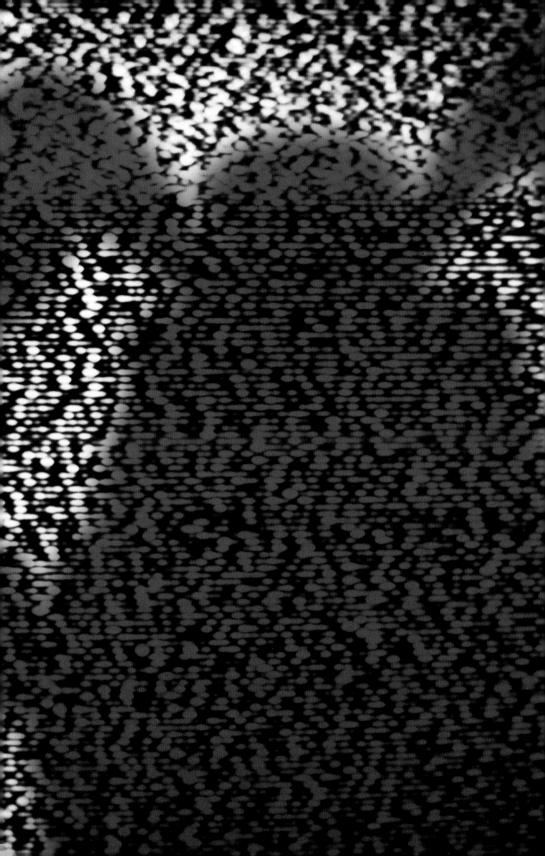

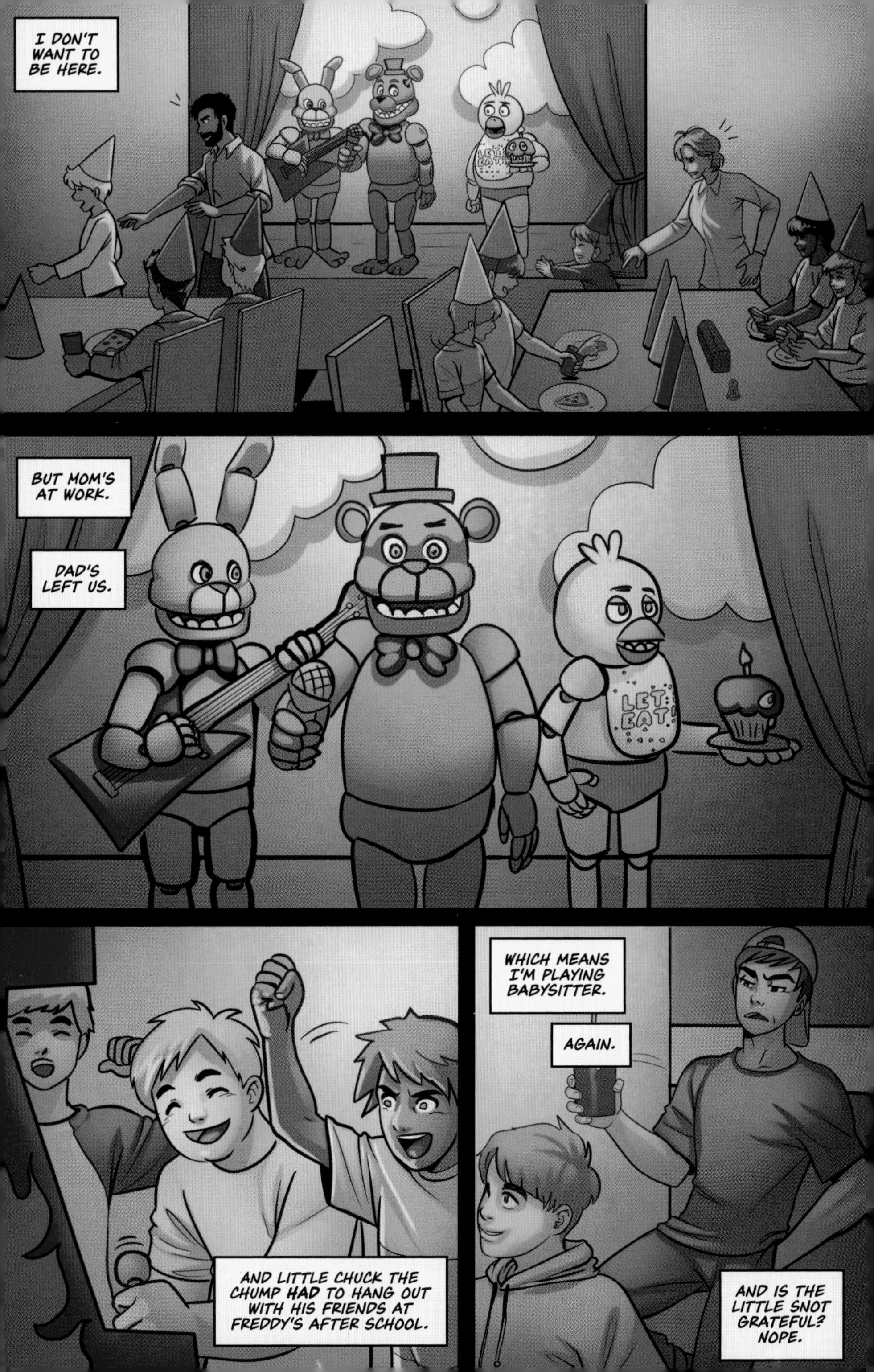
I DON'T WANT TO BE HERE.
BUT MOM'S AT WORK.
DAD'S LEFT US.
LET'S EAT!
AND LITTLE CHUCK THE CHUMP **HAD** TO HANG OUT WITH HIS FRIENDS AT FREDDY'S AFTER SCHOOL.
WHICH MEANS I'M PLAYING BABYSITTER.
AGAIN.
AND IS THE LITTLE SNOT GRATEFUL? NOPE.

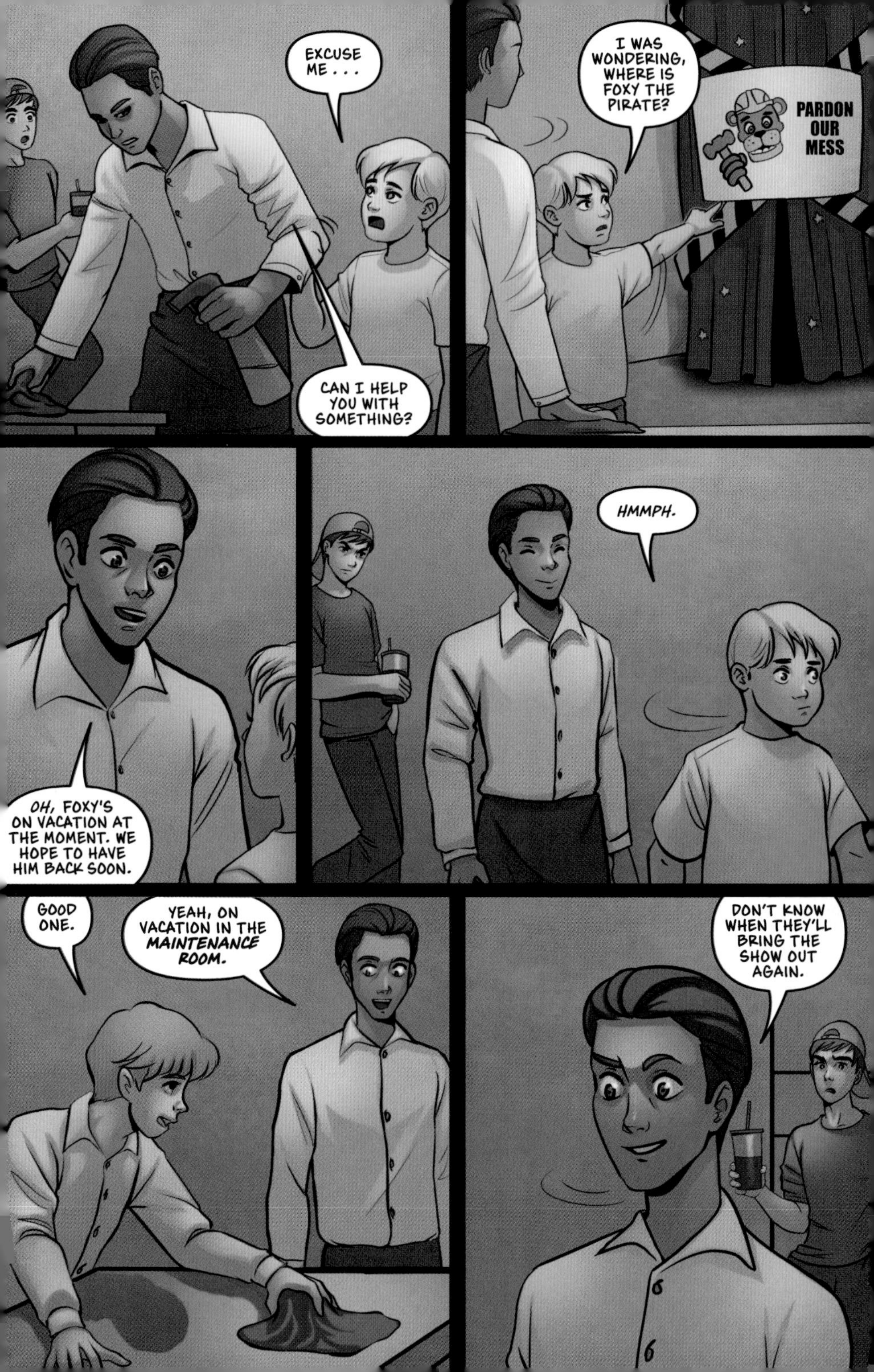
EXCUSE ME . . .
CAN I HELP YOU WITH SOMETHING?
I WAS WONDERING, WHERE IS FOXY THE PIRATE?
PARDON OUR MESS
OH, FOXY'S ON VACATION AT THE MOMENT. WE HOPE TO HAVE HIM BACK SOON.
HMMPH.
GOOD ONE.
YEAH, ON VACATION IN THE MAINTENANCE ROOM.
DON'T KNOW WHEN THEY'LL BRING THE SHOW OUT AGAIN.

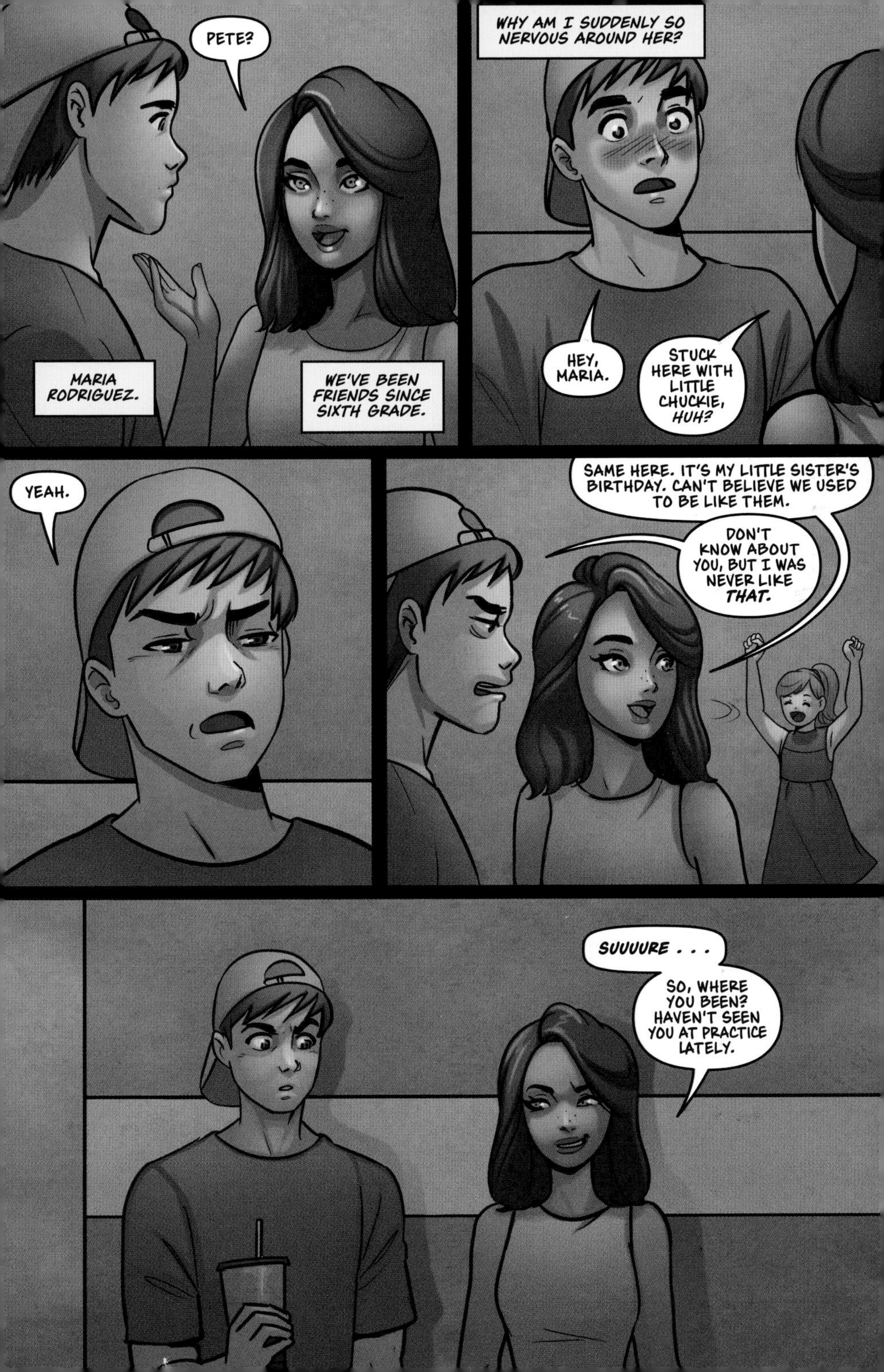
PETE?
MARIA RODRIGUEZ.
WE'VE BEEN FRIENDS SINCE SIXTH GRADE.
WHY AM I SUDDENLY SO NERVOUS AROUND HER?
HEY, MARIA.
STUCK HERE WITH LITTLE CHUCKIE, HUH?
YEAH.
SAME HERE. IT'S MY LITTLE SISTER'S BIRTHDAY. CAN'T BELIEVE WE USED TO BE LIKE THEM.
DON'T KNOW ABOUT YOU, BUT I WAS NEVER LIKE *THAT.*
SUUUURE . . .
SO, WHERE YOU BEEN? HAVEN'T SEEN YOU AT PRACTICE LATELY.

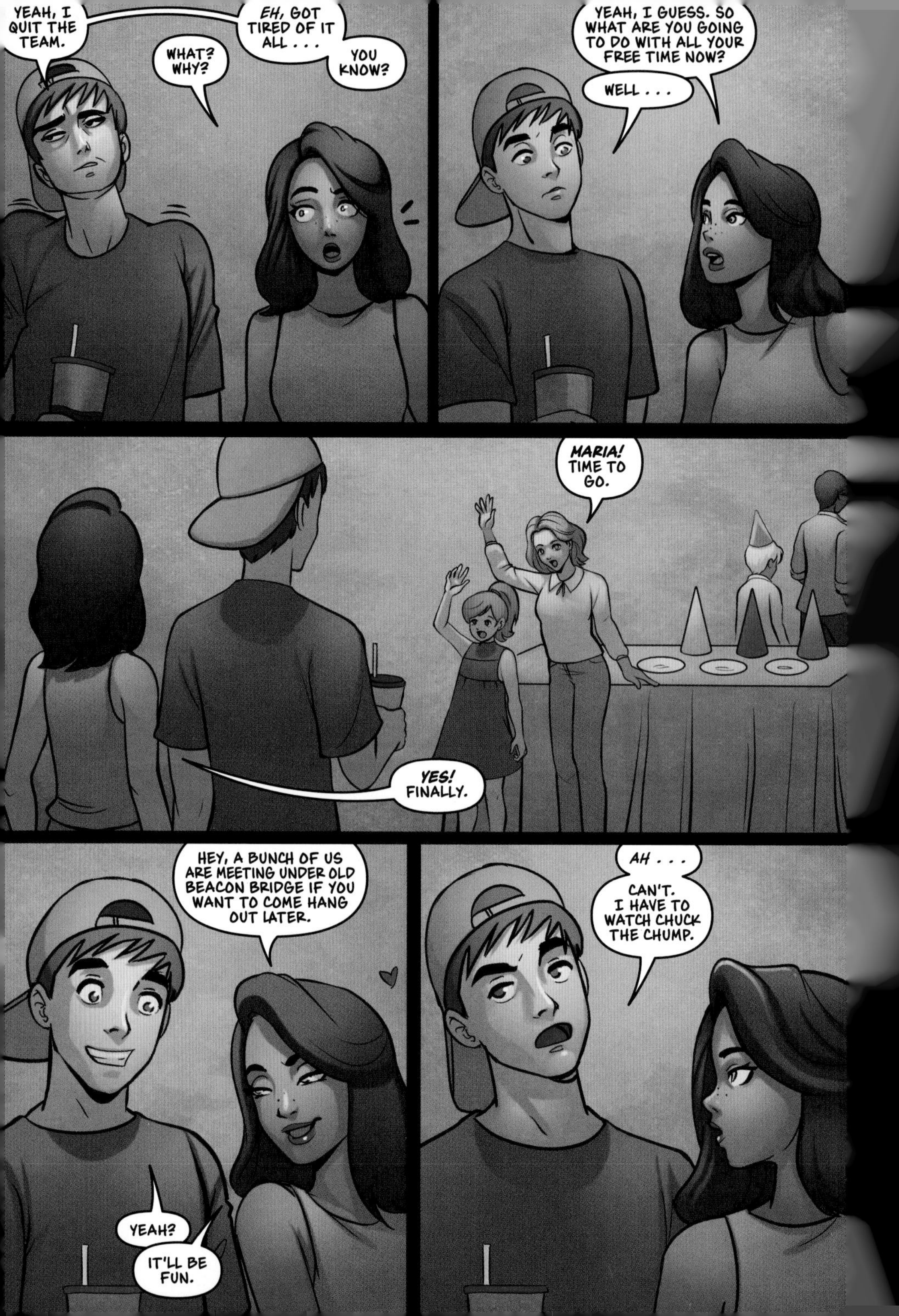
YEAH, I QUIT THE TEAM.
WHAT? WHY?
EH, GOT TIRED OF IT ALL . . .
YOU KNOW?
YEAH, I GUESS. SO WHAT ARE YOU GOING TO DO WITH ALL YOUR FREE TIME NOW?
WELL . . .
MARIA! TIME TO GO.
YES! FINALLY.
HEY, A BUNCH OF US ARE MEETING UNDER OLD BEACON BRIDGE IF YOU WANT TO COME HANG OUT LATER.
YEAH?
IT'LL BE FUN.
AH . . .
CAN'T. I HAVE TO WATCH CHUCK THE CHUMP.

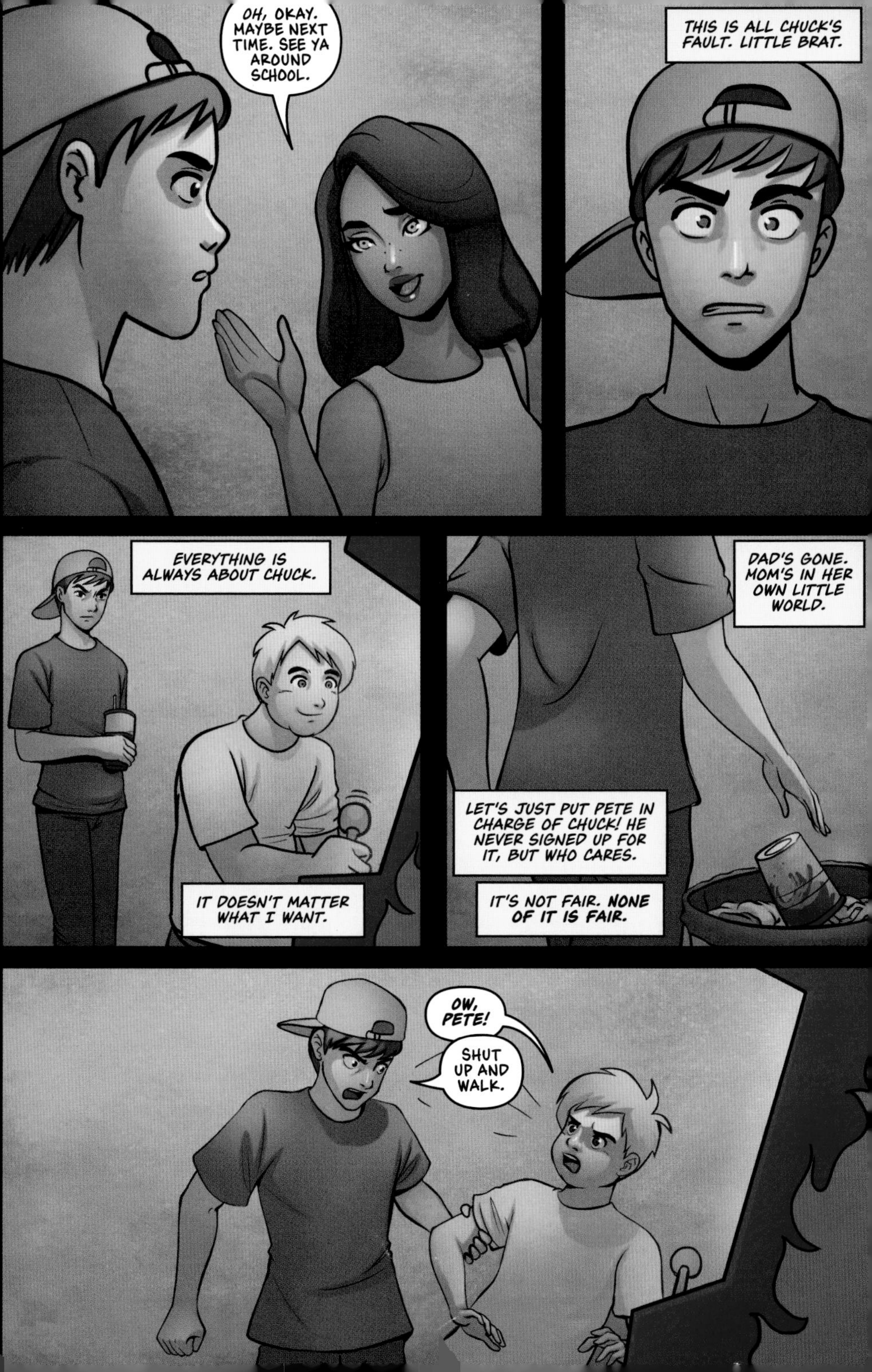
OH, OKAY. MAYBE NEXT TIME. SEE YA AROUND SCHOOL.
THIS IS ALL CHUCK'S FAULT. LITTLE BRAT.
EVERYTHING IS ALWAYS ABOUT CHUCK.
IT DOESN'T MATTER WHAT I WANT.
DAD'S GONE. MOM'S IN HER OWN LITTLE WORLD.
LET'S JUST PUT PETE IN CHARGE OF CHUCK! HE NEVER SIGNED UP FOR IT, BUT WHO CARES.
IT'S NOT FAIR. NONE OF IT IS FAIR.
OW, PETE!
SHUT UP AND WALK.

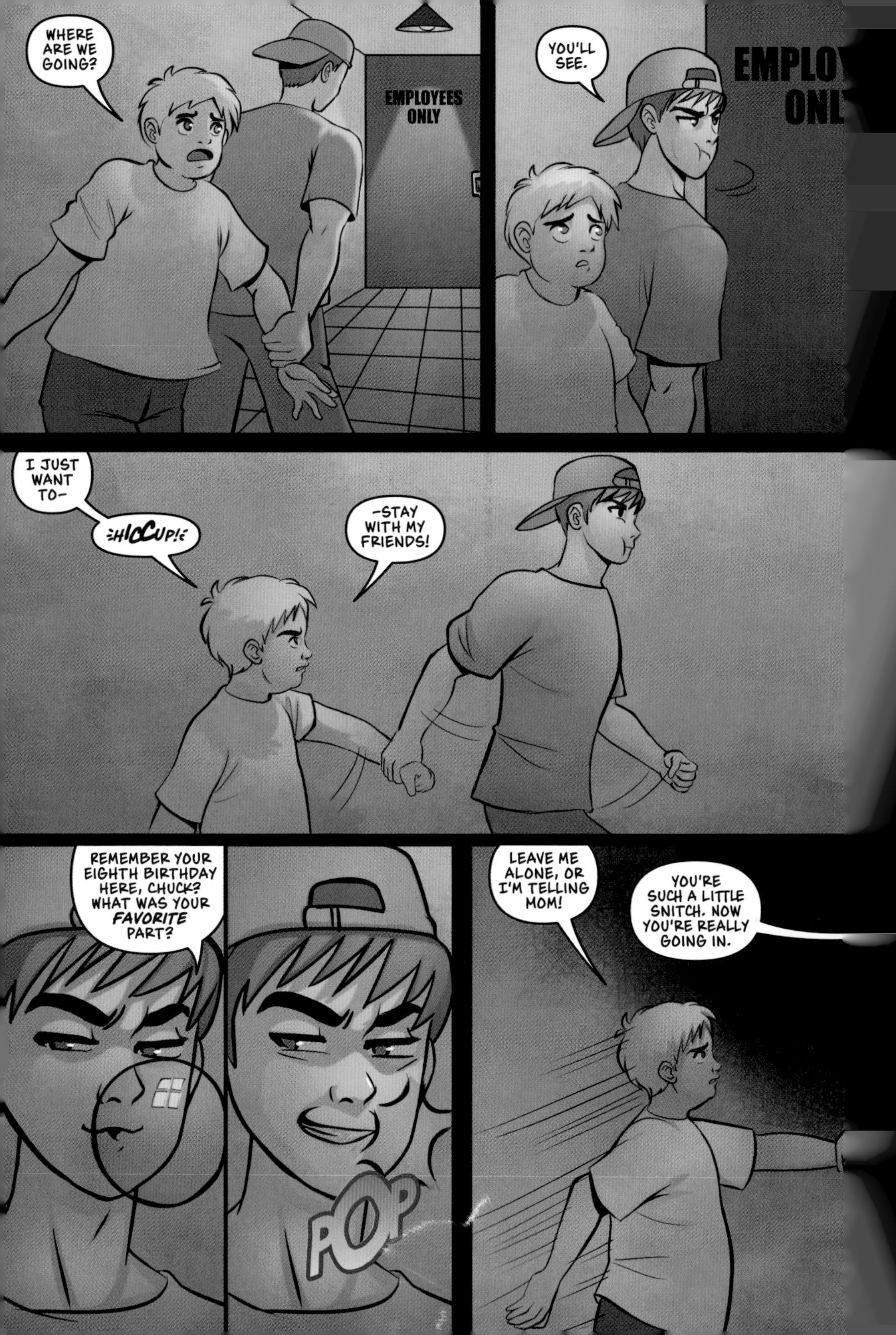
WHERE ARE WE GOING?
EMPLOYEES ONLY
YOU'LL SEE.
I JUST WANT TO-
HICCUP!
-STAY WITH MY FRIENDS!
REMEMBER YOUR EIGHTH BIRTHDAY HERE, CHUCK? WHAT WAS YOUR FAVORITE PART?
POP
LEAVE ME ALONE, OR I'M TELLING MOM!
YOU'RE SUCH A LITTLE SNITCH. NOW YOU'RE REALLY GOING IN.

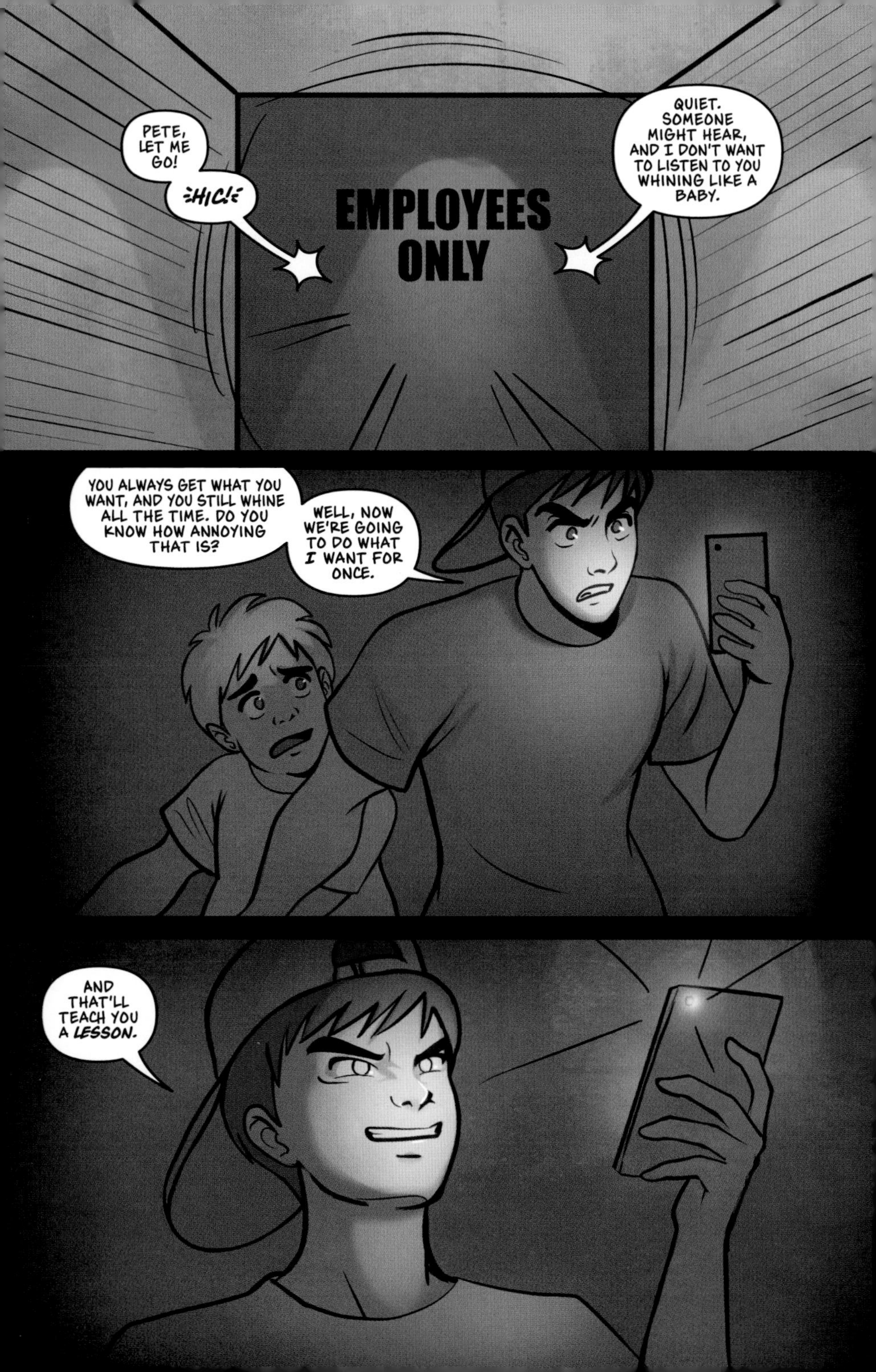
PETE, LET ME GO!
HIC!
QUIET. SOMEONE MIGHT HEAR, AND I DON'T WANT TO LISTEN TO YOU WHINING LIKE A BABY.
EMPLOYEES ONLY
YOU ALWAYS GET WHAT YOU WANT, AND YOU STILL WHINE ALL THE TIME. DO YOU KNOW HOW ANNOYING THAT IS?
WELL, NOW WE'RE GOING TO DO WHAT *I* WANT FOR ONCE.
AND THAT'LL TEACH YOU A *LESSON*.

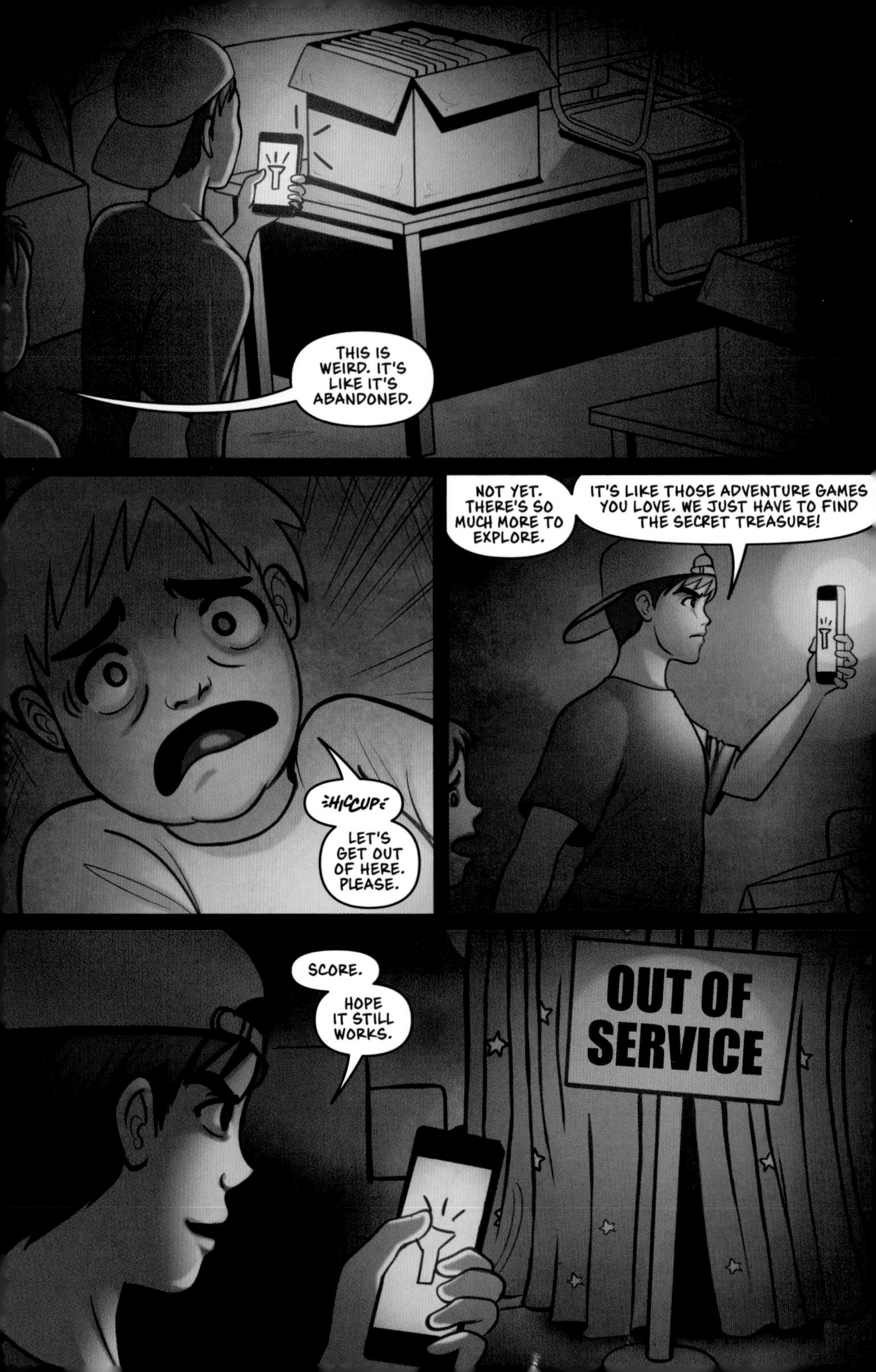
THIS IS WEIRD. IT'S LIKE IT'S ABANDONED.
HICCUP
LET'S GET OUT OF HERE. PLEASE.
NOT YET. THERE'S SO MUCH MORE TO EXPLORE.
IT'S LIKE THOSE ADVENTURE GAMES YOU LOVE. WE JUST HAVE TO FIND THE SECRET TREASURE!
SCORE.
HOPE IT STILL WORKS.
OUT OF SERVICE

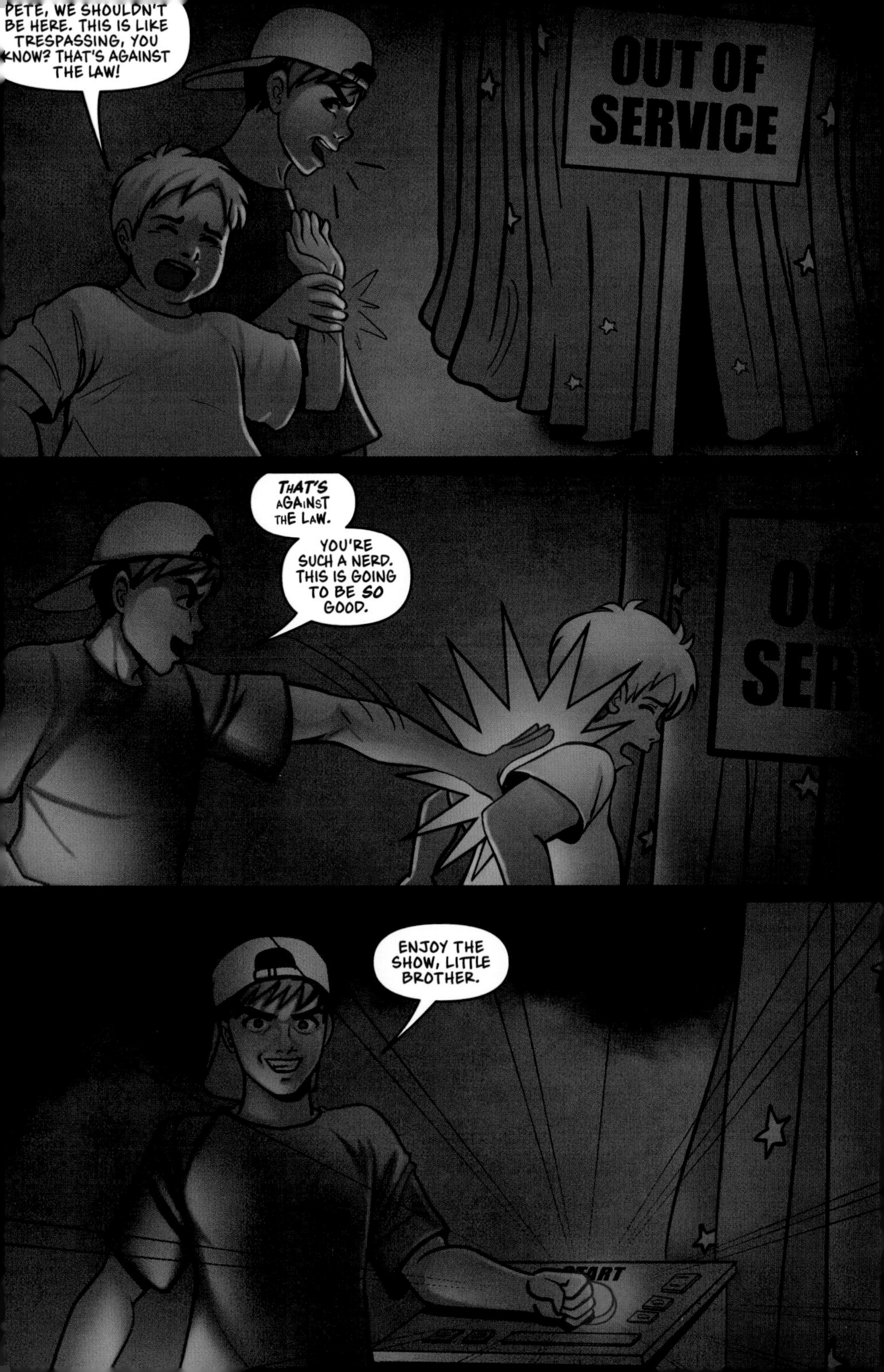
PETE, WE SHOULDN'T BE HERE. THIS IS LIKE TRESPASSING, YOU KNOW? THAT'S AGAINST THE LAW!
OUT OF SERVICE
THAT'S AGAINST THE LAW.
YOU'RE SUCH A NERD. THIS IS GOING TO BE SO GOOD.
ENJOY THE SHOW, LITTLE BROTHER.

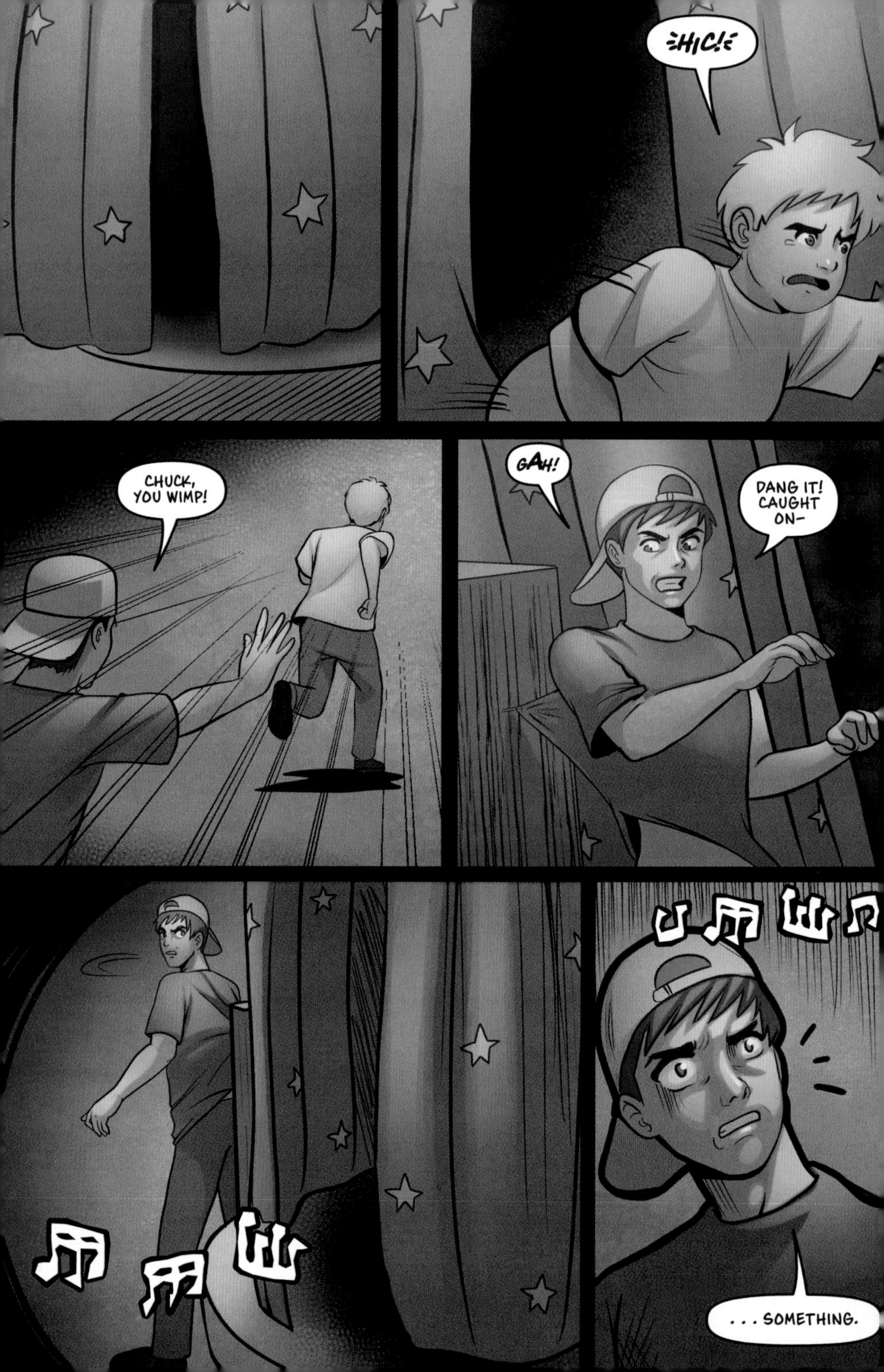
HIC!
CHUCK, YOU WIMP!
GAH!
DANG IT! CAUGHT ON–
. . . SOMETHING.

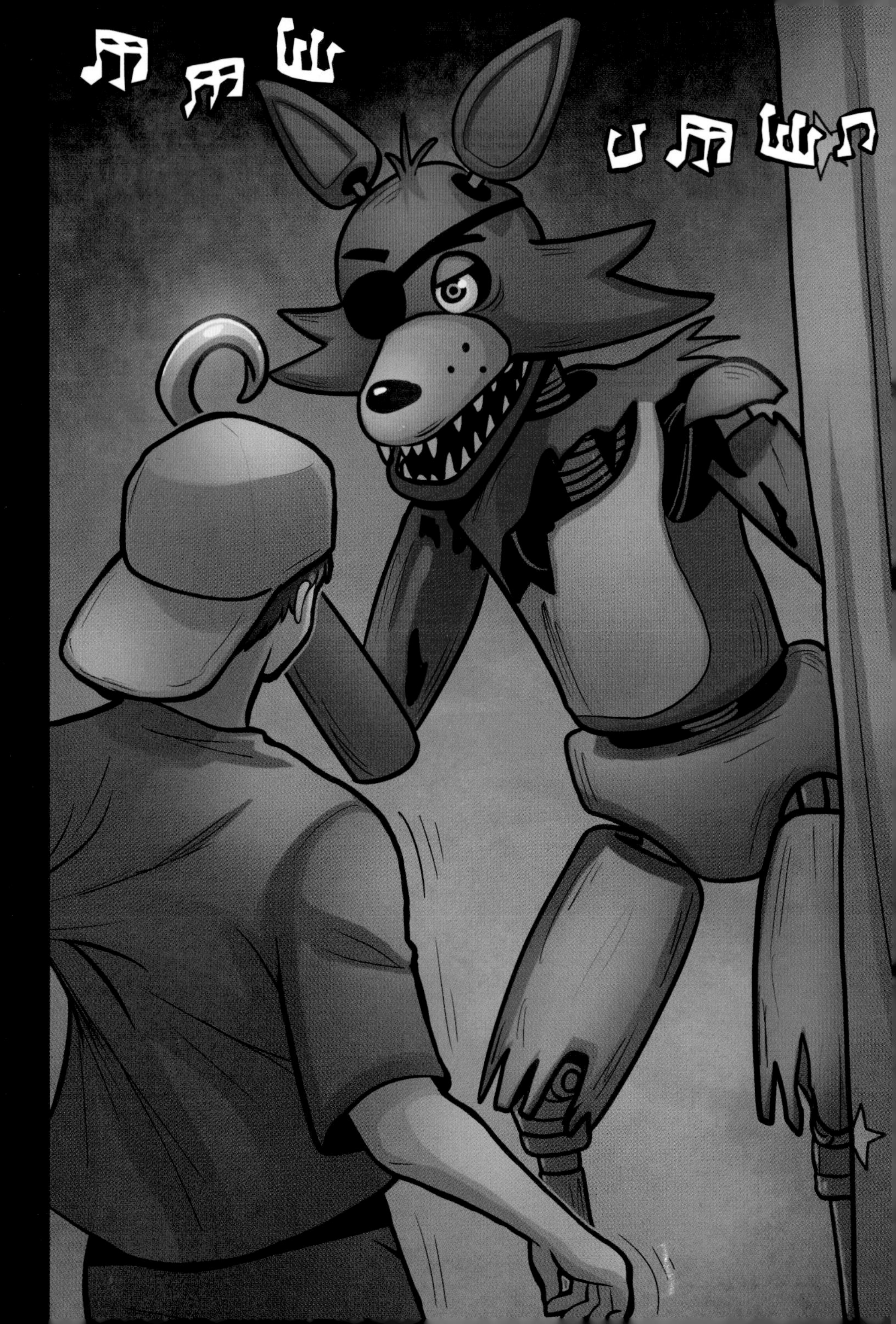

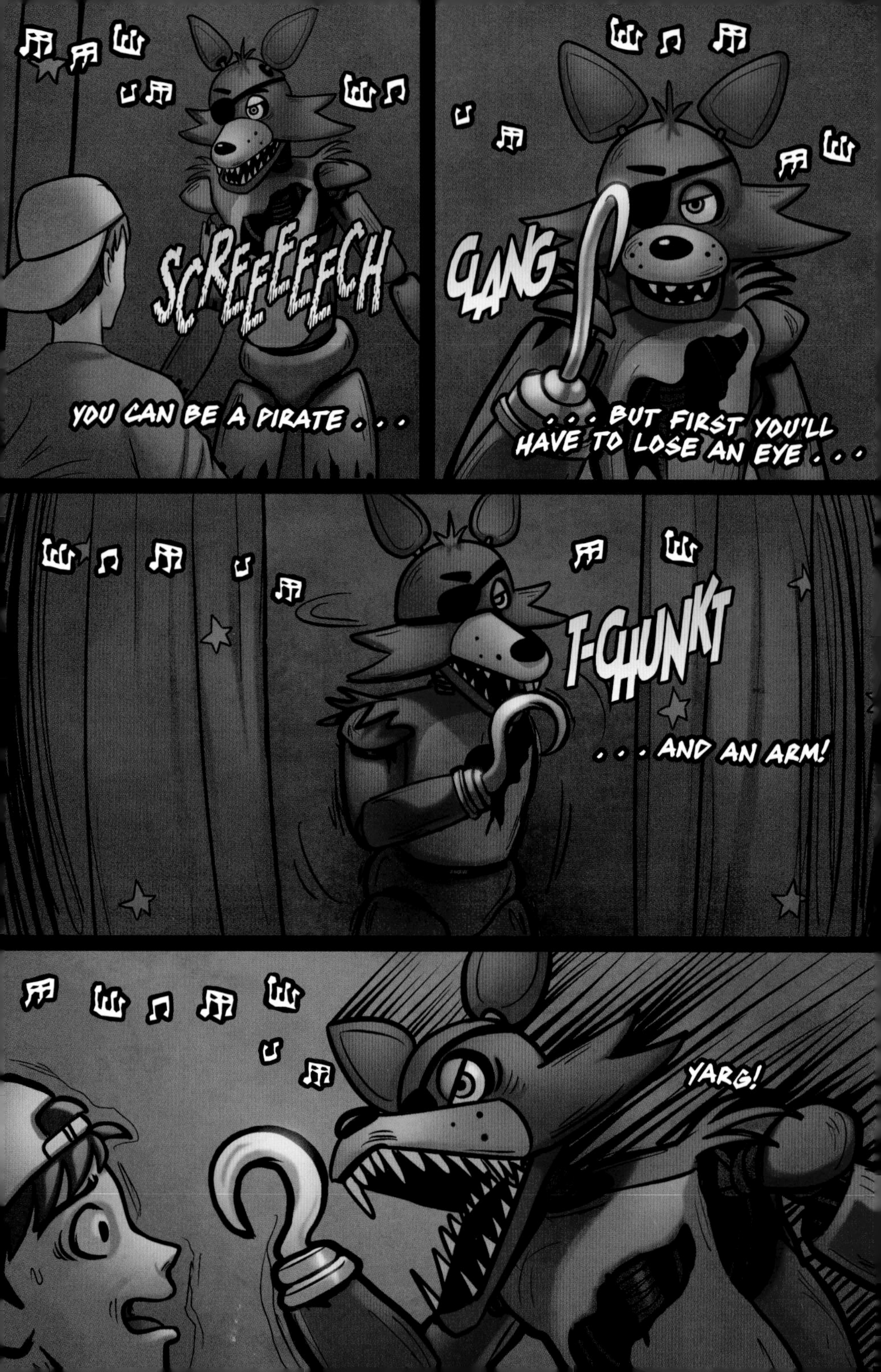
SCREEEEECH
YOU CAN BE A PIRATE . . .
CLANG
. . . BUT FIRST YOU'LL HAVE TO LOSE AN EYE . . .
T-CHUNKT
. . . AND AN ARM!
YARG!

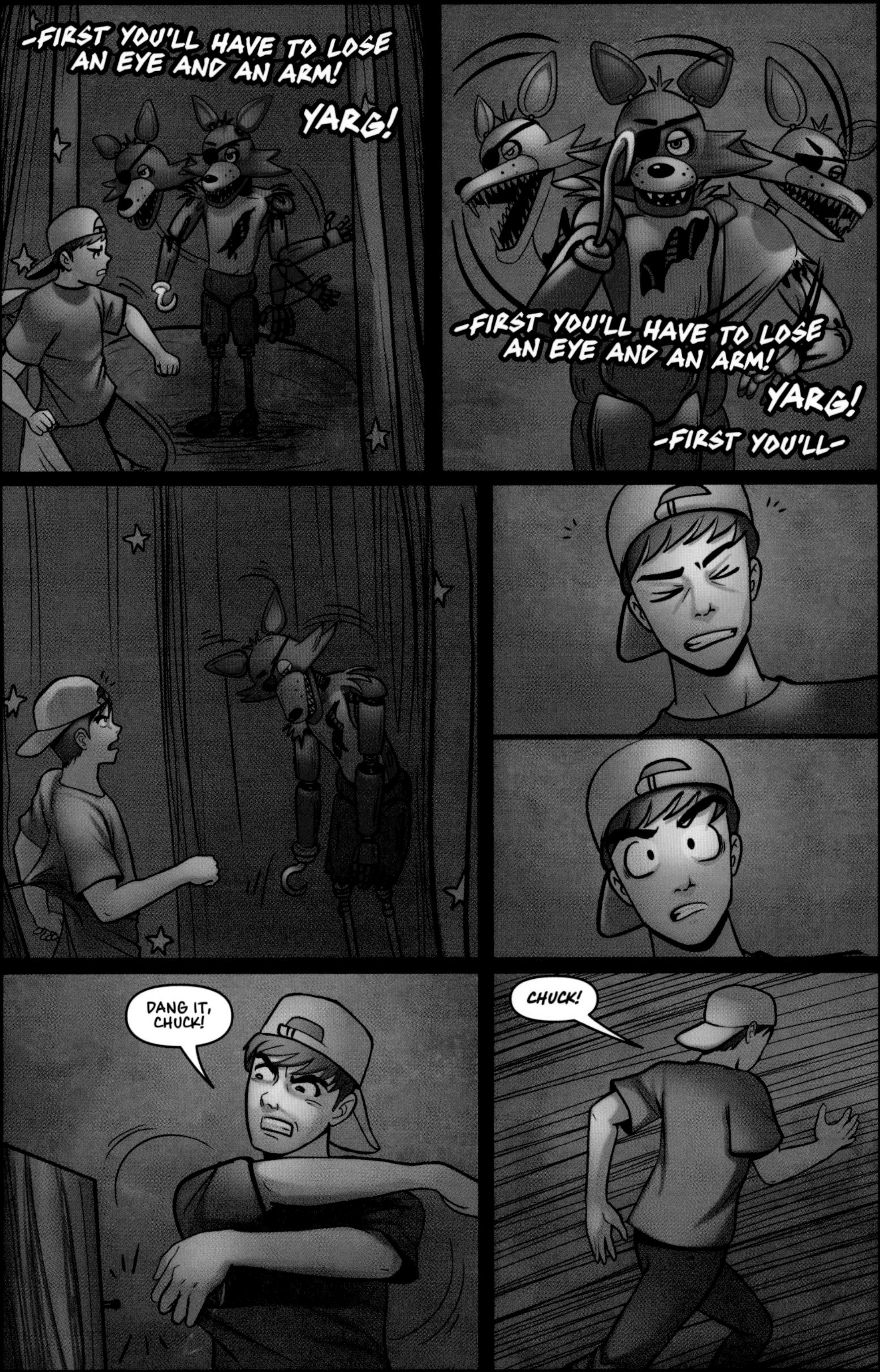
-FIRST YOU'LL HAVE TO LOSE AN EYE AND AN ARM!
YARG!
-FIRST YOU'LL HAVE TO LOSE AN EYE AND AN ARM!
YARG!
-FIRST YOU'LL-
DANG IT, CHUCK!
CHUCK!

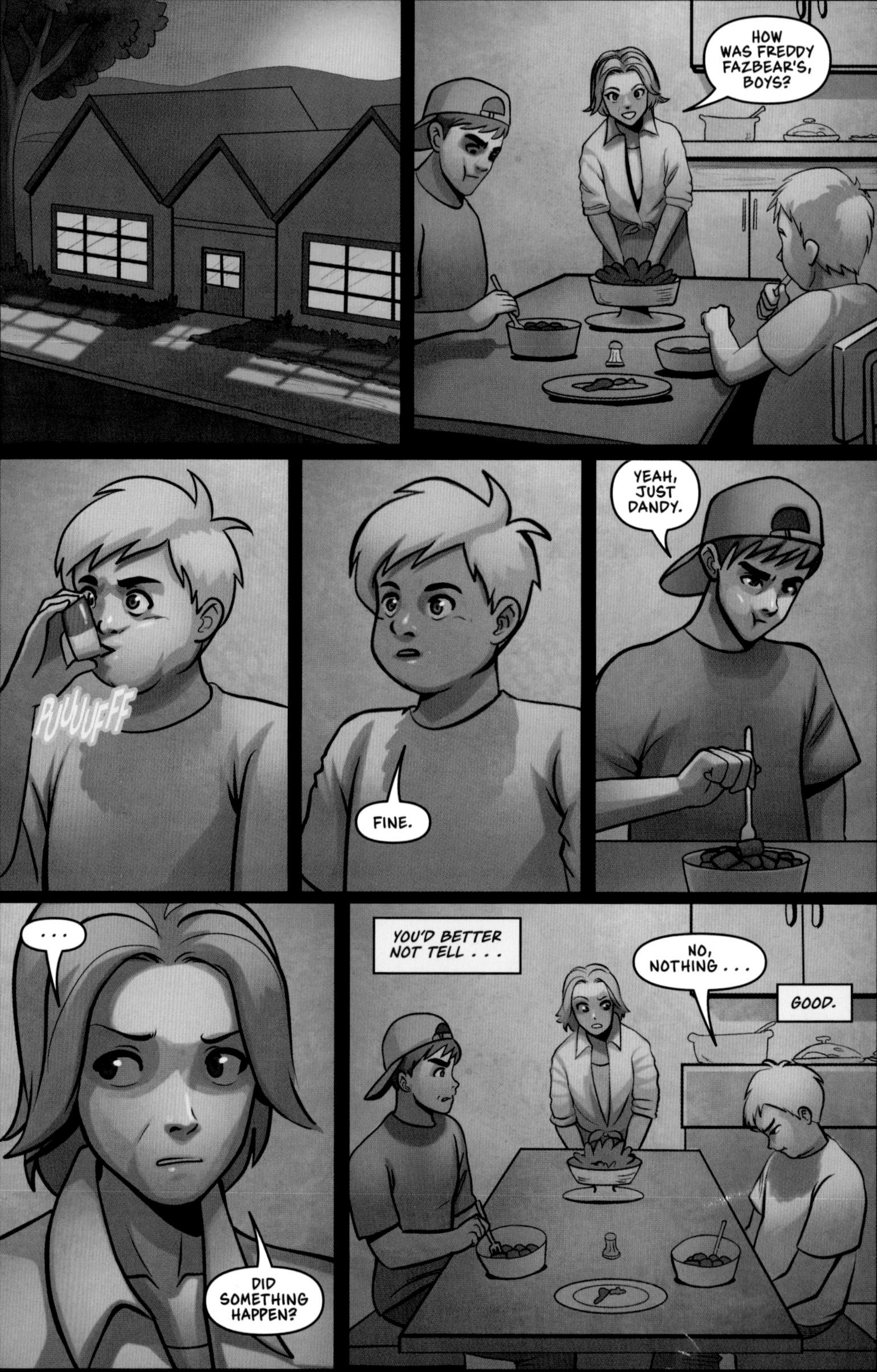
HOW WAS FREDDY FAZBEAR'S, BOYS?
PUUUUFFF
FINE.
YEAH, JUST DANDY.
. . .
DID SOMETHING HAPPEN?
YOU'D BETTER NOT TELL . . .
NO, NOTHING . . .
GOOD.

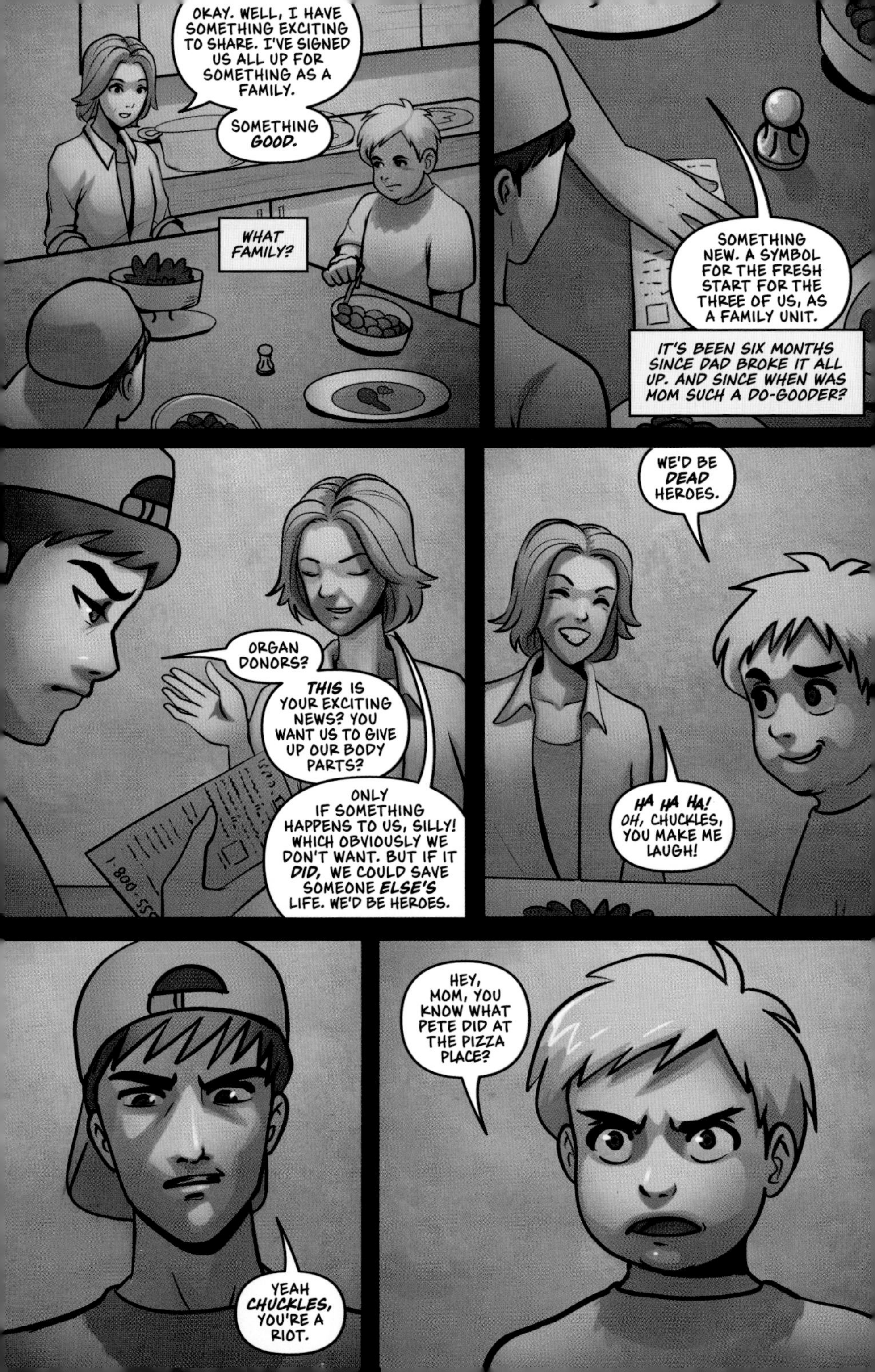
OKAY. WELL, I HAVE SOMETHING EXCITING TO SHARE. I'VE SIGNED US ALL UP FOR SOMETHING AS A FAMILY.
SOMETHING GOOD.
WHAT FAMILY?
SOMETHING NEW. A SYMBOL FOR THE FRESH START FOR THE THREE OF US, AS A FAMILY UNIT.
IT'S BEEN SIX MONTHS SINCE DAD BROKE IT ALL UP. AND SINCE WHEN WAS MOM SUCH A DO-GOODER?
ORGAN DONORS?
THIS IS YOUR EXCITING NEWS? YOU WANT US TO GIVE UP OUR BODY PARTS?
ONLY IF SOMETHING HAPPENS TO US, SILLY! WHICH OBVIOUSLY WE DON'T WANT. BUT IF IT DID, WE COULD SAVE SOMEONE ELSE'S LIFE. WE'D BE HEROES.
WE'D BE DEAD HEROES.
HA HA HA! OH, CHUCKLES, YOU MAKE ME LAUGH!
YEAH CHUCKLES, YOU'RE A RIOT.
HEY, MOM, YOU KNOW WHAT PETE DID AT THE PIZZA PLACE?

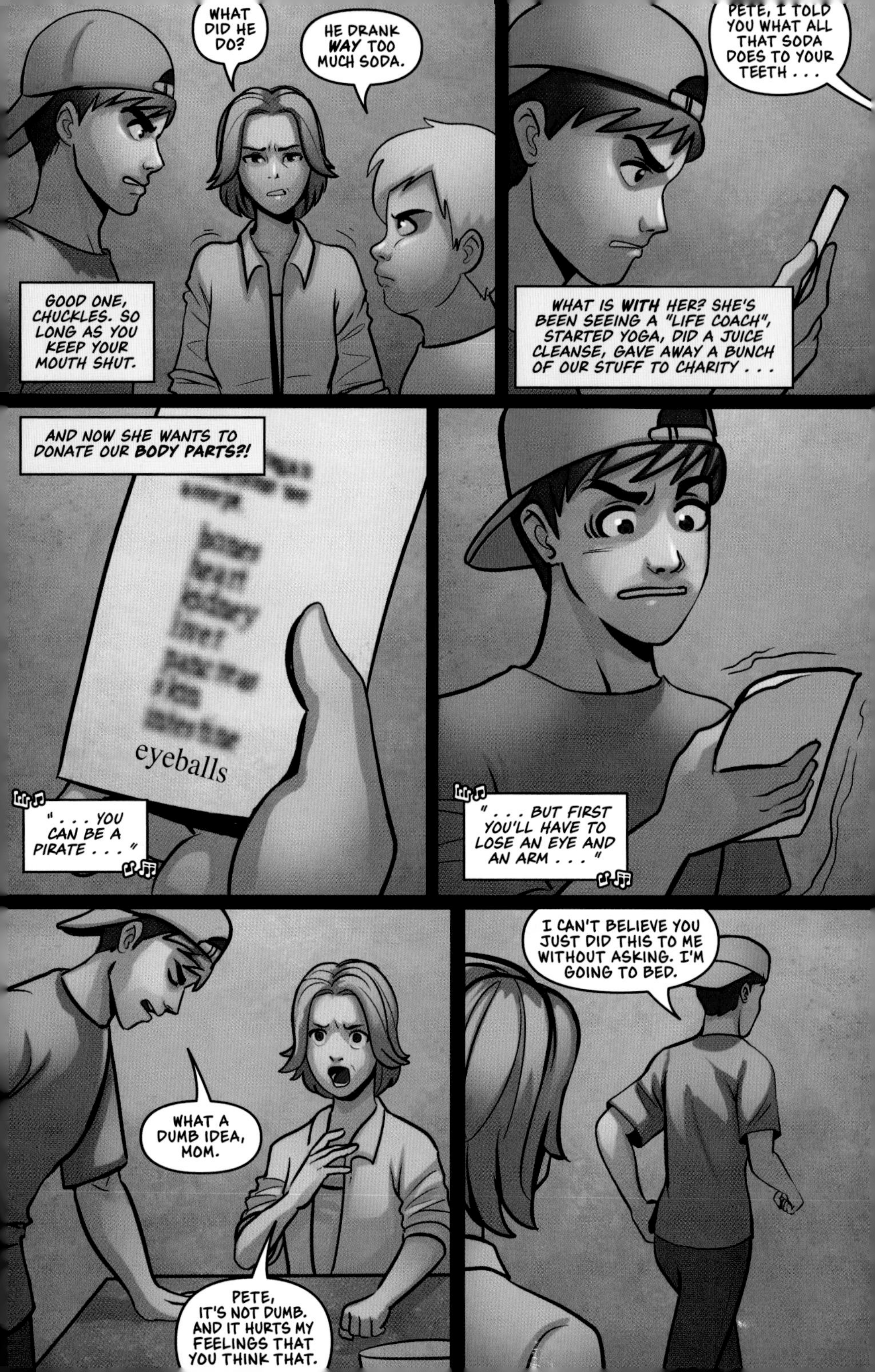
WHAT DID HE DO?
HE DRANK WAY TOO MUCH SODA.
GOOD ONE, CHUCKLES. SO LONG AS YOU KEEP YOUR MOUTH SHUT.
PETE, I TOLD YOU WHAT ALL THAT SODA DOES TO YOUR TEETH . . .
WHAT IS WITH HER? SHE'S BEEN SEEING A "LIFE COACH", STARTED YOGA, DID A JUICE CLEANSE, GAVE AWAY A BUNCH OF OUR STUFF TO CHARITY . . .
AND NOW SHE WANTS TO DONATE OUR BODY PARTS?!
eyeballs
" . . . YOU CAN BE A PIRATE . . . "
" . . . BUT FIRST YOU'LL HAVE TO LOSE AN EYE AND AN ARM . . . "
WHAT A DUMB IDEA, MOM.
PETE, IT'S NOT DUMB. AND IT HURTS MY FEELINGS THAT YOU THINK THAT.
I CAN'T BELIEVE YOU JUST DID THIS TO ME WITHOUT ASKING. I'M GOING TO BED.

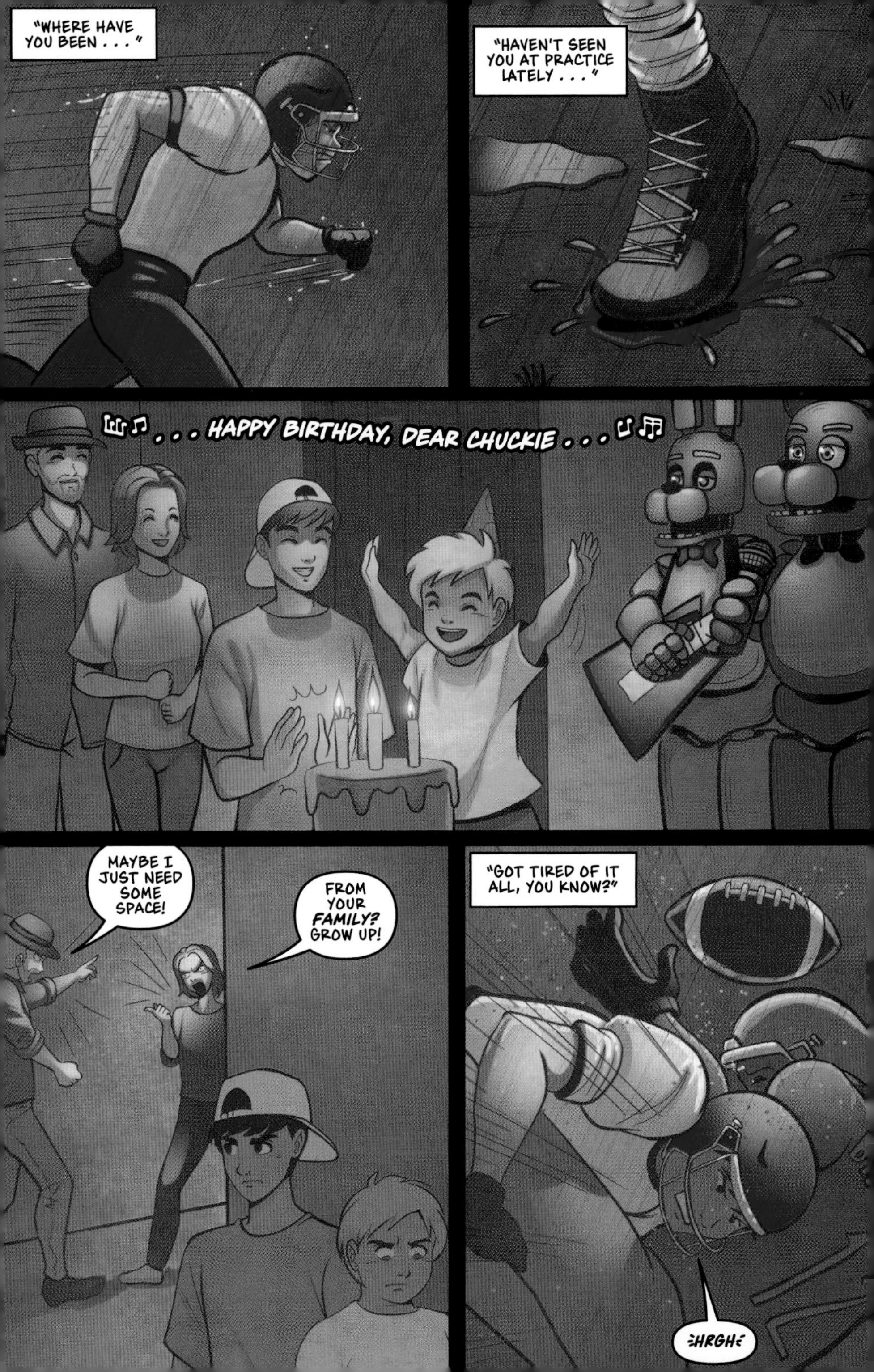
"WHERE HAVE YOU BEEN . . ."
"HAVEN'T SEEN YOU AT PRACTICE LATELY . . ."
. . . HAPPY BIRTHDAY, DEAR CHUCKIE . . .
MAYBE I JUST NEED SOME SPACE!
FROM YOUR FAMILY? GROW UP!
"GOT TIRED OF IT ALL, YOU KNOW?"
HRGH

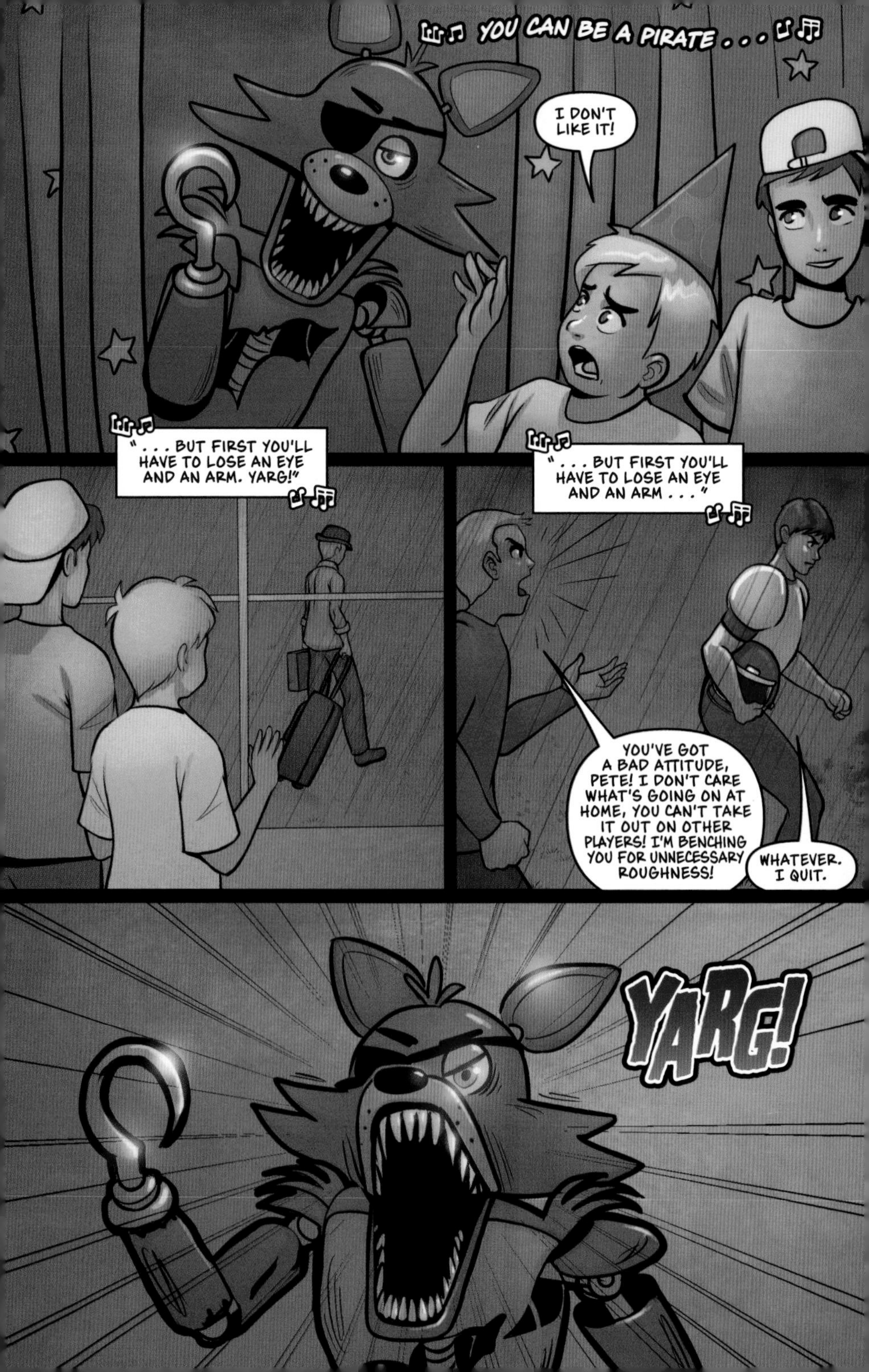
YOU CAN BE A PIRATE . . .
I DON'T LIKE IT!
" . . . BUT FIRST YOU'LL HAVE TO LOSE AN EYE AND AN ARM. YARG!"
" . . . BUT FIRST YOU'LL HAVE TO LOSE AN EYE AND AN ARM . . ."
YOU'VE GOT A BAD ATTITUDE, PETE! I DON'T CARE WHAT'S GOING ON AT HOME, YOU CAN'T TAKE IT OUT ON OTHER PLAYERS! I'M BENCHING YOU FOR UNNECESSARY ROUGHNESS!
WHATEVER. I QUIT.
YARG!

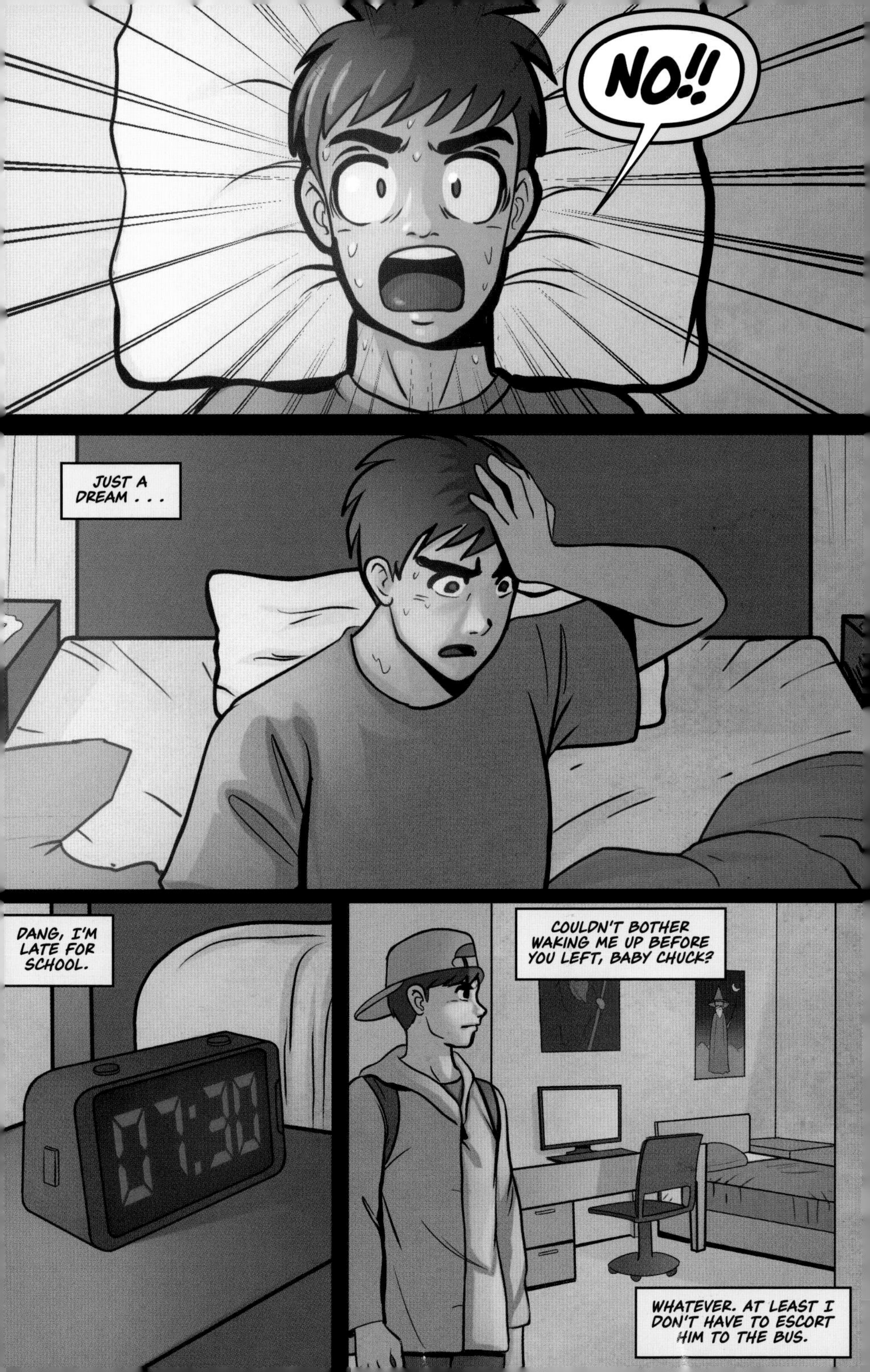
NO!!
JUST A DREAM . . .
DANG, I'M LATE FOR SCHOOL.
COULDN'T BOTHER WAKING ME UP BEFORE YOU LEFT, BABY CHUCK?
WHATEVER. AT LEAST I DON'T HAVE TO ESCORT HIM TO THE BUS.

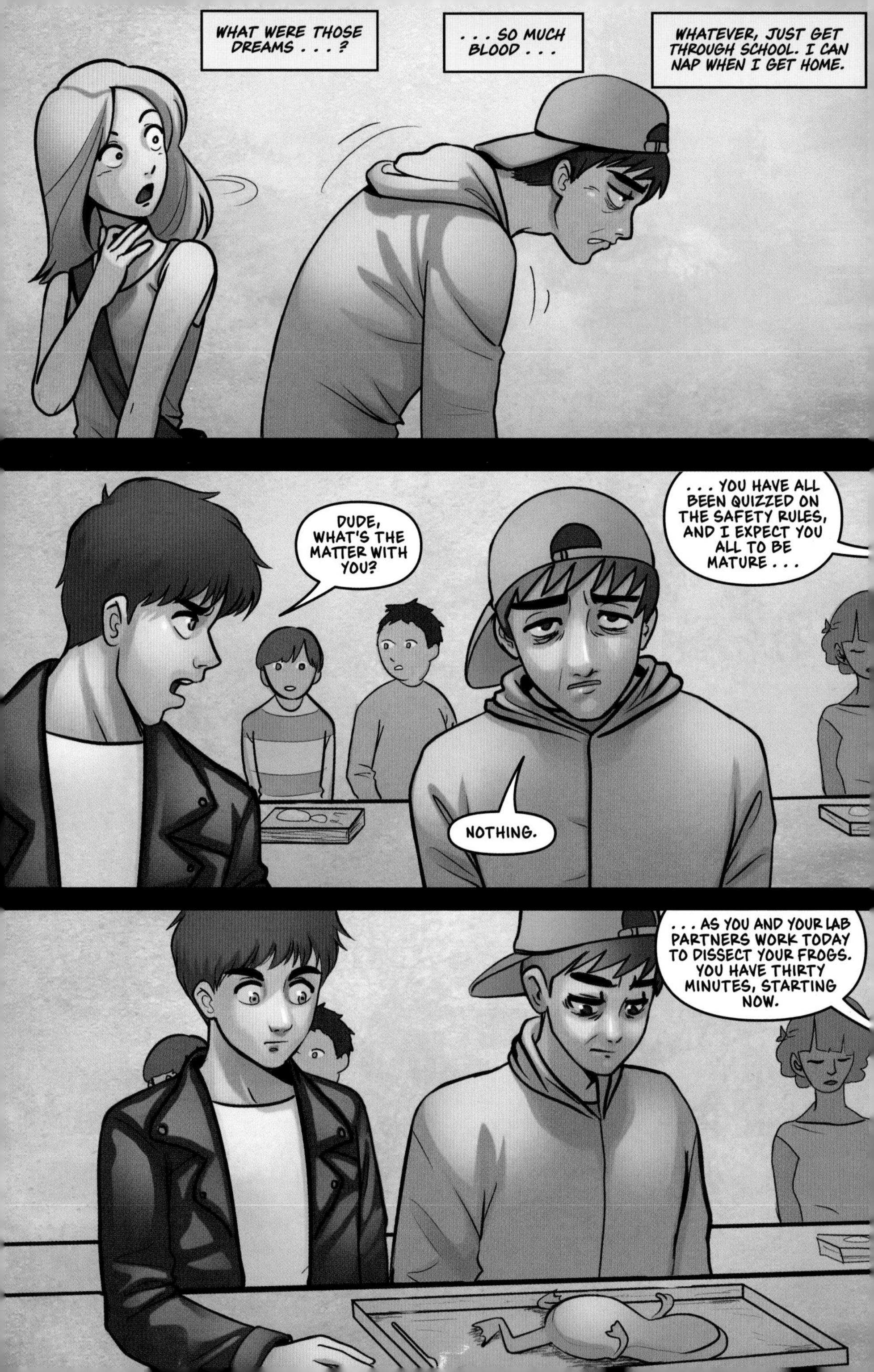
WHAT WERE THOSE DREAMS . . . ?
. . . SO MUCH BLOOD . . .
WHATEVER, JUST GET THROUGH SCHOOL. I CAN NAP WHEN I GET HOME.
DUDE, WHAT'S THE MATTER WITH YOU?
. . . YOU HAVE ALL BEEN QUIZZED ON THE SAFETY RULES, AND I EXPECT YOU ALL TO BE MATURE . . .
NOTHING.
. . . AS YOU AND YOUR LAB PARTNERS WORK TODAY TO DISSECT YOUR FROGS. YOU HAVE THIRTY MINUTES, STARTING NOW.

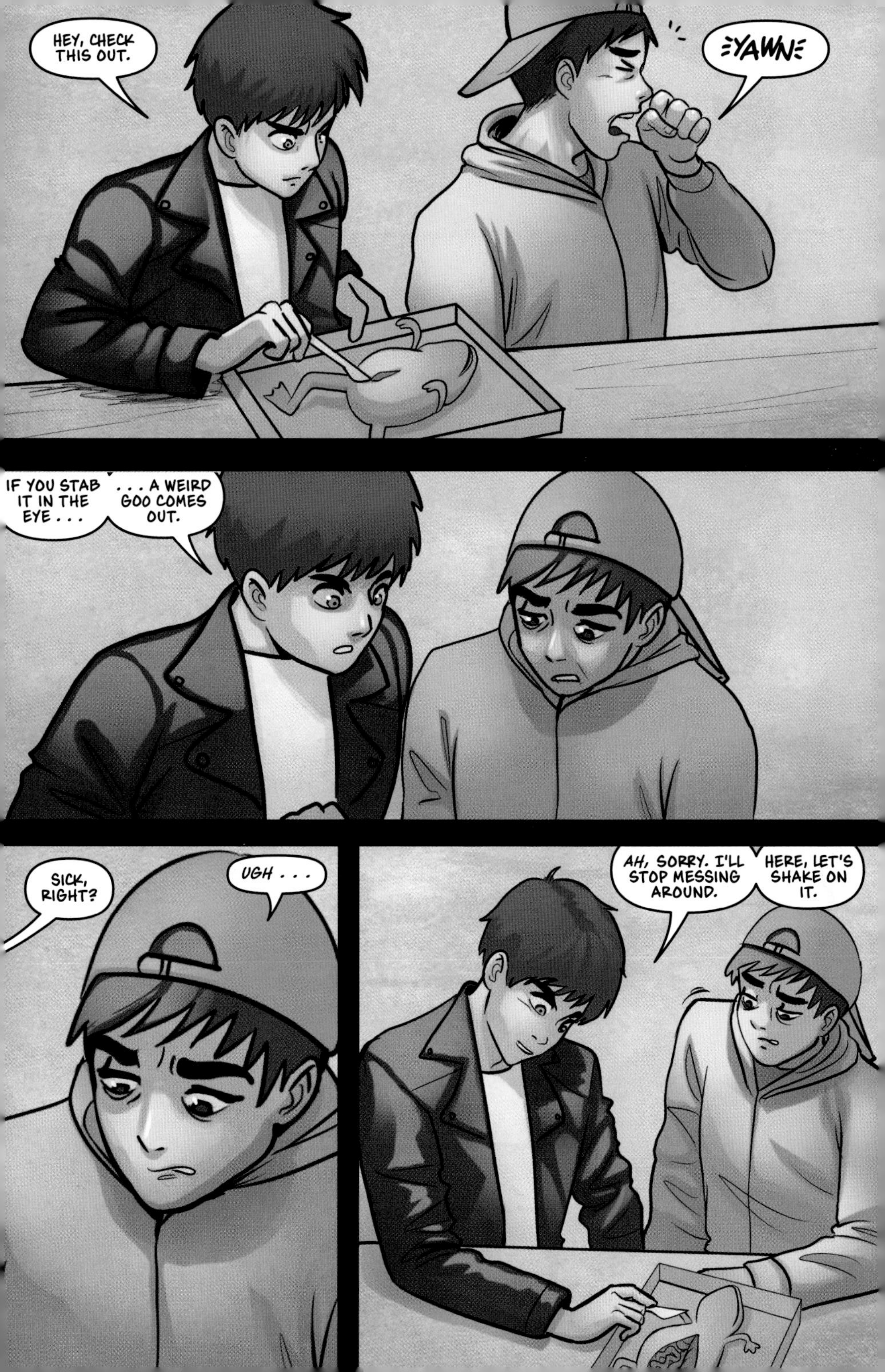
HEY, CHECK THIS OUT.
YAWN
IF YOU STAB IT IN THE EYE . . .
. . . A WEIRD GOO COMES OUT.
SICK, RIGHT?
UGH . . .
AH, SORRY. I'LL STOP MESSING AROUND.
HERE, LET'S SHAKE ON IT.

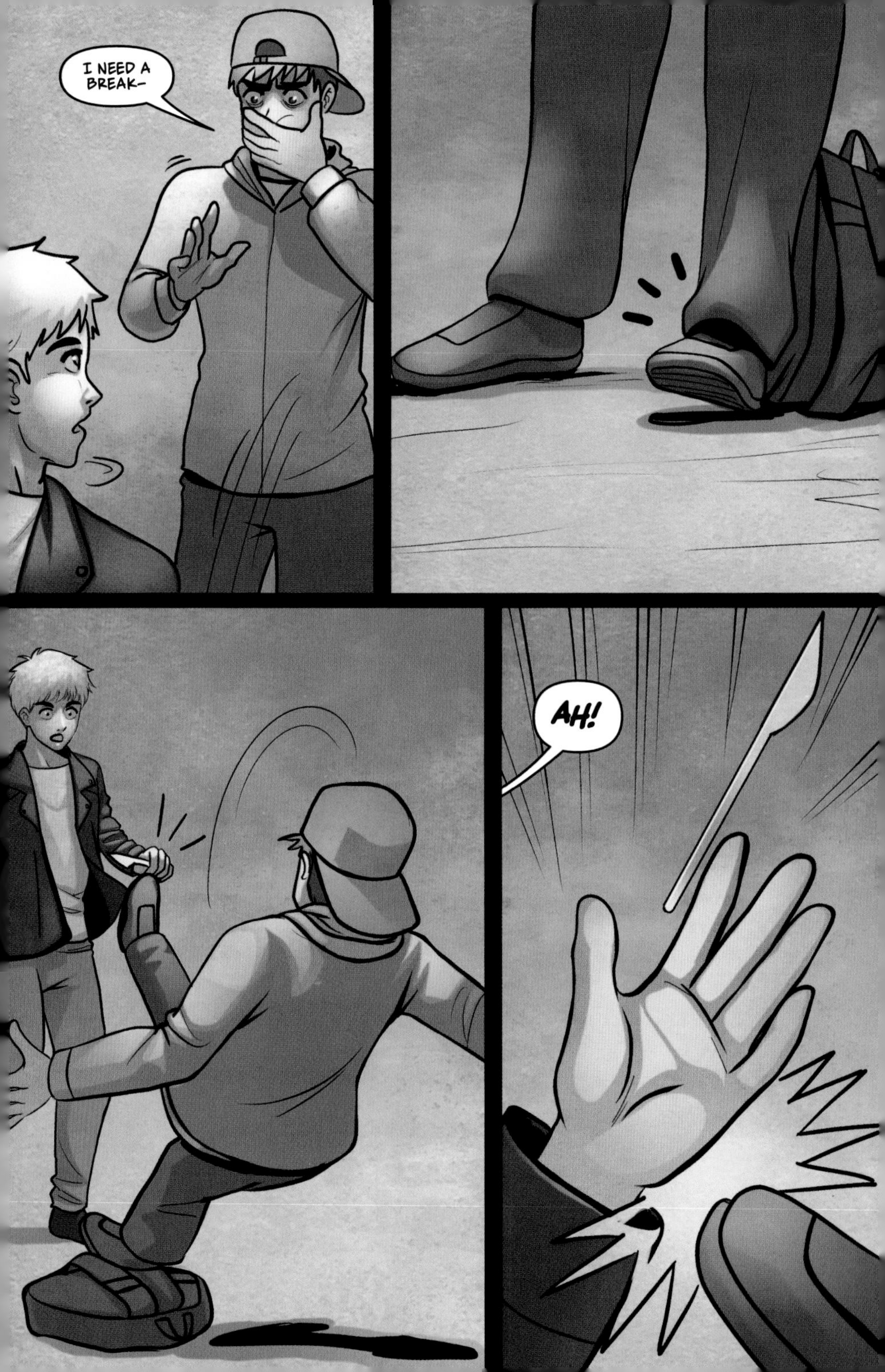
I NEED A BREAK–
AH!

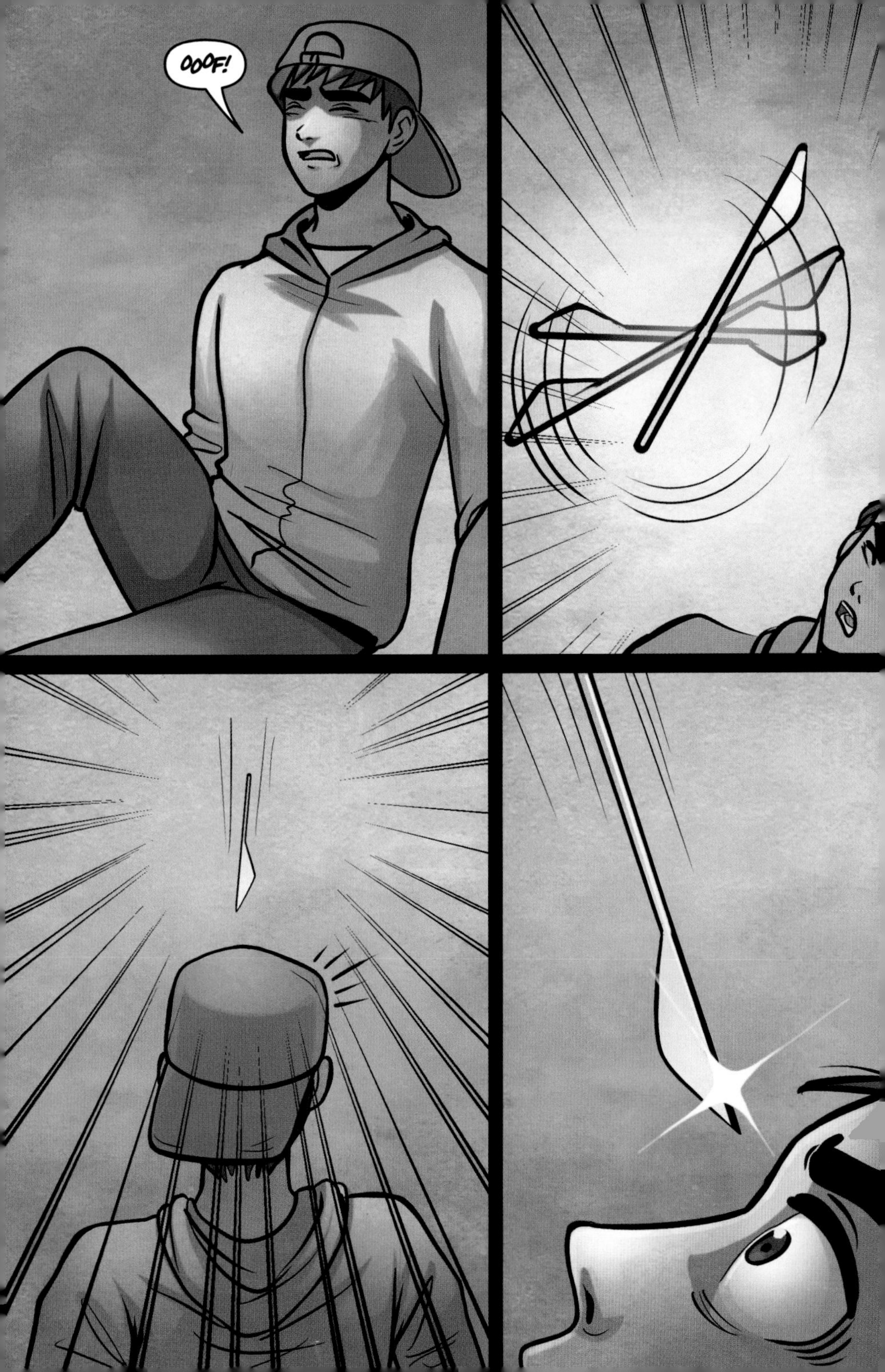
OOOF!

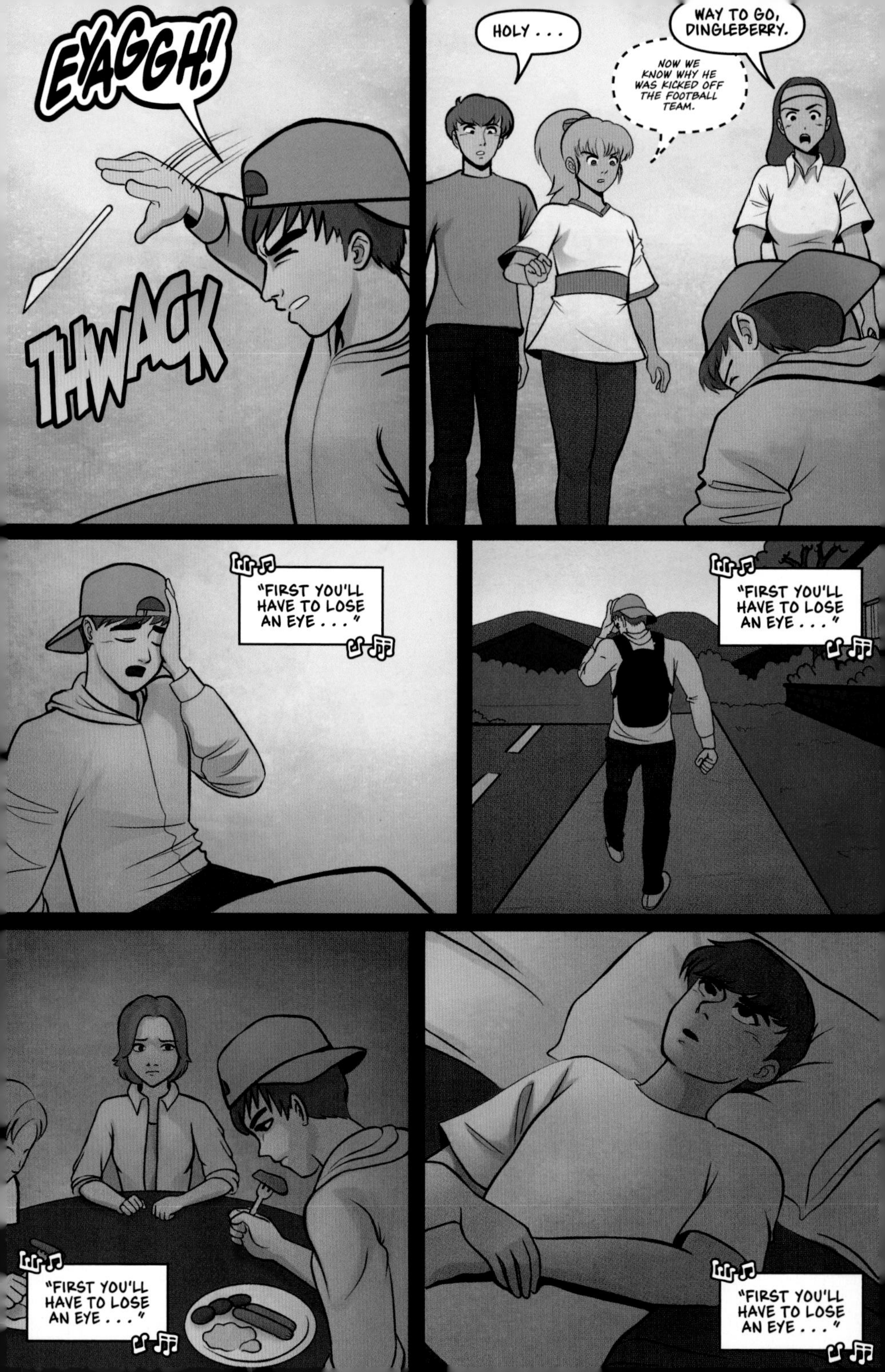

EYAGGH!
THWACK
HOLY . . .
NOW WE KNOW WHY HE WAS KICKED OFF THE FOOTBALL TEAM.
WAY TO GO, DINGLEBERRY.
"FIRST YOU'LL HAVE TO LOSE AN EYE . . ."
"FIRST YOU'LL HAVE TO LOSE AN EYE . . ."
"FIRST YOU'LL HAVE TO LOSE AN EYE . . ."
"FIRST YOU'LL HAVE TO LOSE AN EYE . . ."

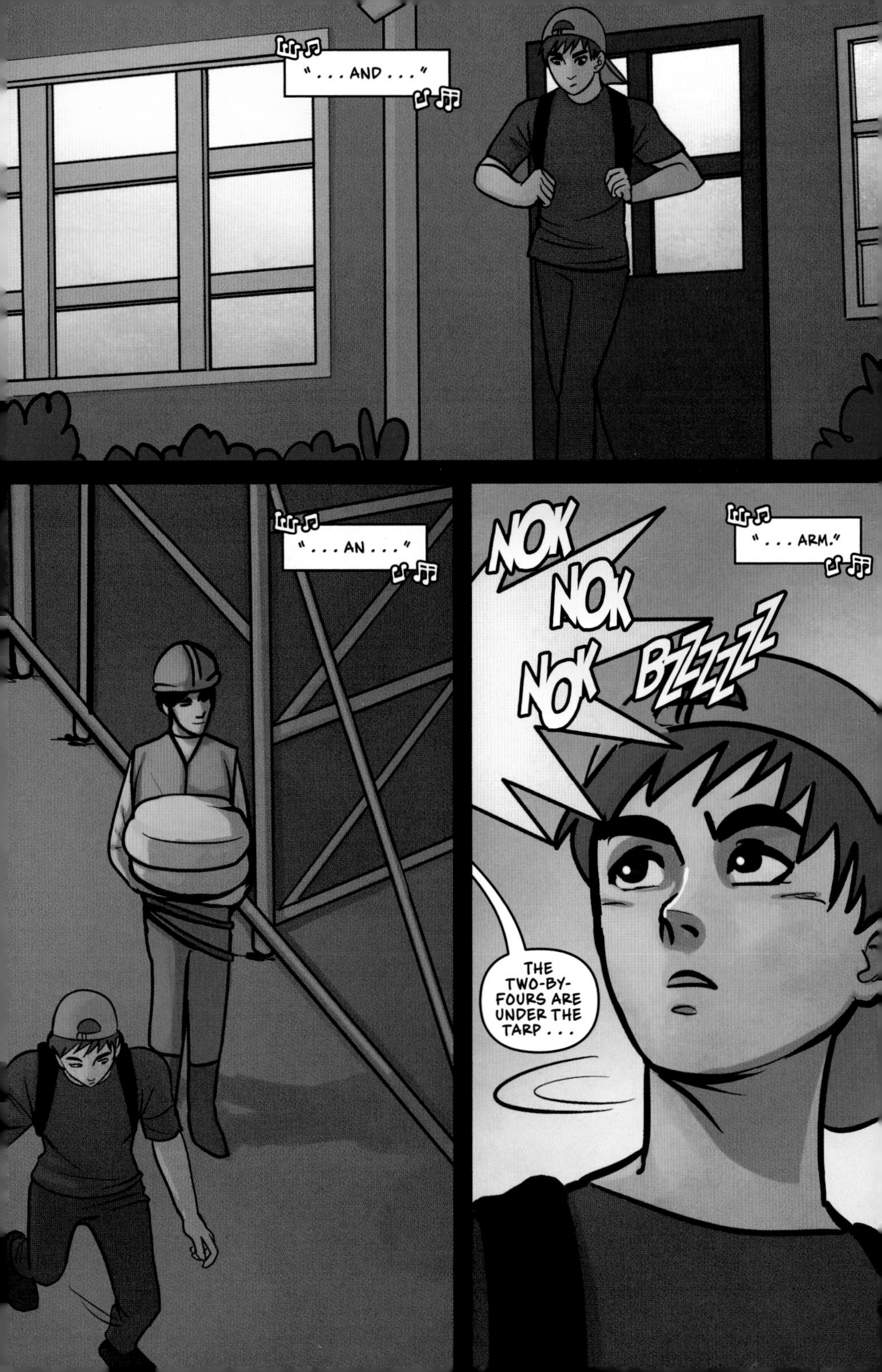
". . . AND . . ."
". . . AN . . ."
NOK NOK NOK BZZZZZ
". . . ARM."
THE TWO-BY-FOURS ARE UNDER THE TARP . . .

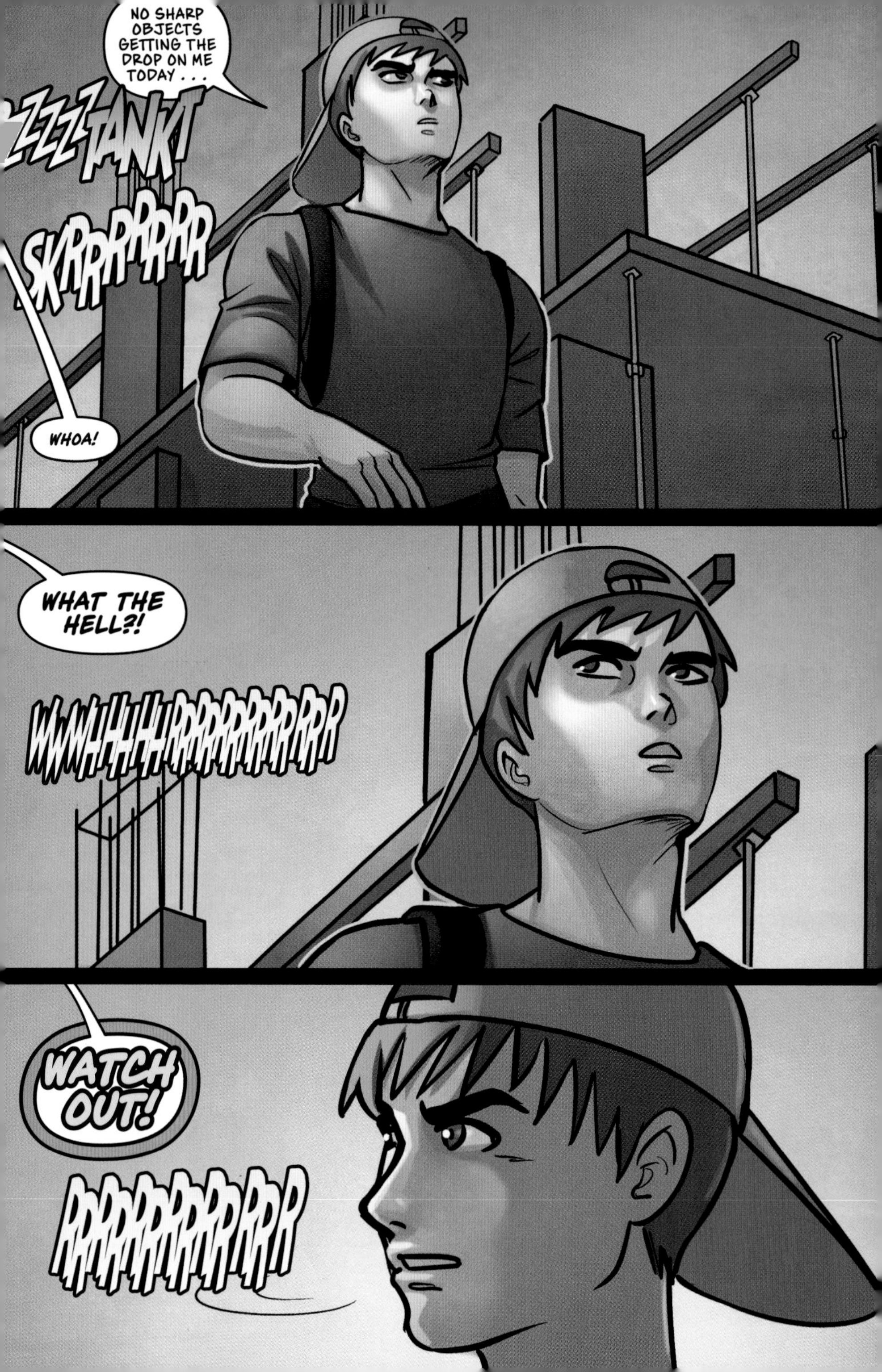

NO SHARP OBJECTS GETTING THE DROP ON ME TODAY . . .
ZZZZTANKT
SKRRRRRRR
WHOA!
WHAT THE HELL?!
WWWHHHHRRRRRRRRRRRR
WATCH OUT!
RRRRRRRRRRRR

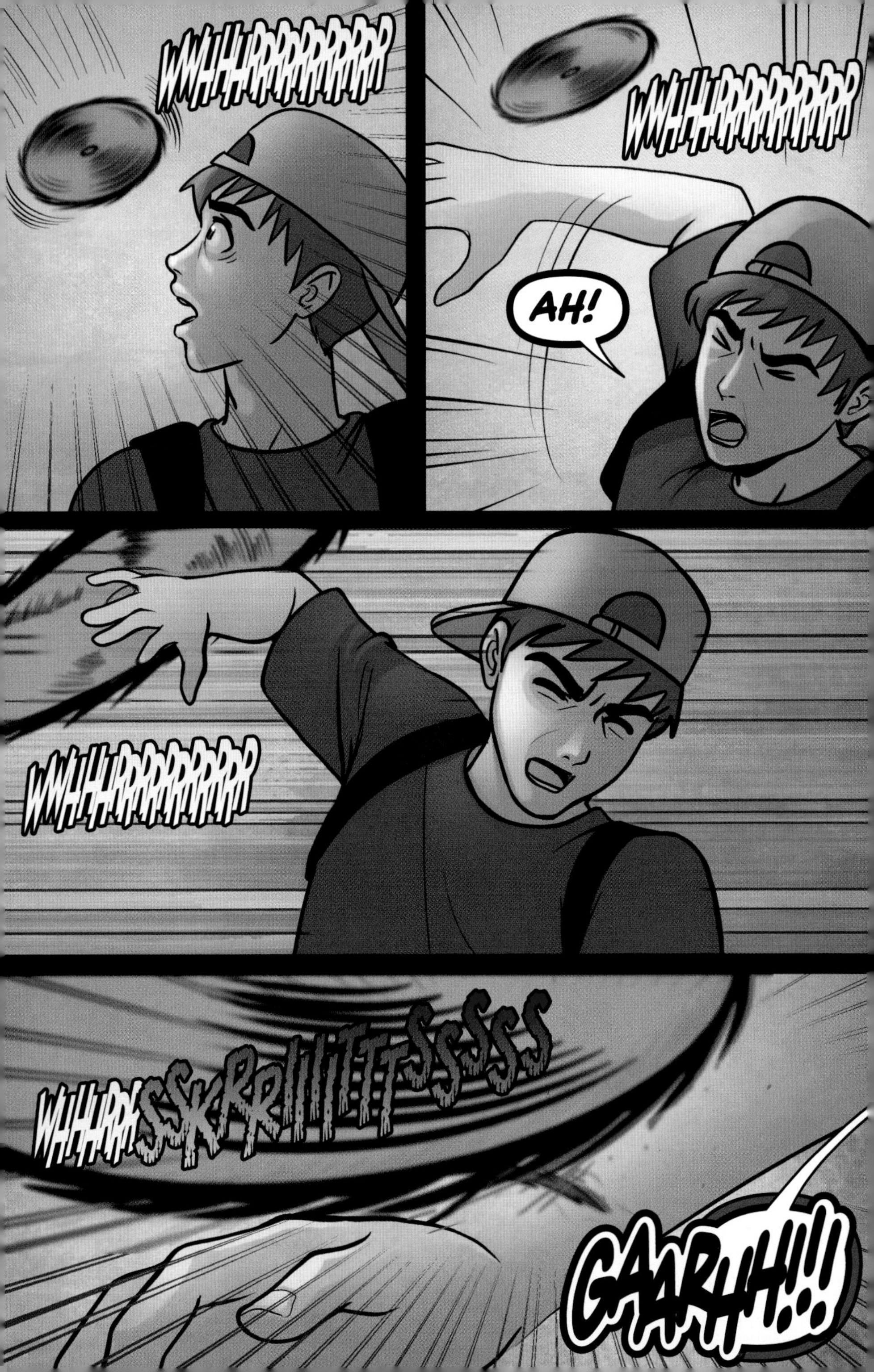
WWHHURRRRRRRRRR
WWHHURRRRRRRRRR
AH!
WWHHURRRRRRRRRR
WHHURRSSKRRIIIITTTSSSSS
GAARHH!!!

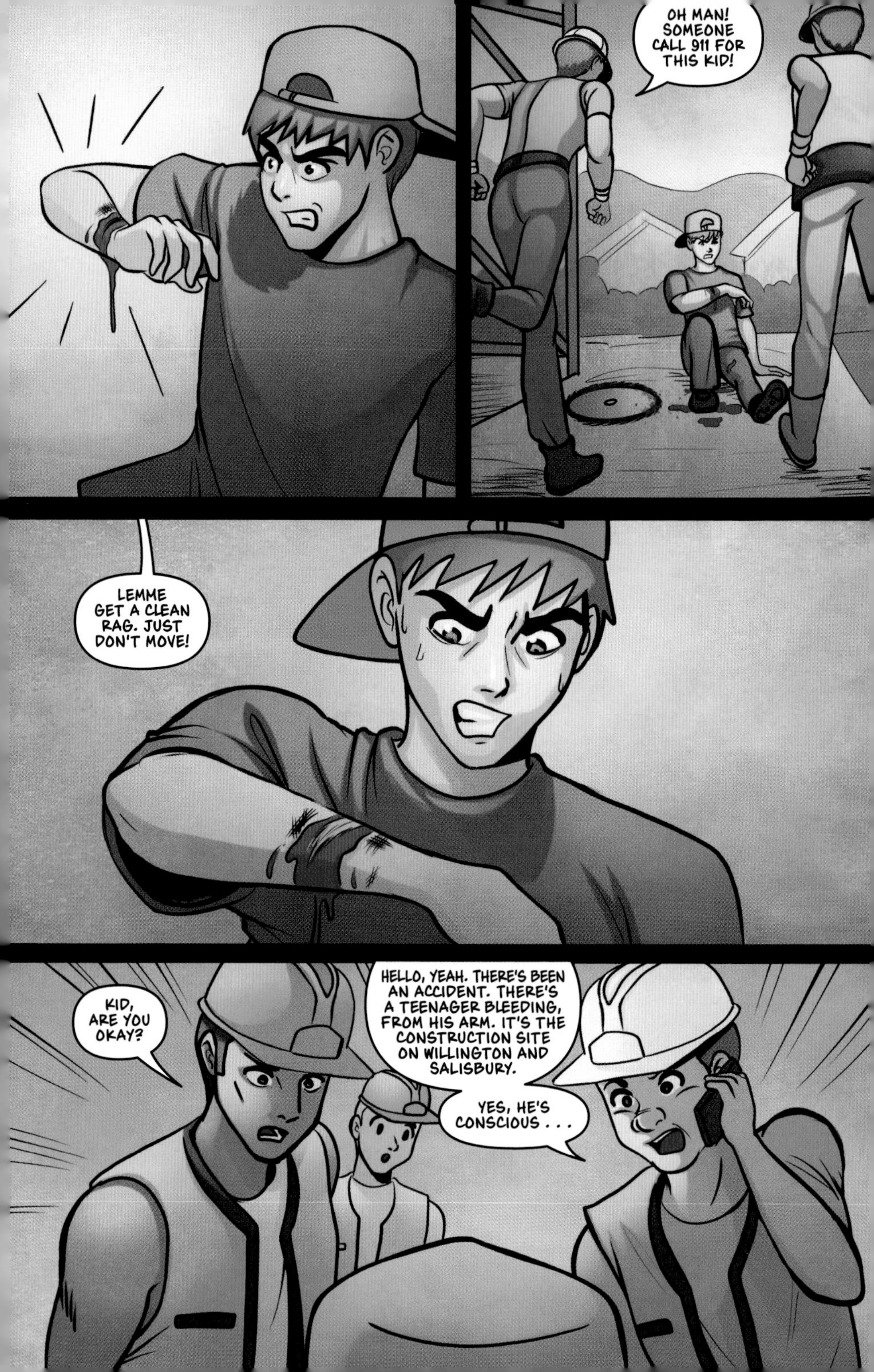
OH MAN! SOMEONE CALL 911 FOR THIS KID!
LEMME GET A CLEAN RAG. JUST DON'T MOVE!
KID, ARE YOU OKAY?
HELLO, YEAH. THERE'S BEEN AN ACCIDENT. THERE'S A TEENAGER BLEEDING, FROM HIS ARM. IT'S THE CONSTRUCTION SITE ON WILLINGTON AND SALISBURY.
YES, HE'S CONSCIOUS . . .

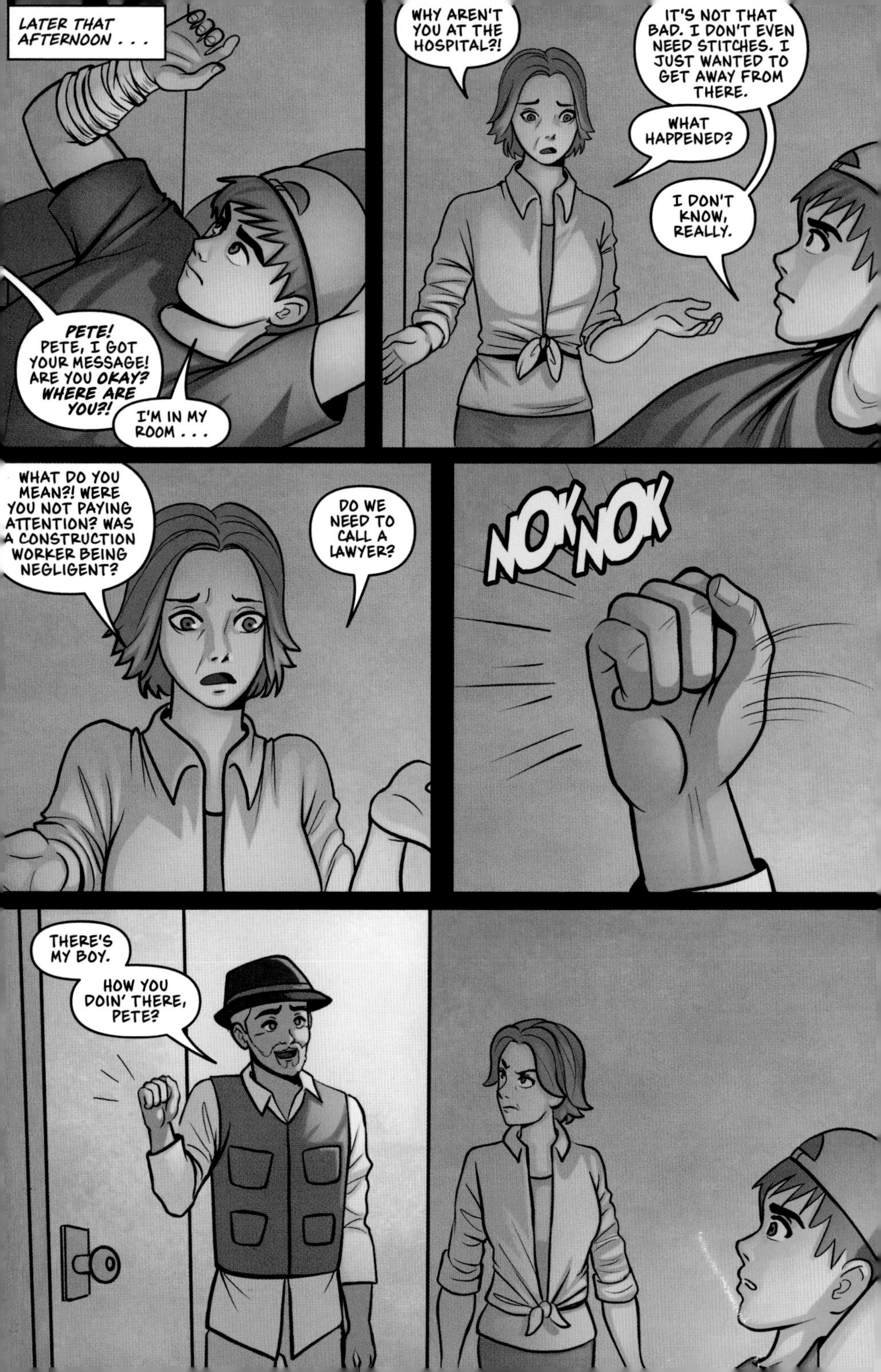

LATER THAT AFTERNOON . . .
PETE! PETE, I GOT YOUR MESSAGE! ARE YOU OKAY? WHERE ARE YOU?!
I'M IN MY ROOM . . .
WHY AREN'T YOU AT THE HOSPITAL?!
IT'S NOT THAT BAD. I DON'T EVEN NEED STITCHES. I JUST WANTED TO GET AWAY FROM THERE.
WHAT HAPPENED?
I DON'T KNOW, REALLY.
WHAT DO YOU MEAN?! WERE YOU NOT PAYING ATTENTION? WAS A CONSTRUCTION WORKER BEING NEGLIGENT?
DO WE NEED TO CALL A LAWYER?
NOK NOK
THERE'S MY BOY.
HOW YOU DOIN' THERE, PETE?

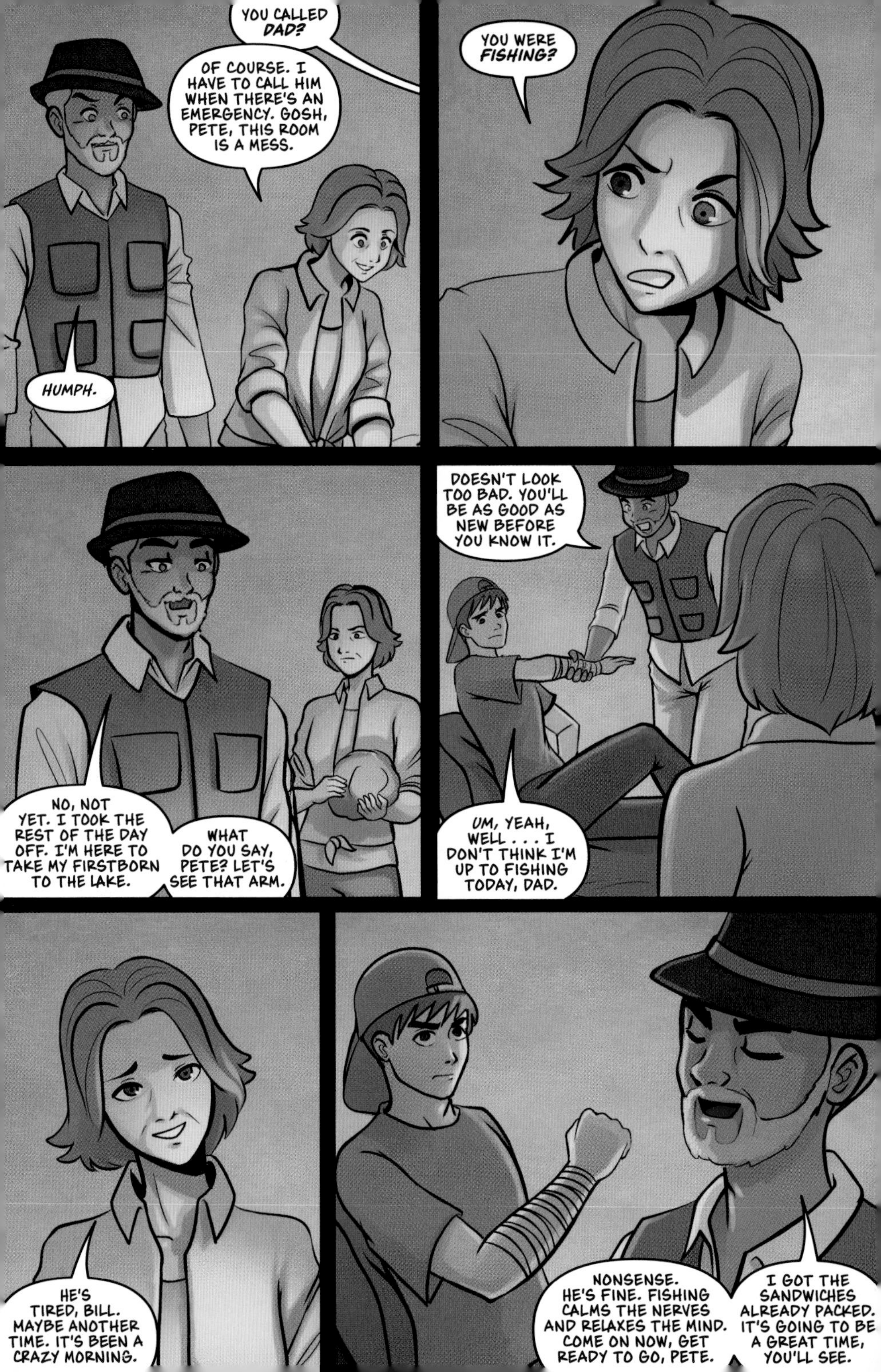
YOU CALLED DAD?
OF COURSE. I HAVE TO CALL HIM WHEN THERE'S AN EMERGENCY. GOSH, PETE, THIS ROOM IS A MESS.
HUMPH.
YOU WERE FISHING?
NO, NOT YET. I TOOK THE REST OF THE DAY OFF. I'M HERE TO TAKE MY FIRSTBORN TO THE LAKE.
WHAT DO YOU SAY, PETE? LET'S SEE THAT ARM.
DOESN'T LOOK TOO BAD. YOU'LL BE AS GOOD AS NEW BEFORE YOU KNOW IT.
UM, YEAH, WELL . . . I DON'T THINK I'M UP TO FISHING TODAY, DAD.
HE'S TIRED, BILL. MAYBE ANOTHER TIME. IT'S BEEN A CRAZY MORNING.
NONSENSE. HE'S FINE. FISHING CALMS THE NERVES AND RELAXES THE MIND. COME ON NOW, GET READY TO GO, PETE.
I GOT THE SANDWICHES ALREADY PACKED. IT'S GOING TO BE A GREAT TIME, YOU'LL SEE.

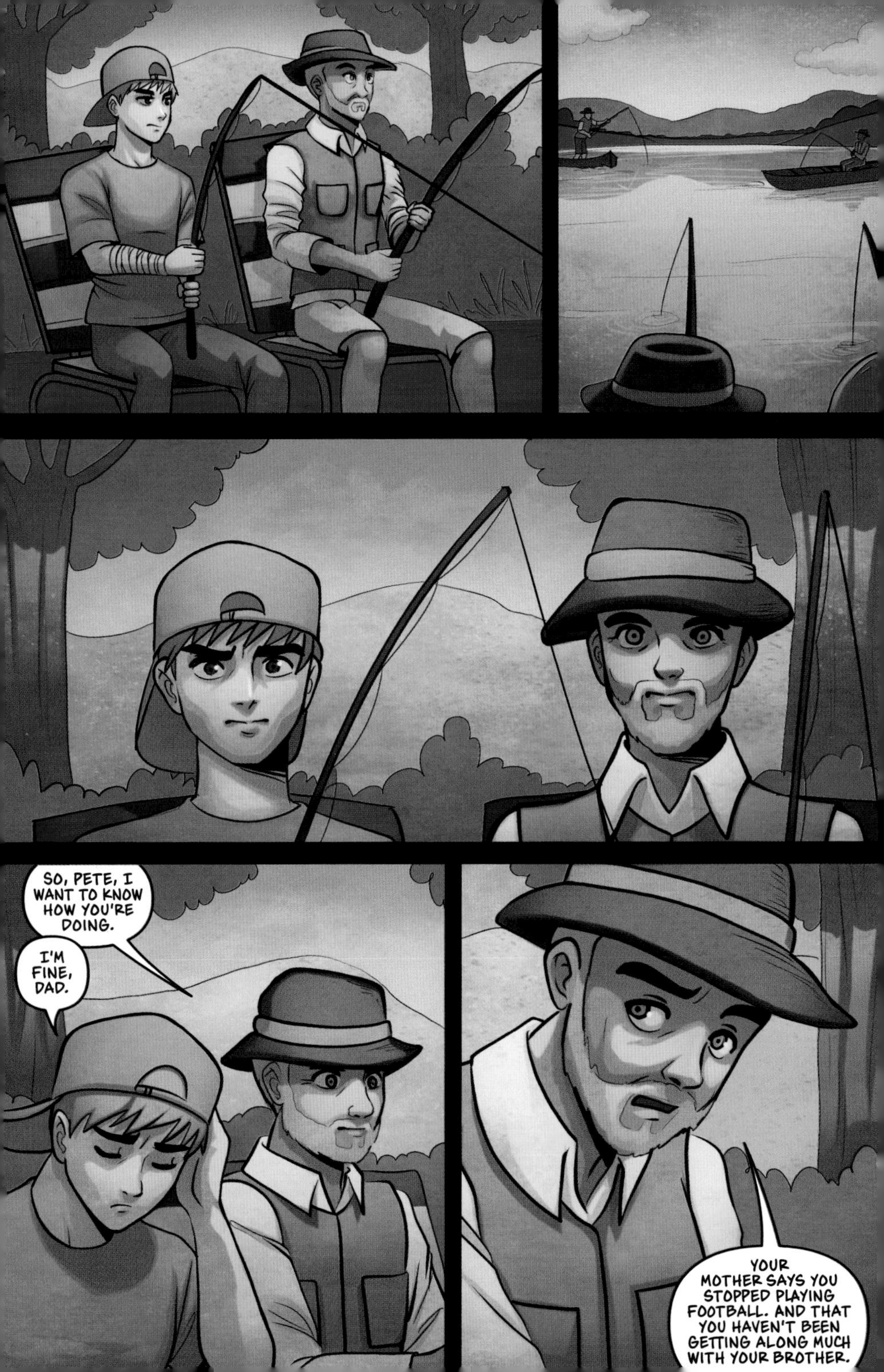
SO, PETE, I WANT TO KNOW HOW YOU'RE DOING.
I'M FINE, DAD.
YOUR MOTHER SAYS YOU STOPPED PLAYING FOOTBALL. AND THAT YOU HAVEN'T BEEN GETTING ALONG MUCH WITH YOUR BROTHER.

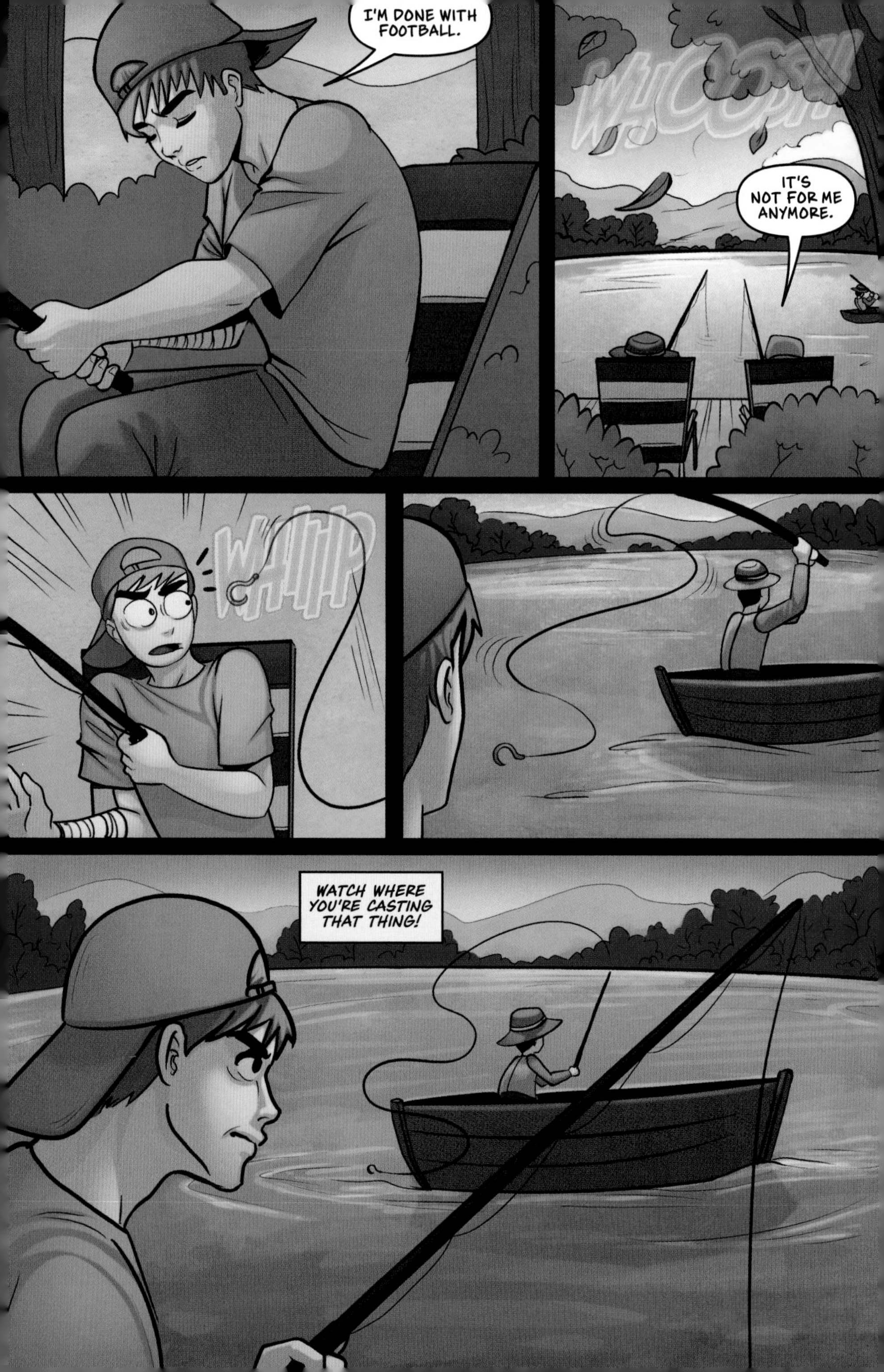
I'M DONE WITH FOOTBALL.
WHOOSH
IT'S NOT FOR ME ANYMORE.
WHIP
WATCH WHERE YOU'RE CASTING THAT THING!

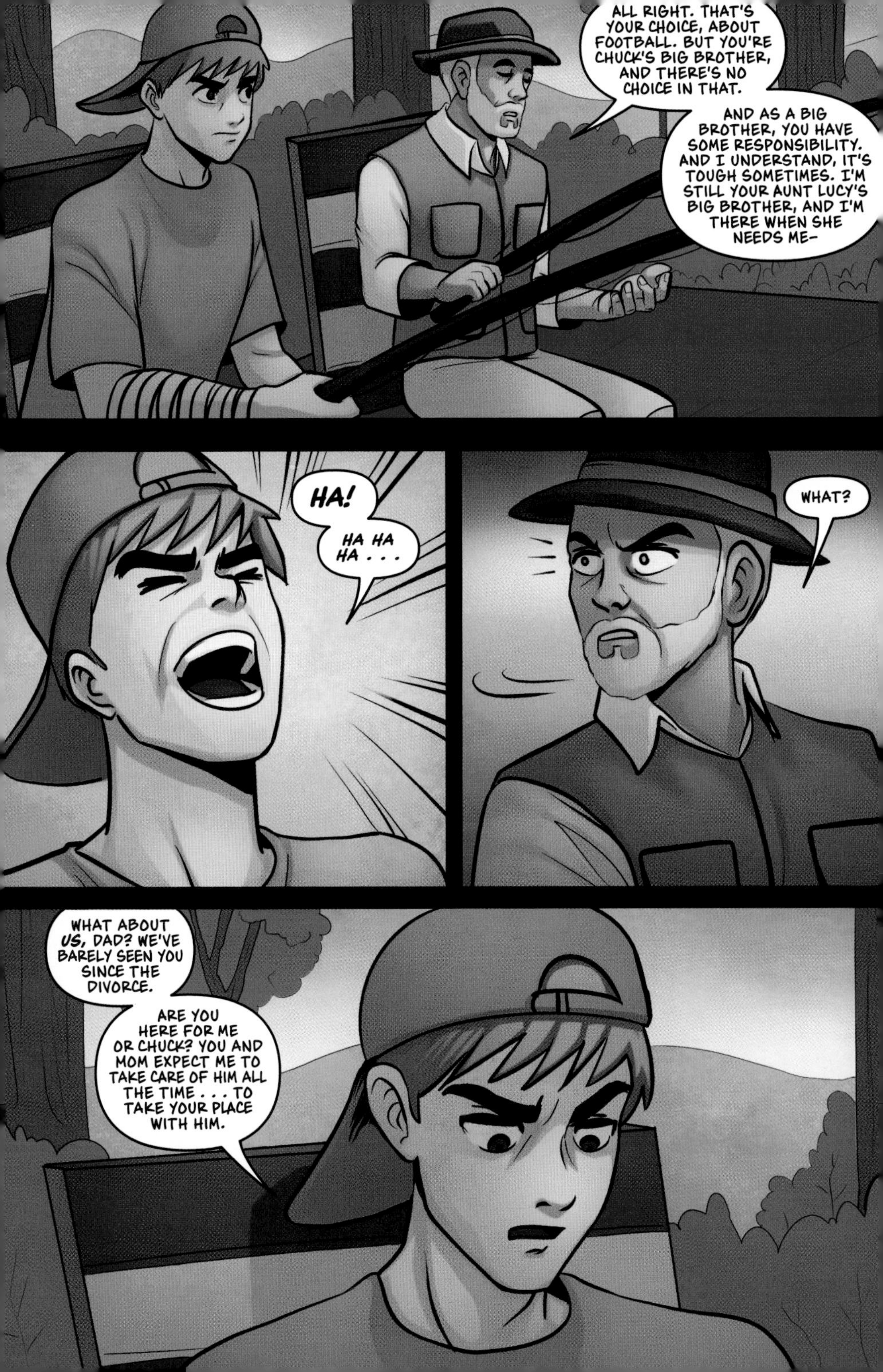
ALL RIGHT. THAT'S YOUR CHOICE, ABOUT FOOTBALL. BUT YOU'RE CHUCK'S BIG BROTHER, AND THERE'S NO CHOICE IN THAT.
AND AS A BIG BROTHER, YOU HAVE SOME RESPONSIBILITY. AND I UNDERSTAND, IT'S TOUGH SOMETIMES. I'M STILL YOUR AUNT LUCY'S BIG BROTHER, AND I'M THERE WHEN SHE NEEDS ME–
HA!
HA HA HA . . .
WHAT?
WHAT ABOUT US, DAD? WE'VE BARELY SEEN YOU SINCE THE DIVORCE.
ARE YOU HERE FOR ME OR CHUCK? YOU AND MOM EXPECT ME TO TAKE CARE OF HIM ALL THE TIME . . . TO TAKE YOUR PLACE WITH HIM.

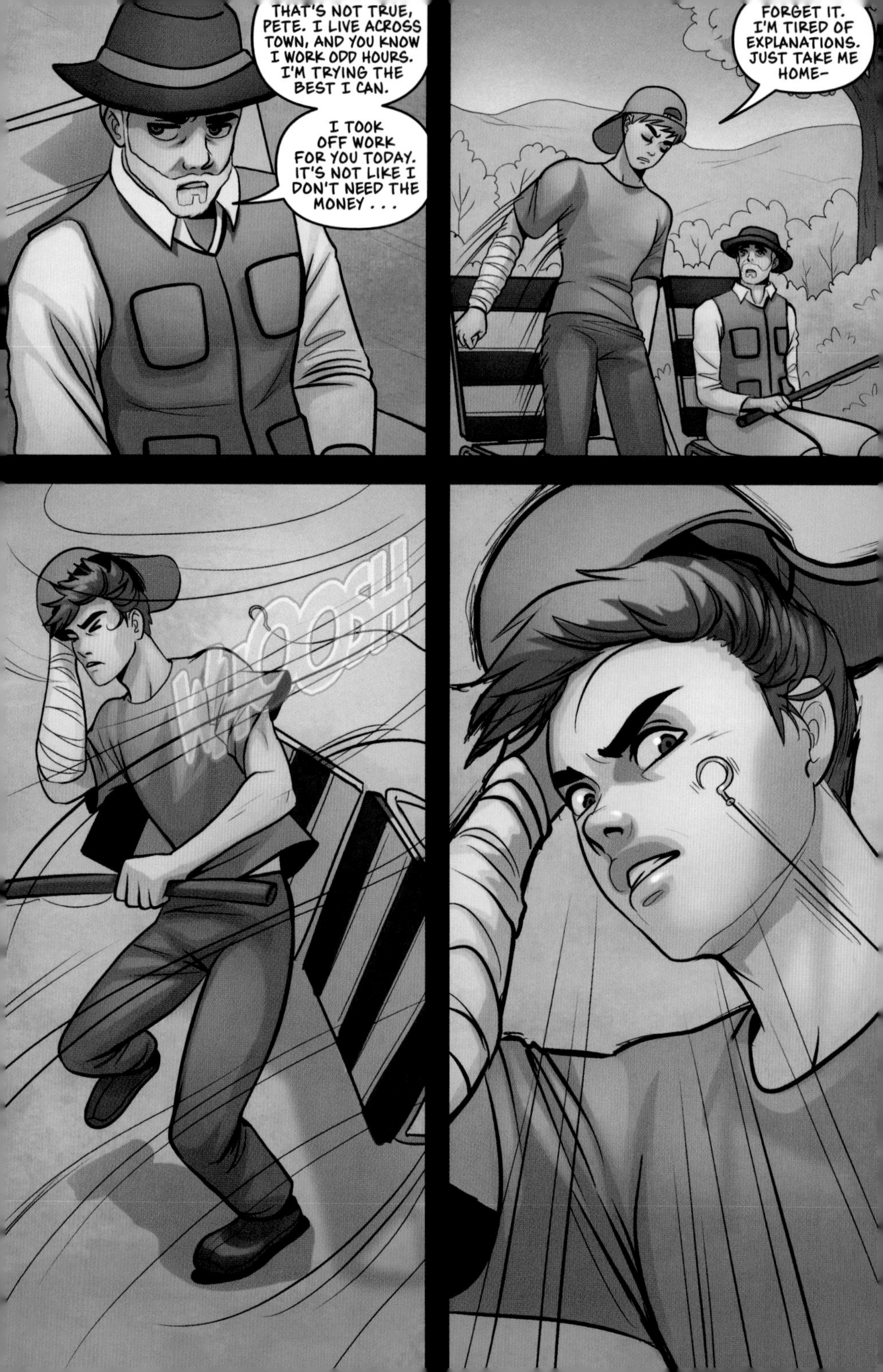
THAT'S NOT TRUE, PETE. I LIVE ACROSS TOWN, AND YOU KNOW I WORK ODD HOURS. I'M TRYING THE BEST I CAN.
I TOOK OFF WORK FOR YOU TODAY. IT'S NOT LIKE I DON'T NEED THE MONEY . . .
FORGET IT. I'M TIRED OF EXPLANATIONS. JUST TAKE ME HOME–
WHOOSH

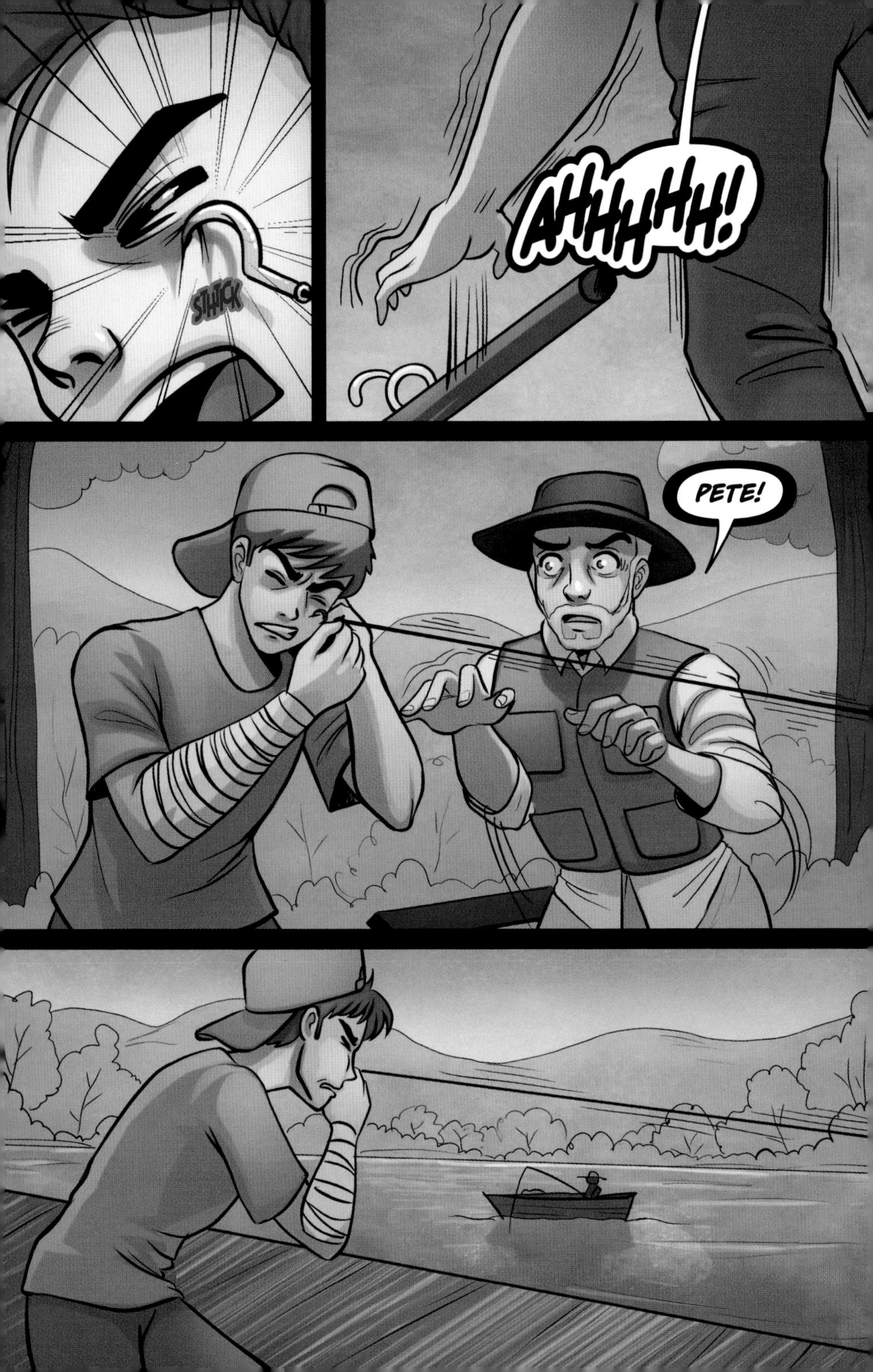
STHTCK
AHHHHH!
PETE!

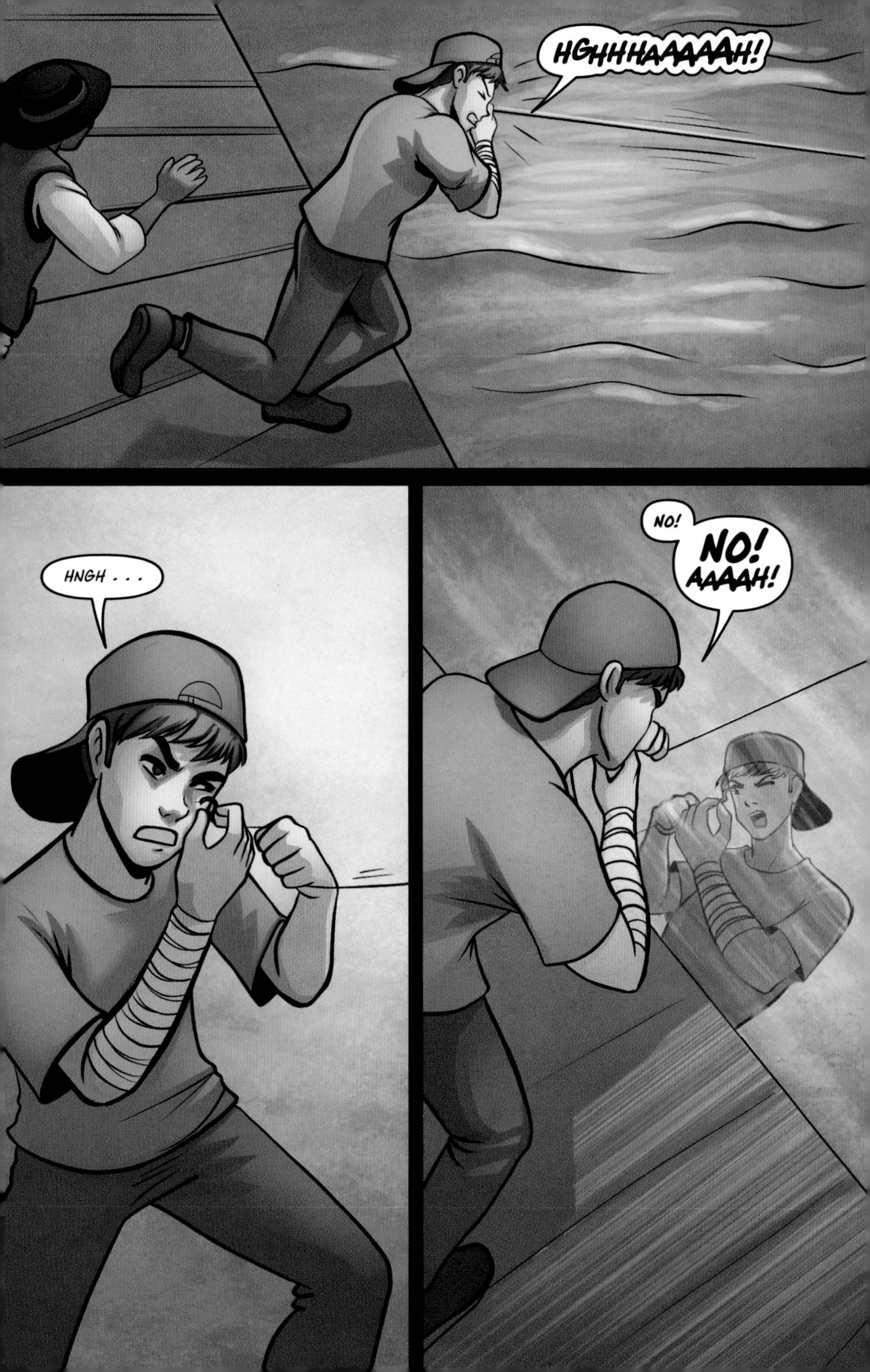
HGHHHAAAAAH!
HNGH . . .
NO!
NO! AAAAH!

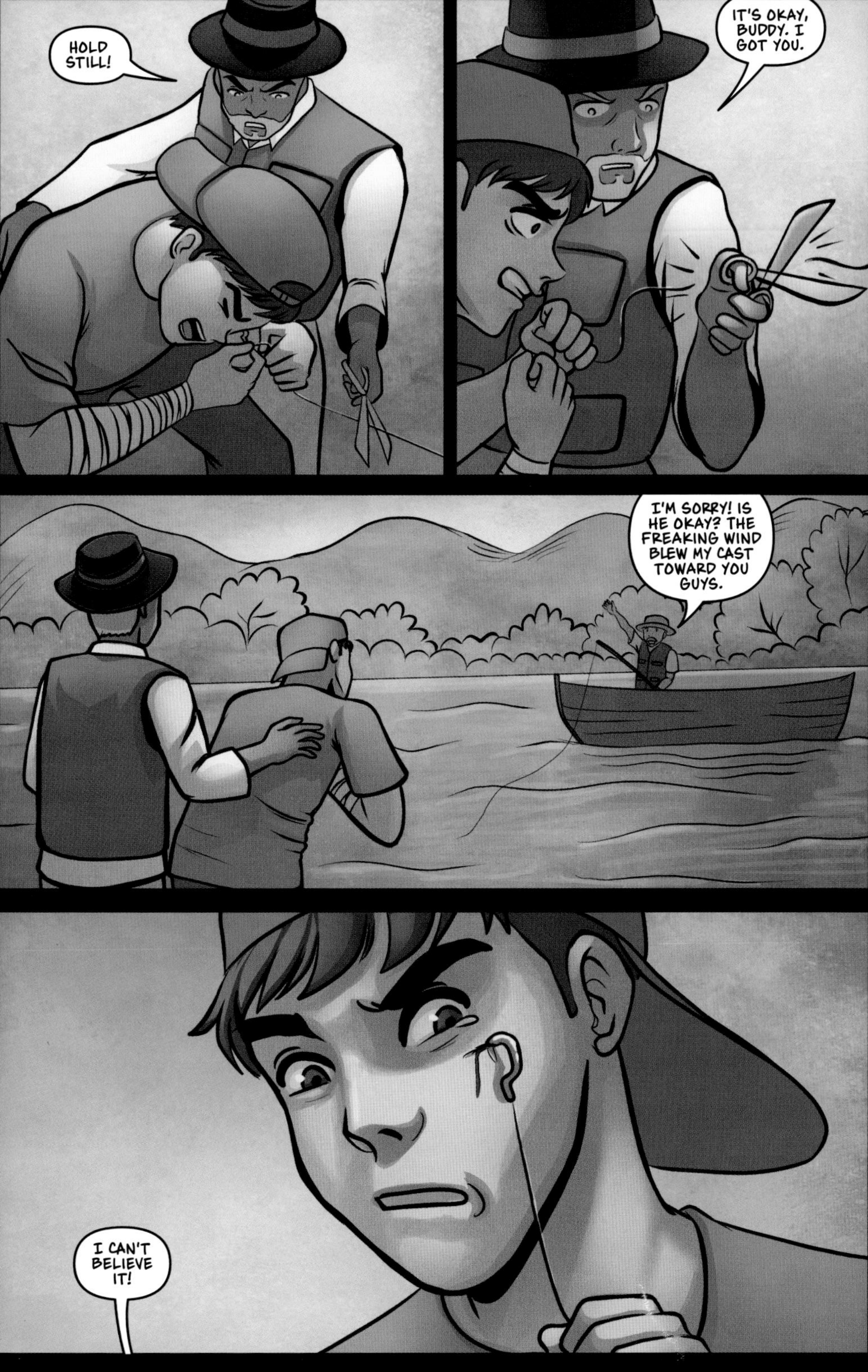
HOLD STILL!
IT'S OKAY, BUDDY. I GOT YOU.
I'M SORRY! IS HE OKAY? THE FREAKING WIND BLEW MY CAST TOWARD YOU GUYS.
I CAN'T BELIEVE IT!

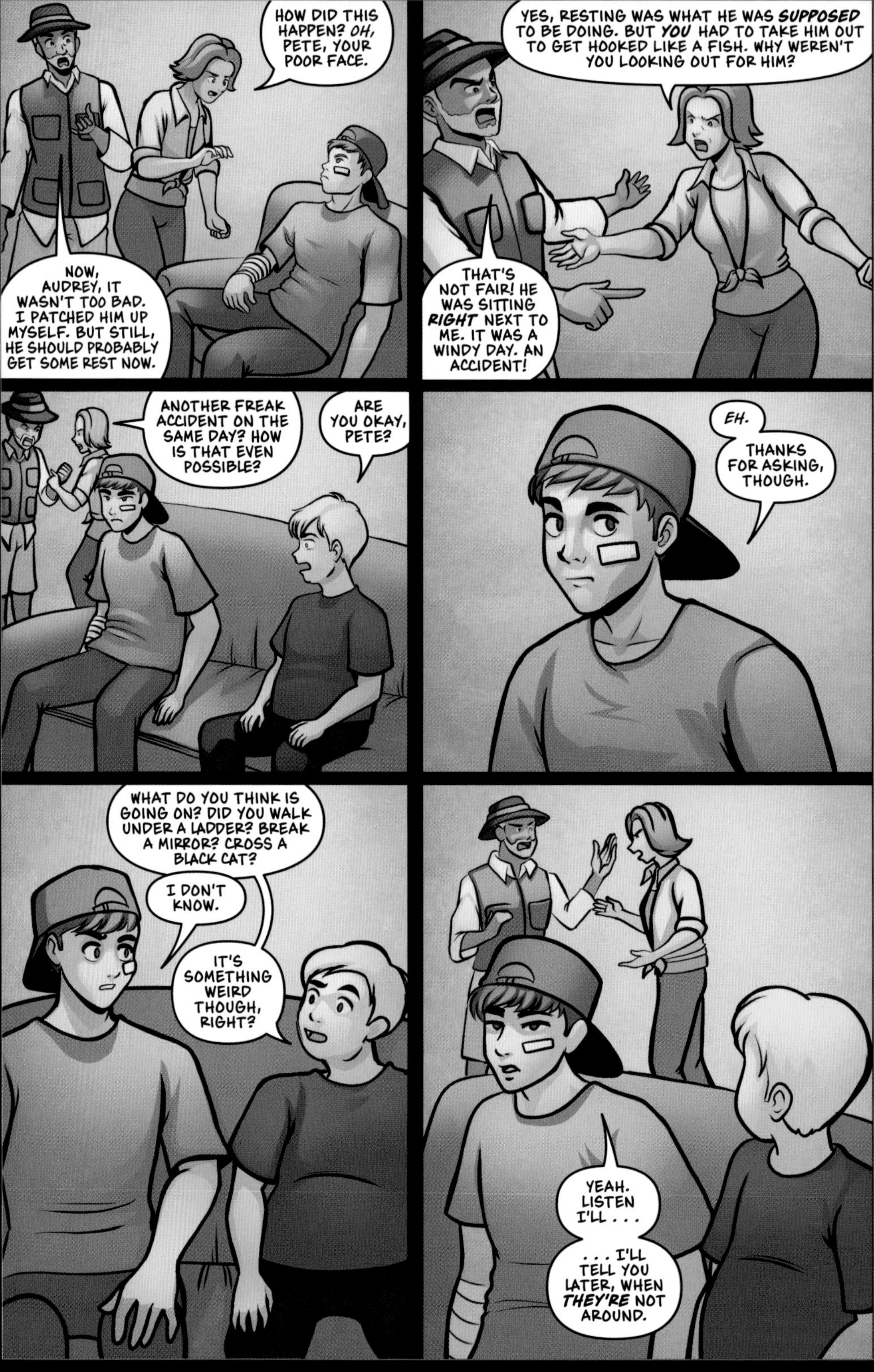
HOW DID THIS HAPPEN? *OH,* PETE, YOUR POOR FACE.
NOW, AUDREY, IT WASN'T TOO BAD. I PATCHED HIM UP MYSELF. BUT STILL, HE SHOULD PROBABLY GET SOME REST NOW.
YES, RESTING WAS WHAT HE WAS ***SUPPOSED*** TO BE DOING. BUT ***YOU*** HAD TO TAKE HIM OUT TO GET HOOKED LIKE A FISH. WHY WEREN'T YOU LOOKING OUT FOR HIM?
THAT'S NOT FAIR! HE WAS SITTING ***RIGHT*** NEXT TO ME. IT WAS A WINDY DAY. AN ACCIDENT!
ANOTHER FREAK ACCIDENT ON THE SAME DAY? HOW IS THAT EVEN POSSIBLE?
ARE YOU OKAY, PETE?
EH.
THANKS FOR ASKING, THOUGH.
WHAT DO YOU THINK IS GOING ON? DID YOU WALK UNDER A LADDER? BREAK A MIRROR? CROSS A BLACK CAT?
I DON'T KNOW.
IT'S SOMETHING WEIRD THOUGH, RIGHT?
YEAH. LISTEN I'LL . . .
. . . I'LL TELL YOU LATER, WHEN ***THEY'RE*** NOT AROUND.

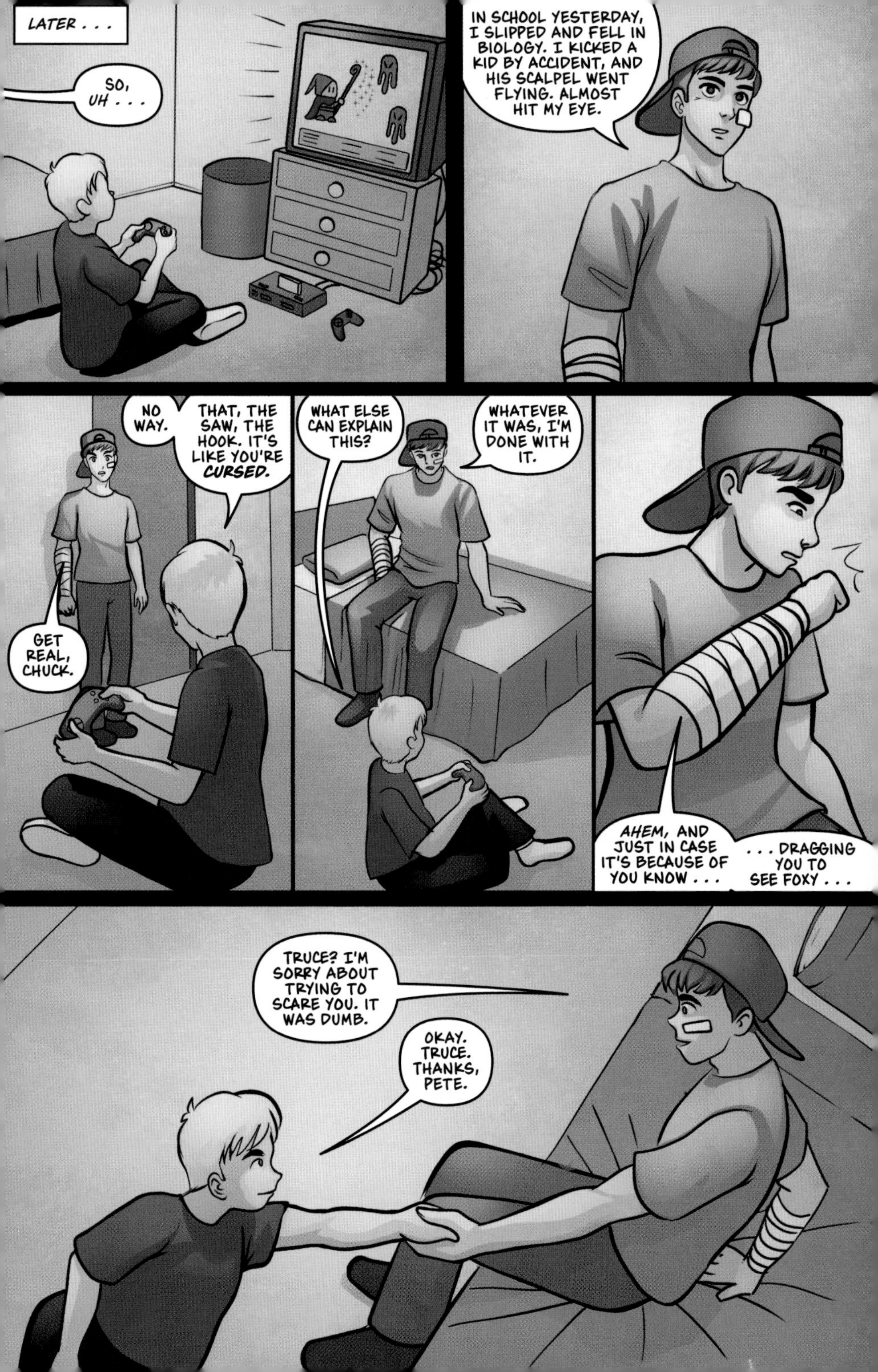
LATER . . .
SO, UH . . .
IN SCHOOL YESTERDAY, I SLIPPED AND FELL IN BIOLOGY. I KICKED A KID BY ACCIDENT, AND HIS SCALPEL WENT FLYING. ALMOST HIT MY EYE.
NO WAY.
THAT, THE SAW, THE HOOK. IT'S LIKE YOU'RE *CURSED.*
GET REAL, CHUCK.
WHAT ELSE CAN EXPLAIN THIS?
WHATEVER IT WAS, I'M DONE WITH IT.
AHEM, AND JUST IN CASE IT'S BECAUSE OF YOU KNOW . . .
. . . DRAGGING YOU TO SEE FOXY . . .
TRUCE? I'M SORRY ABOUT TRYING TO SCARE YOU. IT WAS DUMB.
OKAY. TRUCE. THANKS, PETE.

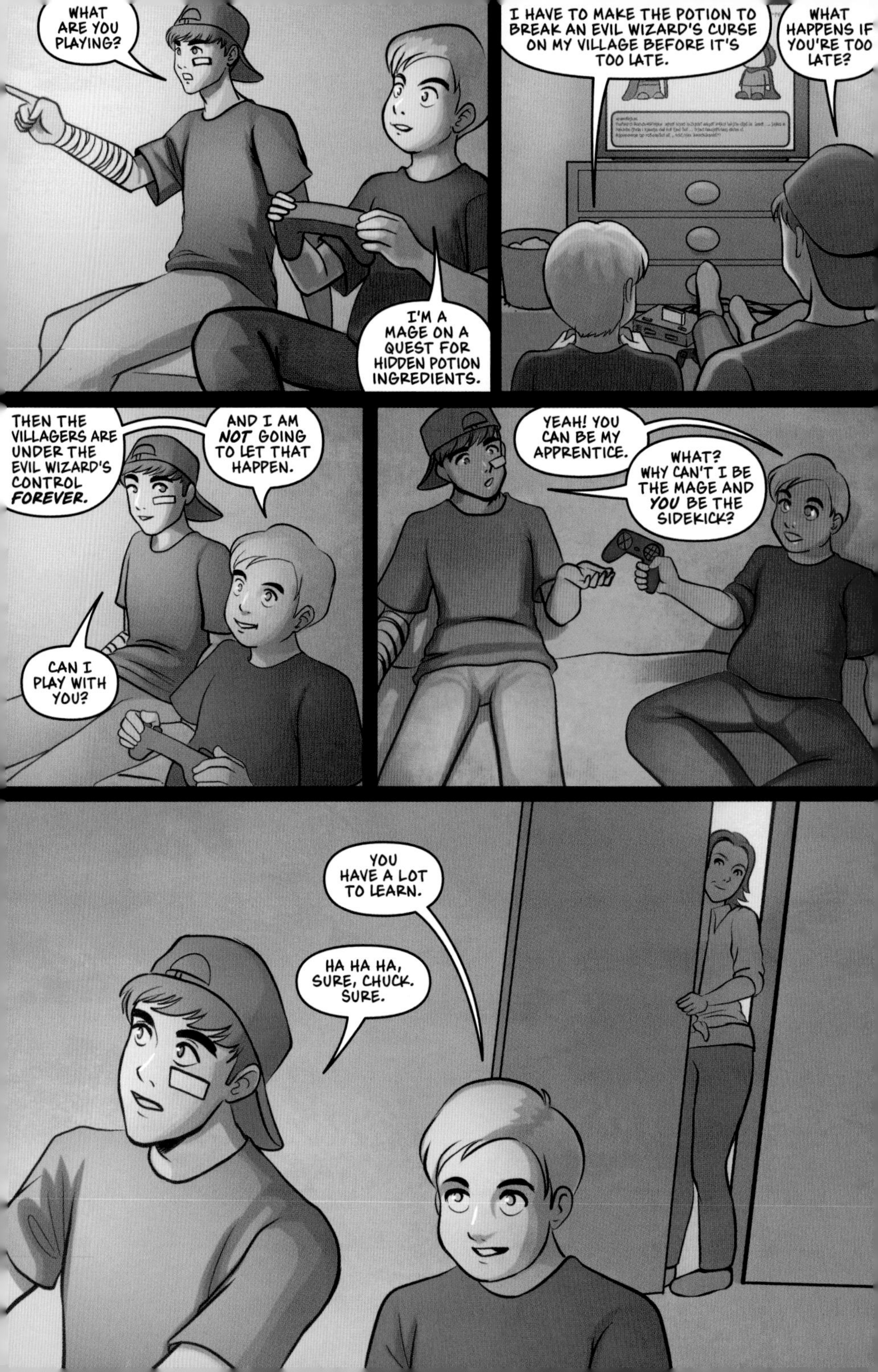
WHAT ARE YOU PLAYING?
I'M A MAGE ON A QUEST FOR HIDDEN POTION INGREDIENTS.
I HAVE TO MAKE THE POTION TO BREAK AN EVIL WIZARD'S CURSE ON MY VILLAGE BEFORE IT'S TOO LATE.
WHAT HAPPENS IF YOU'RE TOO LATE?
THEN THE VILLAGERS ARE UNDER THE EVIL WIZARD'S CONTROL FOREVER.
AND I AM NOT GOING TO LET THAT HAPPEN.
CAN I PLAY WITH YOU?
YEAH! YOU CAN BE MY APPRENTICE.
WHAT? WHY CAN'T I BE THE MAGE AND YOU BE THE SIDEKICK?
YOU HAVE A LOT TO LEARN.
HA HA HA, SURE, CHUCK. SURE.

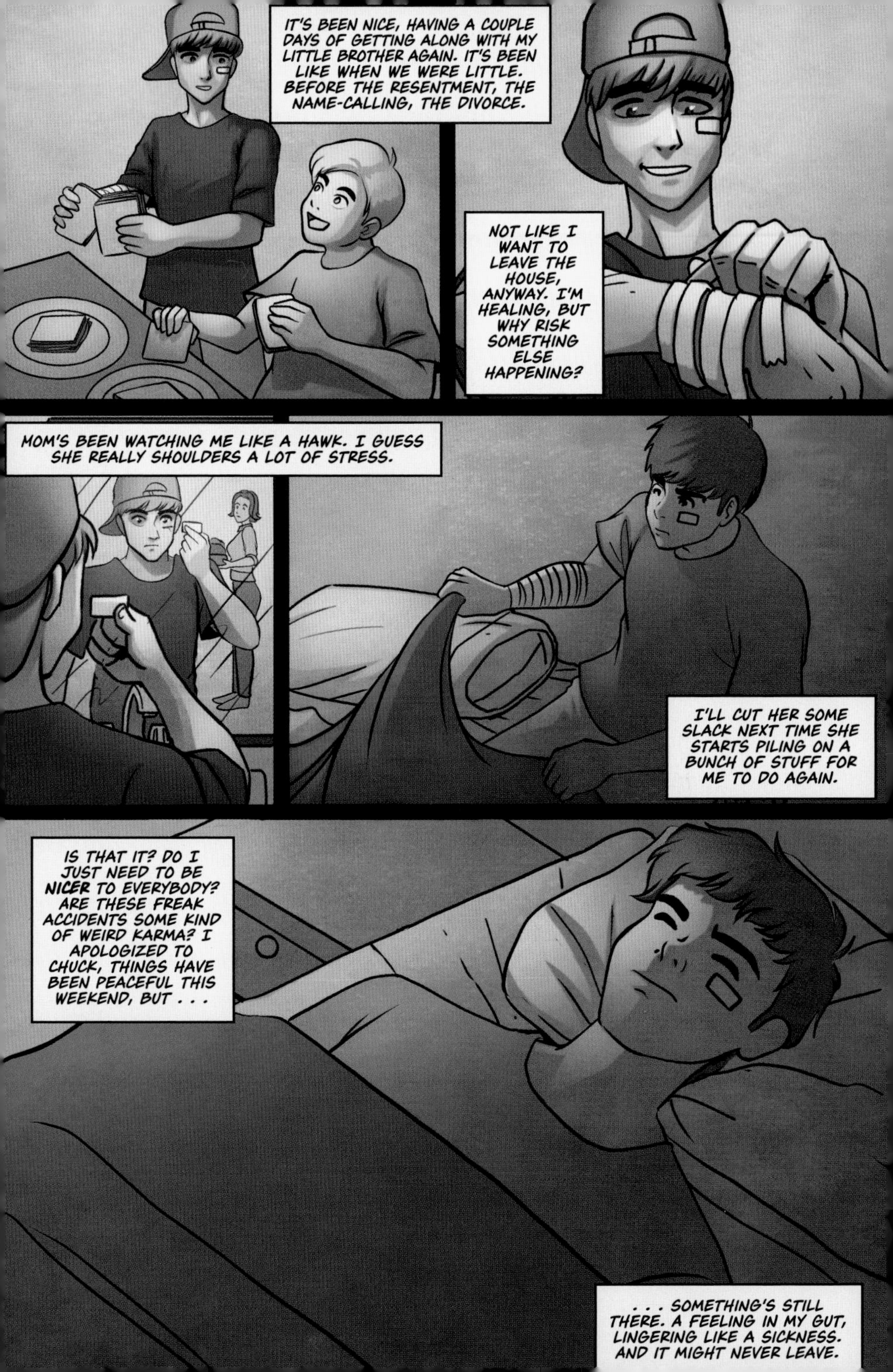
IT'S BEEN NICE, HAVING A COUPLE DAYS OF GETTING ALONG WITH MY LITTLE BROTHER AGAIN. IT'S BEEN LIKE WHEN WE WERE LITTLE. BEFORE THE RESENTMENT, THE NAME-CALLING, THE DIVORCE.
NOT LIKE I WANT TO LEAVE THE HOUSE, ANYWAY. I'M HEALING, BUT WHY RISK SOMETHING ELSE HAPPENING?
MOM'S BEEN WATCHING ME LIKE A HAWK. I GUESS SHE REALLY SHOULDERS A LOT OF STRESS.
I'LL CUT HER SOME SLACK NEXT TIME SHE STARTS PILING ON A BUNCH OF STUFF FOR ME TO DO AGAIN.
IS THAT IT? DO I JUST NEED TO BE **NICER** TO EVERYBODY? ARE THESE FREAK ACCIDENTS SOME KIND OF WEIRD KARMA? I APOLOGIZED TO CHUCK, THINGS HAVE BEEN PEACEFUL THIS WEEKEND, BUT . . .
. . . SOMETHING'S STILL THERE. A FEELING IN MY GUT, LINGERING LIKE A SICKNESS. AND IT MIGHT NEVER LEAVE.

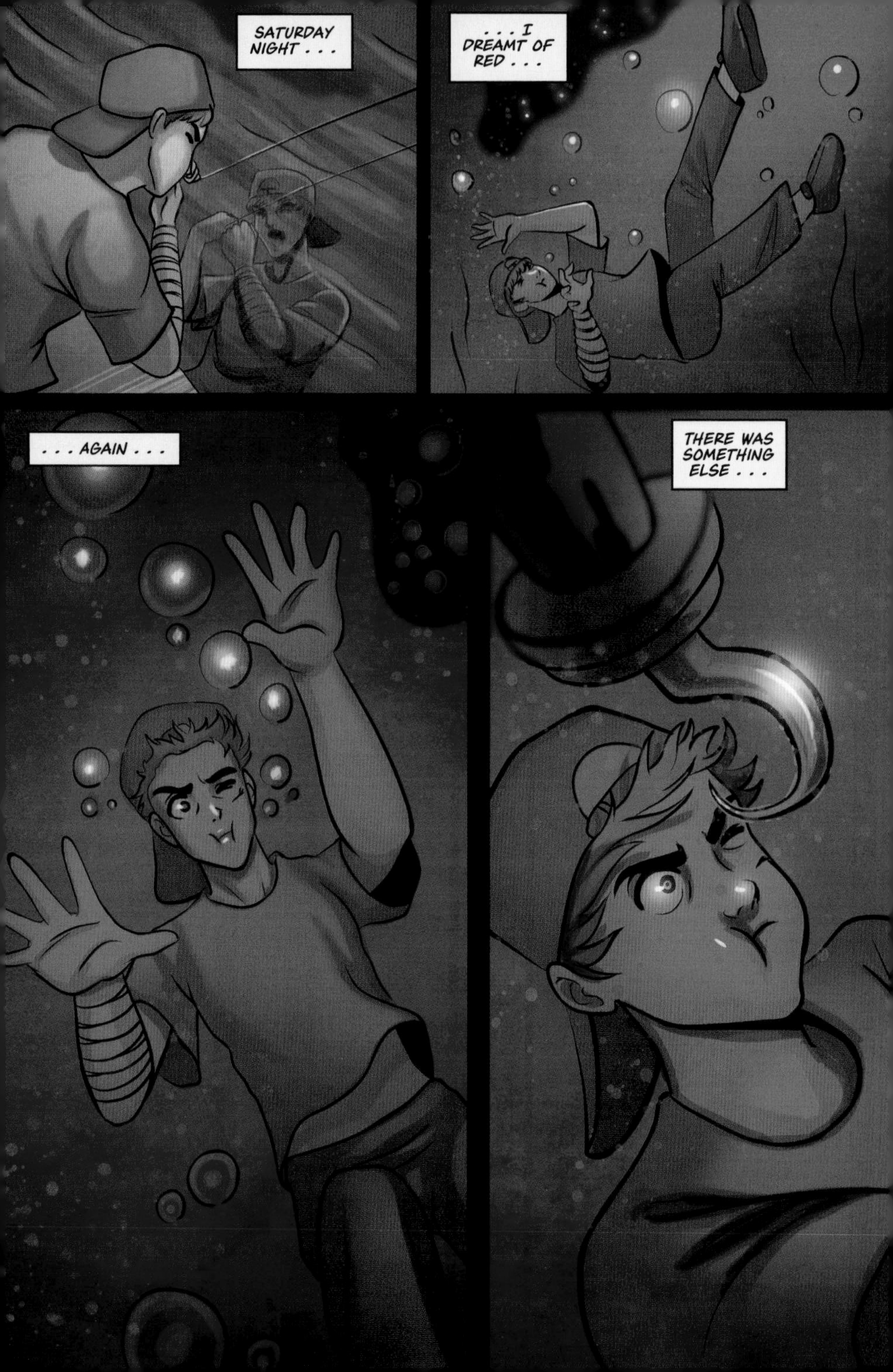
SATURDAY NIGHT . . .
. . . I DREAMT OF RED . . .
. . . AGAIN . . .
THERE WAS SOMETHING ELSE . . .

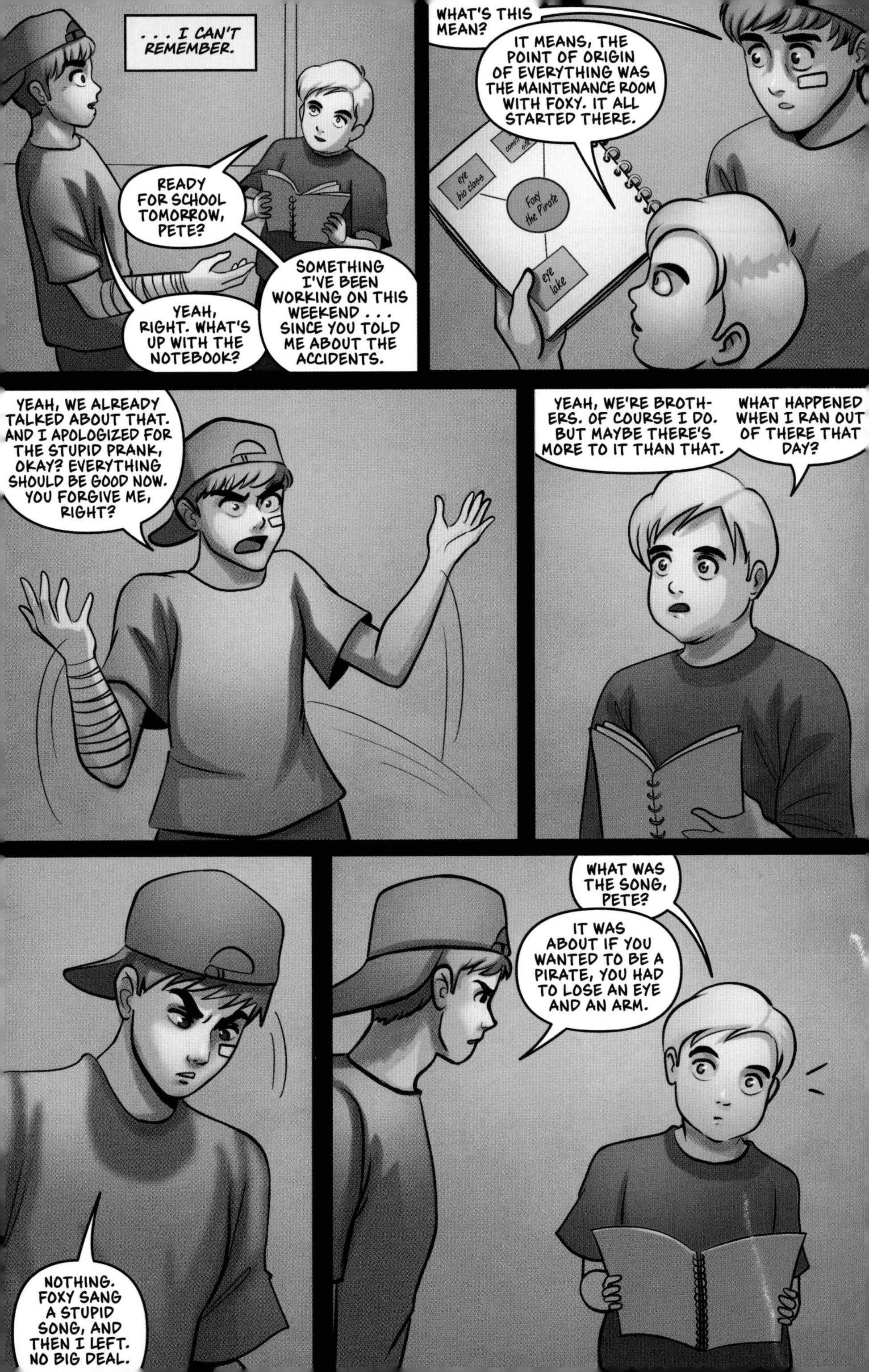
. . . I CAN'T REMEMBER.
READY FOR SCHOOL TOMORROW, PETE?
YEAH, RIGHT. WHAT'S UP WITH THE NOTEBOOK?
SOMETHING I'VE BEEN WORKING ON THIS WEEKEND . . . SINCE YOU TOLD ME ABOUT THE ACCIDENTS.
WHAT'S THIS MEAN?
IT MEANS, THE POINT OF ORIGIN OF EVERYTHING WAS THE MAINTENANCE ROOM WITH FOXY. IT ALL STARTED THERE.
eye bio class
Foxy the Pirate
eye lake
YEAH, WE ALREADY TALKED ABOUT THAT. AND I APOLOGIZED FOR THE STUPID PRANK, OKAY? EVERYTHING SHOULD BE GOOD NOW. YOU FORGIVE ME, RIGHT?
YEAH, WE'RE BROTHERS. OF COURSE I DO. BUT MAYBE THERE'S MORE TO IT THAN THAT.
WHAT HAPPENED WHEN I RAN OUT OF THERE THAT DAY?
NOTHING. FOXY SANG A STUPID SONG, AND THEN I LEFT. NO BIG DEAL.
WHAT WAS THE SONG, PETE?
IT WAS ABOUT IF YOU WANTED TO BE A PIRATE, YOU HAD TO LOSE AN EYE AND AN ARM.

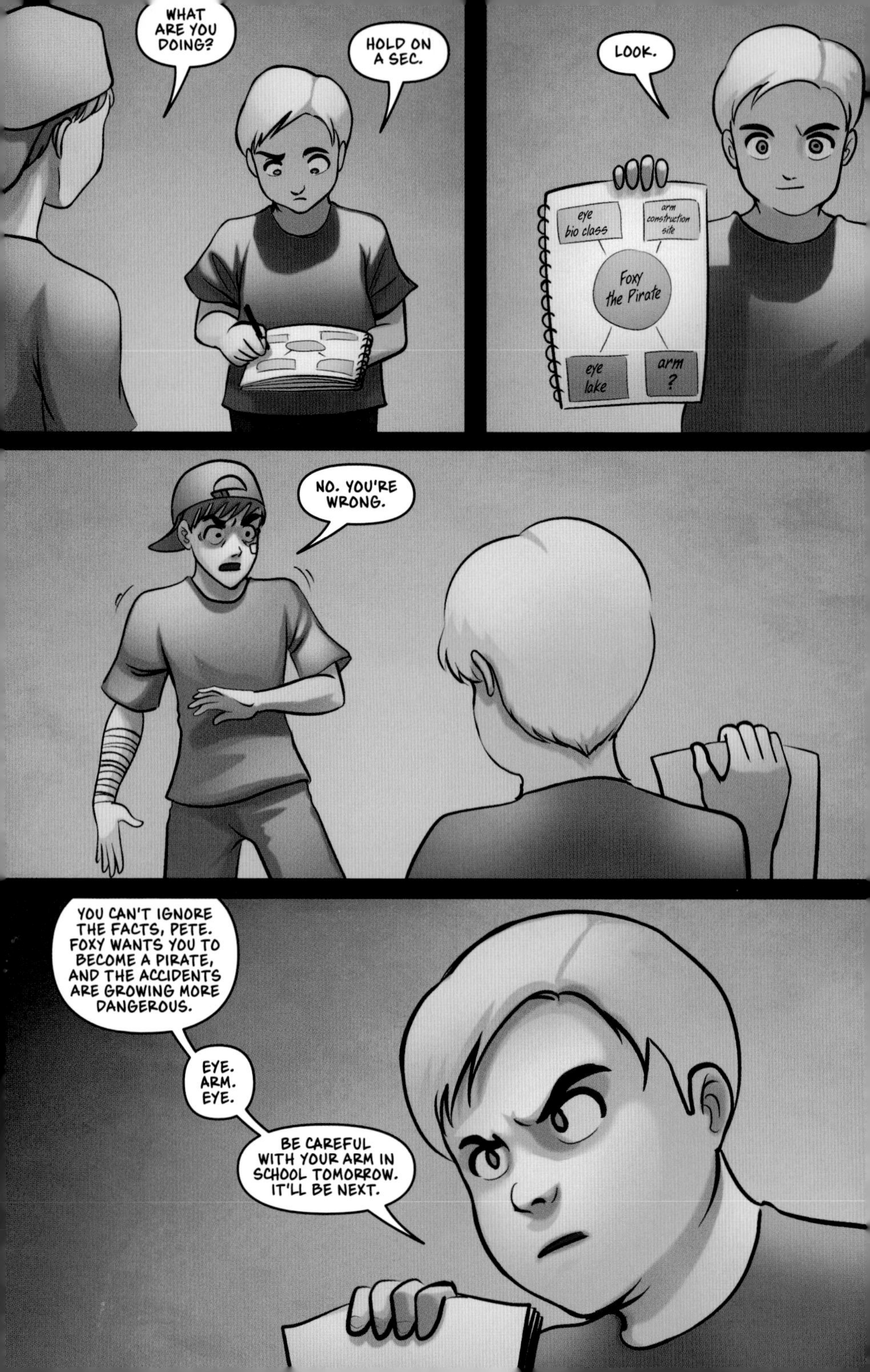

WHAT ARE YOU DOING?
HOLD ON A SEC.
LOOK.
eye bio class
arm construction site
Foxy the Pirate
eye lake
arm ?
NO. YOU'RE WRONG.
YOU CAN'T IGNORE THE FACTS, PETE. FOXY WANTS YOU TO BECOME A PIRATE, AND THE ACCIDENTS ARE GROWING MORE DANGEROUS.
EYE. ARM. EYE.
BE CAREFUL WITH YOUR ARM IN SCHOOL TOMORROW. IT'LL BE NEXT.

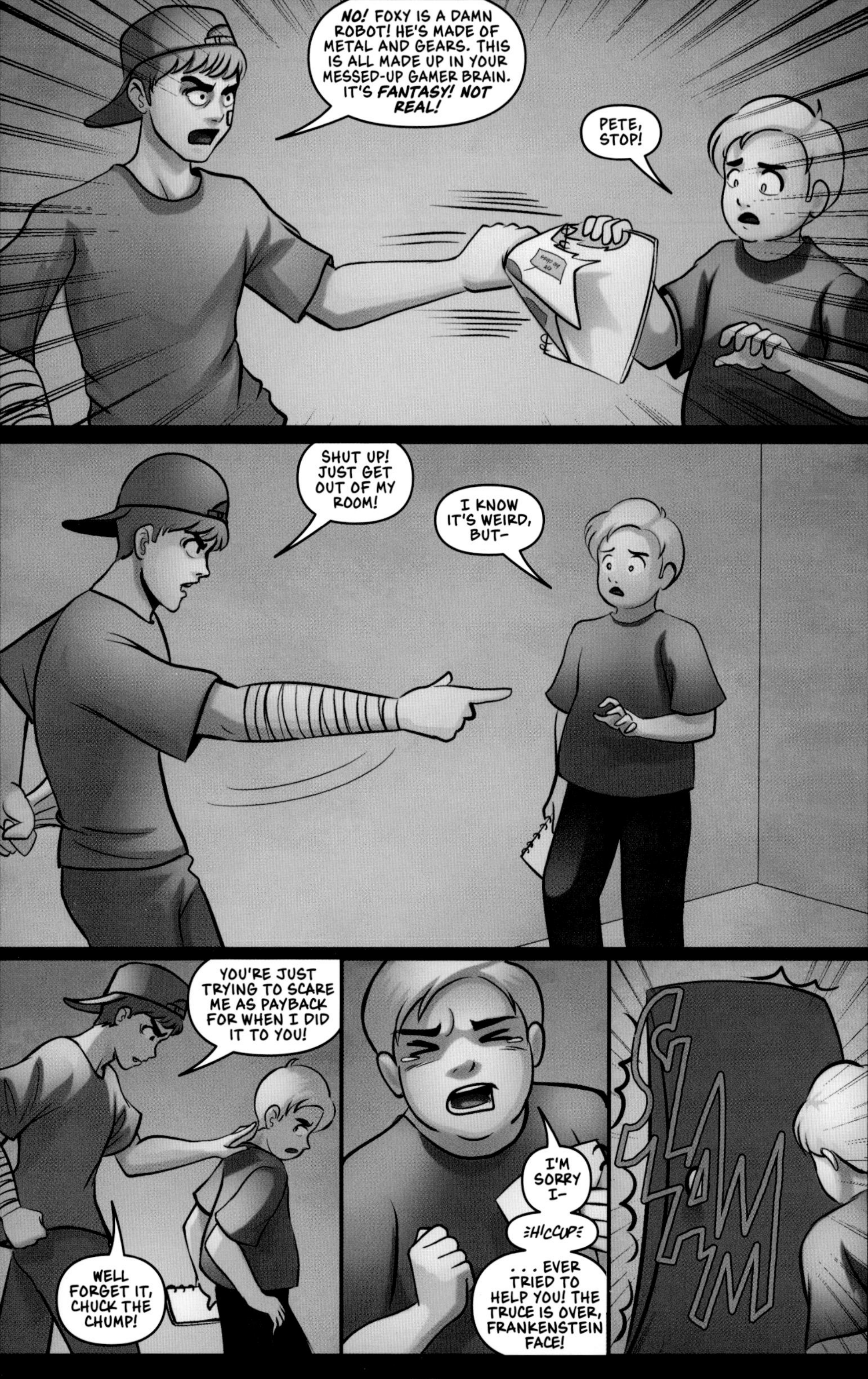
NO! FOXY IS A DAMN ROBOT! HE'S MADE OF METAL AND GEARS. THIS IS ALL MADE UP IN YOUR MESSED-UP GAMER BRAIN. IT'S FANTASY! NOT REAL!
PETE, STOP!
SHUT UP! JUST GET OUT OF MY ROOM!
I KNOW IT'S WEIRD, BUT-
YOU'RE JUST TRYING TO SCARE ME AS PAYBACK FOR WHEN I DID IT TO YOU!
WELL FORGET IT, CHUCK THE CHUMP!
I'M SORRY I-
HICCUP
. . . EVER TRIED TO HELP YOU! THE TRUCE IS OVER, FRANKENSTEIN FACE!
SLAM

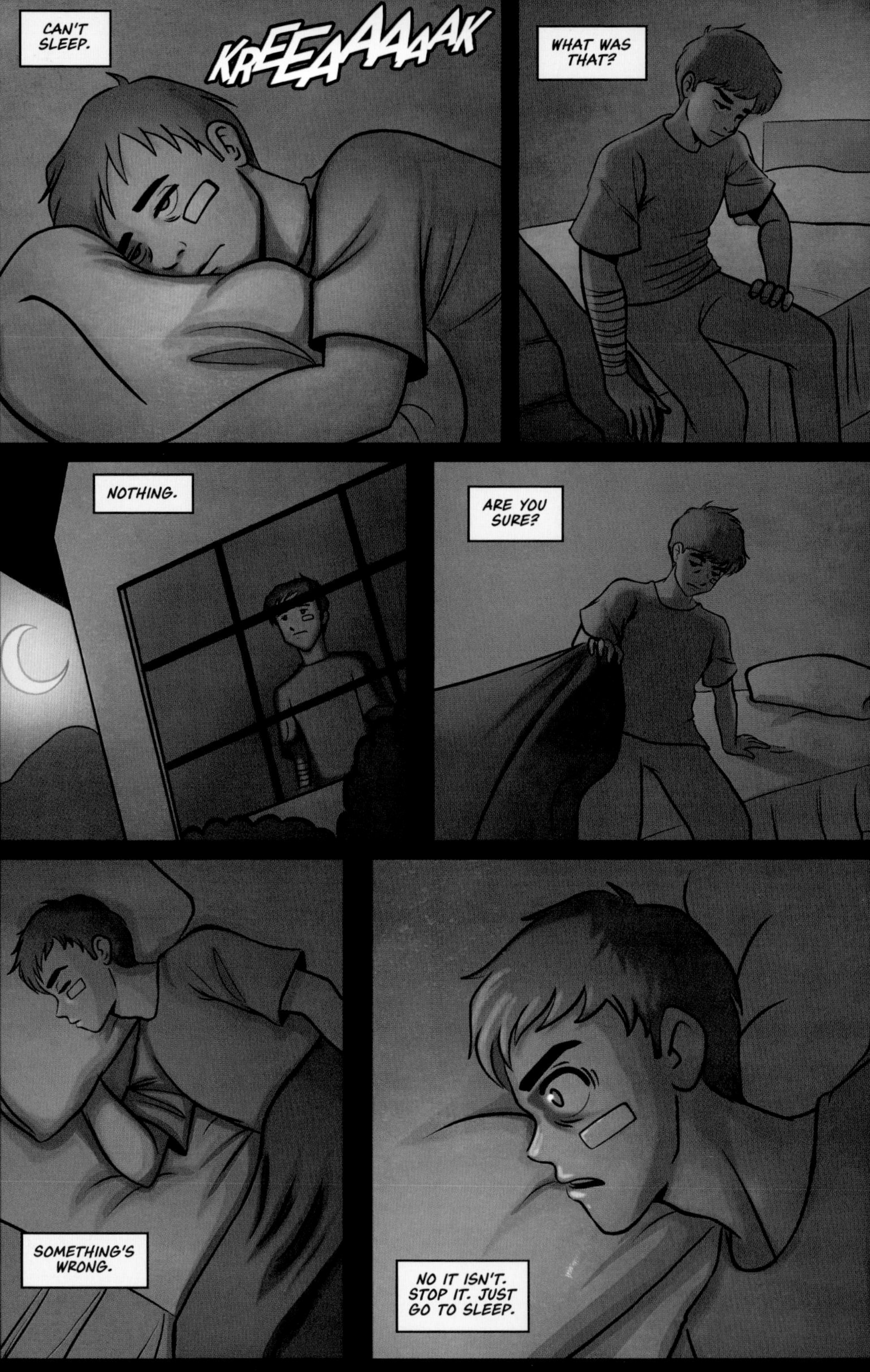
CAN'T SLEEP.
KREEEAAAAAK
WHAT WAS THAT?
NOTHING.
ARE YOU SURE?
SOMETHING'S WRONG.
NO IT ISN'T. STOP IT. JUST GO TO SLEEP.

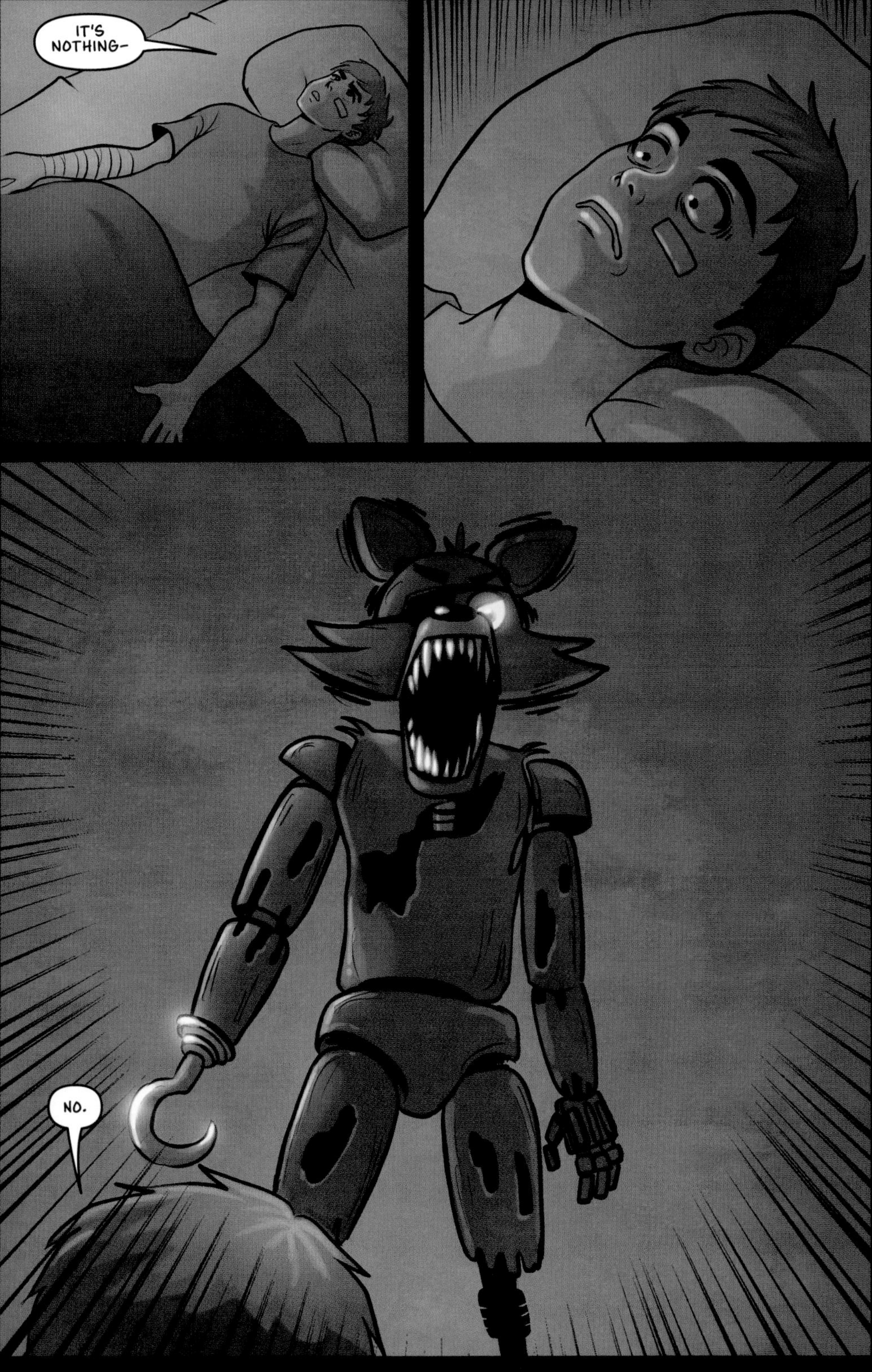
IT'S NOTHING-
NO.

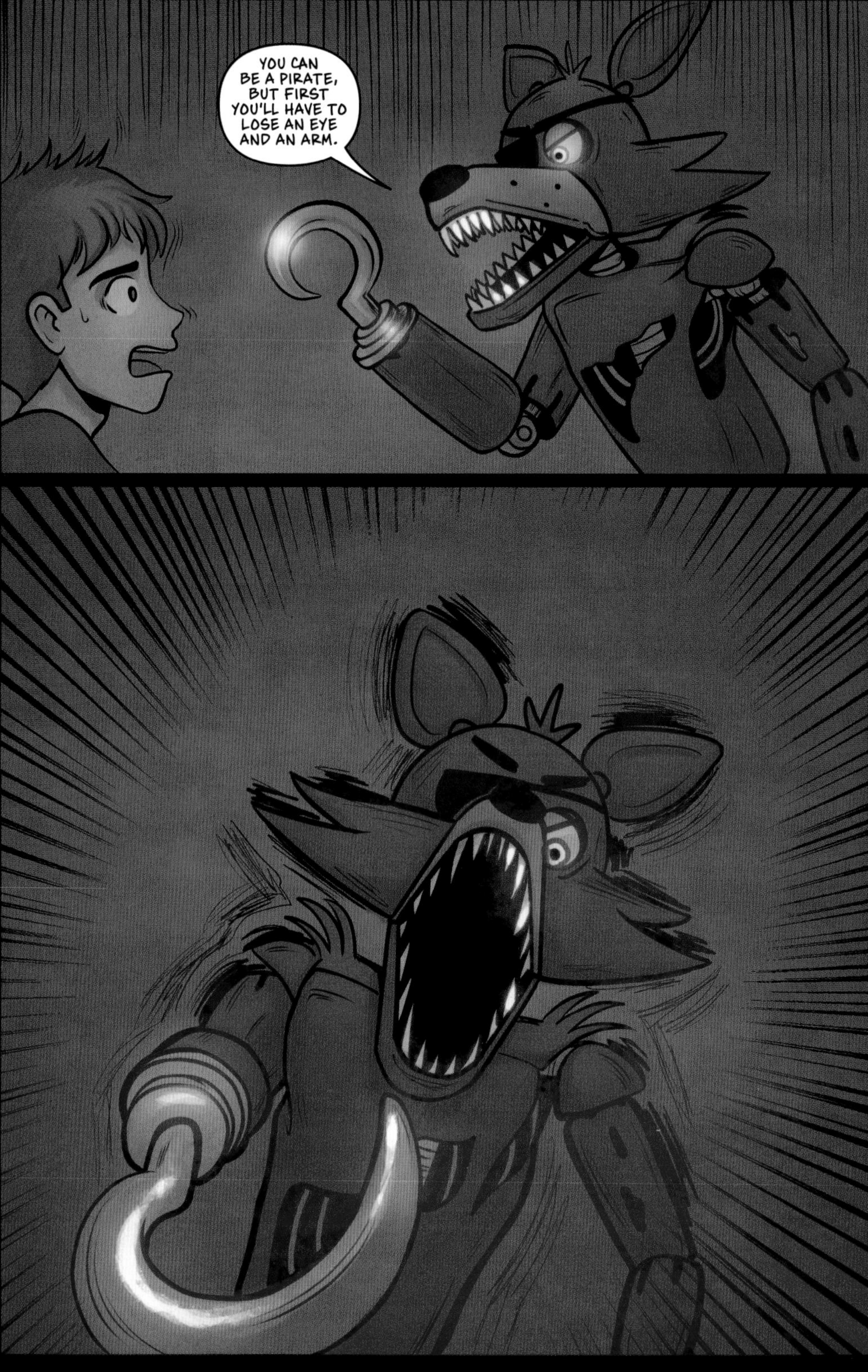
YOU CAN BE A PIRATE, BUT FIRST YOU'LL HAVE TO LOSE AN EYE AND AN ARM.

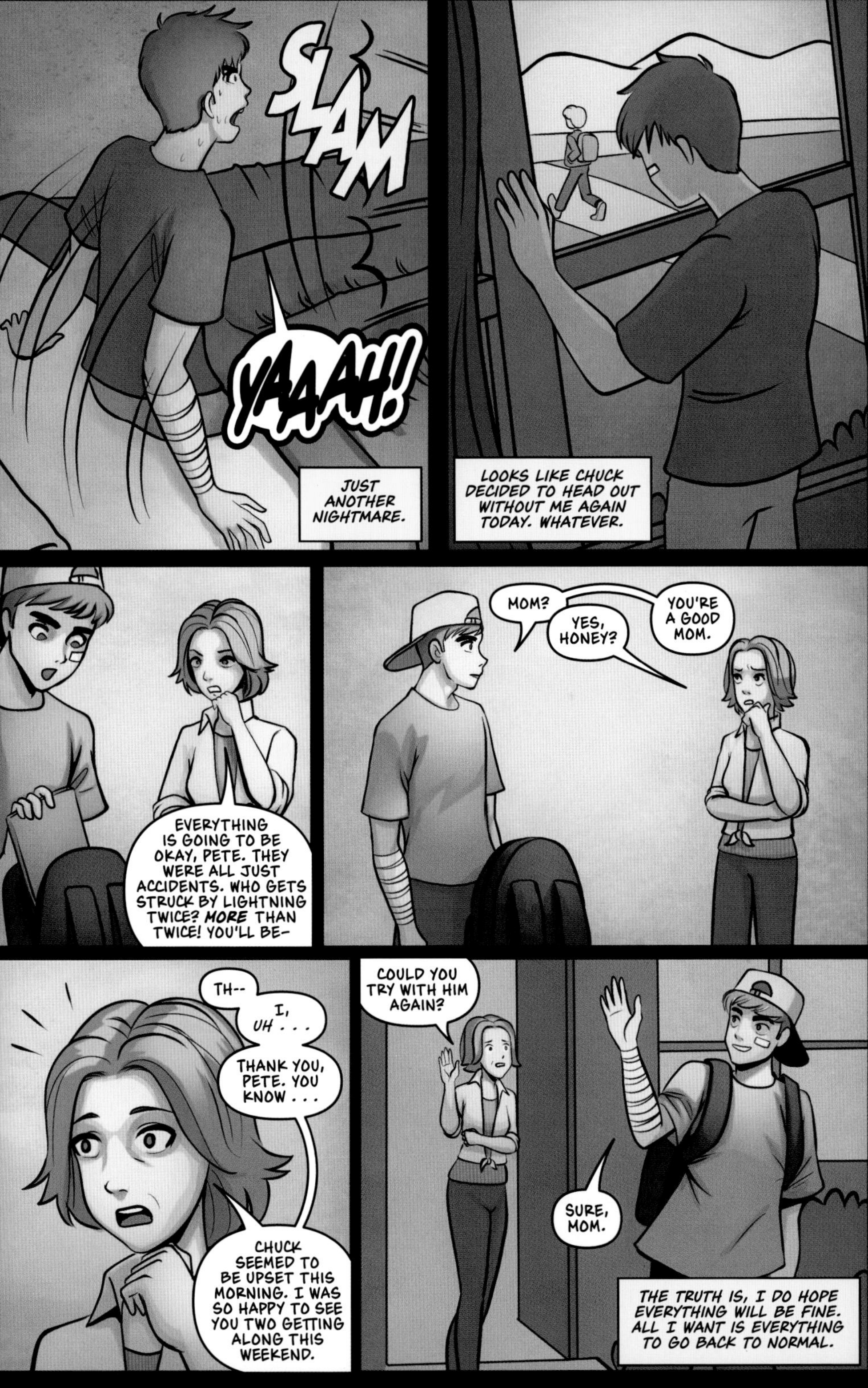
SLAM
YAAAH!
JUST ANOTHER NIGHTMARE.
LOOKS LIKE CHUCK DECIDED TO HEAD OUT WITHOUT ME AGAIN TODAY. WHATEVER.
EVERYTHING IS GOING TO BE OKAY, PETE. THEY WERE ALL JUST ACCIDENTS. WHO GETS STRUCK BY LIGHTNING TWICE? MORE THAN TWICE! YOU'LL BE-
MOM?
YES, HONEY?
YOU'RE A GOOD MOM.
TH--
I, UH . . .
THANK YOU, PETE. YOU KNOW . . .
CHUCK SEEMED TO BE UPSET THIS MORNING. I WAS SO HAPPY TO SEE YOU TWO GETTING ALONG THIS WEEKEND.
COULD YOU TRY WITH HIM AGAIN?
SURE, MOM.
THE TRUTH IS, I DO HOPE EVERYTHING WILL BE FINE. ALL I WANT IS EVERYTHING TO GO BACK TO NORMAL.

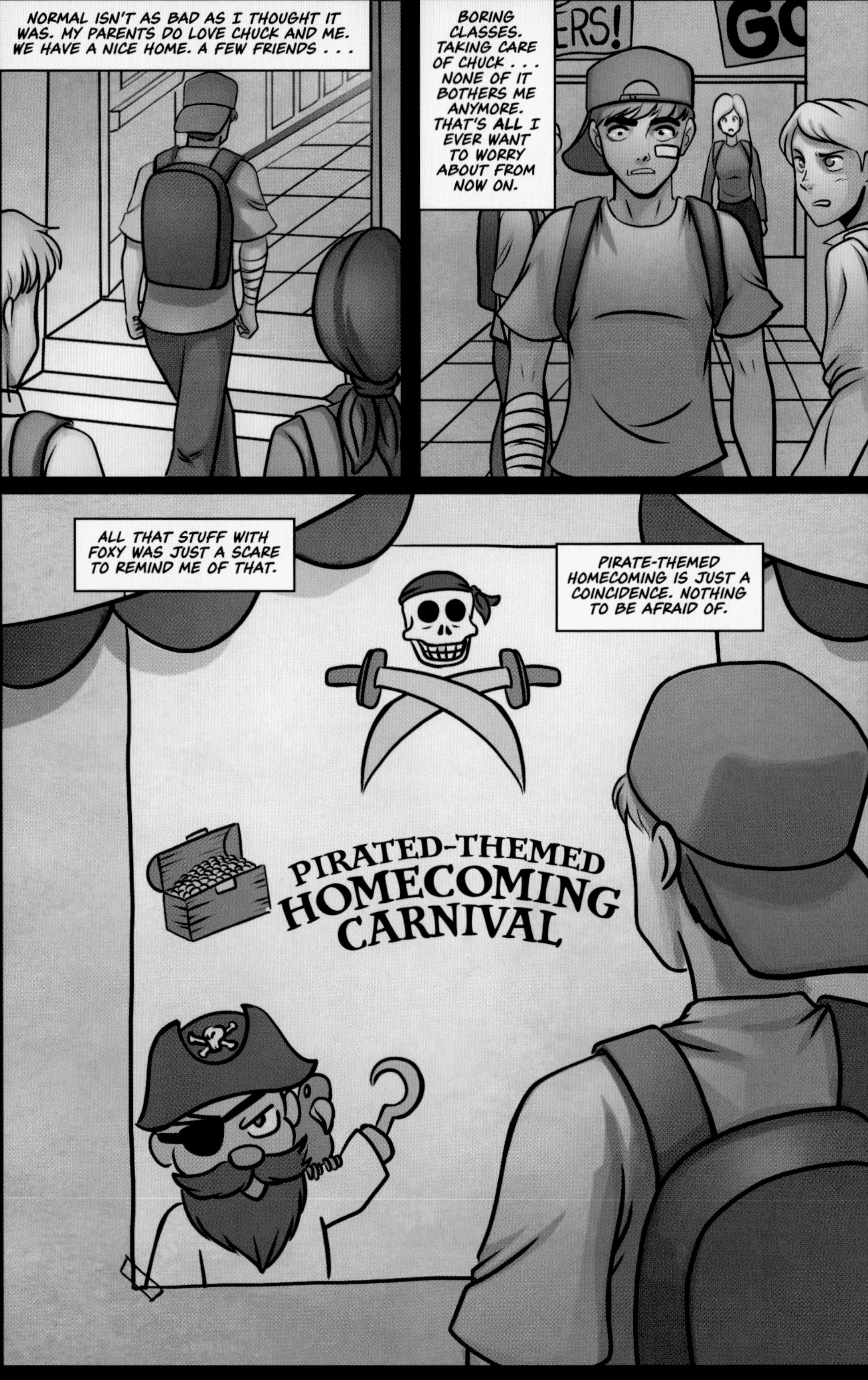
NORMAL ISN'T AS BAD AS I THOUGHT IT WAS. MY PARENTS DO LOVE CHUCK AND ME. WE HAVE A NICE HOME. A FEW FRIENDS . . .
BORING CLASSES. TAKING CARE OF CHUCK . . . NONE OF IT BOTHERS ME ANYMORE. THAT'S ALL I EVER WANT TO WORRY ABOUT FROM NOW ON.
ALL THAT STUFF WITH FOXY WAS JUST A SCARE TO REMIND ME OF THAT.
PIRATE-THEMED HOMECOMING IS JUST A COINCIDENCE. NOTHING TO BE AFRAID OF.
PIRATED-THEMED HOMECOMING CARNIVAL

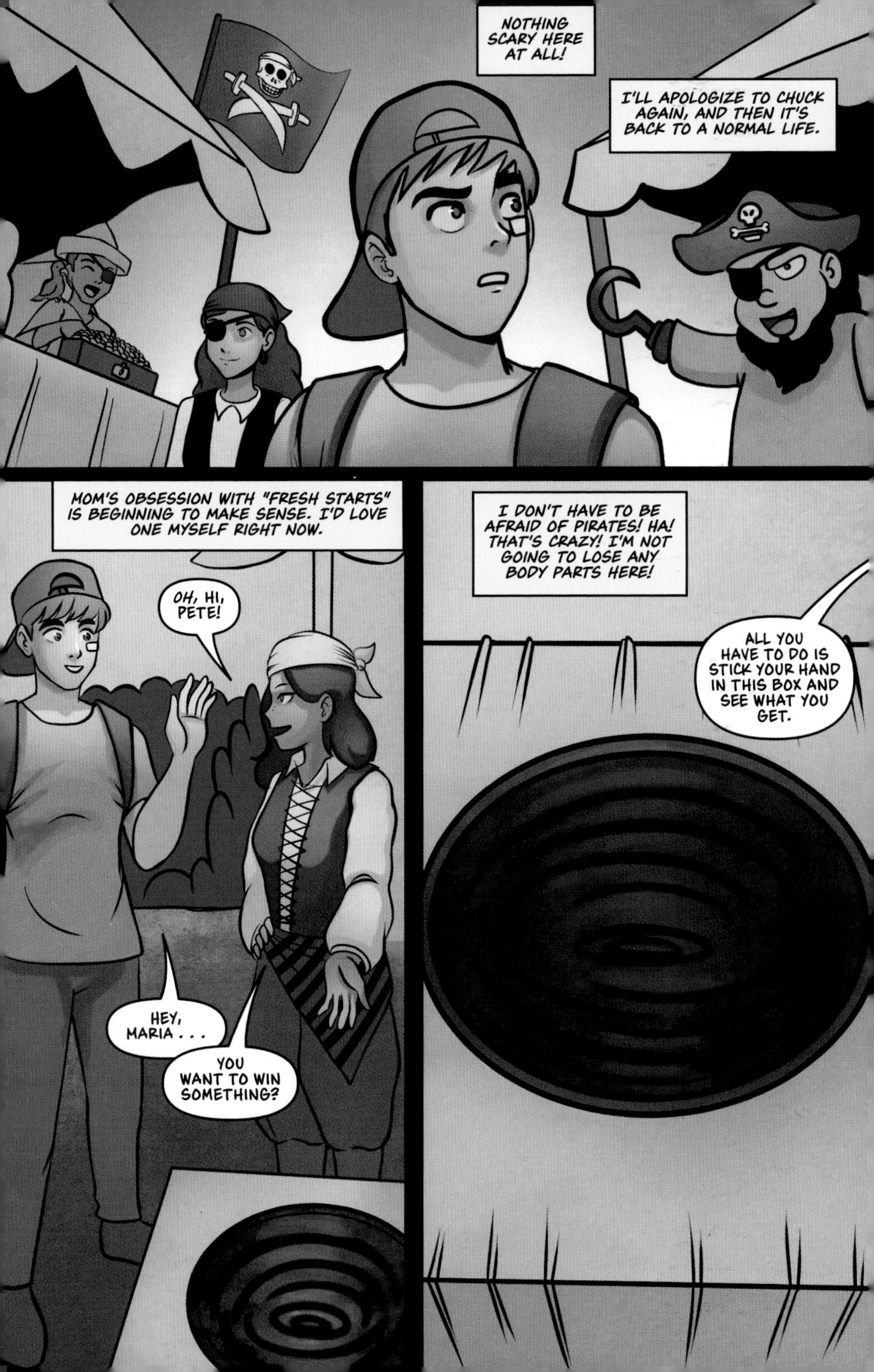
NOTHING SCARY HERE AT ALL!
I'LL APOLOGIZE TO CHUCK AGAIN, AND THEN IT'S BACK TO A NORMAL LIFE.
MOM'S OBSESSION WITH "FRESH STARTS" IS BEGINNING TO MAKE SENSE. I'D LOVE ONE MYSELF RIGHT NOW.
OH, HI, PETE!
HEY, MARIA . . .
YOU WANT TO WIN SOMETHING?
I DON'T HAVE TO BE AFRAID OF PIRATES! HA! THAT'S CRAZY! I'M NOT GOING TO LOSE ANY BODY PARTS HERE!
ALL YOU HAVE TO DO IS STICK YOUR HAND IN THIS BOX AND SEE WHAT YOU GET.

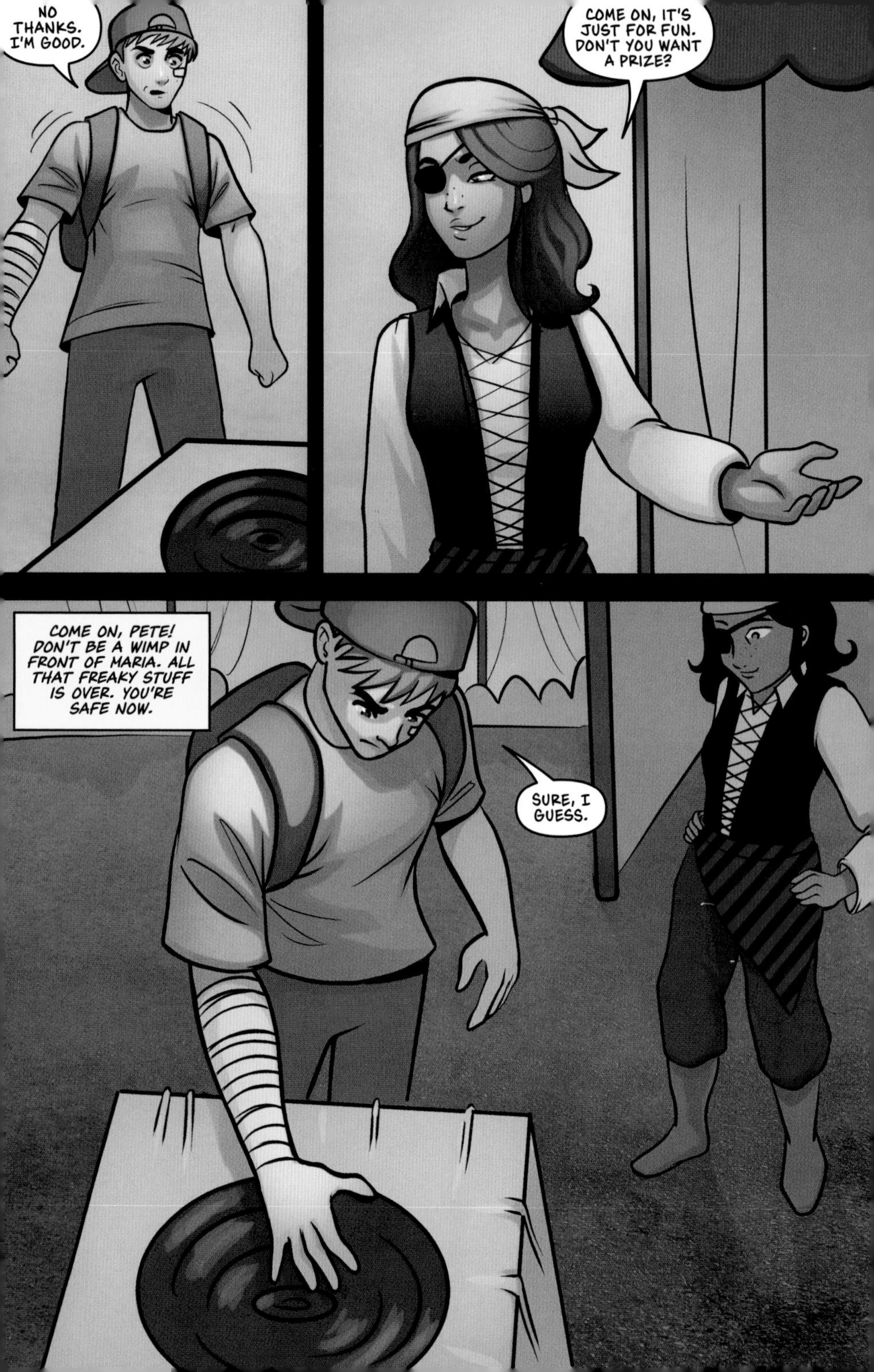
NO THANKS. I'M GOOD.
COME ON, IT'S JUST FOR FUN. DON'T YOU WANT A PRIZE?
COME ON, PETE! DON'T BE A WIMP IN FRONT OF MARIA. ALL THAT FREAKY STUFF IS OVER. YOU'RE SAFE NOW.
SURE, I GUESS.

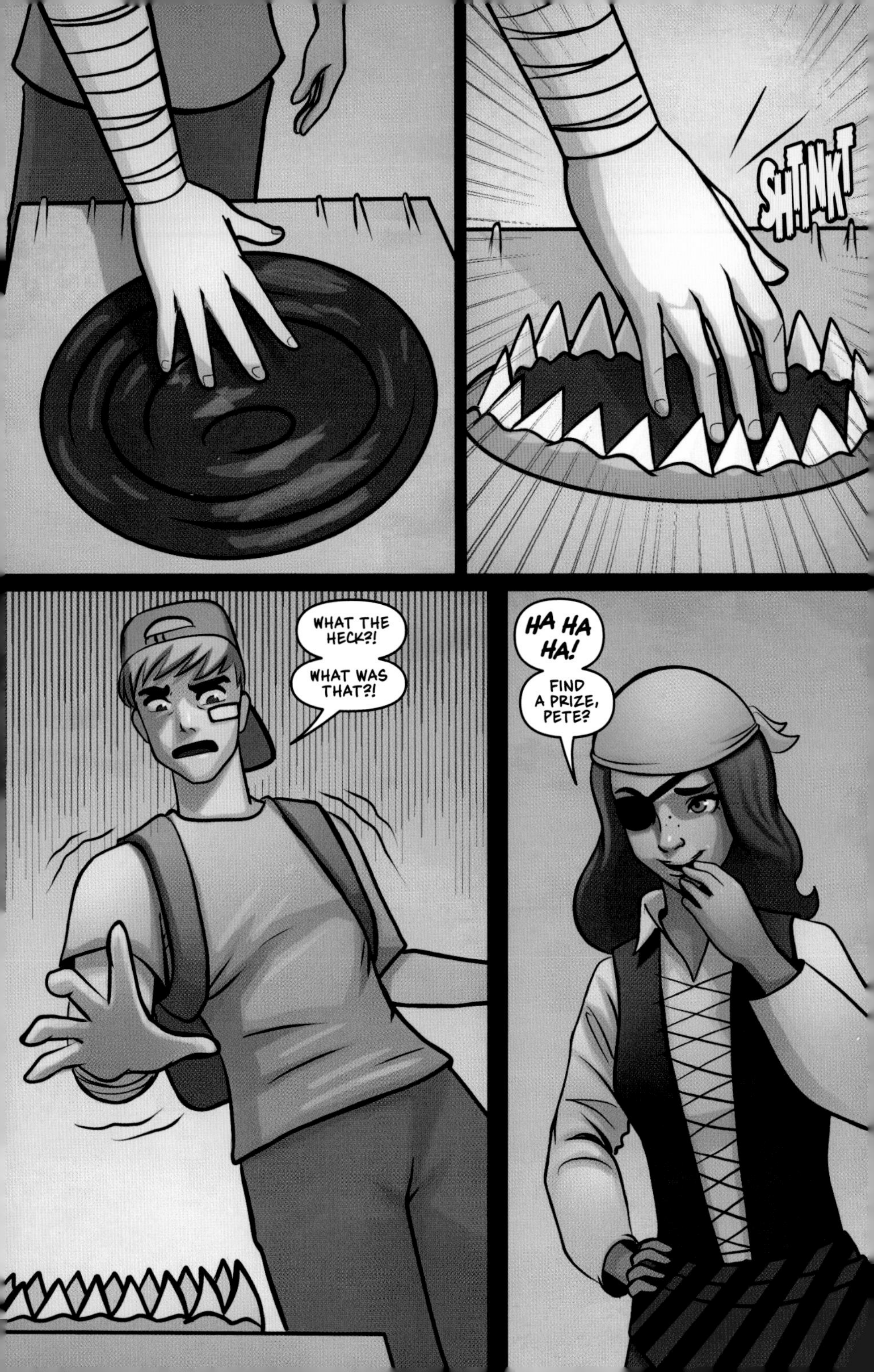
SHTINKT
WHAT THE HECK?!
WHAT WAS THAT?!
HA HA HA!
FIND A PRIZE, PETE?

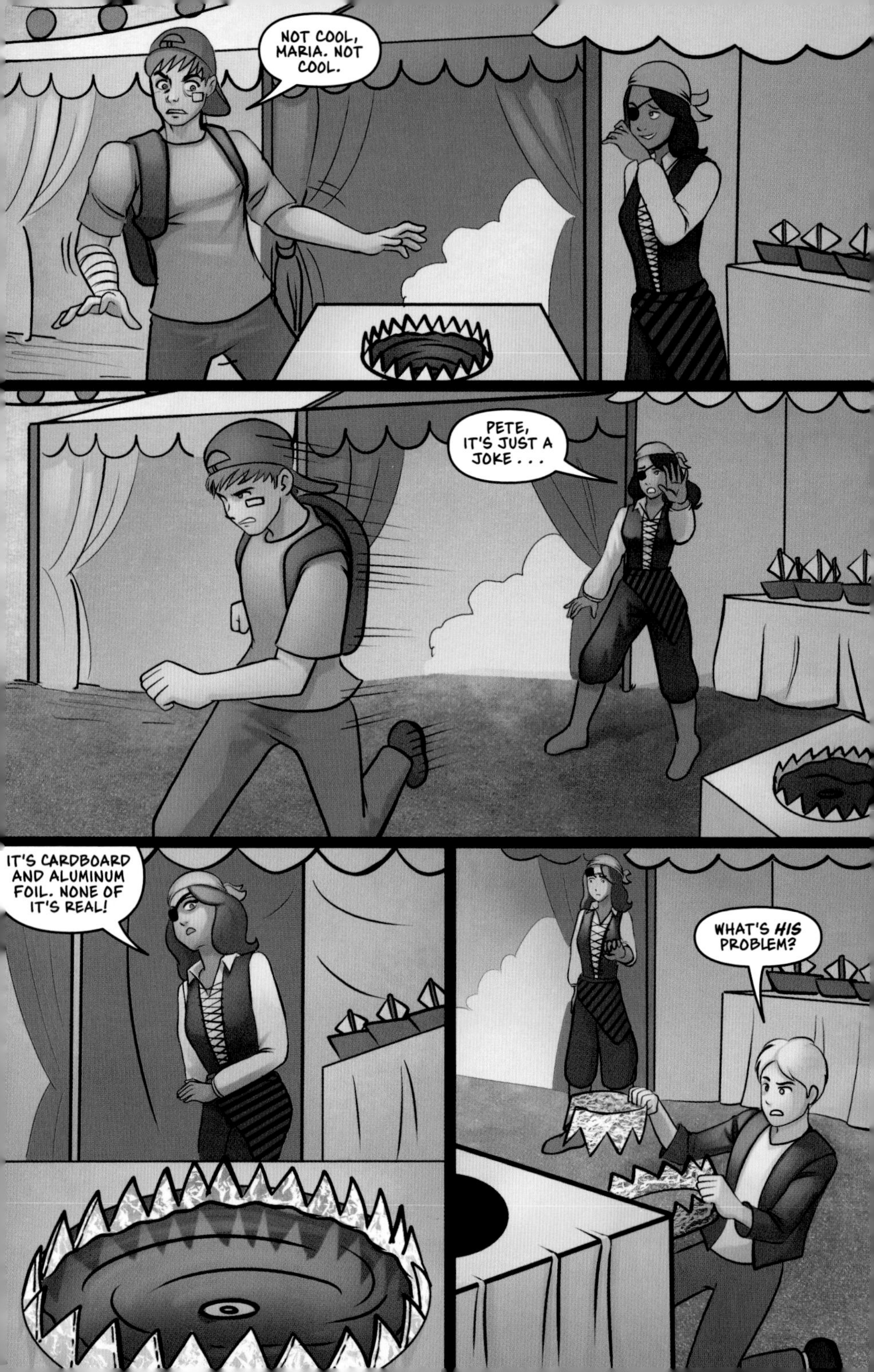
NOT COOL, MARIA. NOT COOL.
PETE, IT'S JUST A JOKE . . .
IT'S CARDBOARD AND ALUMINUM FOIL. NONE OF IT'S REAL!
WHAT'S *HIS* PROBLEM?

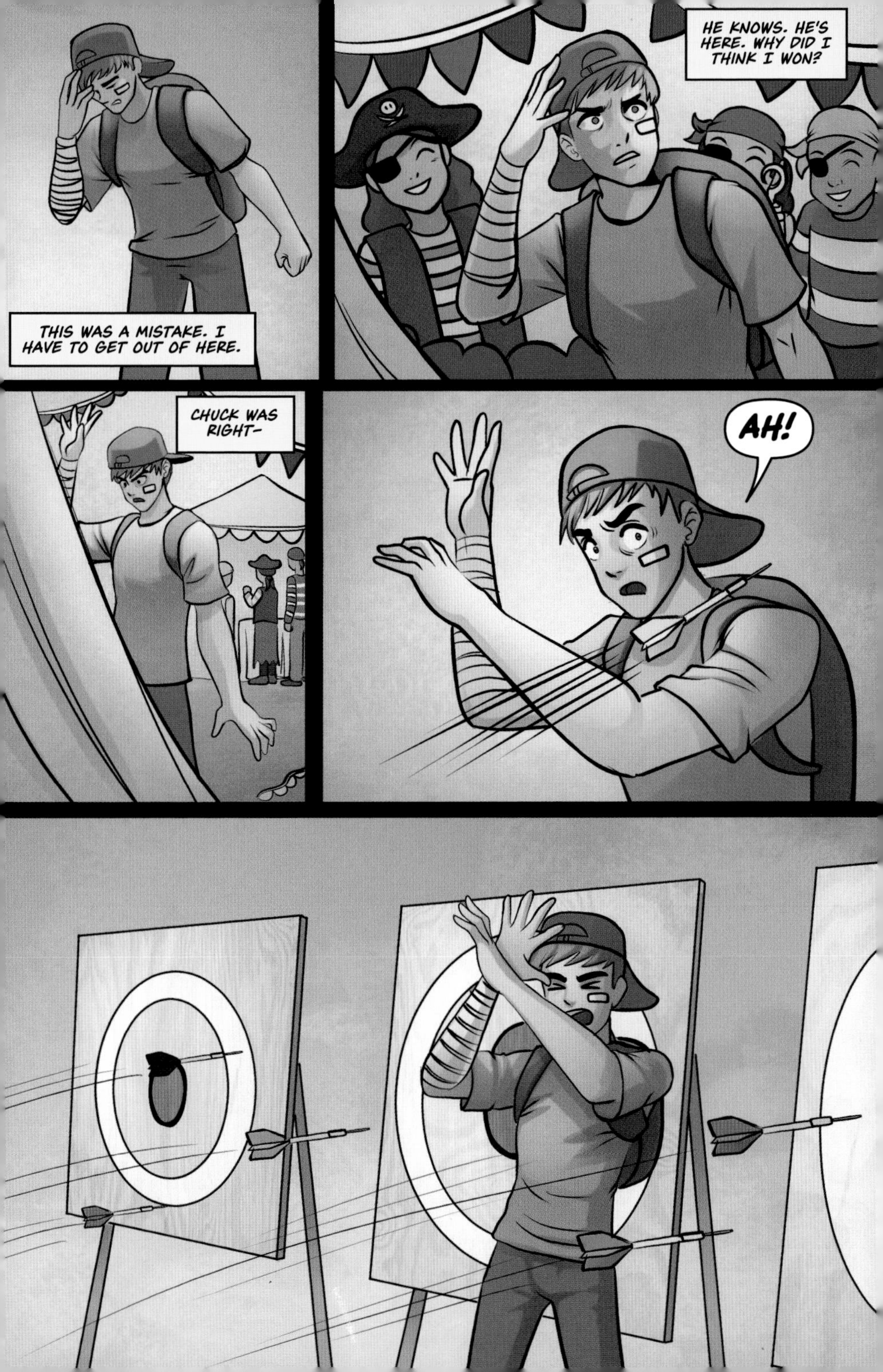
THIS WAS A MISTAKE. I HAVE TO GET OUT OF HERE.
HE KNOWS. HE'S HERE. WHY DID I THINK I WON?
CHUCK WAS RIGHT-
AH!

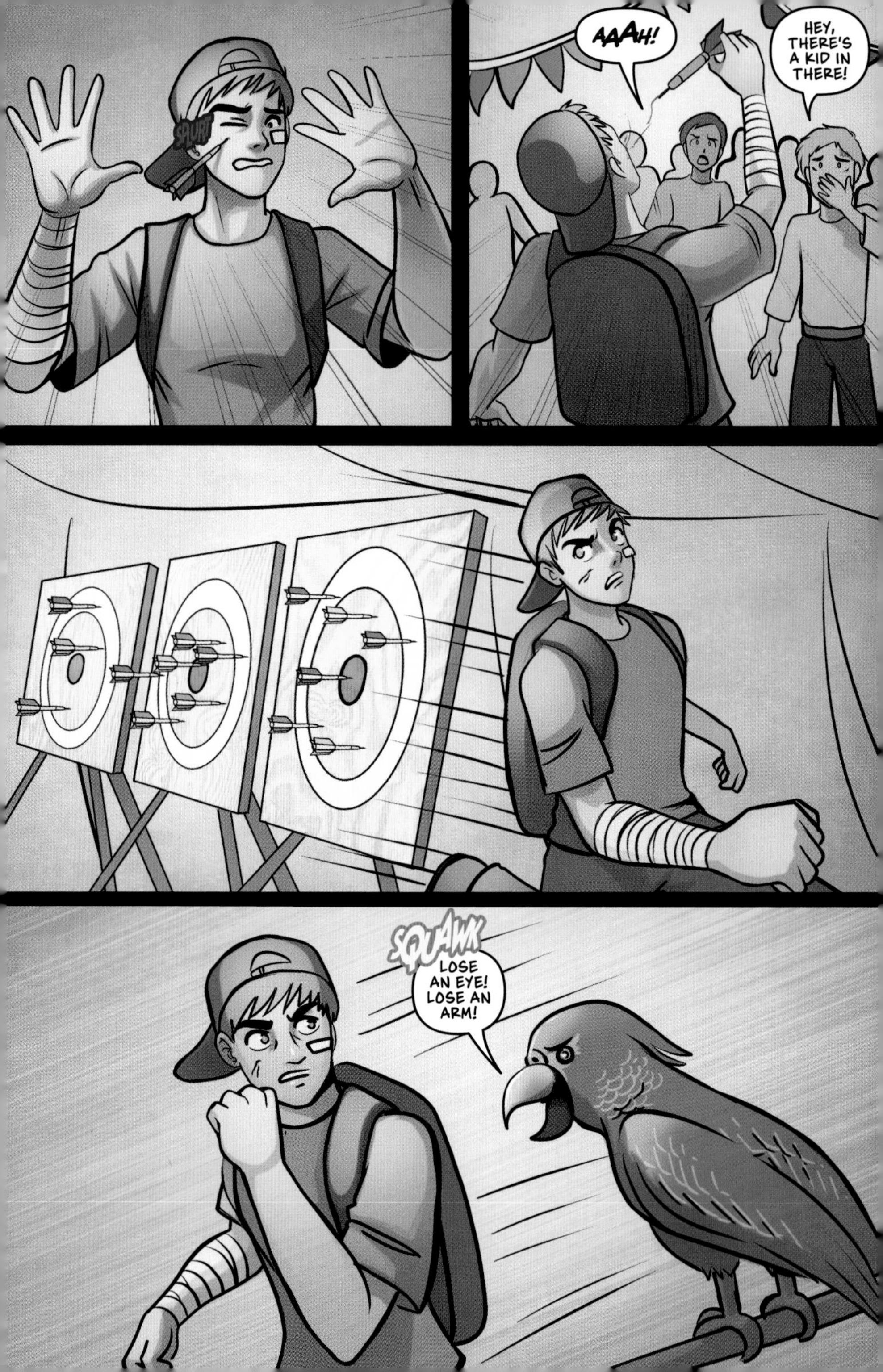
SPLURT
AAAH!
HEY, THERE'S A KID IN THERE!
SQUAWK
LOSE AN EYE! LOSE AN ARM!

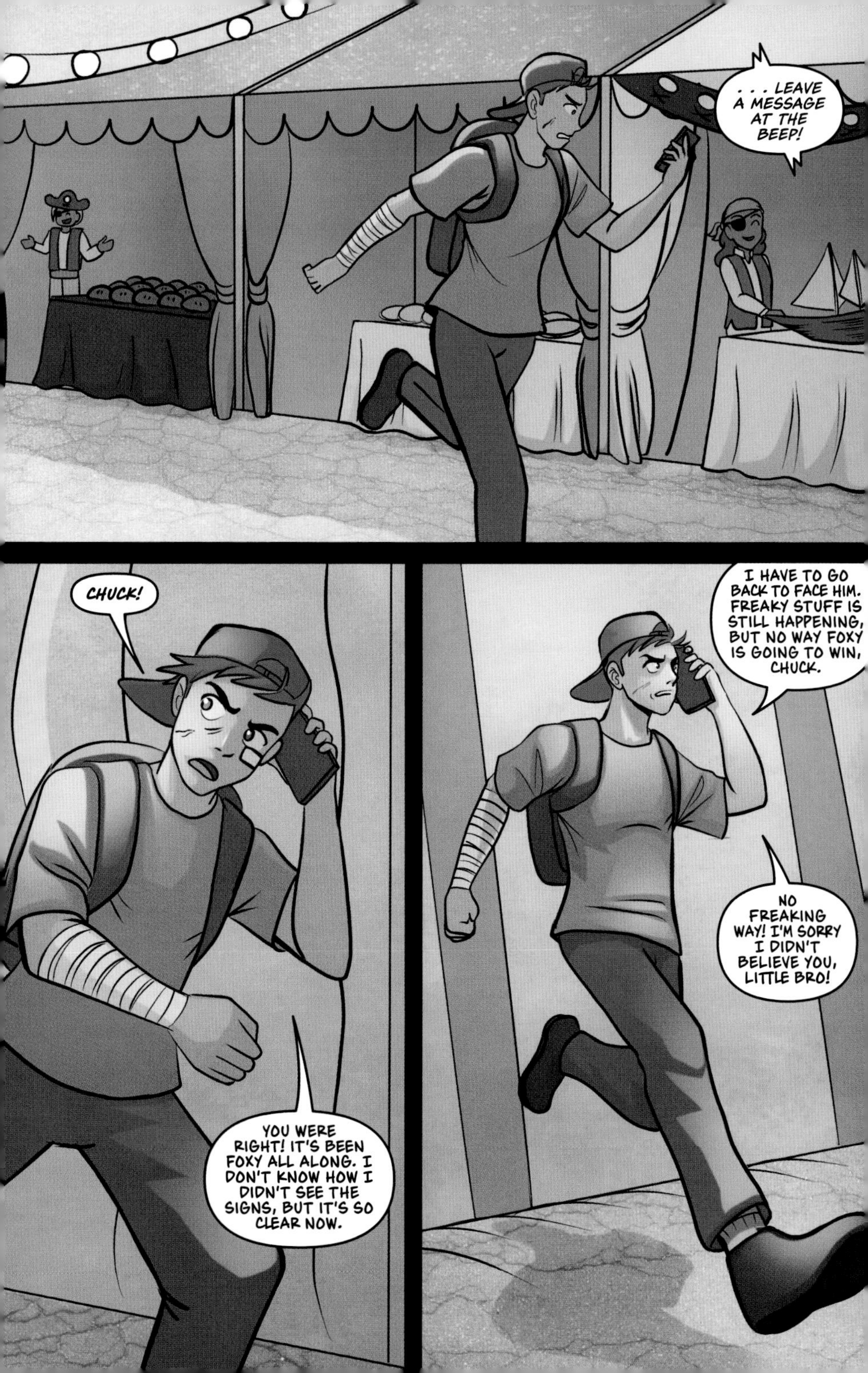
. . . LEAVE A MESSAGE AT THE BEEP!
CHUCK!
YOU WERE RIGHT! IT'S BEEN FOXY ALL ALONG. I DON'T KNOW HOW I DIDN'T SEE THE SIGNS, BUT IT'S SO CLEAR NOW.
I HAVE TO GO BACK TO FACE HIM. FREAKY STUFF IS STILL HAPPENING, BUT NO WAY FOXY IS GOING TO WIN, CHUCK.
NO FREAKING WAY! I'M SORRY I DIDN'T BELIEVE YOU, LITTLE BRO!

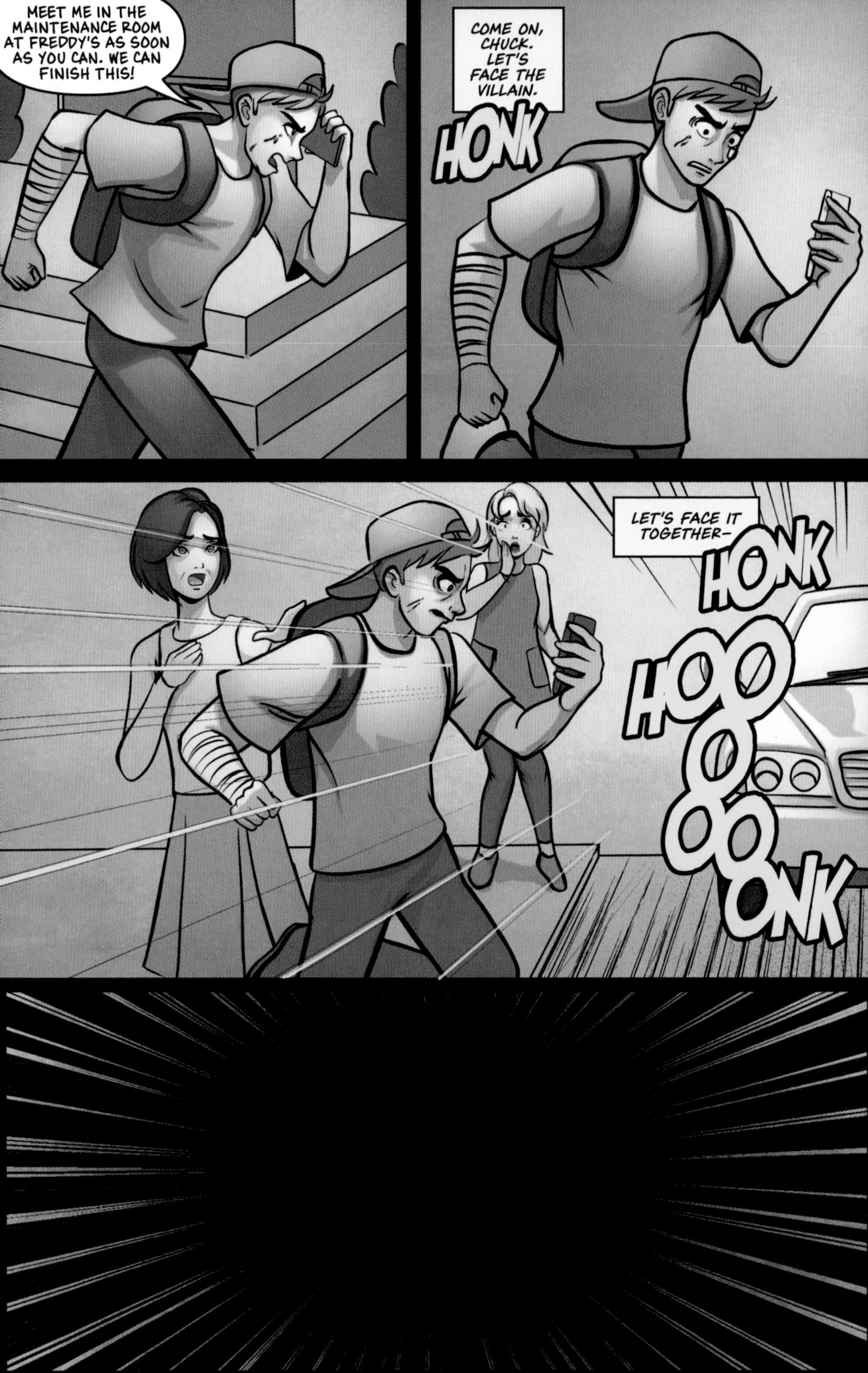
MEET ME IN THE MAINTENANCE ROOM AT FREDDY'S AS SOON AS YOU CAN. WE CAN FINISH THIS!
COME ON, CHUCK. LET'S FACE THE VILLAIN.
HONK
LET'S FACE IT TOGETHER—
HONK
HOOOOOONK

HELLO?
WHERE AM I—

WHAT THE HECK?! I
CAN'T MOVE MY LIPS.

ZZZZUIP

I MUST BE AT
THE HOSPITAL.
I WAS . . .

. . . HIT BY
THAT TRUCK!

ARE YOU A DOCTOR?
DUDE, YOU GOTTA HELP
ME. I FEEL WEIRD . . .

THEY MUST HAVE ME ON
SOME SERIOUS ANESTHESIA.
I CAN'T MOVE A THING.

BUT AT
HERE, AND
TO GET

THEN CHUC
I CAN FAC
TOGETHER,
WILL ALL B

A F
JU
A

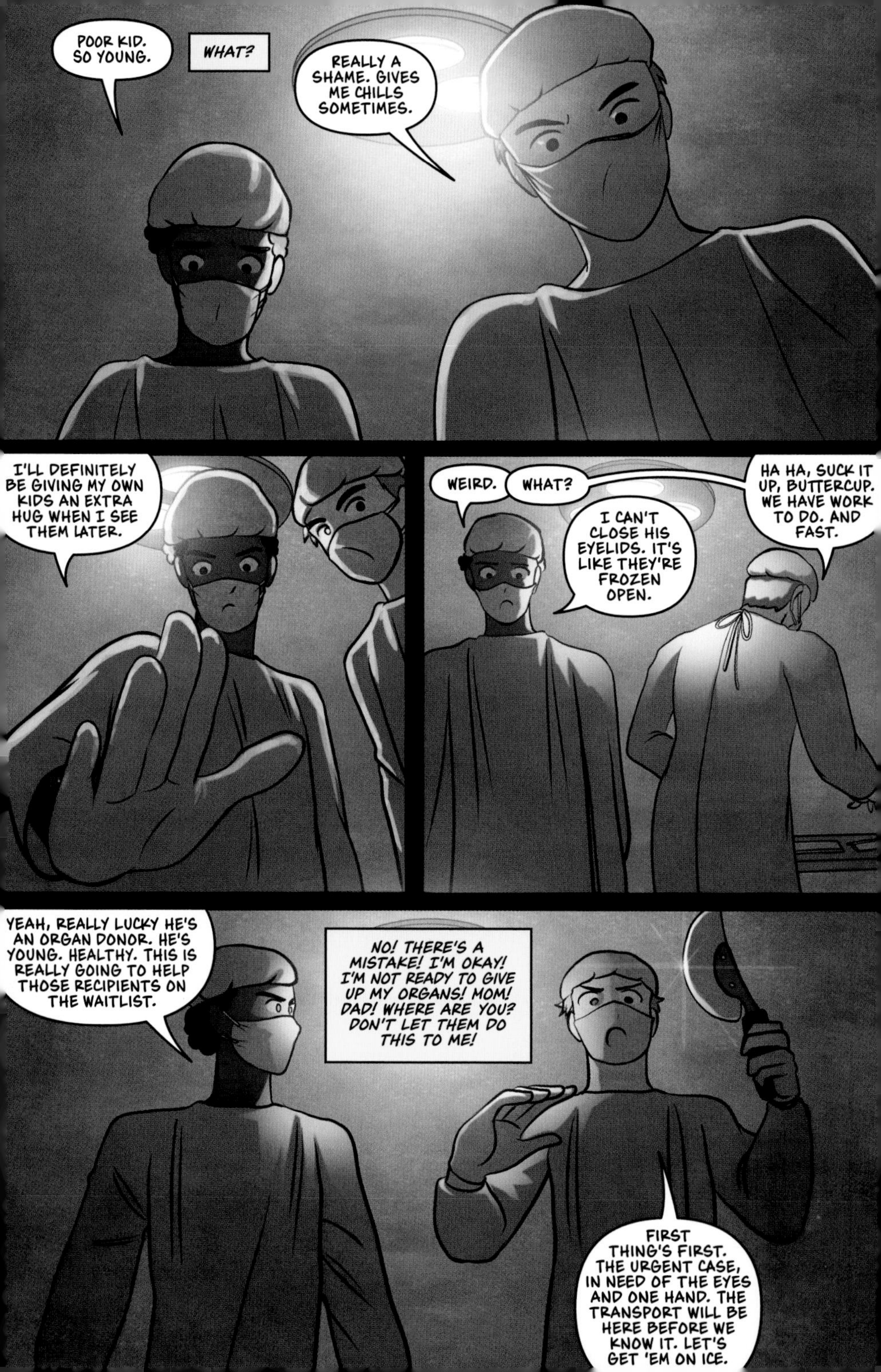
POOR KID. SO YOUNG.
WHAT?
REALLY A SHAME. GIVES ME CHILLS SOMETIMES.
I'LL DEFINITELY BE GIVING MY OWN KIDS AN EXTRA HUG WHEN I SEE THEM LATER.
WEIRD.
WHAT?
I CAN'T CLOSE HIS EYELIDS. IT'S LIKE THEY'RE FROZEN OPEN.
HA HA, SUCK IT UP, BUTTERCUP. WE HAVE WORK TO DO. AND FAST.
YEAH, REALLY LUCKY HE'S AN ORGAN DONOR. HE'S YOUNG. HEALTHY. THIS IS REALLY GOING TO HELP THOSE RECIPIENTS ON THE WAITLIST.
NO! THERE'S A MISTAKE! I'M OKAY! I'M NOT READY TO GIVE UP MY ORGANS! MOM! DAD! WHERE ARE YOU? DON'T LET THEM DO THIS TO ME!
FIRST THING'S FIRST. THE URGENT CASE, IN NEED OF THE EYES AND ONE HAND. THE TRANSPORT WILL BE HERE BEFORE WE KNOW IT. LET'S GET 'EM ON ICE.

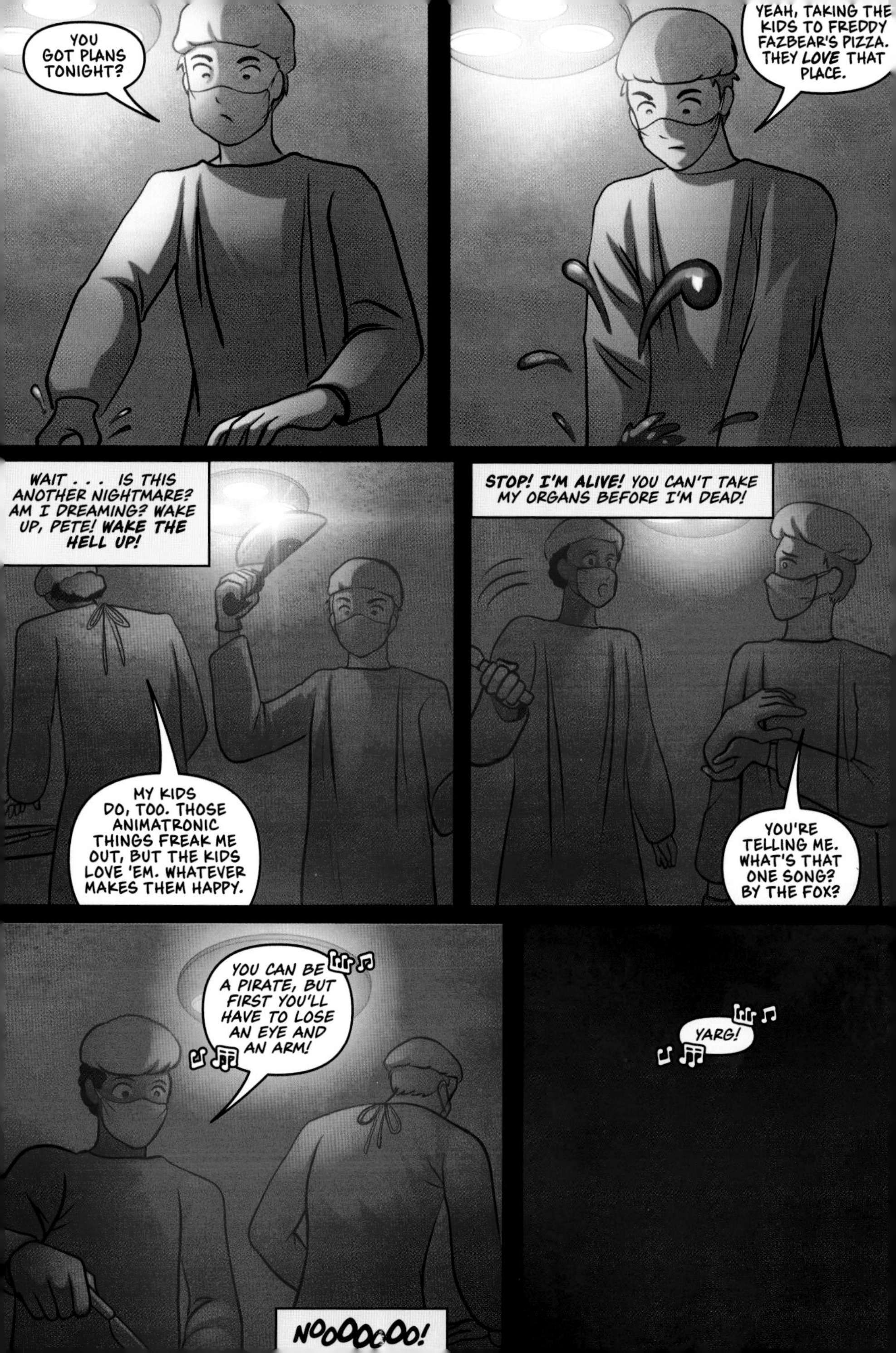
YOU GOT PLANS TONIGHT?
YEAH, TAKING THE KIDS TO FREDDY FAZBEAR'S PIZZA. THEY LOVE THAT PLACE.
WAIT . . . IS THIS ANOTHER NIGHTMARE? AM I DREAMING? WAKE UP, PETE! WAKE THE HELL UP!
MY KIDS DO, TOO. THOSE ANIMATRONIC THINGS FREAK ME OUT, BUT THE KIDS LOVE 'EM. WHATEVER MAKES THEM HAPPY.
STOP! I'M ALIVE! YOU CAN'T TAKE MY ORGANS BEFORE I'M DEAD!
YOU'RE TELLING ME. WHAT'S THAT ONE SONG? BY THE FOX?
YOU CAN BE A PIRATE, BUT FIRST YOU'LL HAVE TO LOSE AN EYE AND AN ARM!
NOOOOOOO!
YARG!

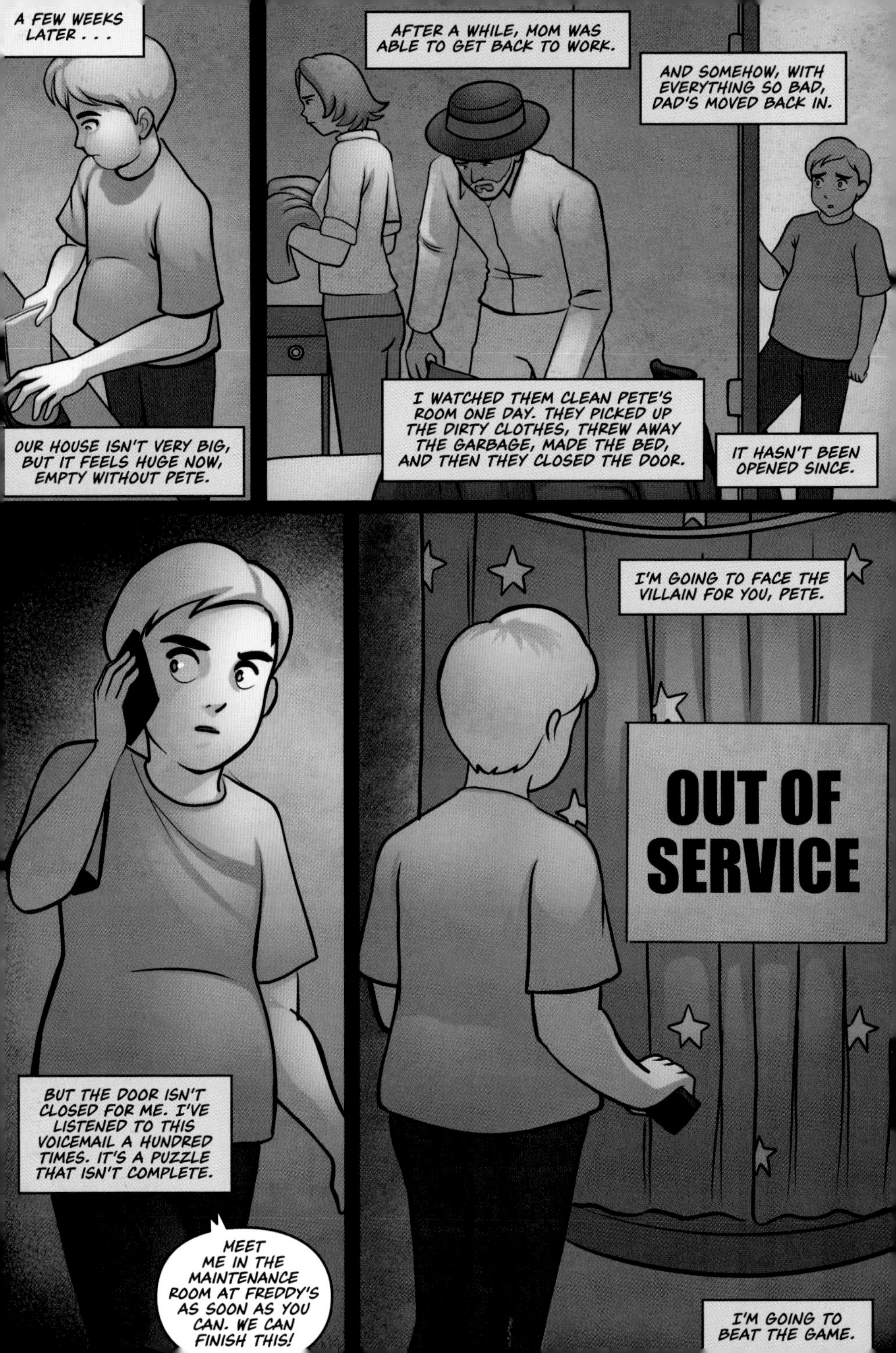
A FEW WEEKS LATER . . .
OUR HOUSE ISN'T VERY BIG, BUT IT FEELS HUGE NOW, EMPTY WITHOUT PETE.
AFTER A WHILE, MOM WAS ABLE TO GET BACK TO WORK.
AND SOMEHOW, WITH EVERYTHING SO BAD, DAD'S MOVED BACK IN.
I WATCHED THEM CLEAN PETE'S ROOM ONE DAY. THEY PICKED UP THE DIRTY CLOTHES, THREW AWAY THE GARBAGE, MADE THE BED, AND THEN THEY CLOSED THE DOOR.
IT HASN'T BEEN OPENED SINCE.
BUT THE DOOR ISN'T CLOSED FOR ME. I'VE LISTENED TO THIS VOICEMAIL A HUNDRED TIMES. IT'S A PUZZLE THAT ISN'T COMPLETE.
MEET ME IN THE MAINTENANCE ROOM AT FREDDY'S AS SOON AS YOU CAN. WE CAN FINISH THIS!
I'M GOING TO FACE THE VILLAIN FOR YOU, PETE.
OUT OF SERVICE
I'M GOING TO BEAT THE GAME.

BUNNY CALL

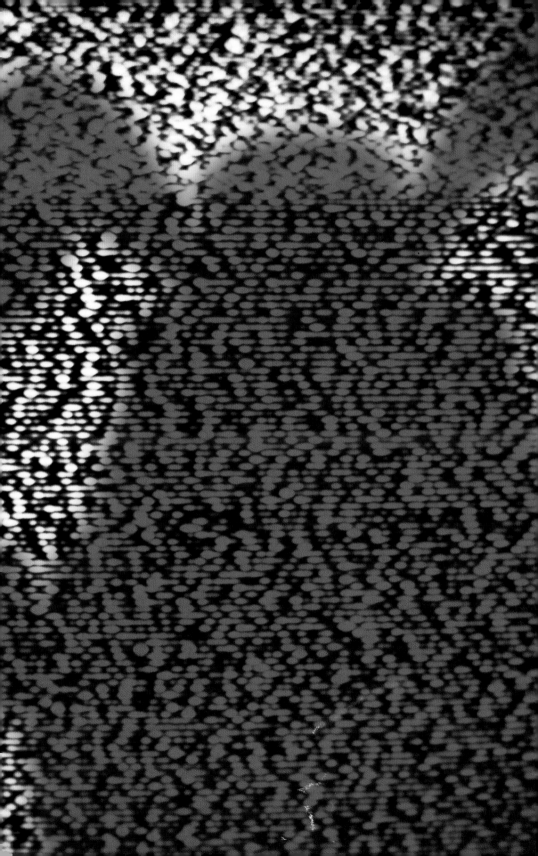

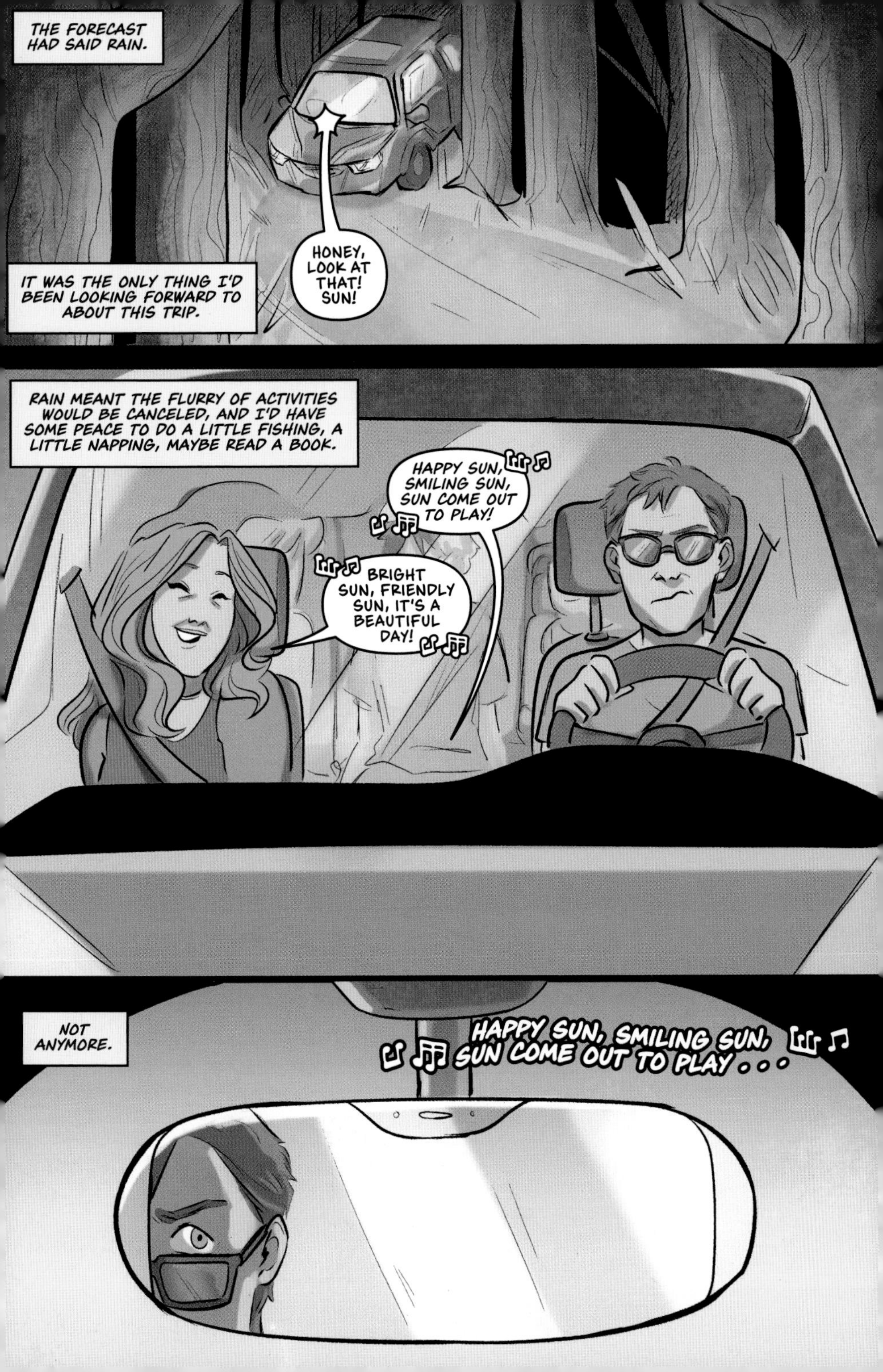
THE FORECAST HAD SAID RAIN.
IT WAS THE ONLY THING I'D BEEN LOOKING FORWARD TO ABOUT THIS TRIP.
HONEY, LOOK AT THAT! SUN!
RAIN MEANT THE FLURRY OF ACTIVITIES WOULD BE CANCELED, AND I'D HAVE SOME PEACE TO DO A LITTLE FISHING, A LITTLE NAPPING, MAYBE READ A BOOK.
HAPPY SUN, SMILING SUN, SUN COME OUT TO PLAY!
BRIGHT SUN, FRIENDLY SUN, IT'S A BEAUTIFUL DAY!
NOT ANYMORE.
HAPPY SUN, SMILING SUN, SUN COME OUT TO PLAY . . .

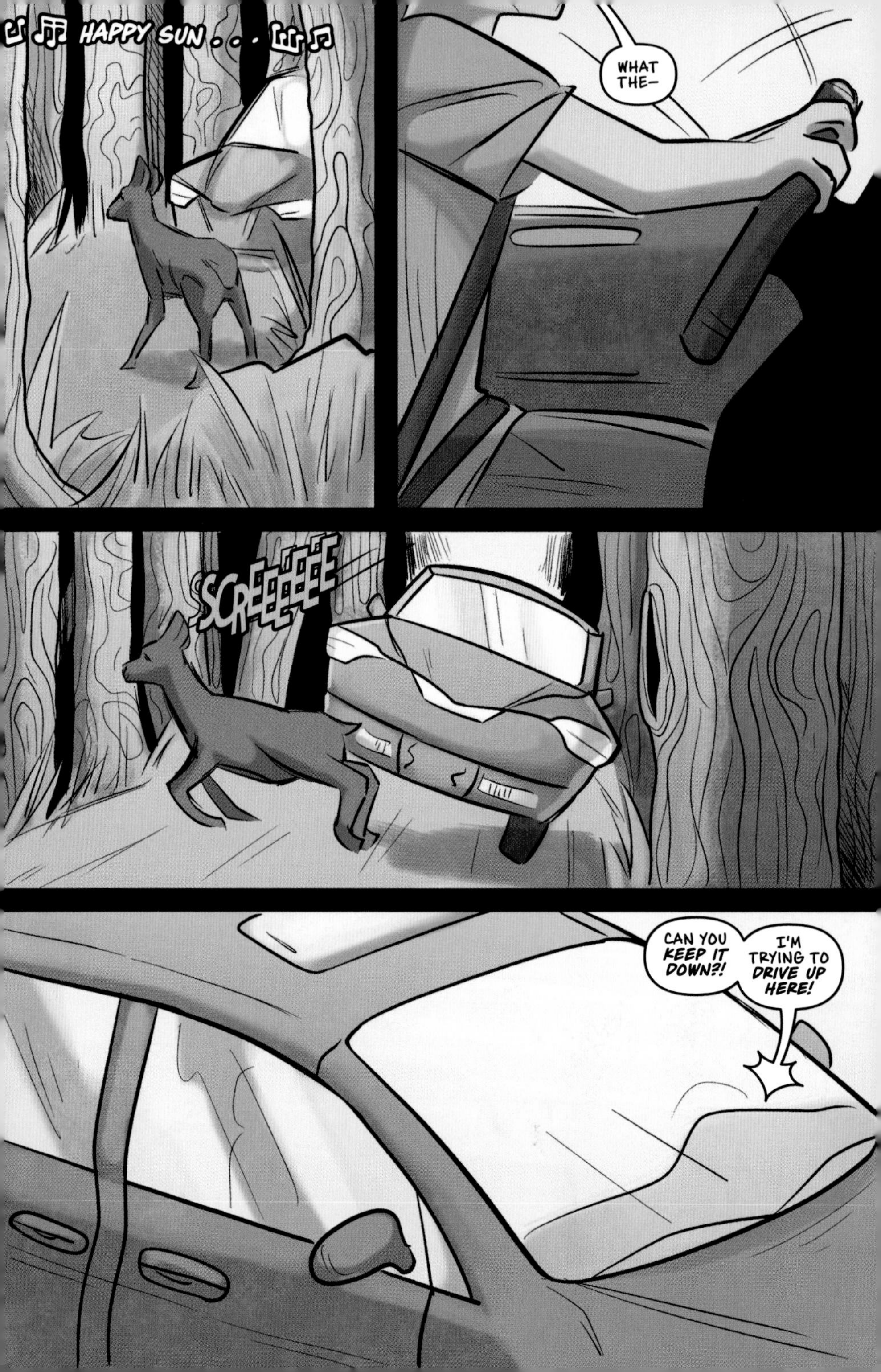
HAPPY SUN . . .
WHAT THE—
SCREEEEEEE
CAN YOU KEEP IT DOWN?!
I'M TRYING TO DRIVE UP HERE!

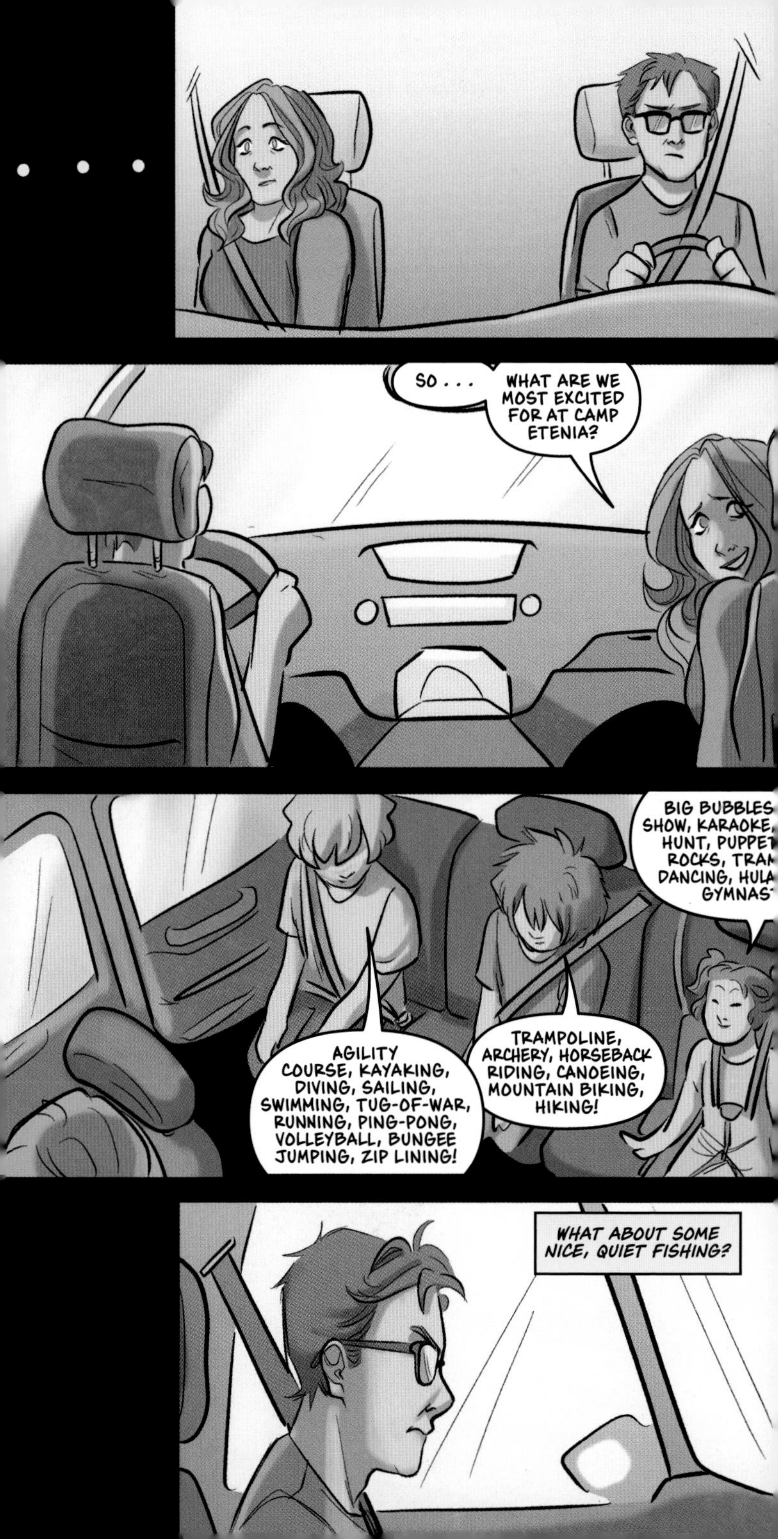
. . .
SO . . .
WHAT ARE WE MOST EXCITED FOR AT CAMP ETENIA?
BIG BUBBLES SHOW, KARAOKE, HUNT, PUPPET ROCKS, TRAM DANCING, HULA GYMNAS
AGILITY COURSE, KAYAKING, DIVING, SAILING, SWIMMING, TUG-OF-WAR, RUNNING, PING-PONG, VOLLEYBALL, BUNGEE JUMPING, ZIP LINING!
TRAMPOLINE, ARCHERY, HORSEBACK RIDING, CANOEING, MOUNTAIN BIKING, HIKING!
WHAT ABOUT SOME NICE, QUIET FISHING?

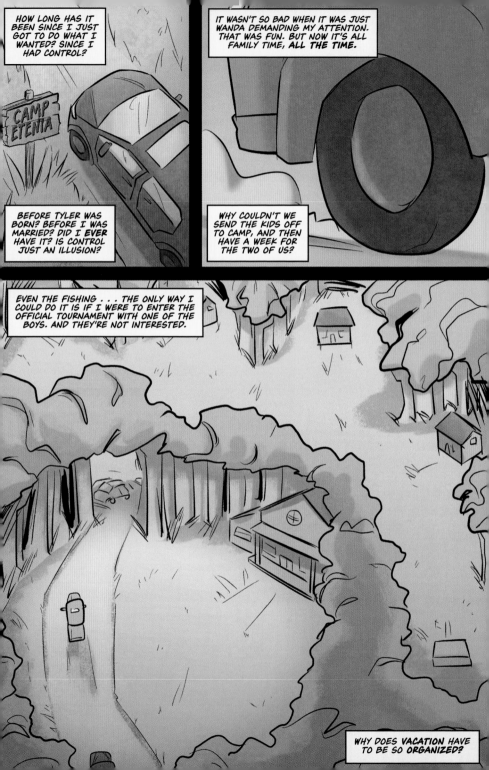

HOW LONG HAS IT BEEN SINCE I JUST GOT TO DO WHAT I WANTED? SINCE I HAD CONTROL?

IT WASN'T SO BAD WHEN IT WAS JUST WANDA DEMANDING MY ATTENTION. THAT WAS FUN. BUT NOW IT'S ALL FAMILY TIME, ALL THE TIME.

CAMP ETENIA

BEFORE TYLER WAS BORN? BEFORE I WAS MARRIED? DID I EVER HAVE IT? IS CONTROL JUST AN ILLUSION?

WHY COULDN'T WE SEND THE KIDS OFF TO CAMP, AND THEN HAVE A WEEK FOR THE TWO OF US?

EVEN THE FISHING . . . THE ONLY WAY I COULD DO IT IS IF I WERE TO ENTER THE OFFICIAL TOURNAMENT WITH ONE OF THE BOYS. AND THEY'RE NOT INTERESTED.

WHY DOES VACATION HAVE TO BE SO ORGANIZED?

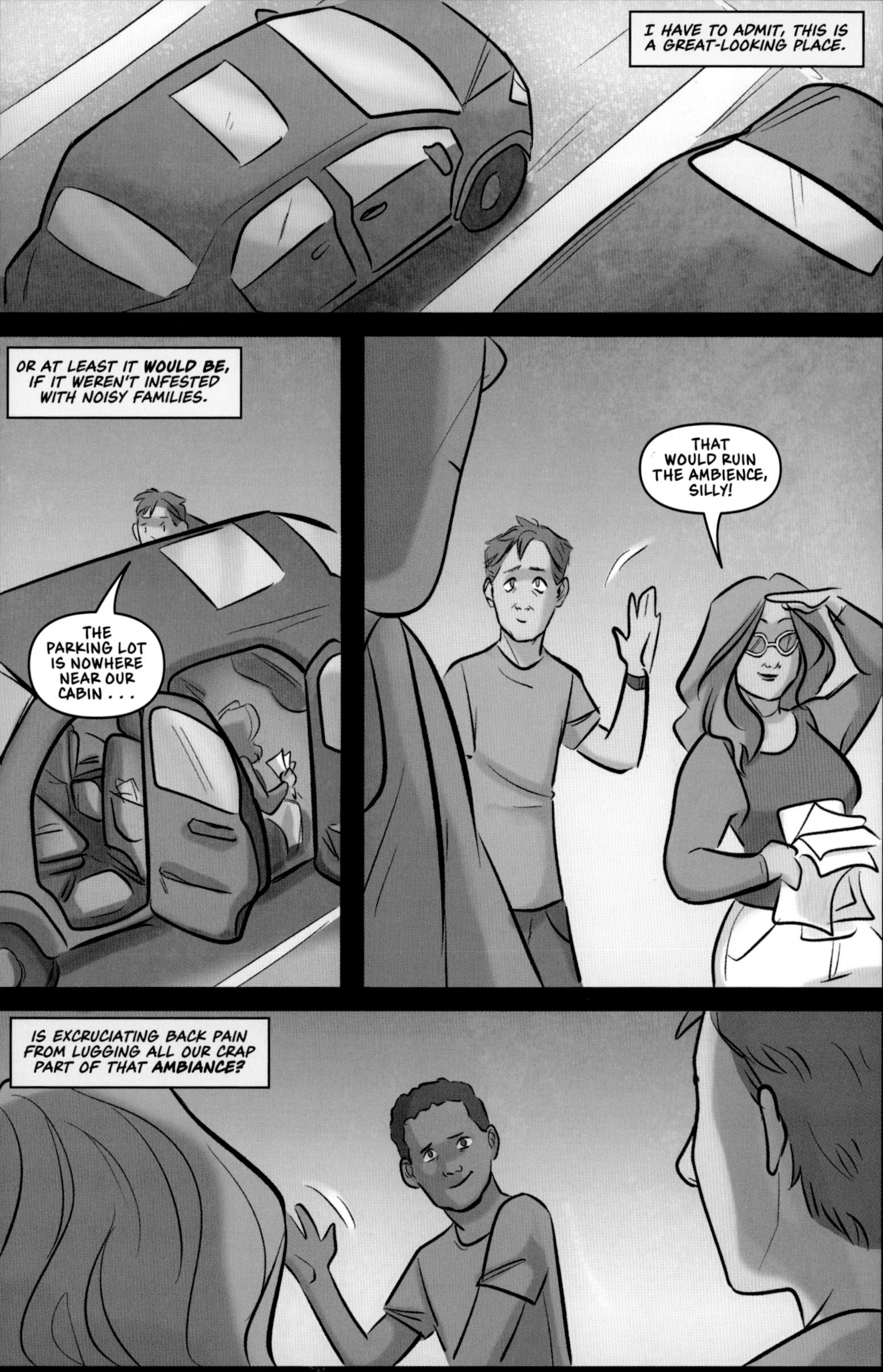
I HAVE TO ADMIT, THIS IS A GREAT-LOOKING PLACE.
OR AT LEAST IT WOULD BE, IF IT WEREN'T INFESTED WITH NOISY FAMILIES.
THE PARKING LOT IS NOWHERE NEAR OUR CABIN . . .
THAT WOULD RUIN THE AMBIENCE, SILLY!
IS EXCRUCIATING BACK PAIN FROM LUGGING ALL OUR CRAP PART OF THAT AMBIANCE?

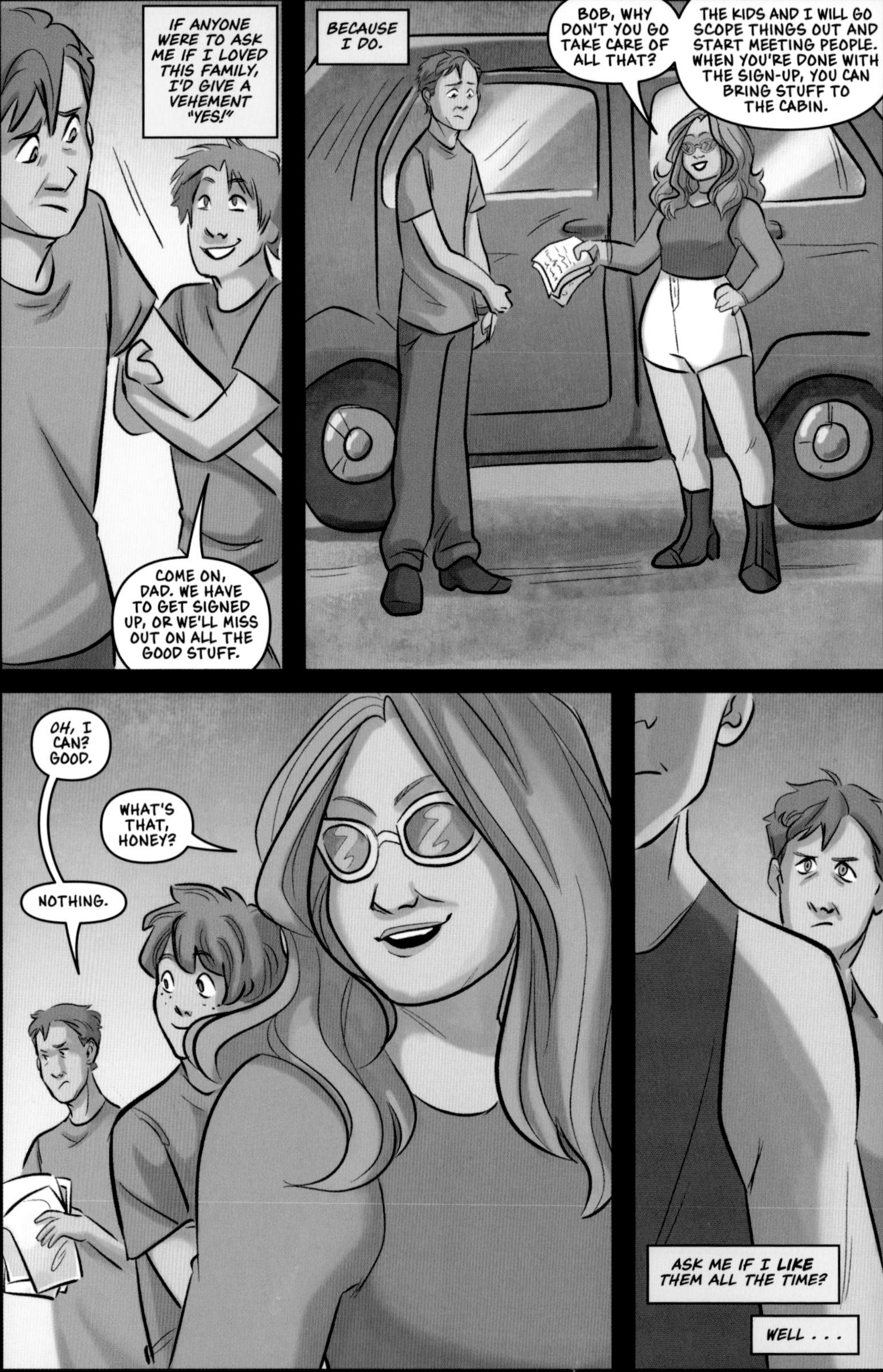
IF ANYONE WERE TO ASK ME IF I LOVED THIS FAMILY, I'D GIVE A VEHEMENT "YES!"
COME ON, DAD. WE HAVE TO GET SIGNED UP, OR WE'LL MISS OUT ON ALL THE GOOD STUFF.
BECAUSE I DO.
BOB, WHY DON'T YOU GO TAKE CARE OF ALL THAT?
THE KIDS AND I WILL GO SCOPE THINGS OUT AND START MEETING PEOPLE. WHEN YOU'RE DONE WITH THE SIGN-UP, YOU CAN BRING STUFF TO THE CABIN.
OH, I CAN? GOOD.
WHAT'S THAT, HONEY?
NOTHING.
ASK ME IF I LIKE THEM ALL THE TIME?
WELL . . .

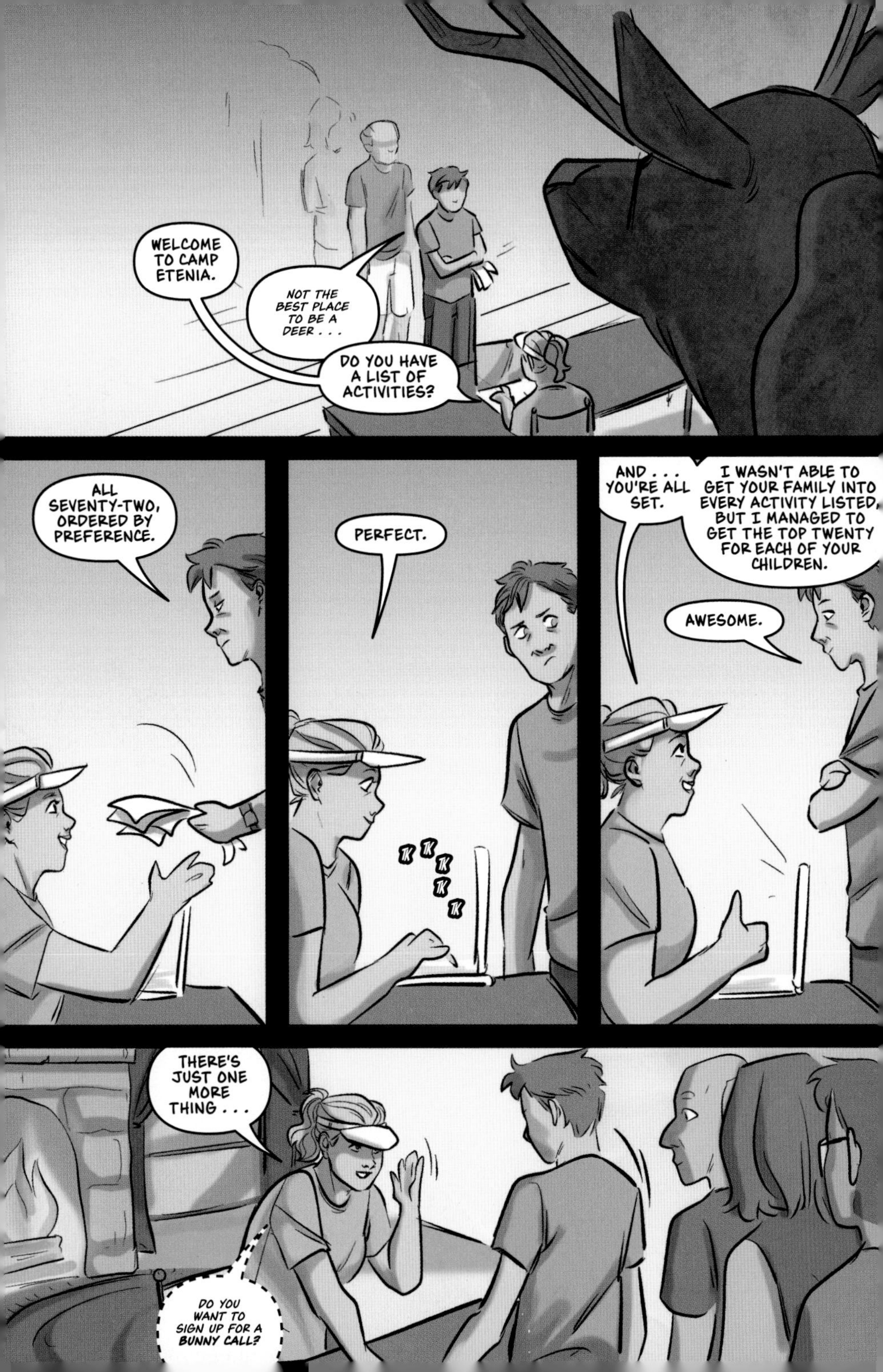
WELCOME TO CAMP ETENIA.
NOT THE BEST PLACE TO BE A DEER . . .
DO YOU HAVE A LIST OF ACTIVITIES?
ALL SEVENTY-TWO, ORDERED BY PREFERENCE.
PERFECT.
TK TK TK TK TK
AND . . . YOU'RE ALL SET.
I WASN'T ABLE TO GET YOUR FAMILY INTO EVERY ACTIVITY LISTED, BUT I MANAGED TO GET THE TOP TWENTY FOR EACH OF YOUR CHILDREN.
AWESOME.
THERE'S JUST ONE MORE THING . . .
DO YOU WANT TO SIGN UP FOR A BUNNY CALL?

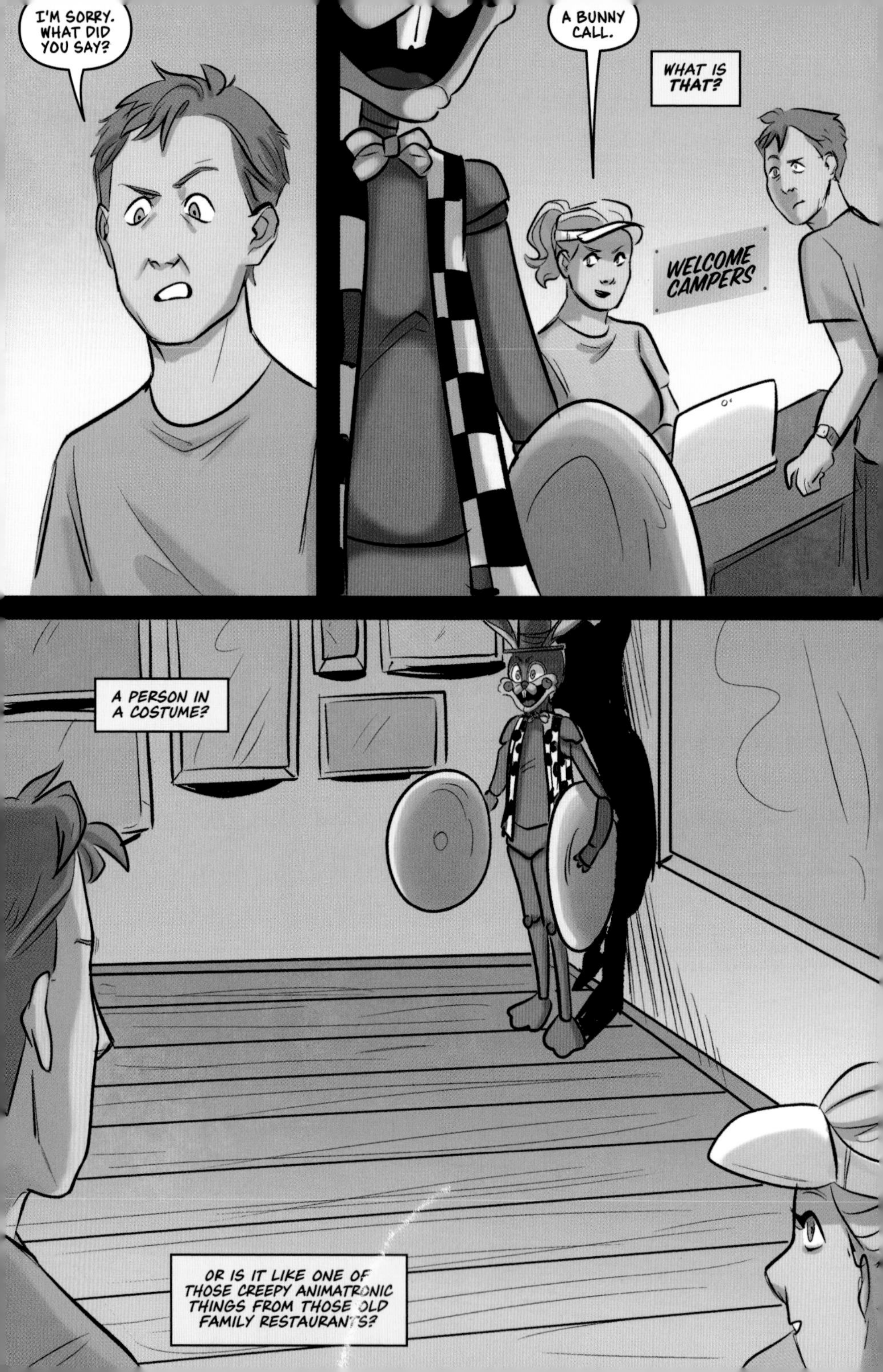
I'M SORRY. WHAT DID YOU SAY?
A BUNNY CALL.
WHAT IS THAT?
WELCOME CAMPERS
A PERSON IN A COSTUME?
OR IS IT LIKE ONE OF THOSE CREEPY ANIMATRONIC THINGS FROM THOSE OLD FAMILY RESTAURANTS?

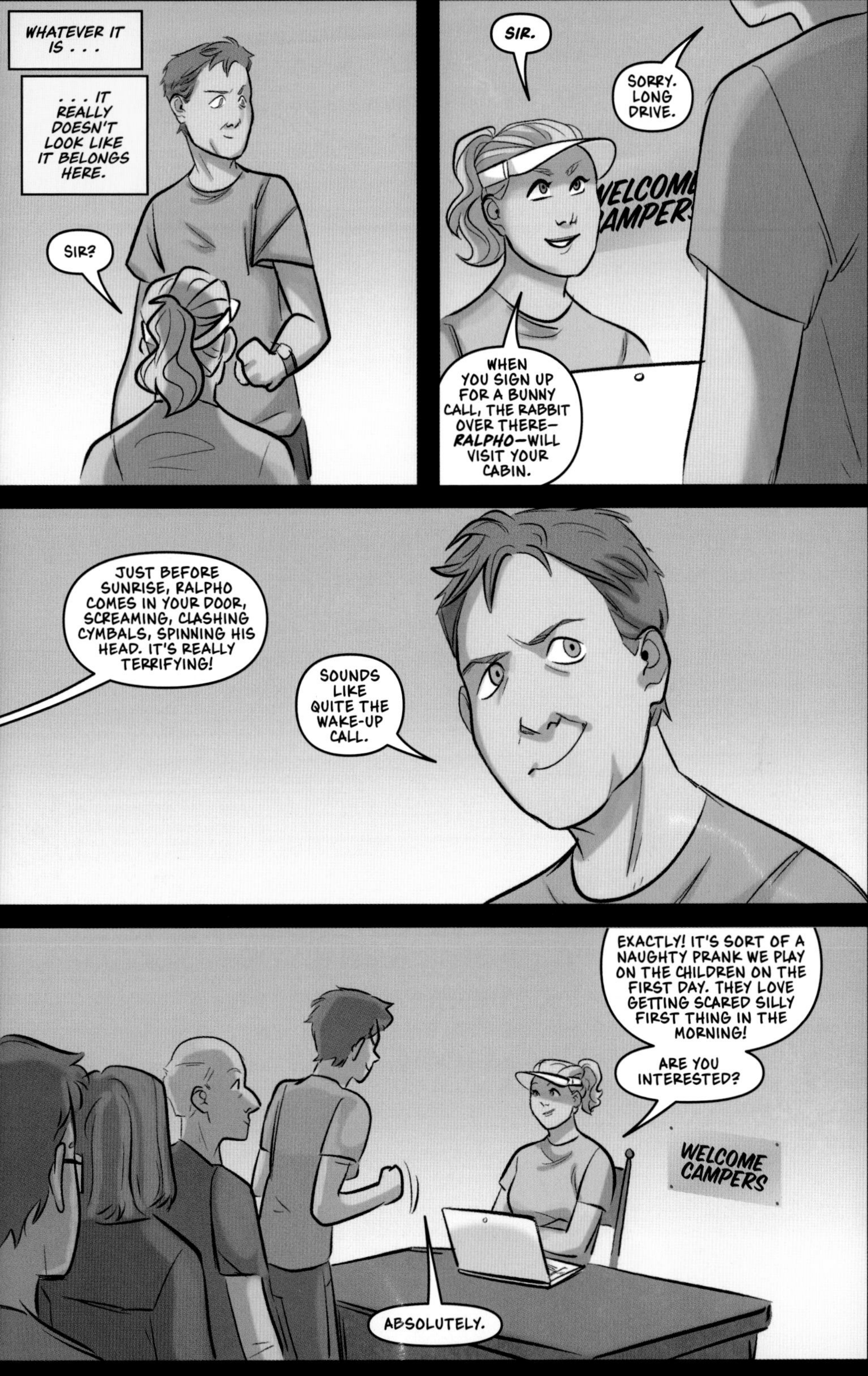
WHATEVER IT IS . . .
. . . IT REALLY DOESN'T LOOK LIKE IT BELONGS HERE.
SIR?
SIR.
SORRY. LONG DRIVE.
WELCOME CAMPERS
WHEN YOU SIGN UP FOR A BUNNY CALL, THE RABBIT OVER THERE—RALPHO—WILL VISIT YOUR CABIN.
JUST BEFORE SUNRISE, RALPHO COMES IN YOUR DOOR, SCREAMING, CLASHING CYMBALS, SPINNING HIS HEAD. IT'S REALLY TERRIFYING!
SOUNDS LIKE QUITE THE WAKE-UP CALL.
EXACTLY! IT'S SORT OF A NAUGHTY PRANK WE PLAY ON THE CHILDREN ON THE FIRST DAY. THEY LOVE GETTING SCARED SILLY FIRST THING IN THE MORNING!
ARE YOU INTERESTED?
WELCOME CAMPERS
ABSOLUTELY.

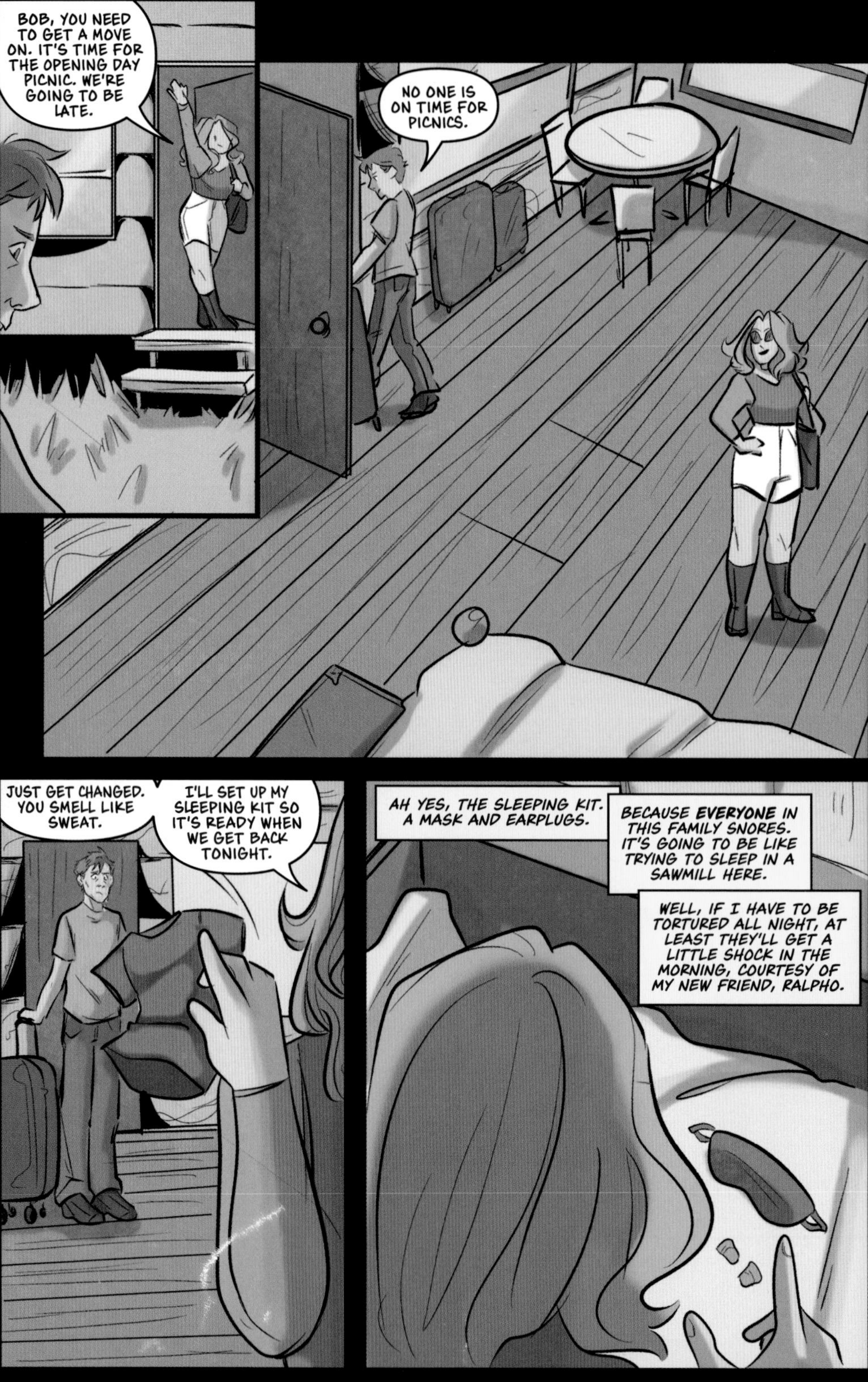
BOB, YOU NEED TO GET A MOVE ON. IT'S TIME FOR THE OPENING DAY PICNIC. WE'RE GOING TO BE LATE.
NO ONE IS ON TIME FOR PICNICS.
JUST GET CHANGED. YOU SMELL LIKE SWEAT.
I'LL SET UP MY SLEEPING KIT SO IT'S READY WHEN WE GET BACK TONIGHT.
AH YES, THE SLEEPING KIT. A MASK AND EARPLUGS.
BECAUSE EVERYONE IN THIS FAMILY SNORES. IT'S GOING TO BE LIKE TRYING TO SLEEP IN A SAWMILL HERE.
WELL, IF I HAVE TO BE TORTURED ALL NIGHT, AT LEAST THEY'LL GET A LITTLE SHOCK IN THE MORNING, COURTESY OF MY NEW FRIEND, RALPHO.

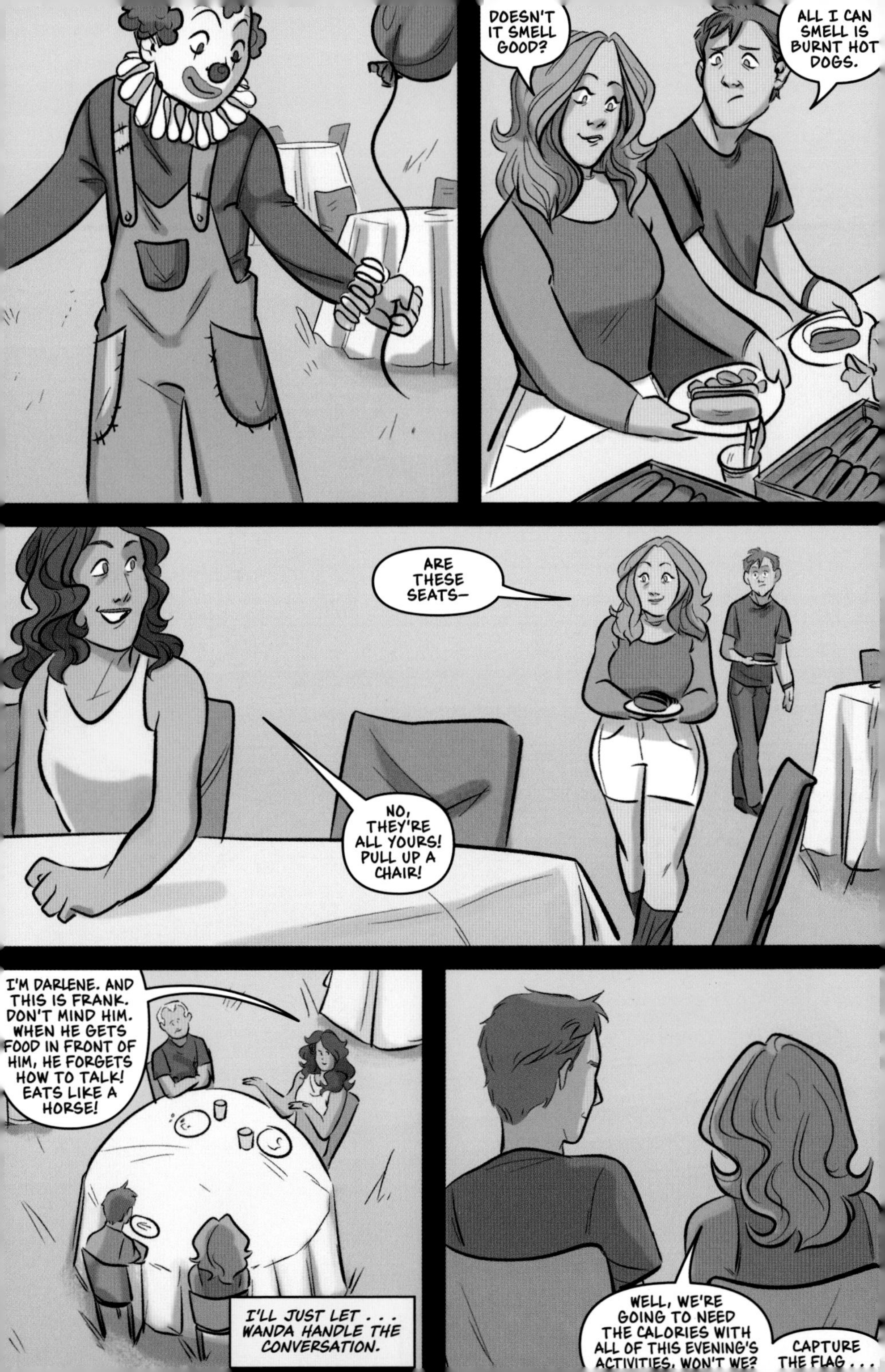
DOESN'T IT SMELL GOOD?
ALL I CAN SMELL IS BURNT HOT DOGS.
ARE THESE SEATS—
NO, THEY'RE ALL YOURS! PULL UP A CHAIR!
I'M DARLENE. AND THIS IS FRANK. DON'T MIND HIM. WHEN HE GETS FOOD IN FRONT OF HIM, HE FORGETS HOW TO TALK! EATS LIKE A HORSE!
I'LL JUST LET . . . WANDA HANDLE THE CONVERSATION.
WELL, WE'RE GOING TO NEED THE CALORIES WITH ALL OF THIS EVENING'S ACTIVITIES, WON'T WE?
CAPTURE THE FLAG . . .

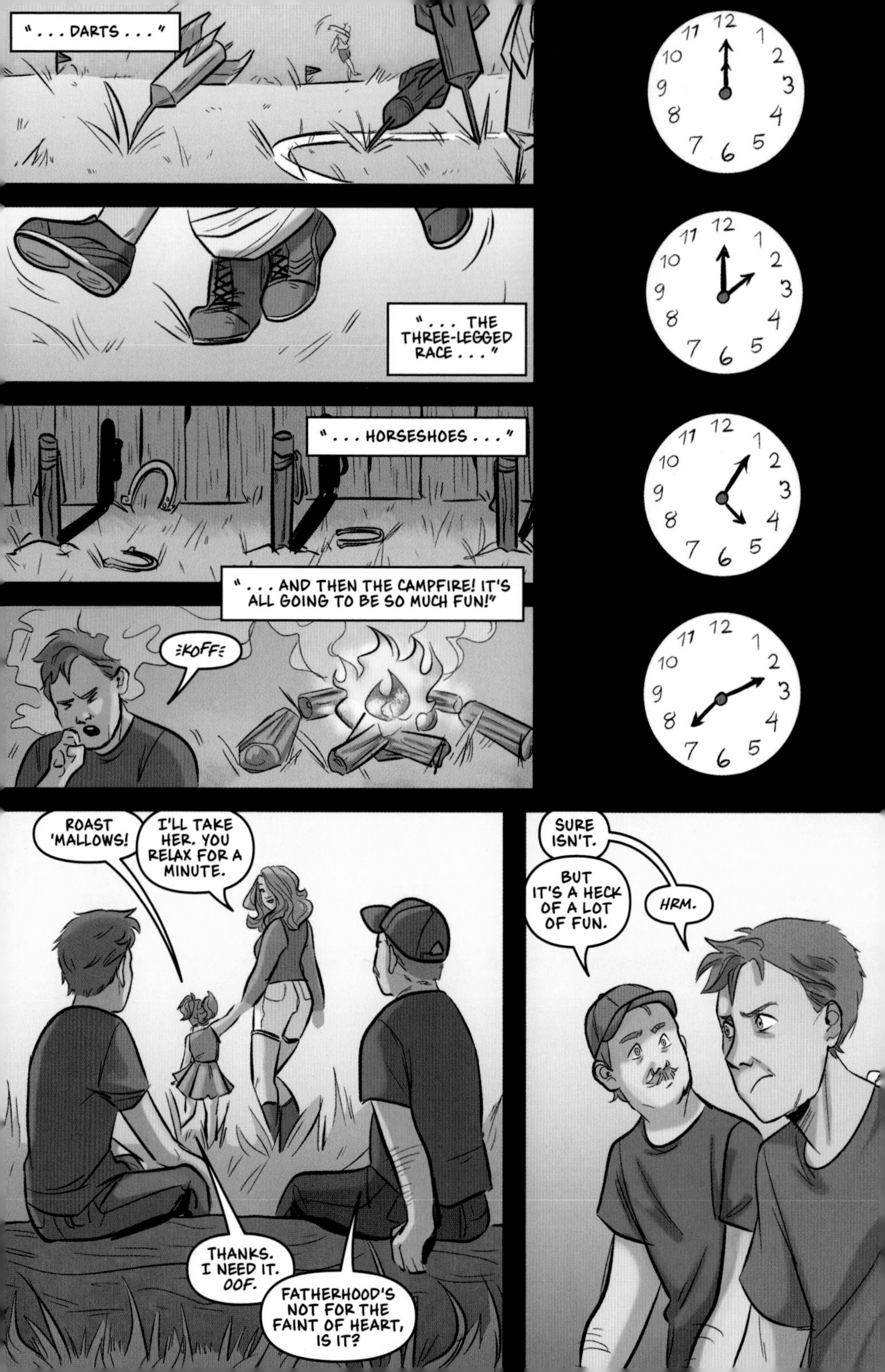
"...DARTS..."
"...THE THREE-LEGGED RACE..."
"...HORSESHOES..."
"...AND THEN THE CAMPFIRE! IT'S ALL GOING TO BE SO MUCH FUN!"
KOFF
ROAST 'MALLOWS!
I'LL TAKE HER. YOU RELAX FOR A MINUTE.
THANKS. I NEED IT. OOF.
FATHERHOOD'S NOT FOR THE FAINT OF HEART, IS IT?
SURE ISN'T.
BUT IT'S A HECK OF A LOT OF FUN.
HRM.

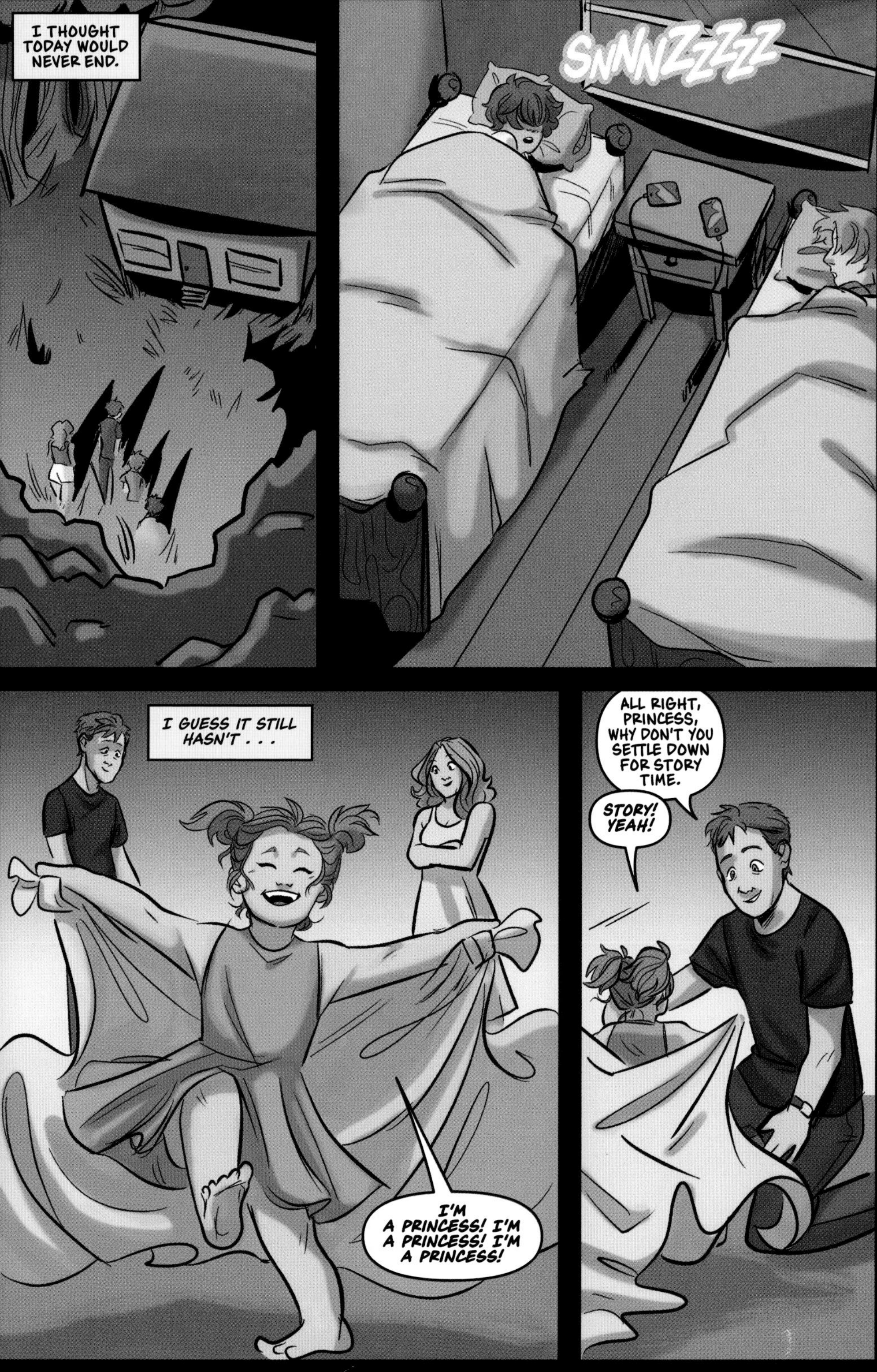
I THOUGHT TODAY WOULD NEVER END.
SNNNZZZZZ
I GUESS IT STILL HASN'T . . .
I'M A PRINCESS! I'M A PRINCESS! I'M A PRINCESS!
ALL RIGHT, PRINCESS, WHY DON'T YOU SETTLE DOWN FOR STORY TIME.
STORY! YEAH!

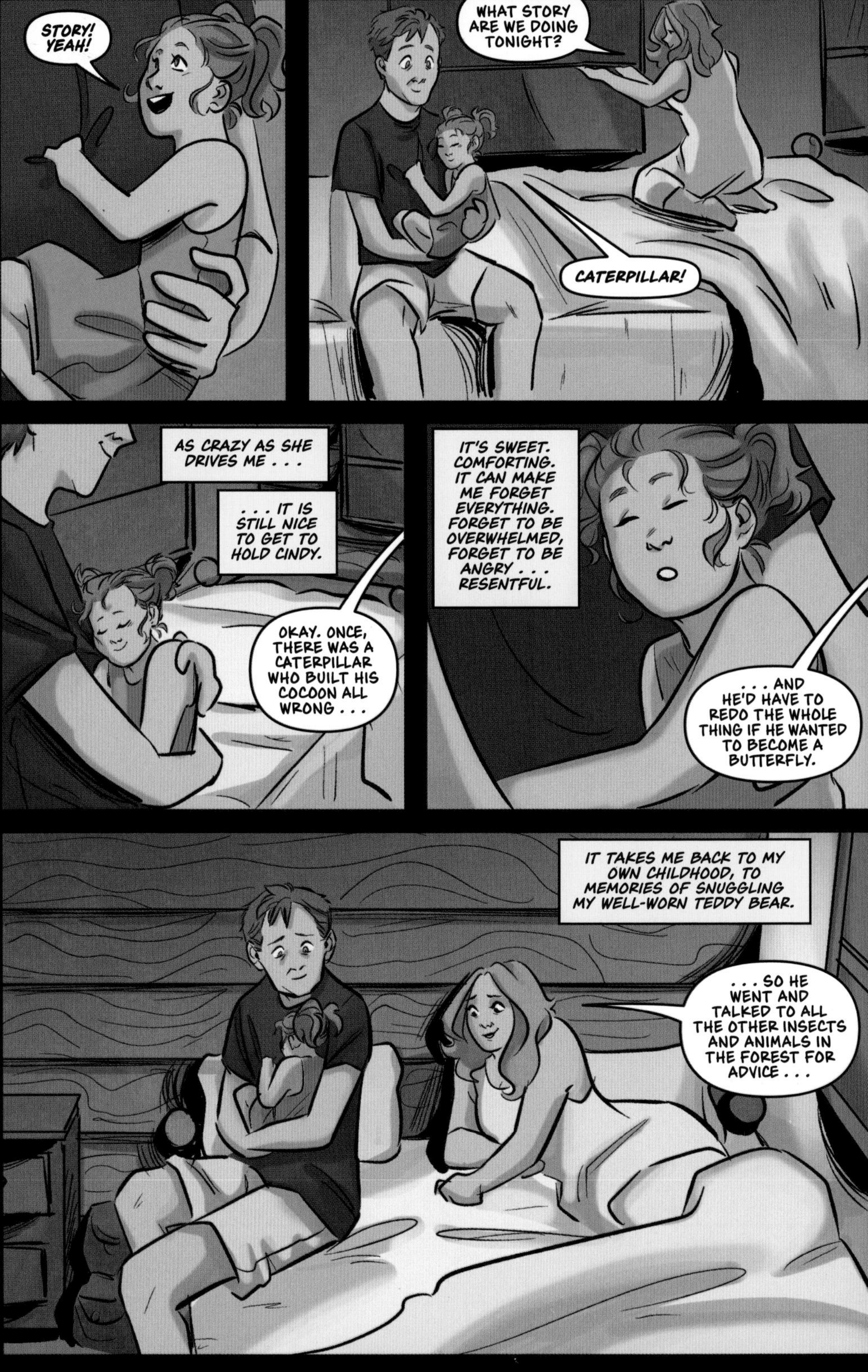
STORY! YEAH!
WHAT STORY ARE WE DOING TONIGHT?
CATERPILLAR!
AS CRAZY AS SHE DRIVES ME . . .
. . . IT IS STILL NICE TO GET TO HOLD CINDY.
OKAY. ONCE, THERE WAS A CATERPILLAR WHO BUILT HIS COCOON ALL WRONG . . .
IT'S SWEET. COMFORTING. IT CAN MAKE ME FORGET EVERYTHING. FORGET TO BE OVERWHELMED, FORGET TO BE ANGRY . . . RESENTFUL.
. . . AND HE'D HAVE TO REDO THE WHOLE THING IF HE WANTED TO BECOME A BUTTERFLY.
IT TAKES ME BACK TO MY OWN CHILDHOOD, TO MEMORIES OF SNUGGLING MY WELL-WORN TEDDY BEAR.
. . . SO HE WENT AND TALKED TO ALL THE OTHER INSECTS AND ANIMALS IN THE FOREST FOR ADVICE . . .

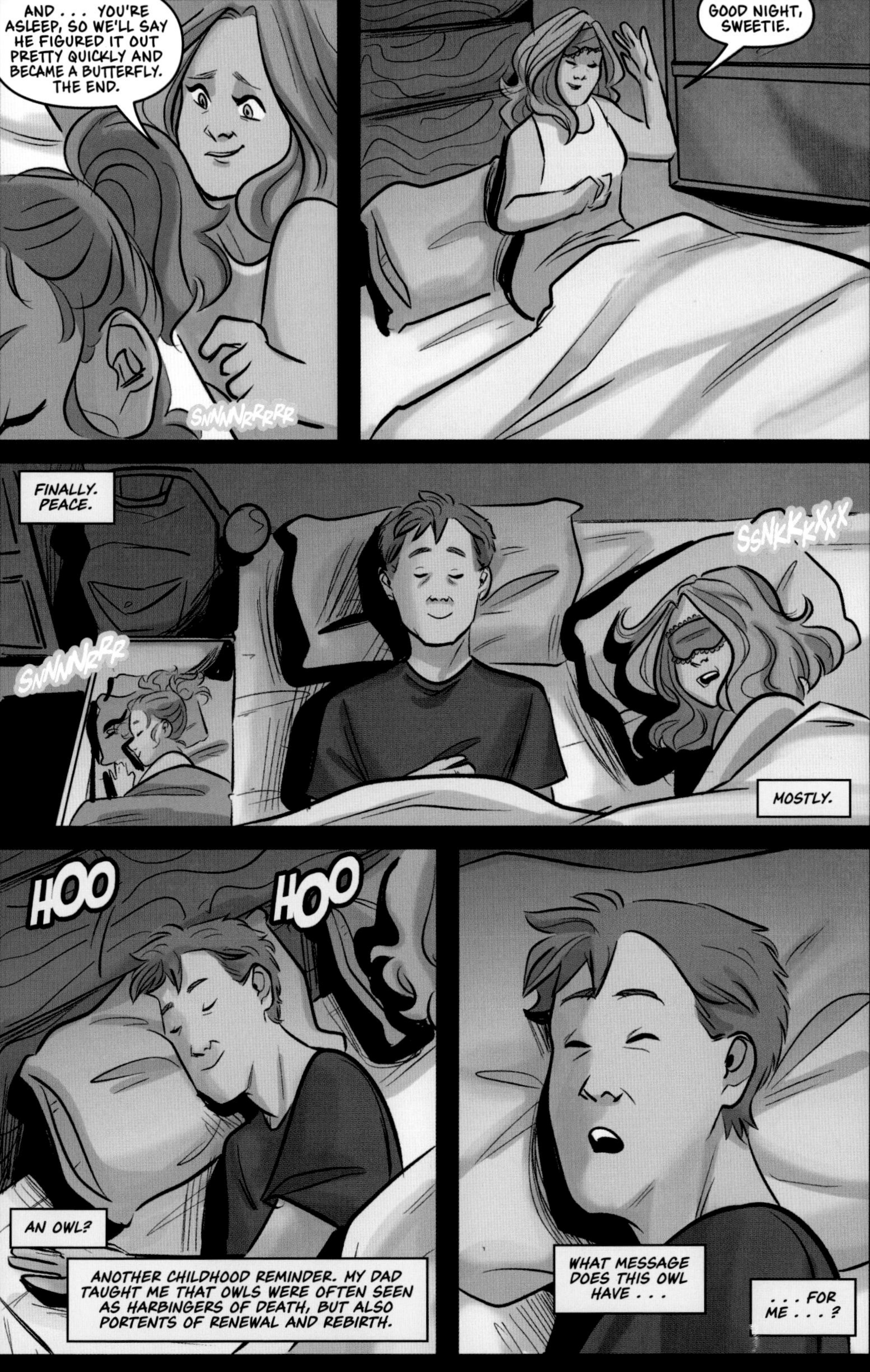
AND . . . YOU'RE ASLEEP, SO WE'LL SAY HE FIGURED IT OUT PRETTY QUICKLY AND BECAME A BUTTERFLY. THE END.
SNNNNRRRR
GOOD NIGHT, SWEETIE.
FINALLY. PEACE.
SSNKKKXXX
SNNNNRRR
MOSTLY.
HOO
HOO
AN OWL?
ANOTHER CHILDHOOD REMINDER. MY DAD TAUGHT ME THAT OWLS WERE OFTEN SEEN AS HARBINGERS OF DEATH, BUT ALSO PORTENTS OF RENEWAL AND REBIRTH.
WHAT MESSAGE DOES THIS OWL HAVE . . .
. . . FOR ME . . . ?

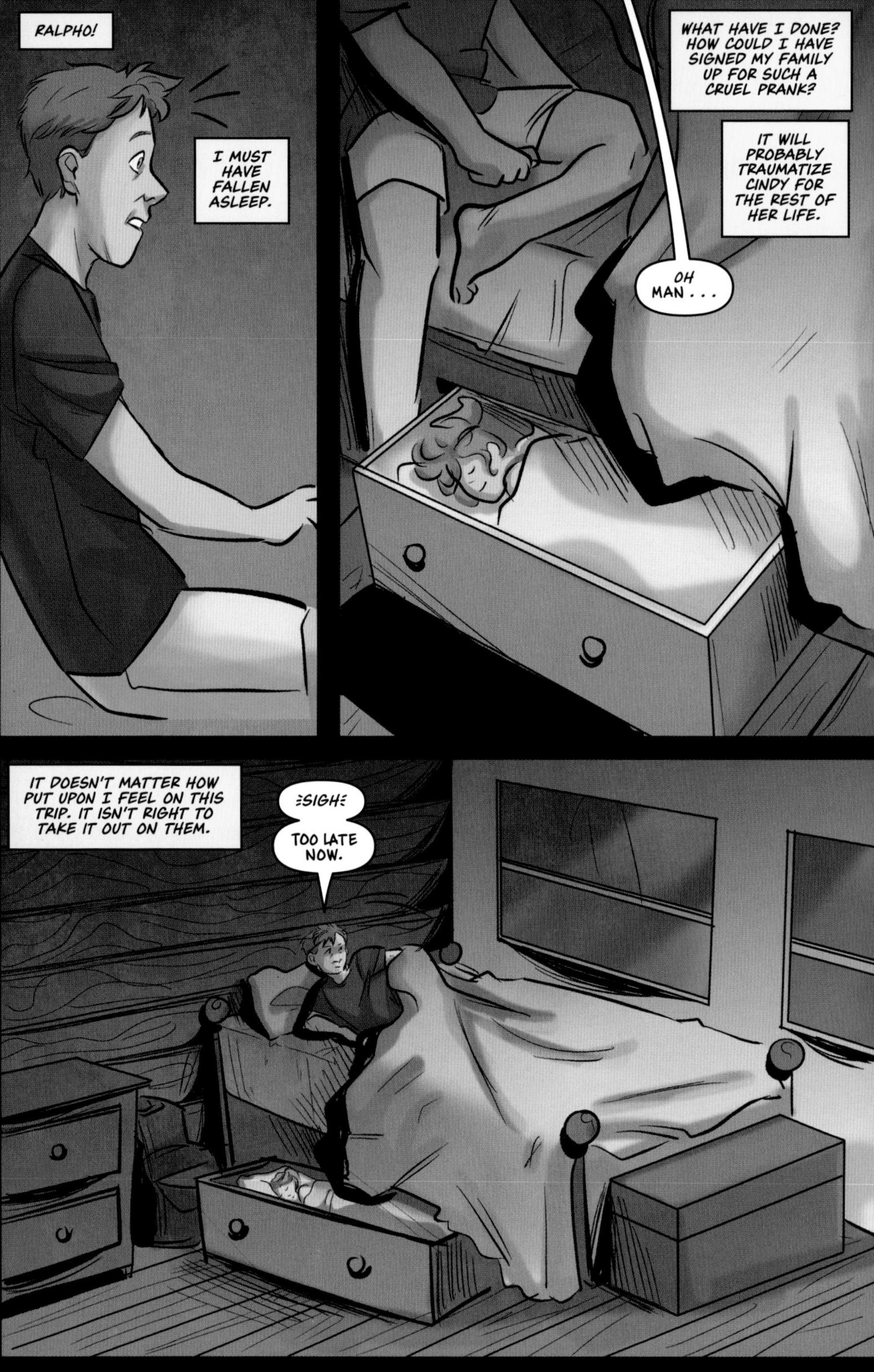
RALPHO!
I MUST HAVE FALLEN ASLEEP.
WHAT HAVE I DONE? HOW COULD I HAVE SIGNED MY FAMILY UP FOR SUCH A CRUEL PRANK?
IT WILL PROBABLY TRAUMATIZE CINDY FOR THE REST OF HER LIFE.
OH MAN . . .
IT DOESN'T MATTER HOW PUT UPON I FEEL ON THIS TRIP. IT ISN'T RIGHT TO TAKE IT OUT ON THEM.
SIGH
TOO LATE NOW.

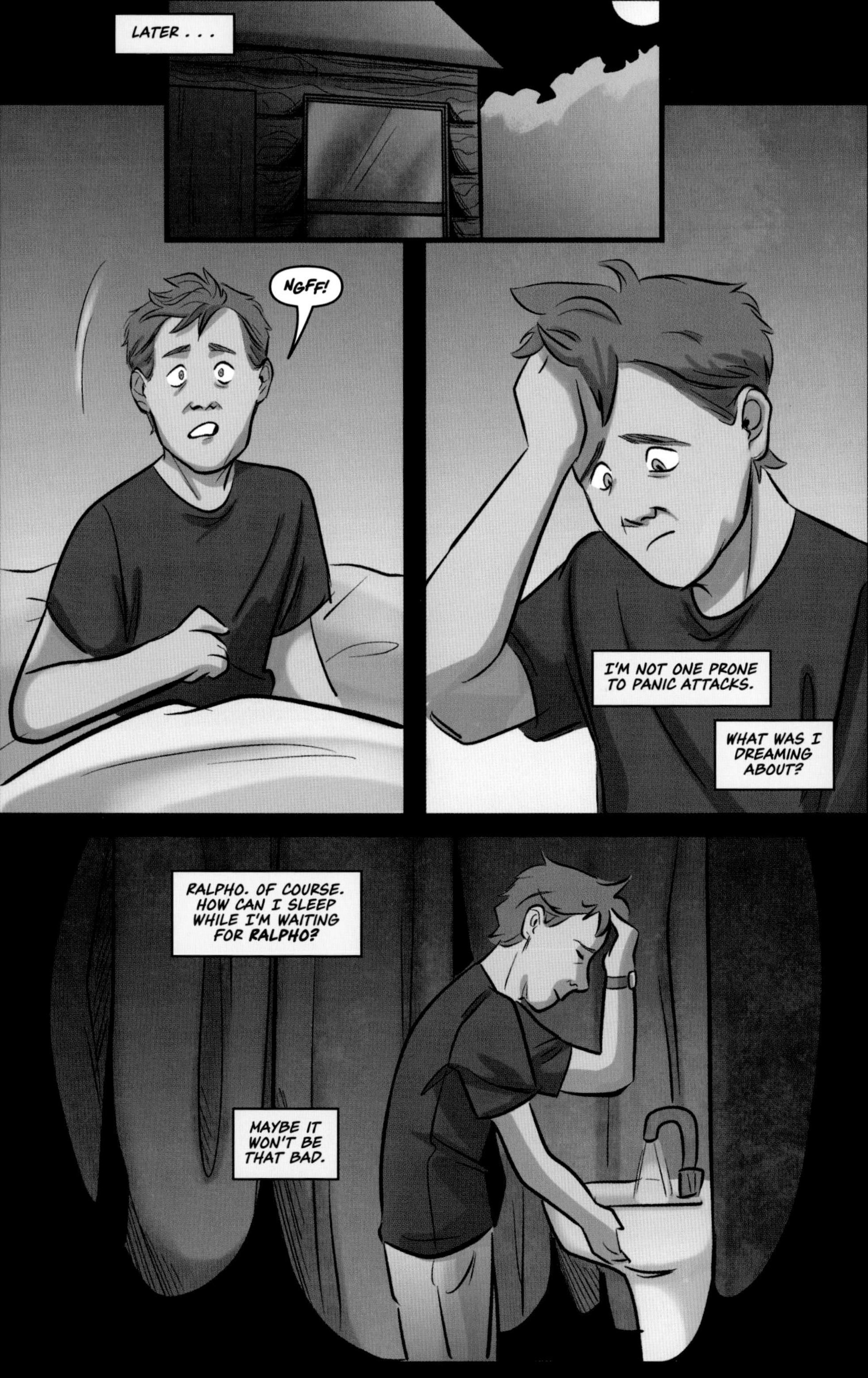
LATER . . .
NGFF!
I'M NOT ONE PRONE TO PANIC ATTACKS.
WHAT WAS I DREAMING ABOUT?
RALPHO. OF COURSE. HOW CAN I SLEEP WHILE I'M WAITING FOR RALPHO?
MAYBE IT WON'T BE THAT BAD.

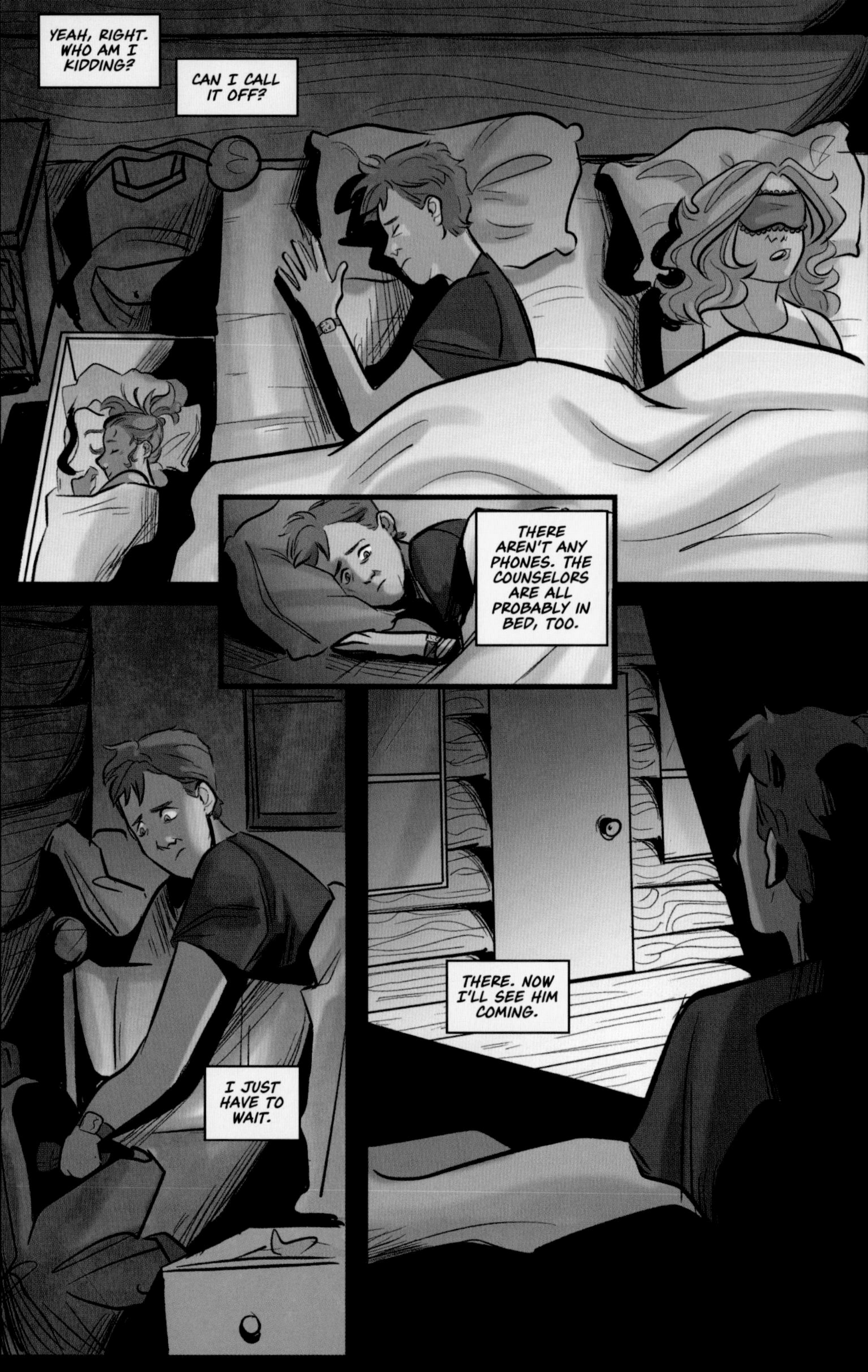
YEAH, RIGHT. WHO AM I KIDDING?
CAN I CALL IT OFF?
THERE AREN'T ANY PHONES. THE COUNSELORS ARE ALL PROBABLY IN BED, TOO.
I JUST HAVE TO WAIT.
THERE. NOW I'LL SEE HIM COMING.

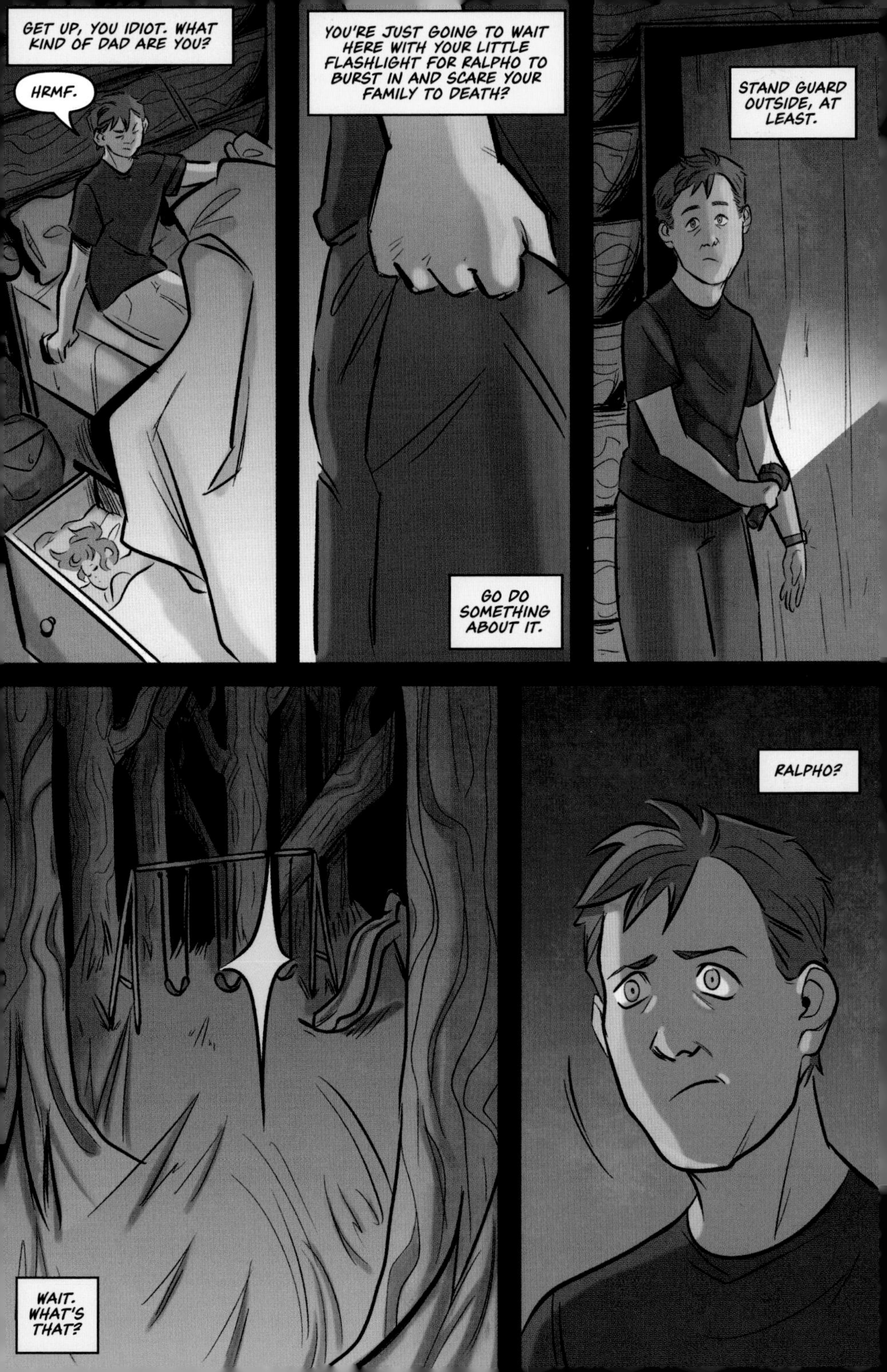
GET UP, YOU IDIOT. WHAT KIND OF DAD ARE YOU?
HRMF.
YOU'RE JUST GOING TO WAIT HERE WITH YOUR LITTLE FLASHLIGHT FOR RALPHO TO BURST IN AND SCARE YOUR FAMILY TO DEATH?
GO DO SOMETHING ABOUT IT.
STAND GUARD OUTSIDE, AT LEAST.
WAIT. WHAT'S THAT?
RALPHO?

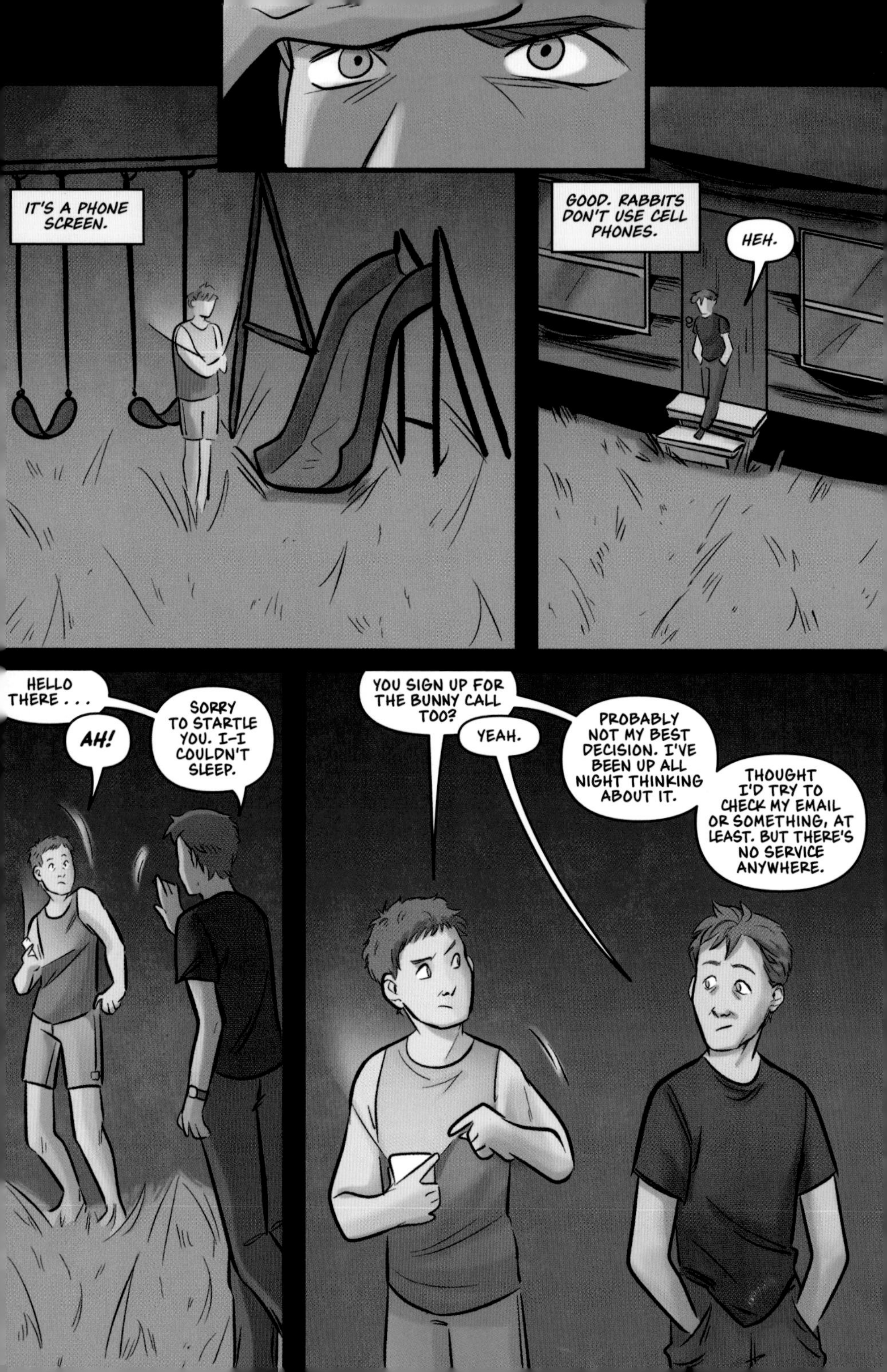
IT'S A PHONE SCREEN.
GOOD. RABBITS DON'T USE CELL PHONES.
HEH.
HELLO THERE . . .
AH!
SORRY TO STARTLE YOU. I-I COULDN'T SLEEP.
YOU SIGN UP FOR THE BUNNY CALL TOO?
YEAH.
PROBABLY NOT MY BEST DECISION. I'VE BEEN UP ALL NIGHT THINKING ABOUT IT.
THOUGHT I'D TRY TO CHECK MY EMAIL OR SOMETHING, AT LEAST. BUT THERE'S NO SERVICE ANYWHERE.

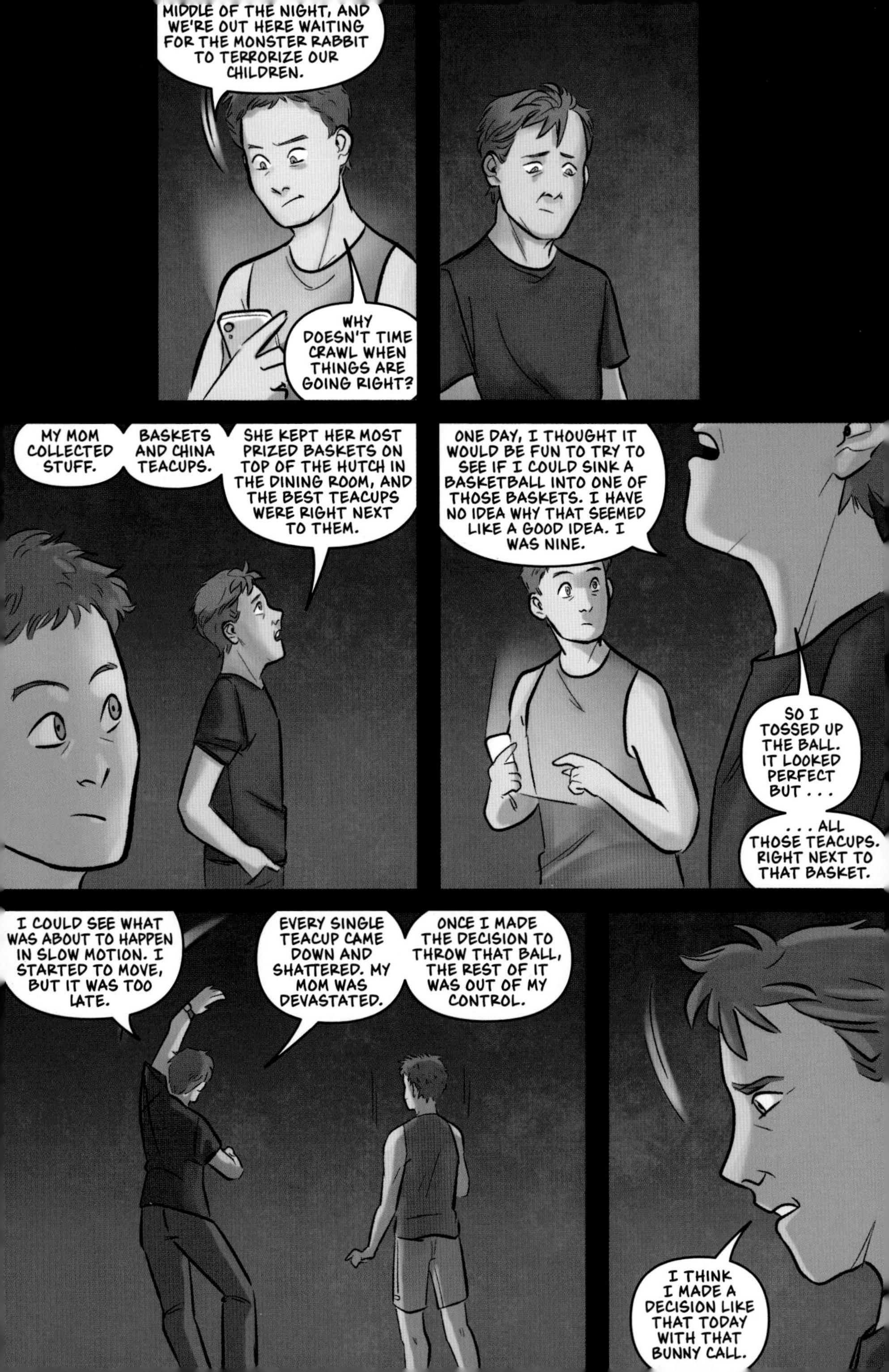
MIDDLE OF THE NIGHT, AND WE'RE OUT HERE WAITING FOR THE MONSTER RABBIT TO TERRORIZE OUR CHILDREN.
WHY DOESN'T TIME CRAWL WHEN THINGS ARE GOING RIGHT?
MY MOM COLLECTED STUFF.
BASKETS AND CHINA TEACUPS.
SHE KEPT HER MOST PRIZED BASKETS ON TOP OF THE HUTCH IN THE DINING ROOM, AND THE BEST TEACUPS WERE RIGHT NEXT TO THEM.
ONE DAY, I THOUGHT IT WOULD BE FUN TO TRY TO SEE IF I COULD SINK A BASKETBALL INTO ONE OF THOSE BASKETS. I HAVE NO IDEA WHY THAT SEEMED LIKE A GOOD IDEA. I WAS NINE.
SO I TOSSED UP THE BALL. IT LOOKED PERFECT BUT . . .
. . . ALL THOSE TEACUPS. RIGHT NEXT TO THAT BASKET.
I COULD SEE WHAT WAS ABOUT TO HAPPEN IN SLOW MOTION. I STARTED TO MOVE, BUT IT WAS TOO LATE.
EVERY SINGLE TEACUP CAME DOWN AND SHATTERED. MY MOM WAS DEVASTATED.
ONCE I MADE THE DECISION TO THROW THAT BALL, THE REST OF IT WAS OUT OF MY CONTROL.
I THINK I MADE A DECISION LIKE THAT TODAY WITH THAT BUNNY CALL.

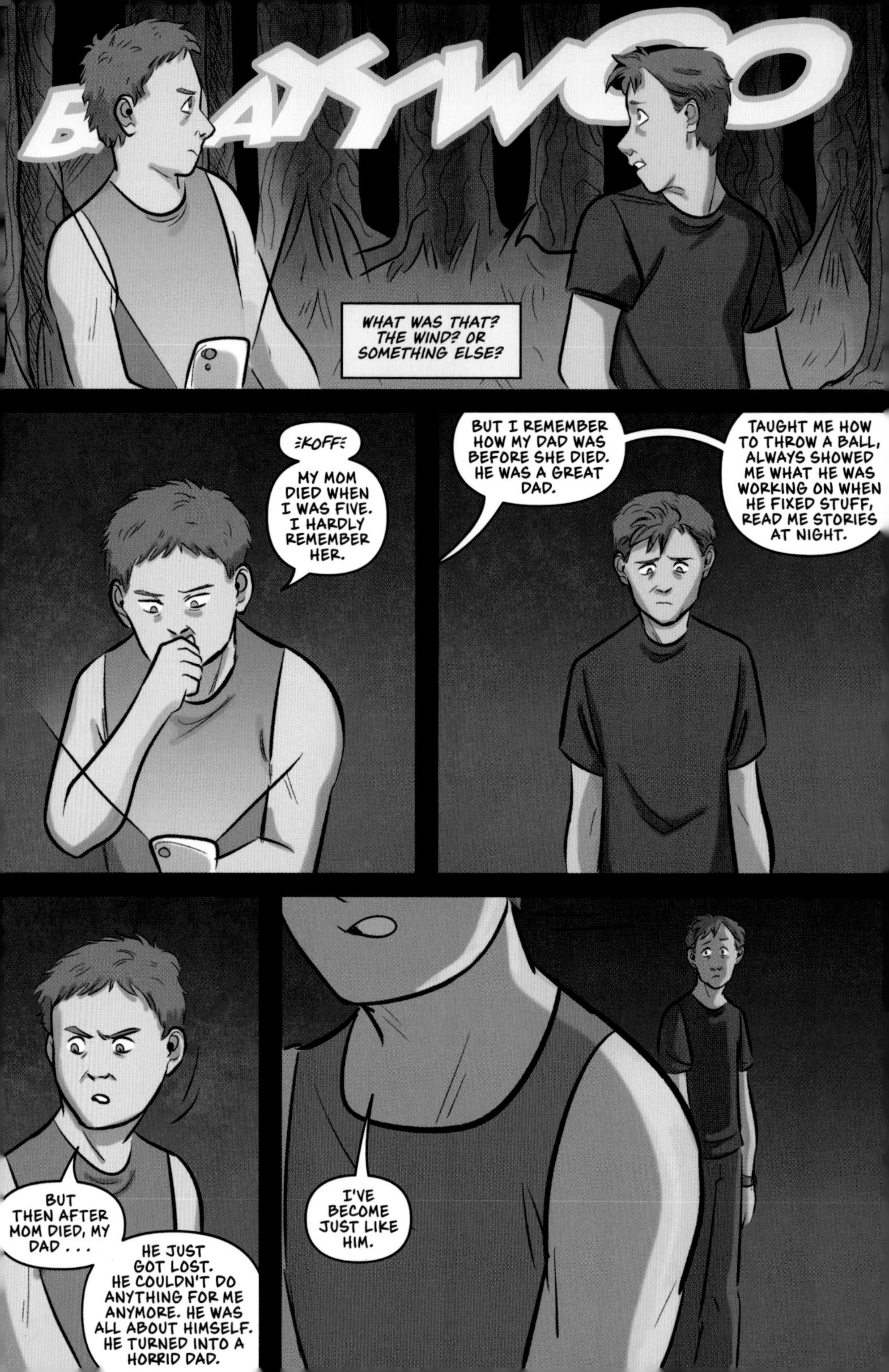
BRAYWOO
WHAT WAS THAT? THE WIND? OR SOMETHING ELSE?
KOFF
MY MOM DIED WHEN I WAS FIVE. I HARDLY REMEMBER HER.
BUT I REMEMBER HOW MY DAD WAS BEFORE SHE DIED. HE WAS A GREAT DAD.
TAUGHT ME HOW TO THROW A BALL, ALWAYS SHOWED ME WHAT HE WAS WORKING ON WHEN HE FIXED STUFF, READ ME STORIES AT NIGHT.
BUT THEN AFTER MOM DIED, MY DAD . . .
HE JUST GOT LOST. HE COULDN'T DO ANYTHING FOR ME ANYMORE. HE WAS ALL ABOUT HIMSELF. HE TURNED INTO A HORRID DAD.
I'VE BECOME JUST LIKE HIM.

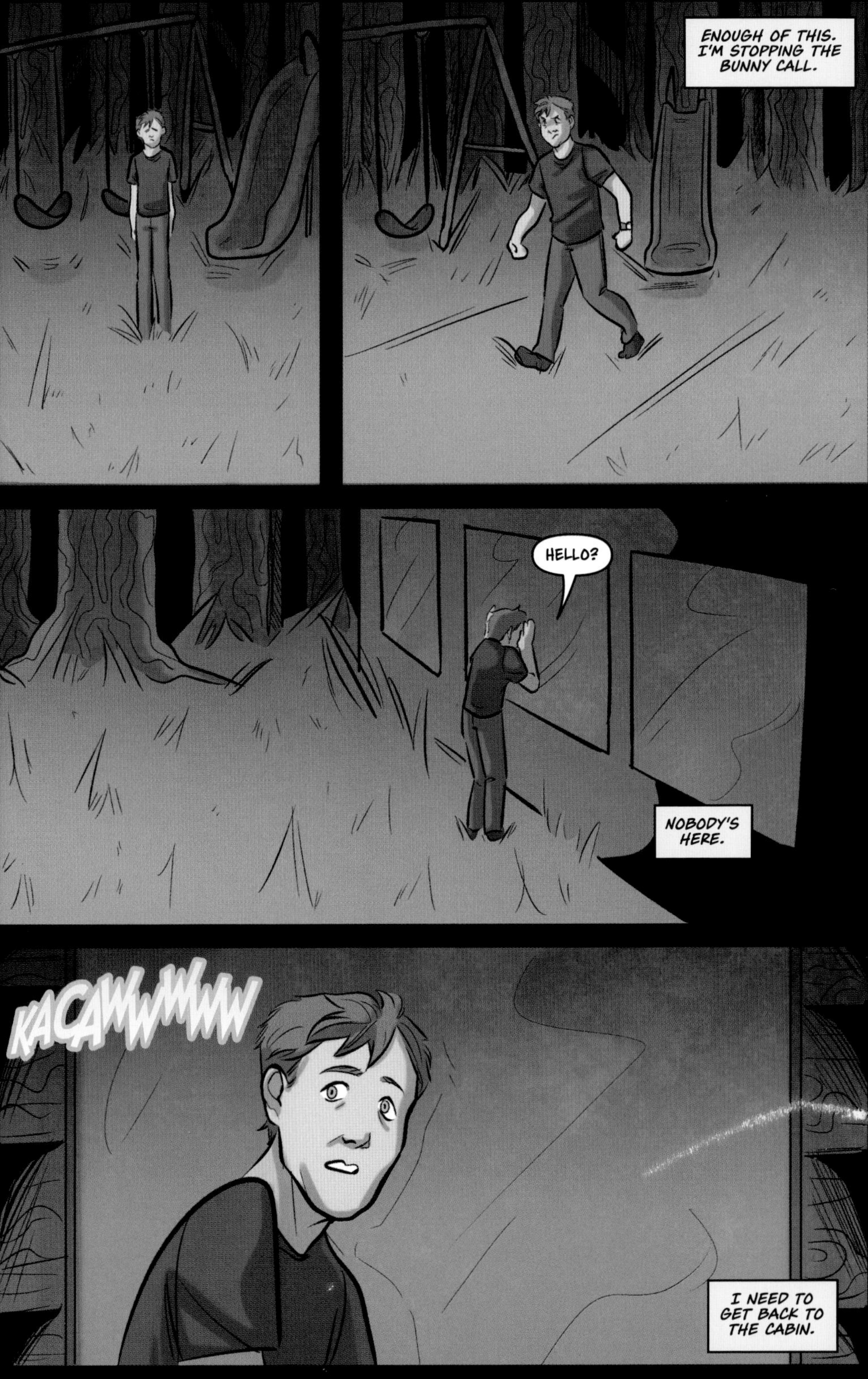
ENOUGH OF THIS. I'M STOPPING THE BUNNY CALL.
HELLO?
NOBODY'S HERE.
KACAWWWWW
I NEED TO GET BACK TO THE CABIN.

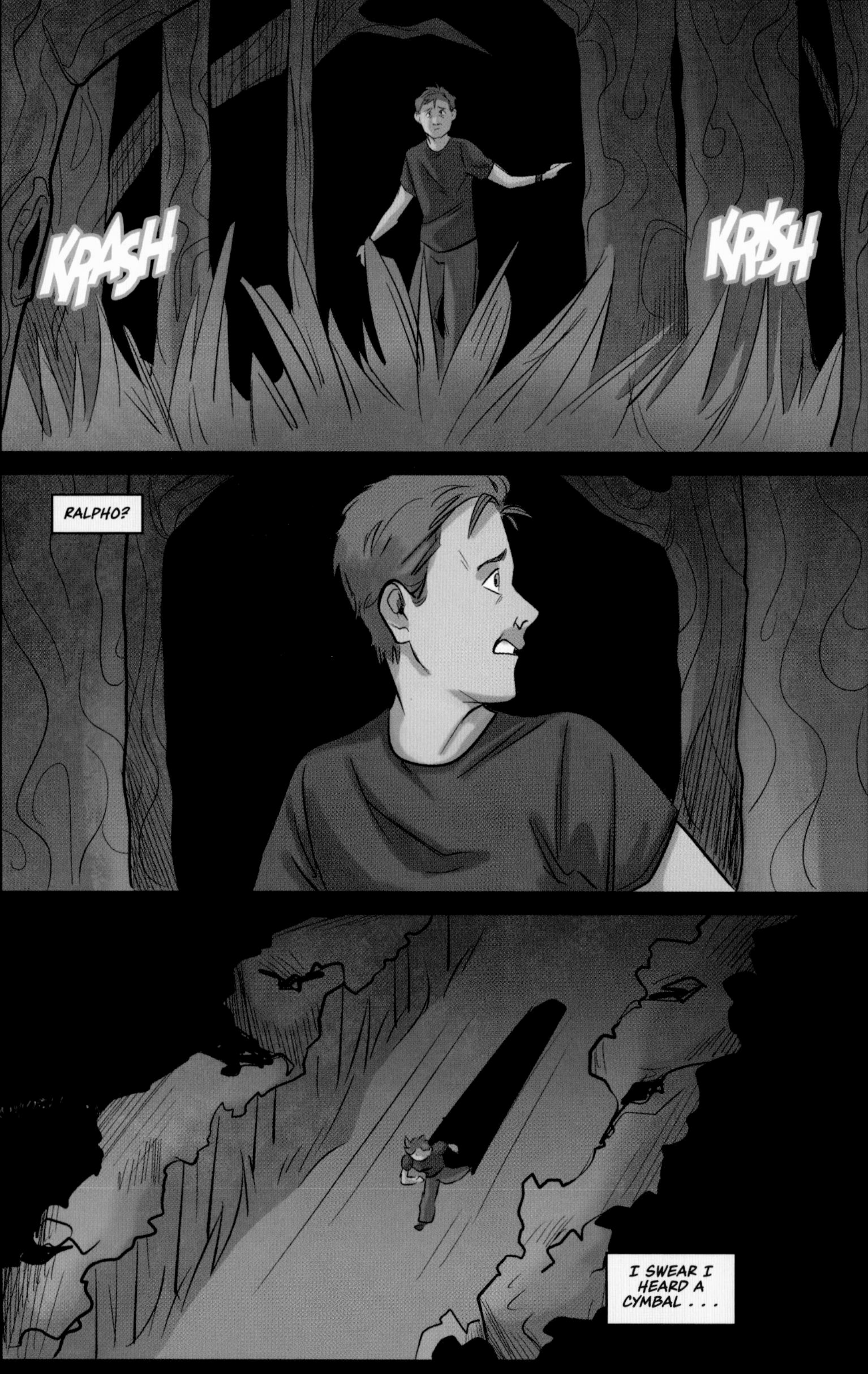
KRASH
KRISH
RALPHO?
I SWEAR I HEARD A CYMBAL . . .

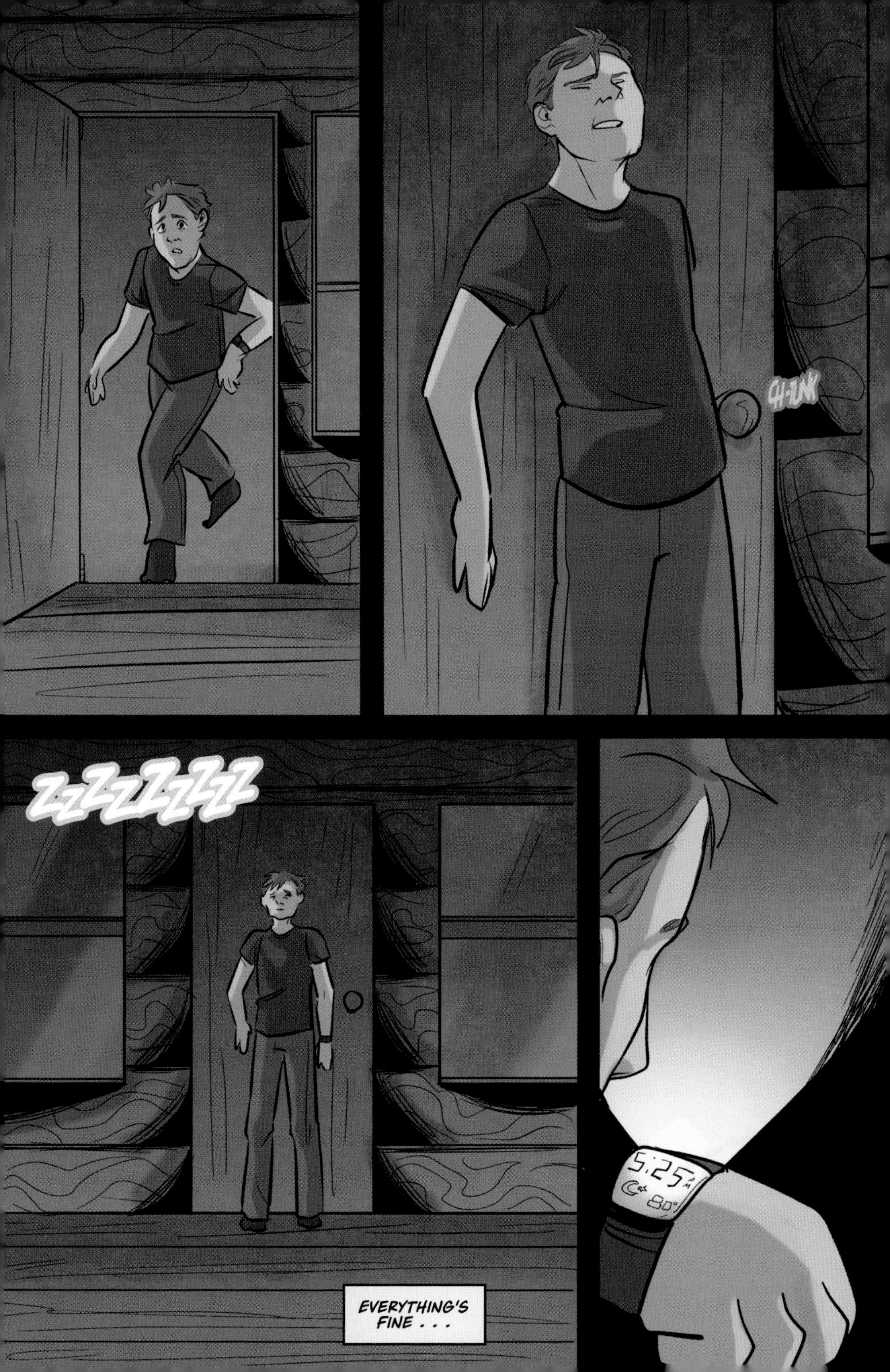
CH-TUNK
ZZZZZZZZZZ
5:25 AM
80°
EVERYTHING'S FINE . . .

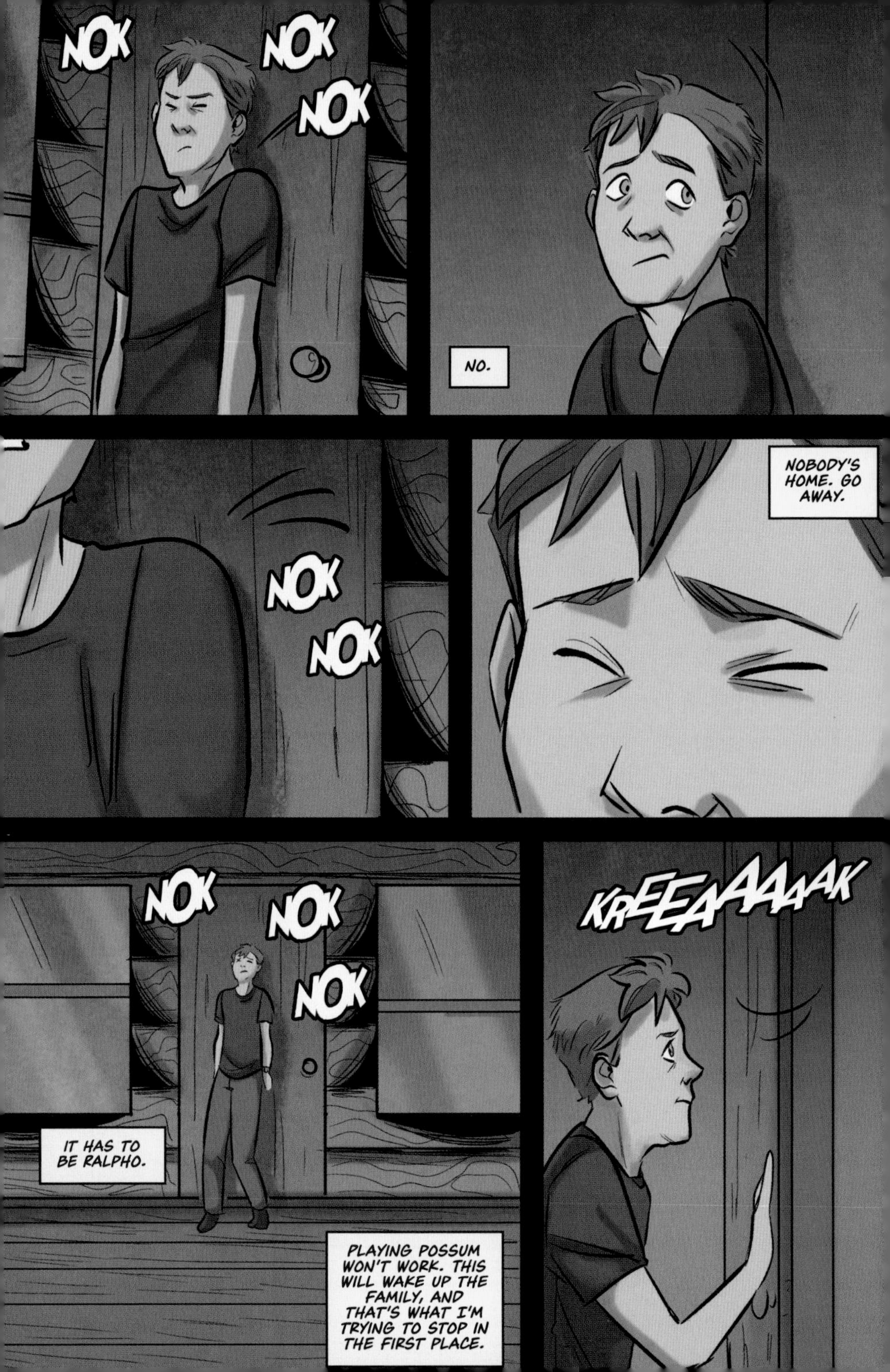
NOK
NOK
NOK
NO.
NOK
NOK
NOBODY'S HOME. GO AWAY.
NOK
NOK
NOK
IT HAS TO BE RALPHO.
PLAYING POSSUM WON'T WORK. THIS WILL WAKE UP THE FAMILY, AND THAT'S WHAT I'M TRYING TO STOP IN THE FIRST PLACE.
KREEAAAAAK

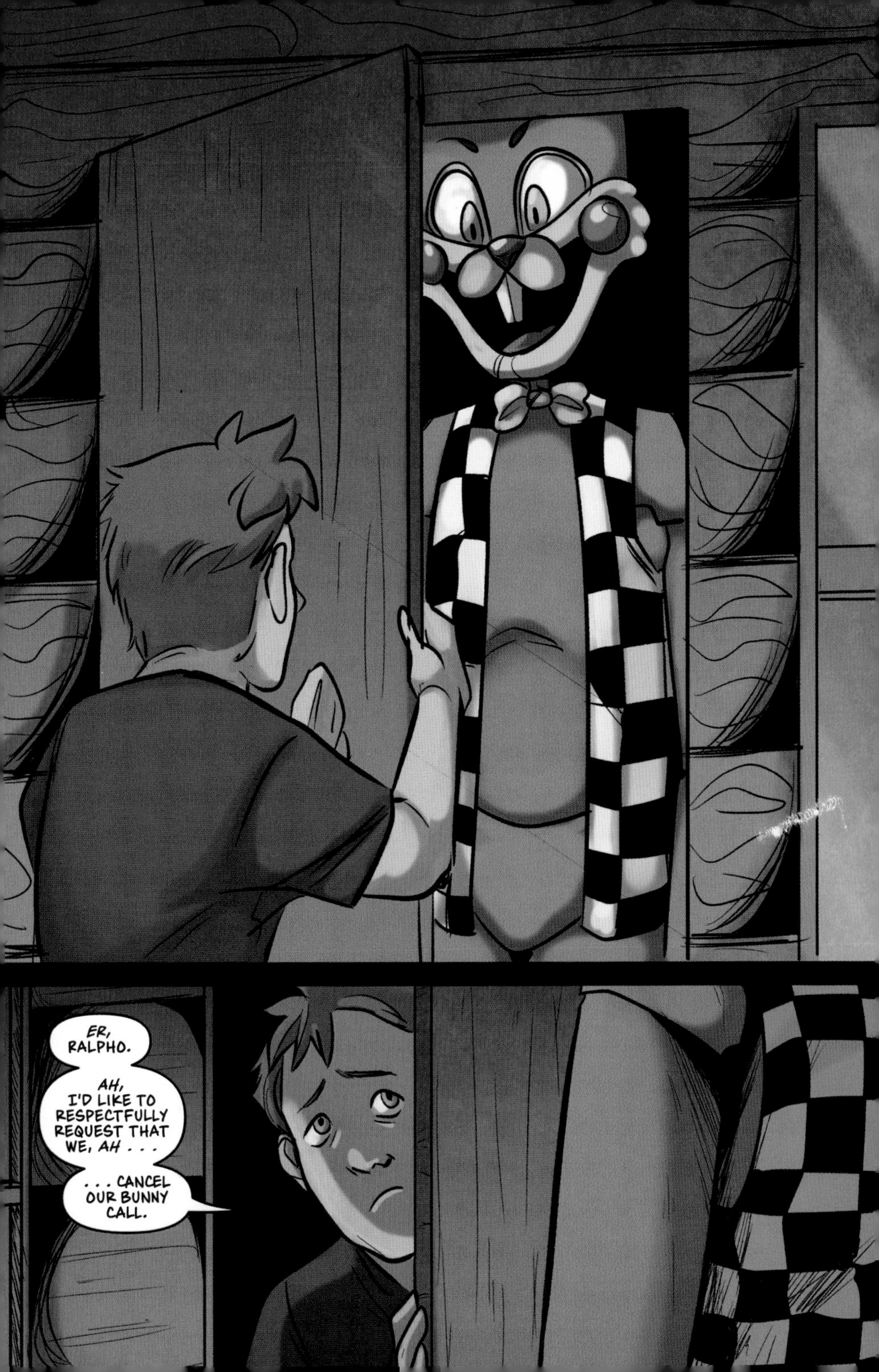
ER, RALPHO.
AH, I'D LIKE TO RESPECTFULLY REQUEST THAT WE, AH . . .
. . . CANCEL OUR BUNNY CALL.

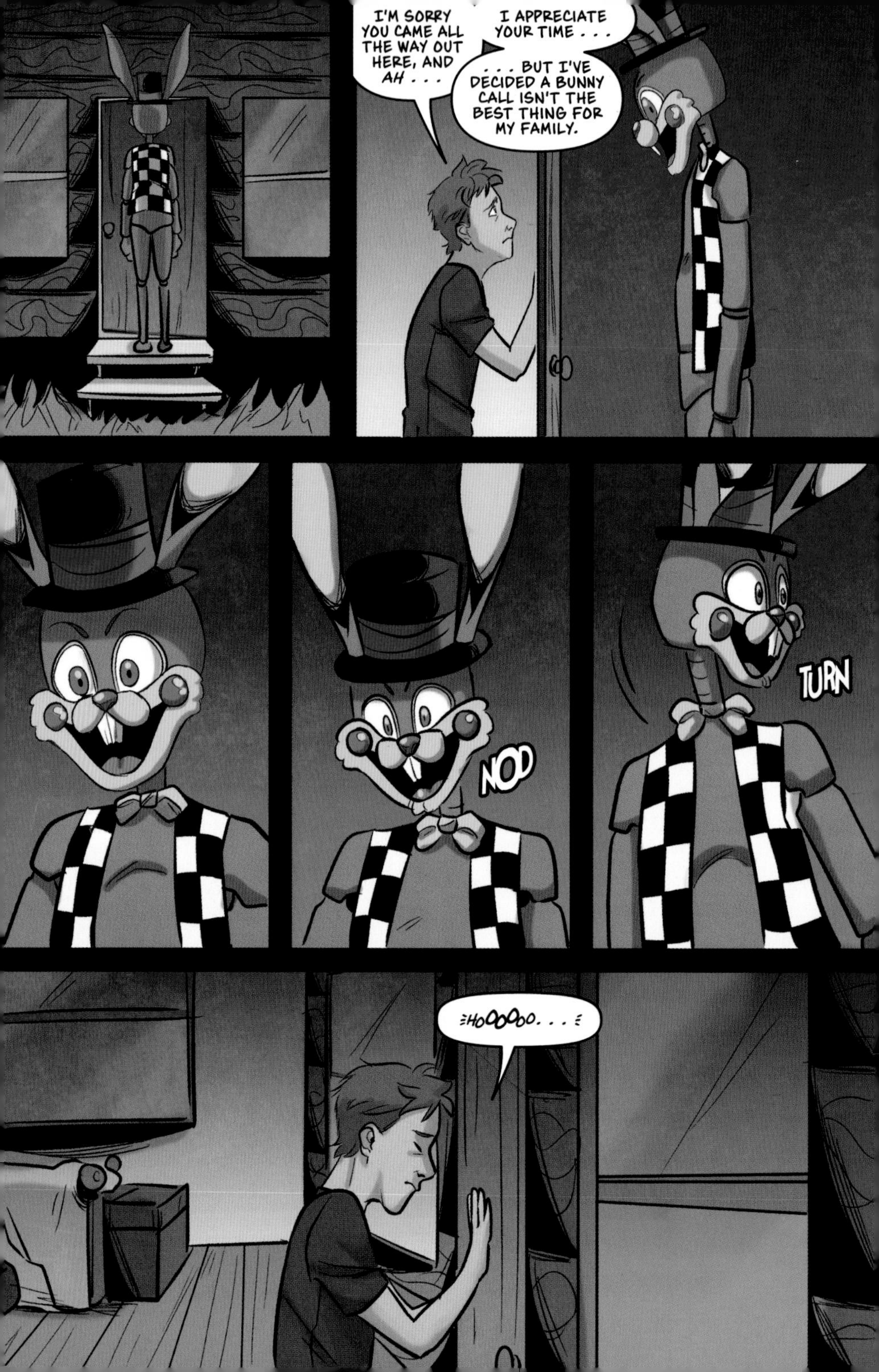
I'M SORRY YOU CAME ALL THE WAY OUT HERE, AND AH . . .
I APPRECIATE YOUR TIME . . .
. . . BUT I'VE DECIDED A BUNNY CALL ISN'T THE BEST THING FOR MY FAMILY.
NOD
TURN
HOOOOO. . .

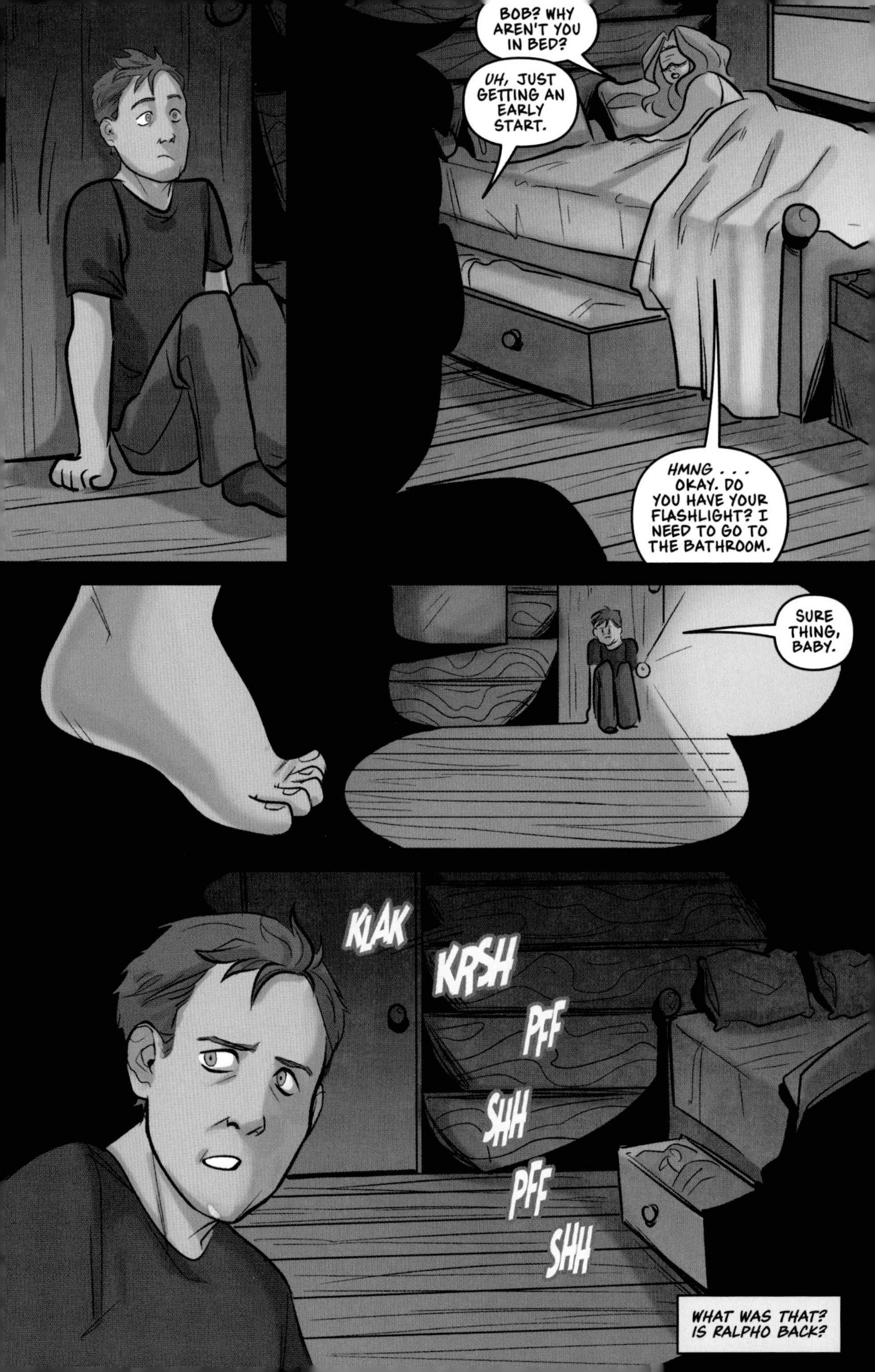
BOB? WHY AREN'T YOU IN BED?
UH, JUST GETTING AN EARLY START.
HMNG . . . OKAY. DO YOU HAVE YOUR FLASHLIGHT? I NEED TO GO TO THE BATHROOM.
SURE THING, BABY.
KLAK
KRSH
PFF
SHH
PFF
SHH
WHAT WAS THAT? IS RALPHO BACK?

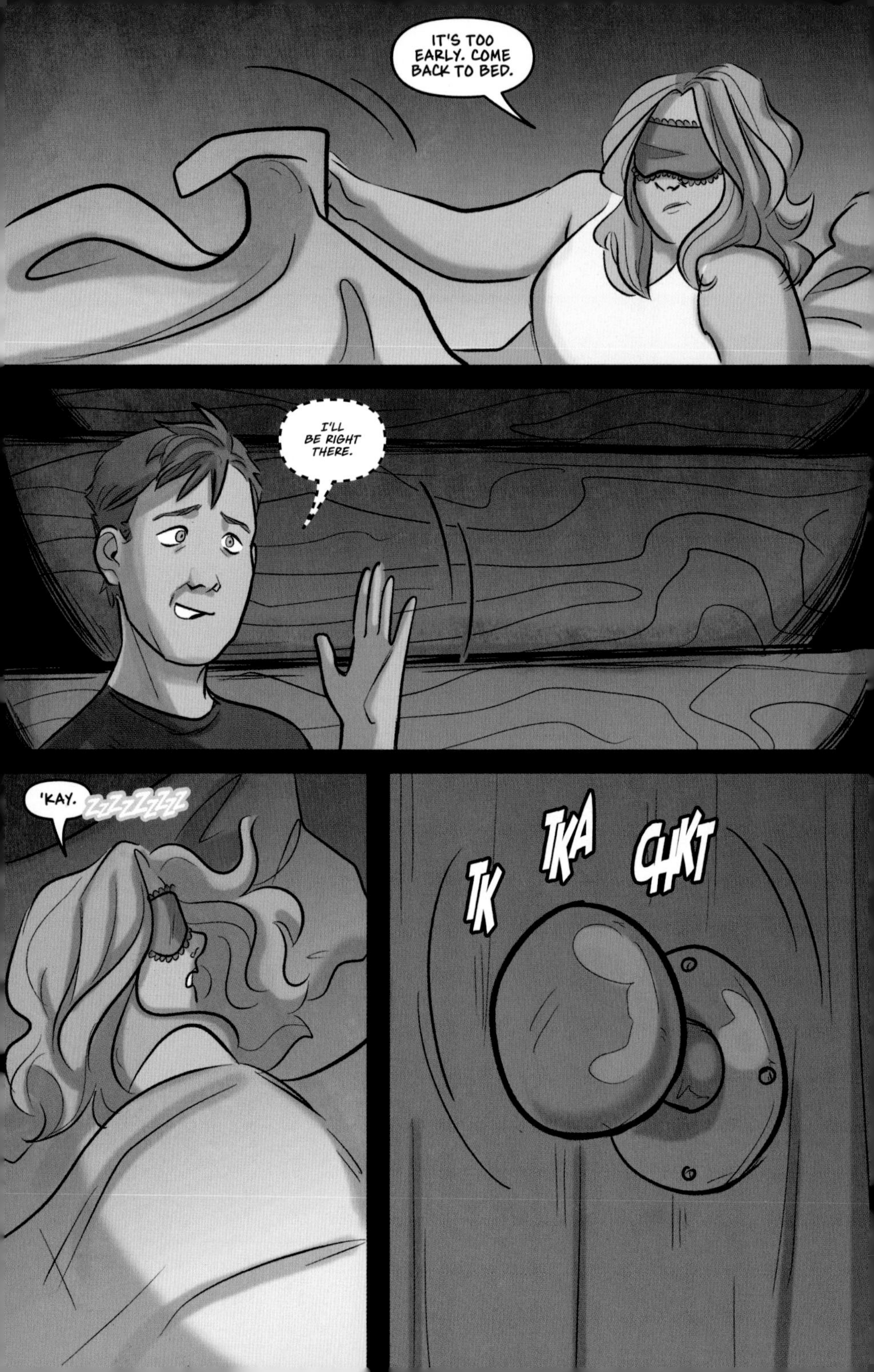
IT'S TOO EARLY. COME BACK TO BED.
I'LL BE RIGHT THERE.
'KAY.
ZZZZZZZZ
TK
TKA
CHKT

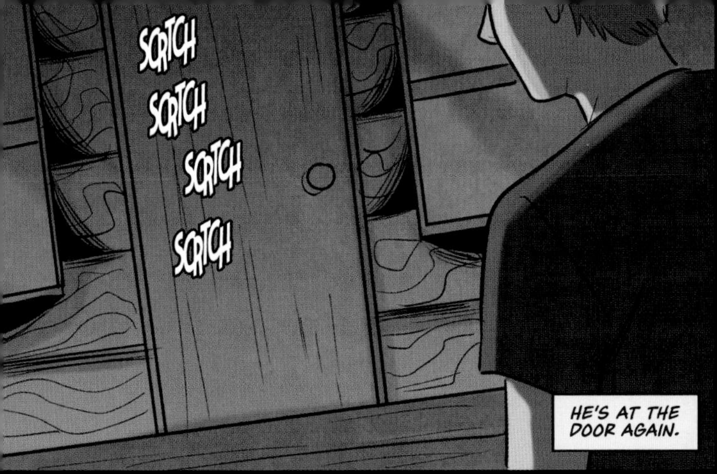
SCRITCH
SCRITCH
SCRITCH
SCRITCH
HE'S AT THE DOOR AGAIN.

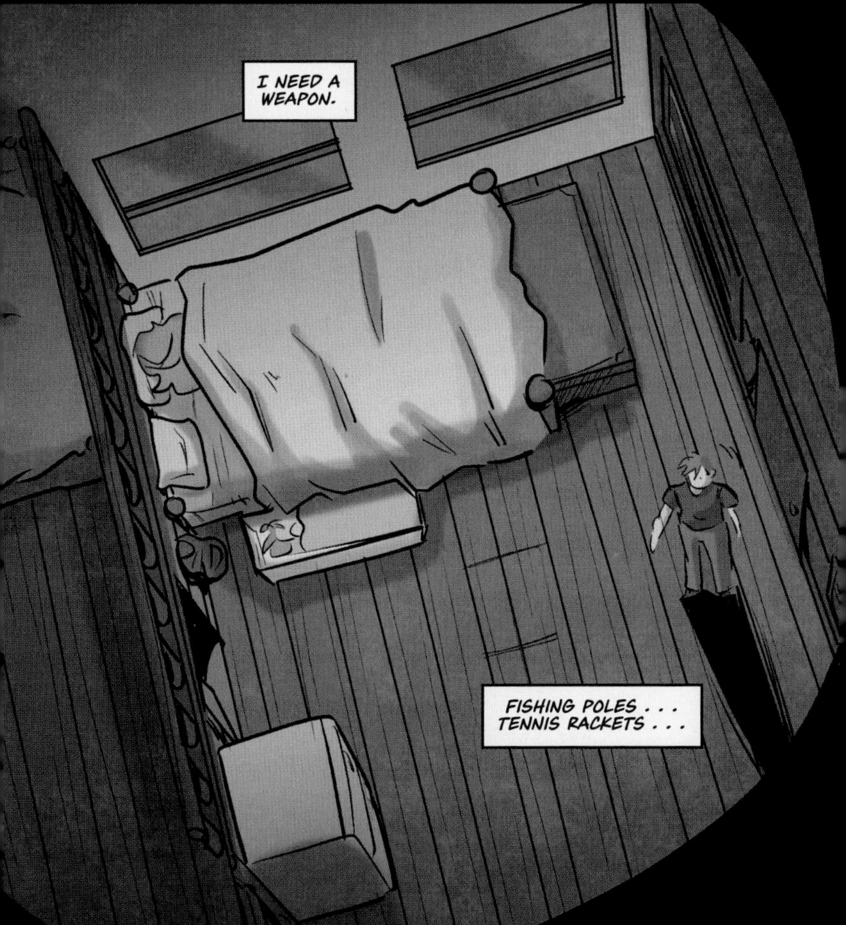
I NEED A WEAPON.
FISHING POLES . . . TENNIS RACKETS . . .
THAT'LL DO A LOT OF GOOD, ONE IN EACH HAND . . .

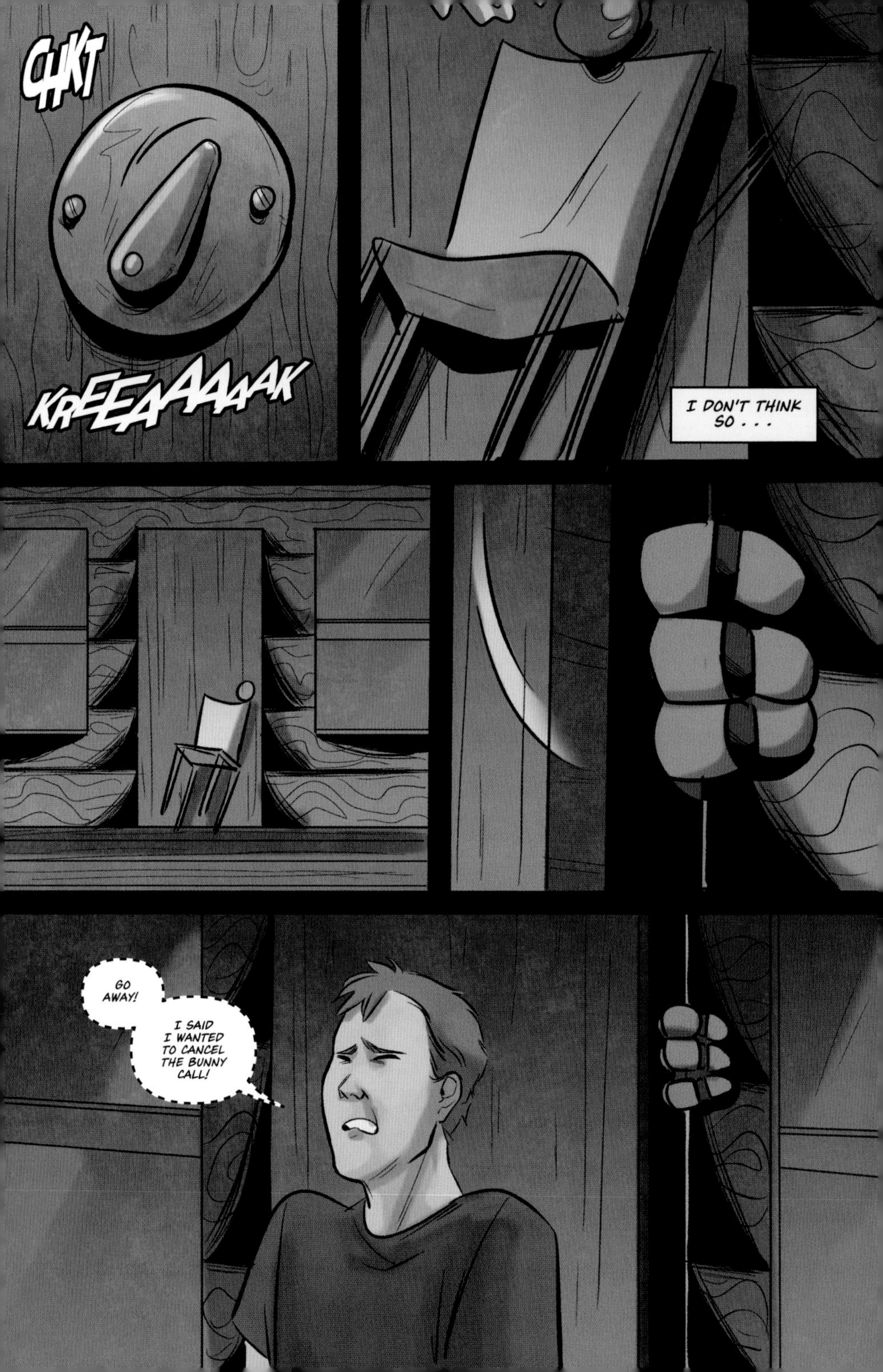
CHKT
KREEAAAAAK
I DON'T THINK SO . . .
GO AWAY!
I SAID I WANTED TO CANCEL THE BUNNY CALL!

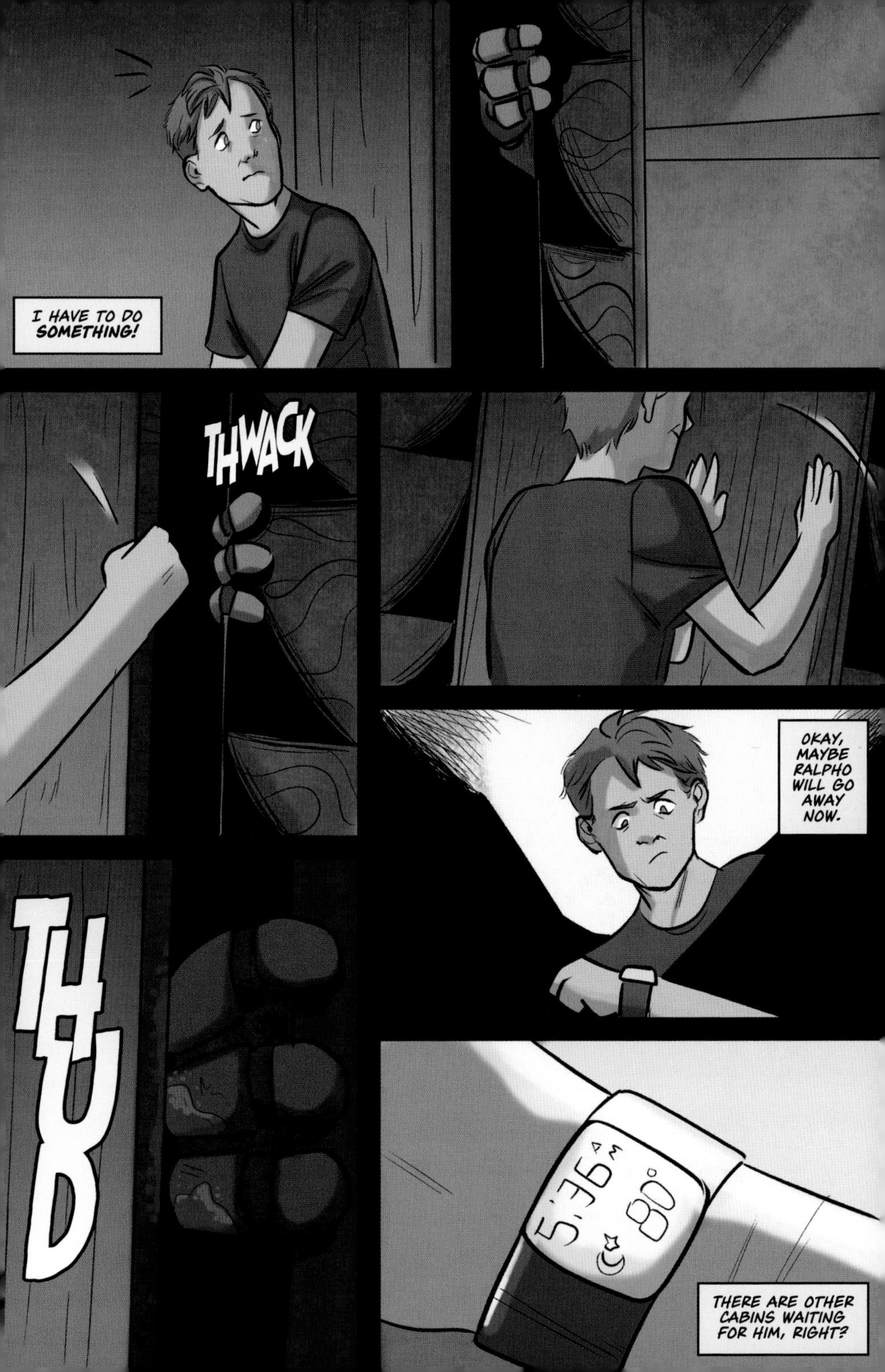
I HAVE TO DO SOMETHING!
THWACK
OKAY, MAYBE RALPHO WILL GO AWAY NOW.
THUD
5:36
80°
THERE ARE OTHER CABINS WAITING FOR HIM, RIGHT?

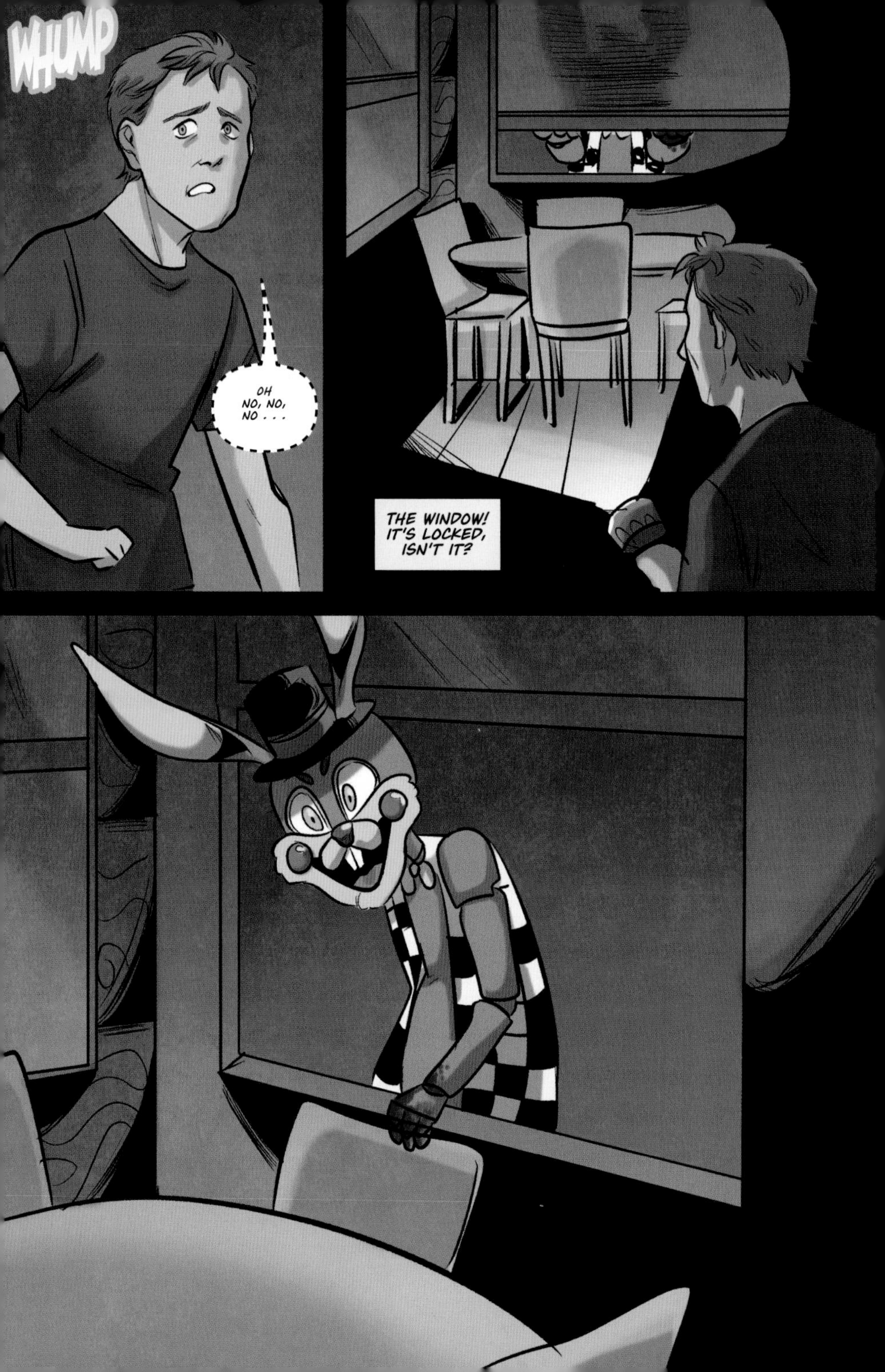
WHUMP
OH NO, NO, NO . . .
THE WINDOW! IT'S LOCKED, ISN'T IT?

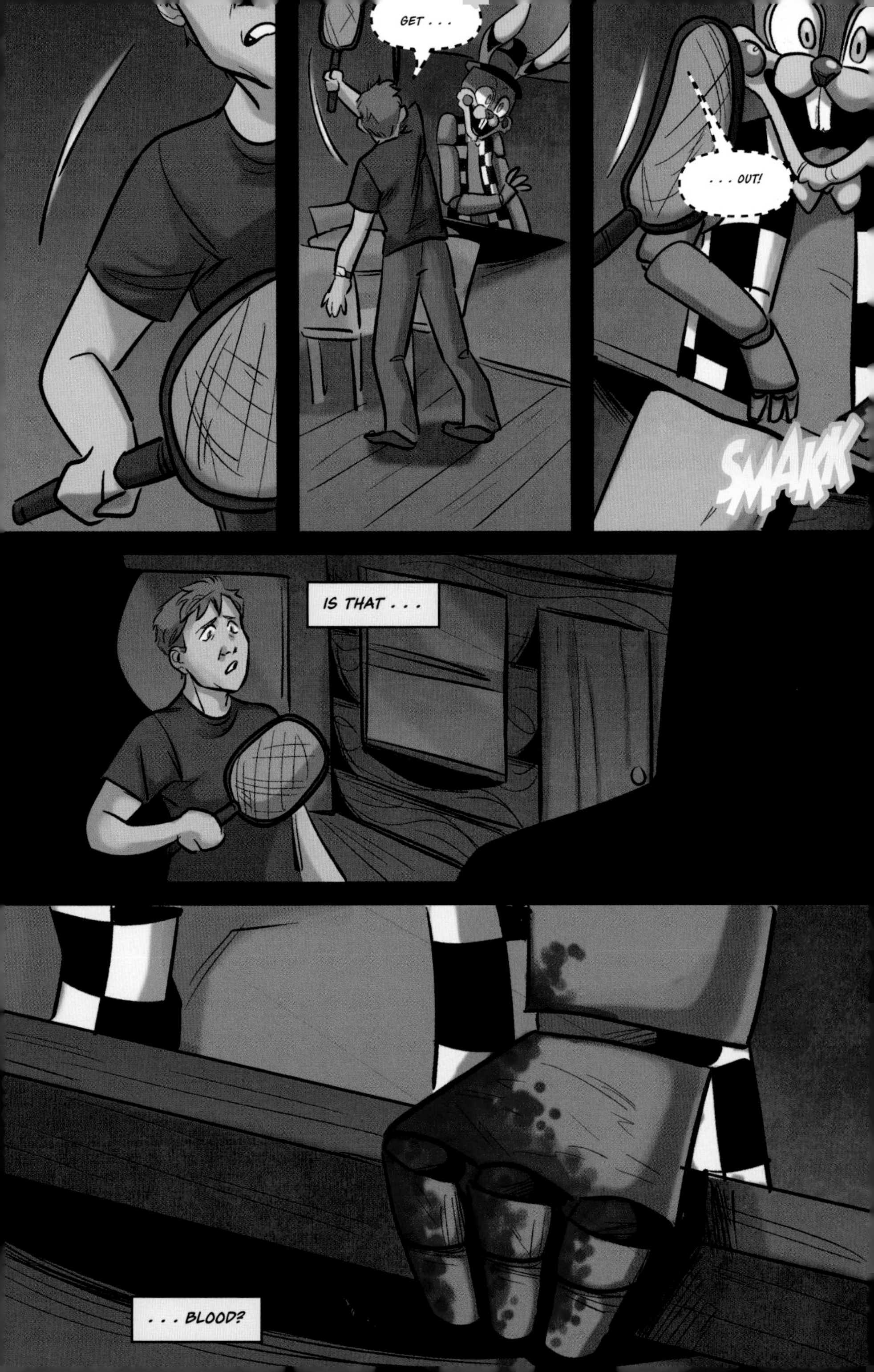
GET . . .
. . . OUT!
SMAKK
IS THAT . . .
. . . BLOOD?

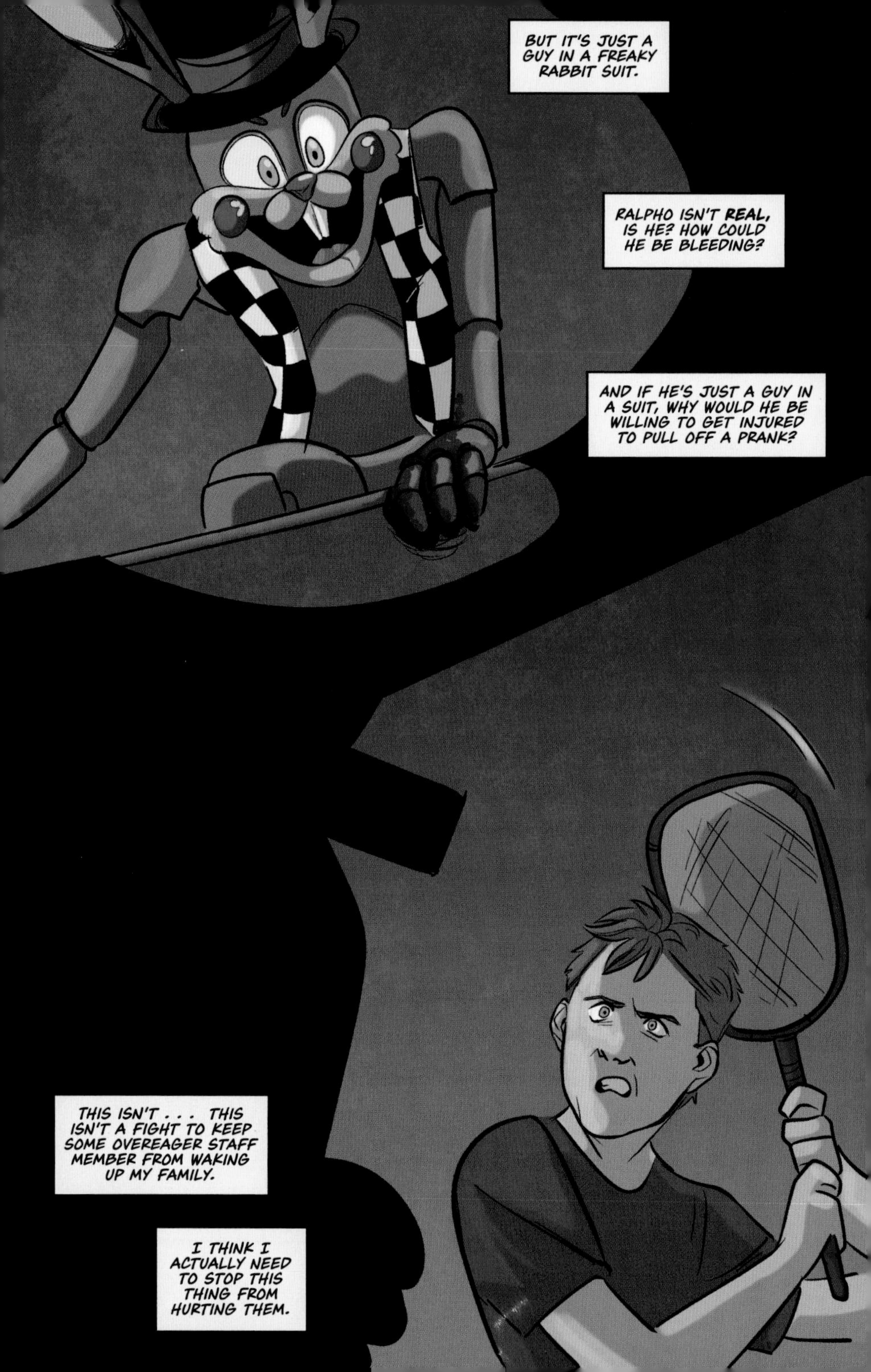
BUT IT'S JUST A GUY IN A FREAKY RABBIT SUIT.
RALPHO ISN'T REAL, IS HE? HOW COULD HE BE BLEEDING?
AND IF HE'S JUST A GUY IN A SUIT, WHY WOULD HE BE WILLING TO GET INJURED TO PULL OFF A PRANK?
THIS ISN'T . . . THIS ISN'T A FIGHT TO KEEP SOME OVEREAGER STAFF MEMBER FROM WAKING UP MY FAMILY.
I THINK I ACTUALLY NEED TO STOP THIS THING FROM HURTING THEM.

ERRRAAGH!

KLAK

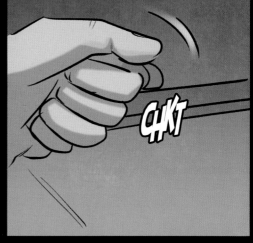

CLIKT

HUFF . . .
HUFF . . .
HUFF

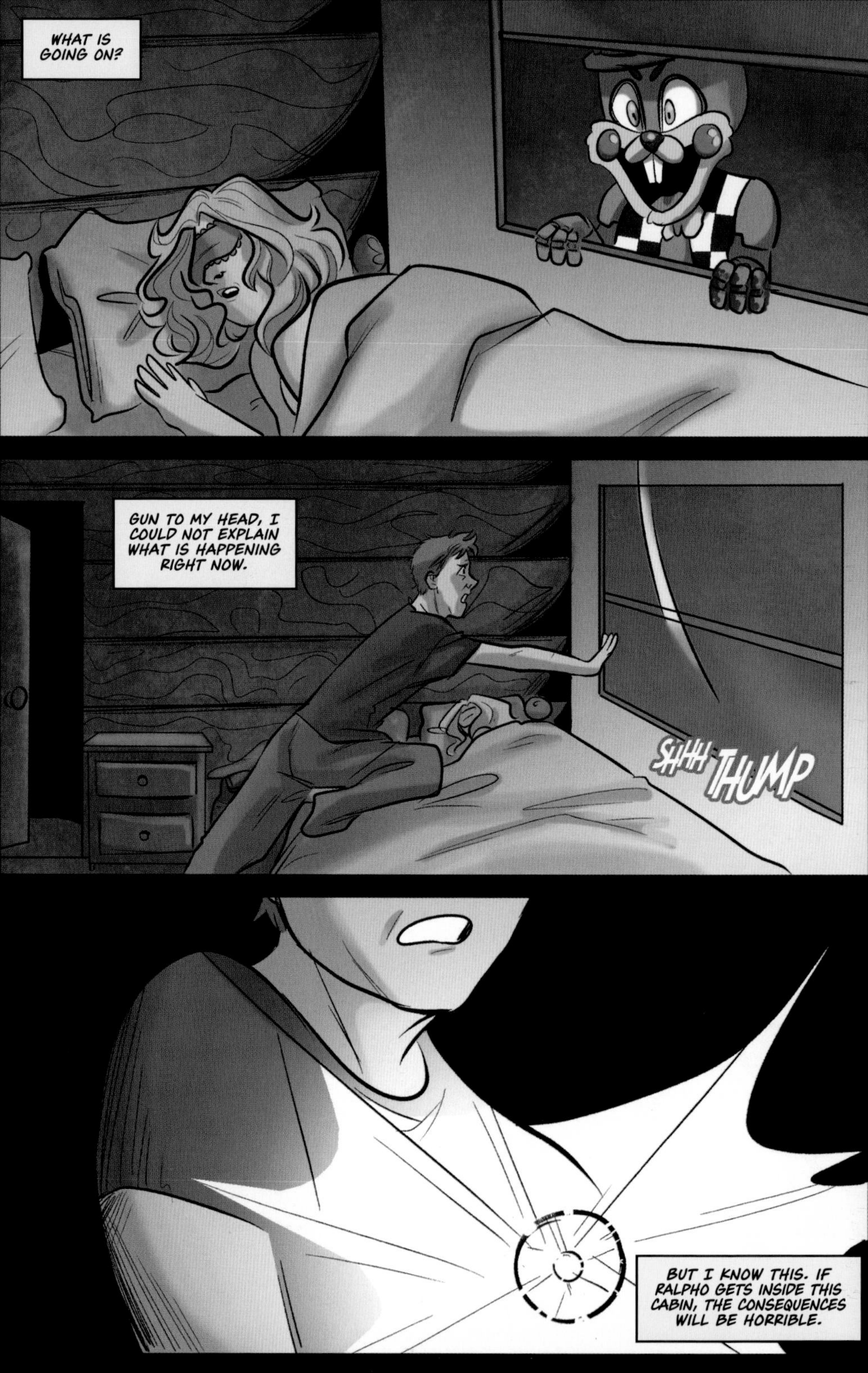
WHAT IS GOING ON?
GUN TO MY HEAD, I COULD NOT EXPLAIN WHAT IS HAPPENING RIGHT NOW.
SHHH THUMP
BUT I KNOW THIS. IF RALPHO GETS INSIDE THIS CABIN, THE CONSEQUENCES WILL BE HORRIBLE.

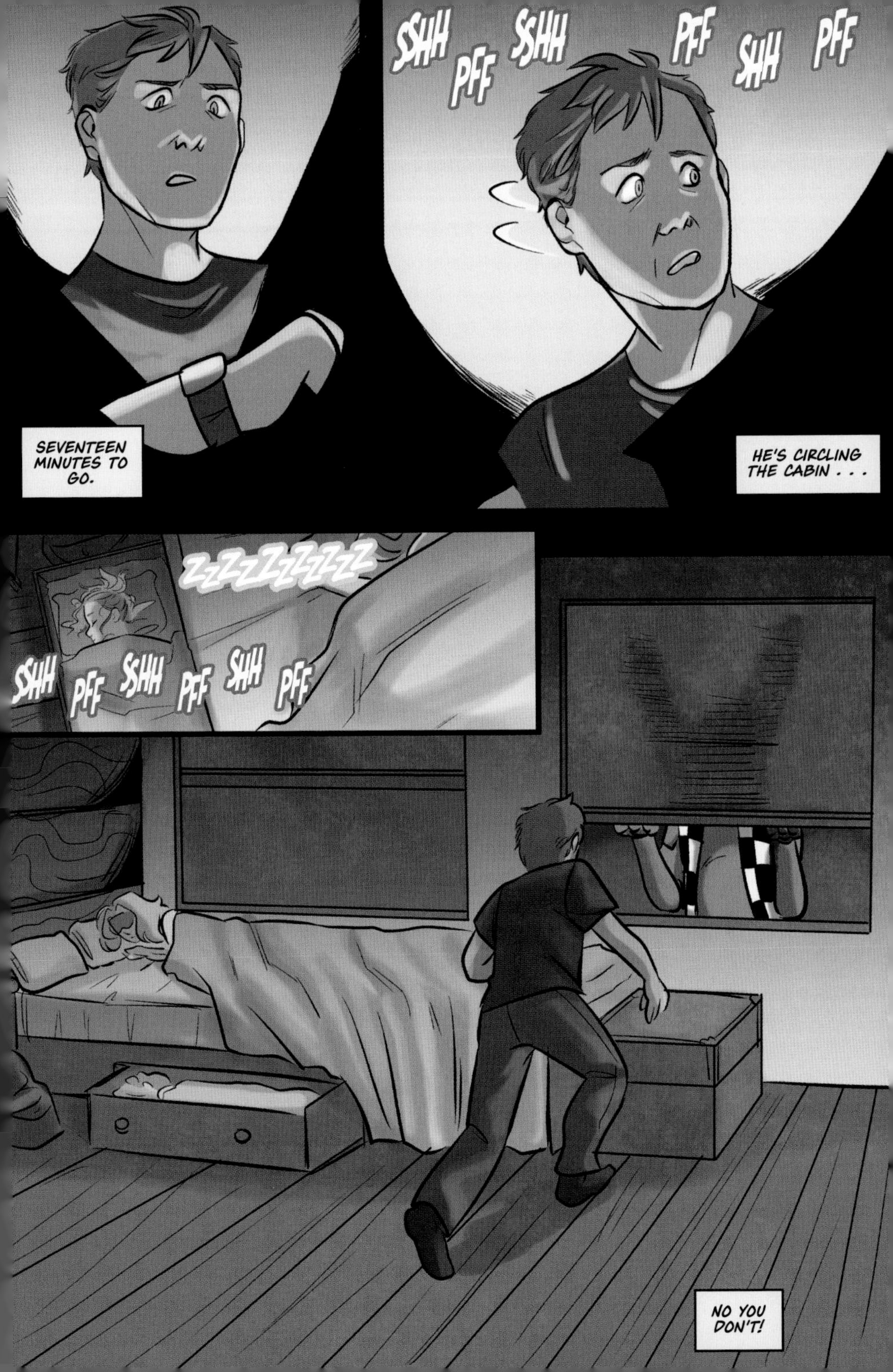
SEVENTEEN MINUTES TO GO.
SSHH PFF SSHH PFF SHH PFF
HE'S CIRCLING THE CABIN . . .
ZZZZZZZZZZZZ
SSHH PFF SSHH PFF SHH PFF
NO YOU DON'T!

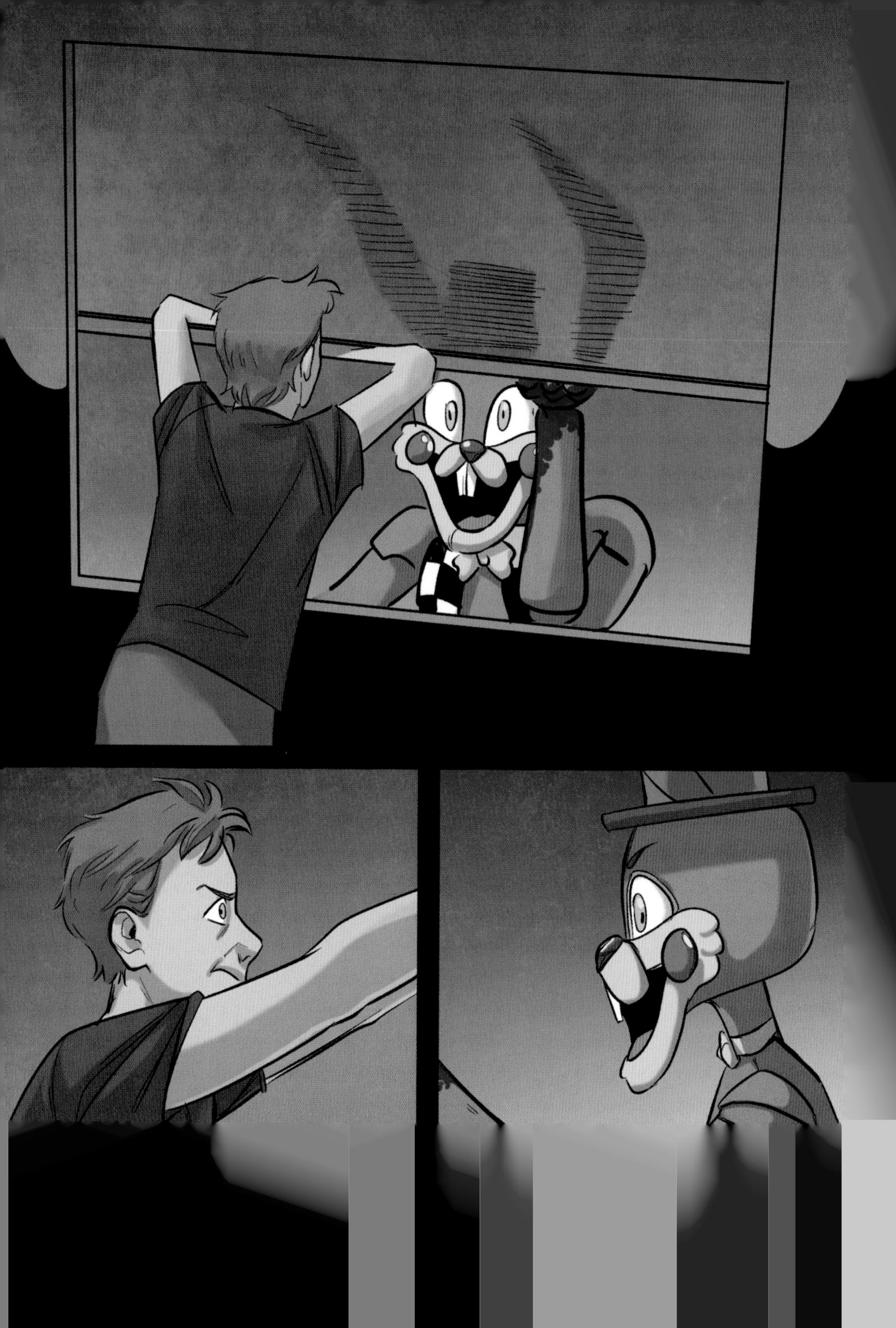

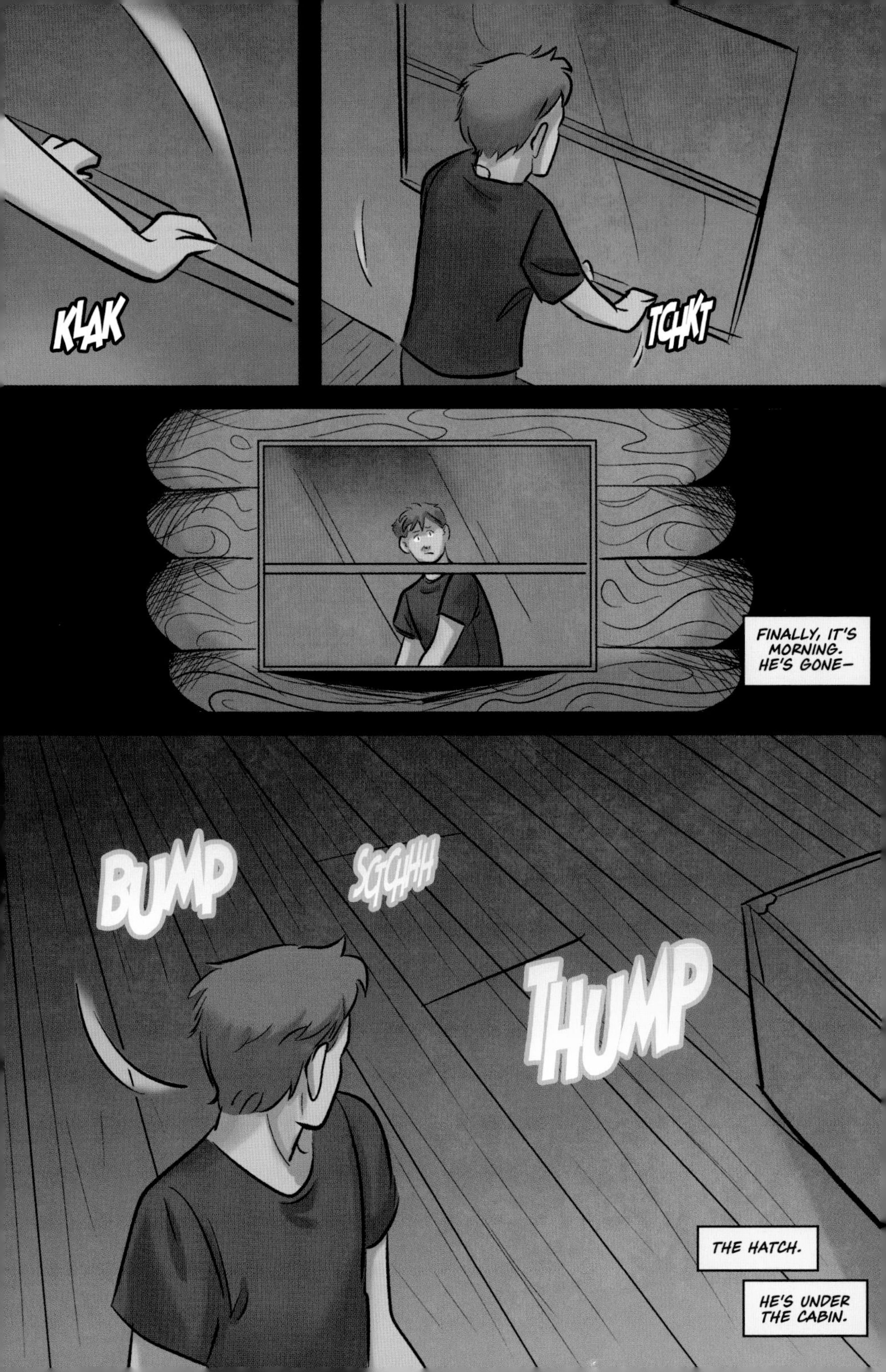
KLAK
TCHKT
FINALLY, IT'S MORNING. HE'S GONE—
BUMP
SGCHHH
THUMP
THE HATCH.
HE'S UNDER THE CABIN.

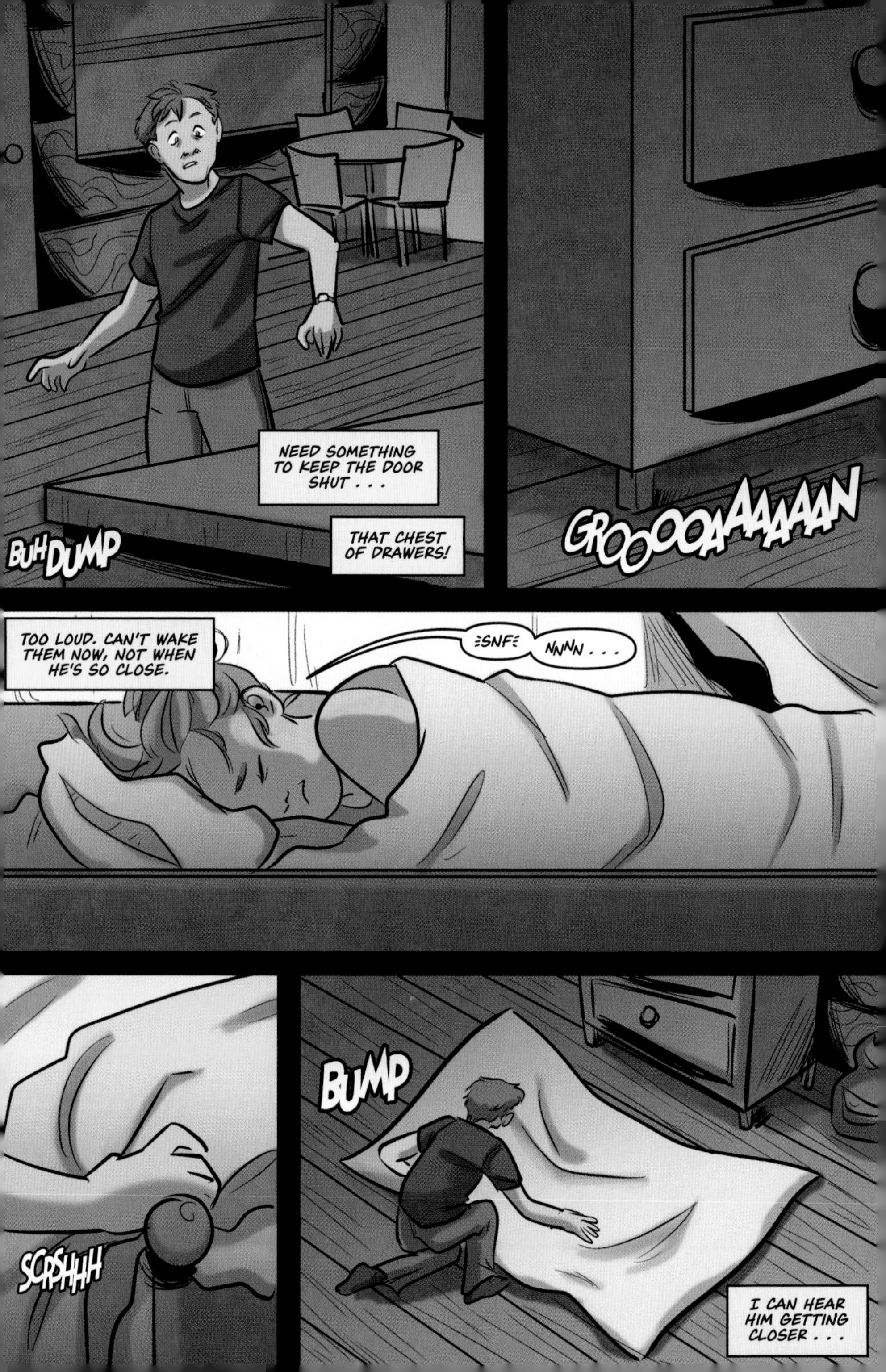
NEED SOMETHING TO KEEP THE DOOR SHUT . . .
THAT CHEST OF DRAWERS!
BUHDUMP
GROOOOOAAAAAAN
TOO LOUD. CAN'T WAKE THEM NOW, NOT WHEN HE'S SO CLOSE.
SNF
NNNN . . .
SCRSHHH
BUMP
I CAN HEAR HIM GETTING CLOSER . . .

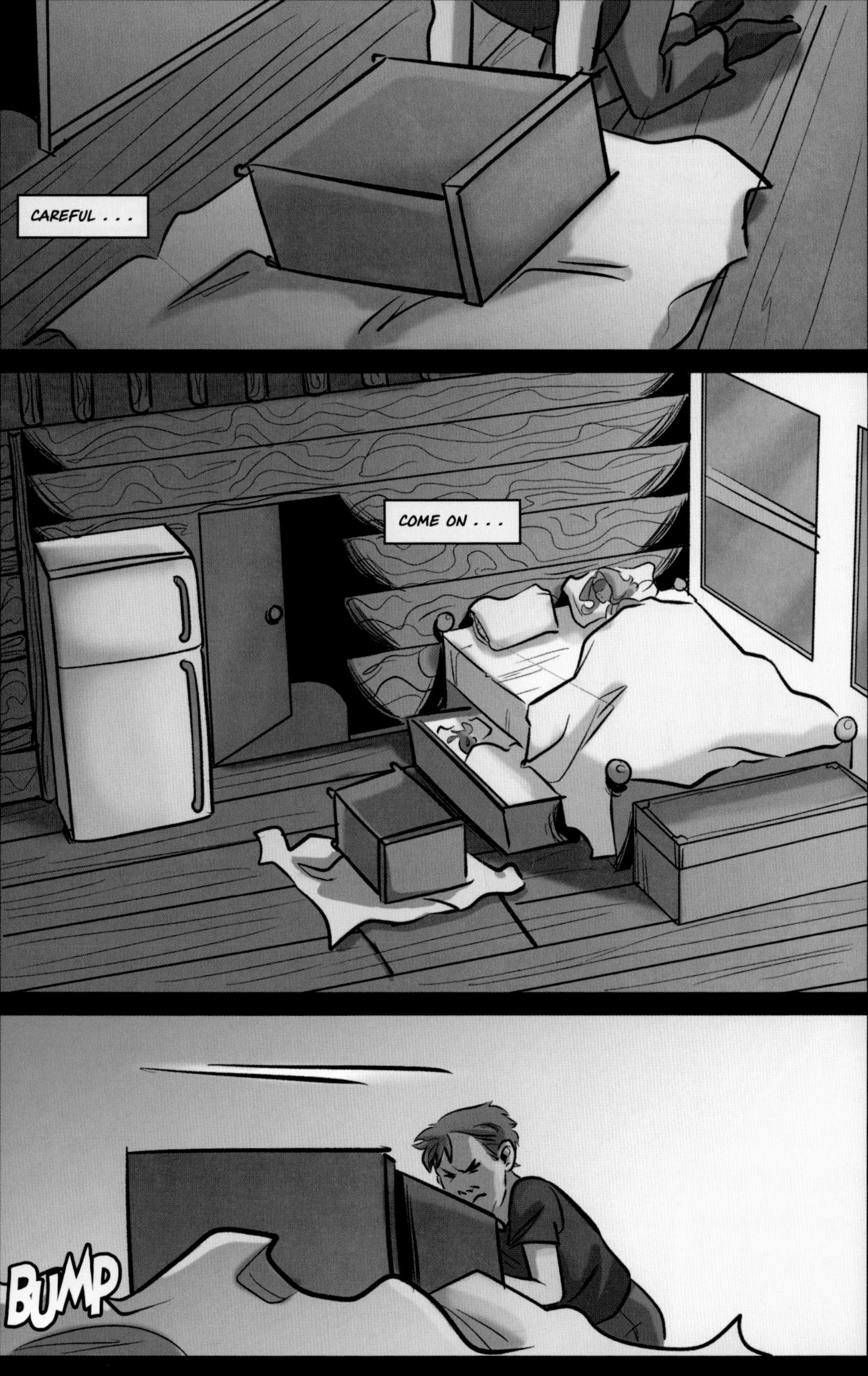
CAREFUL . . .
COME ON . . .
BUMP

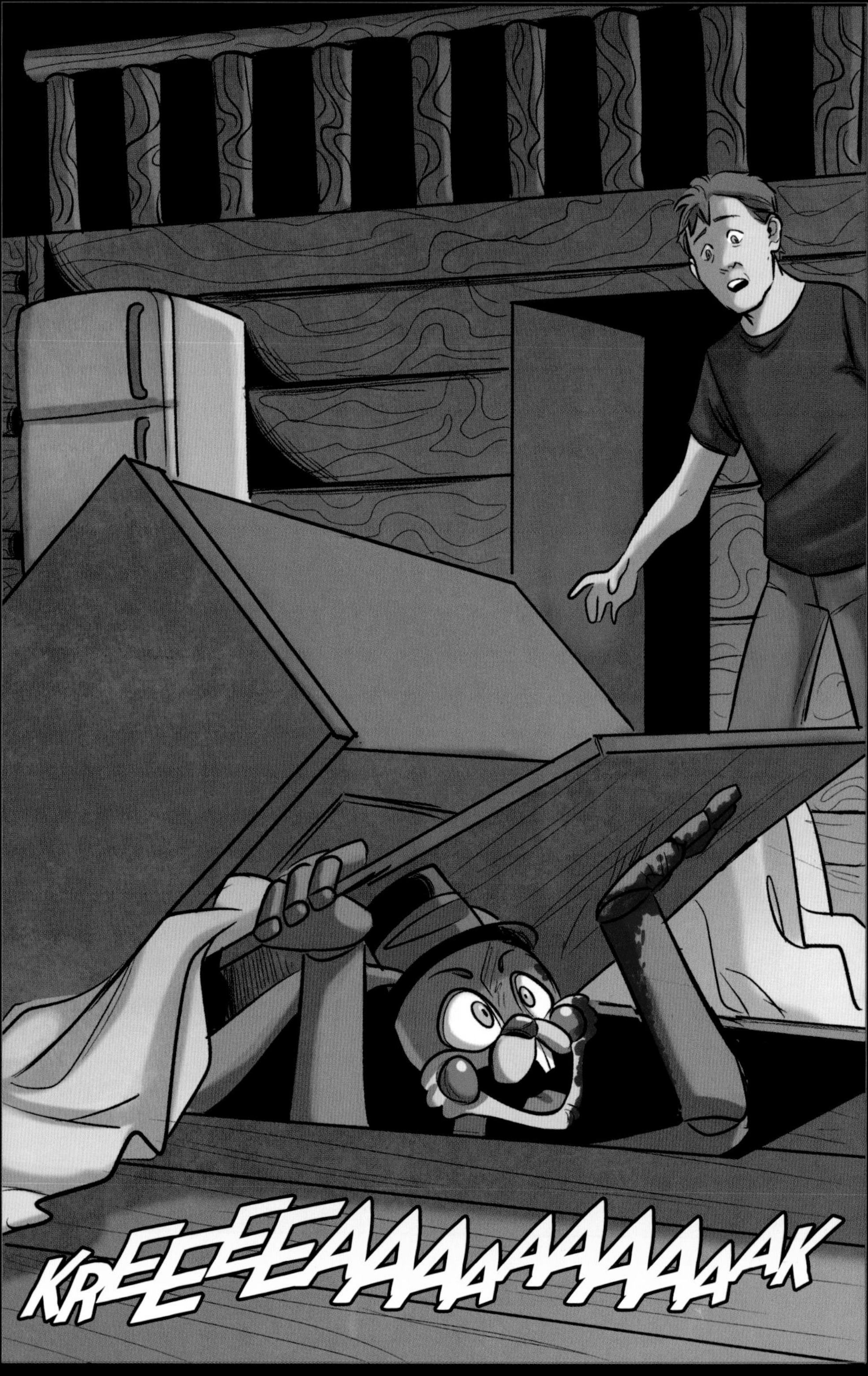
KREEEAAAAAAAAAAAK

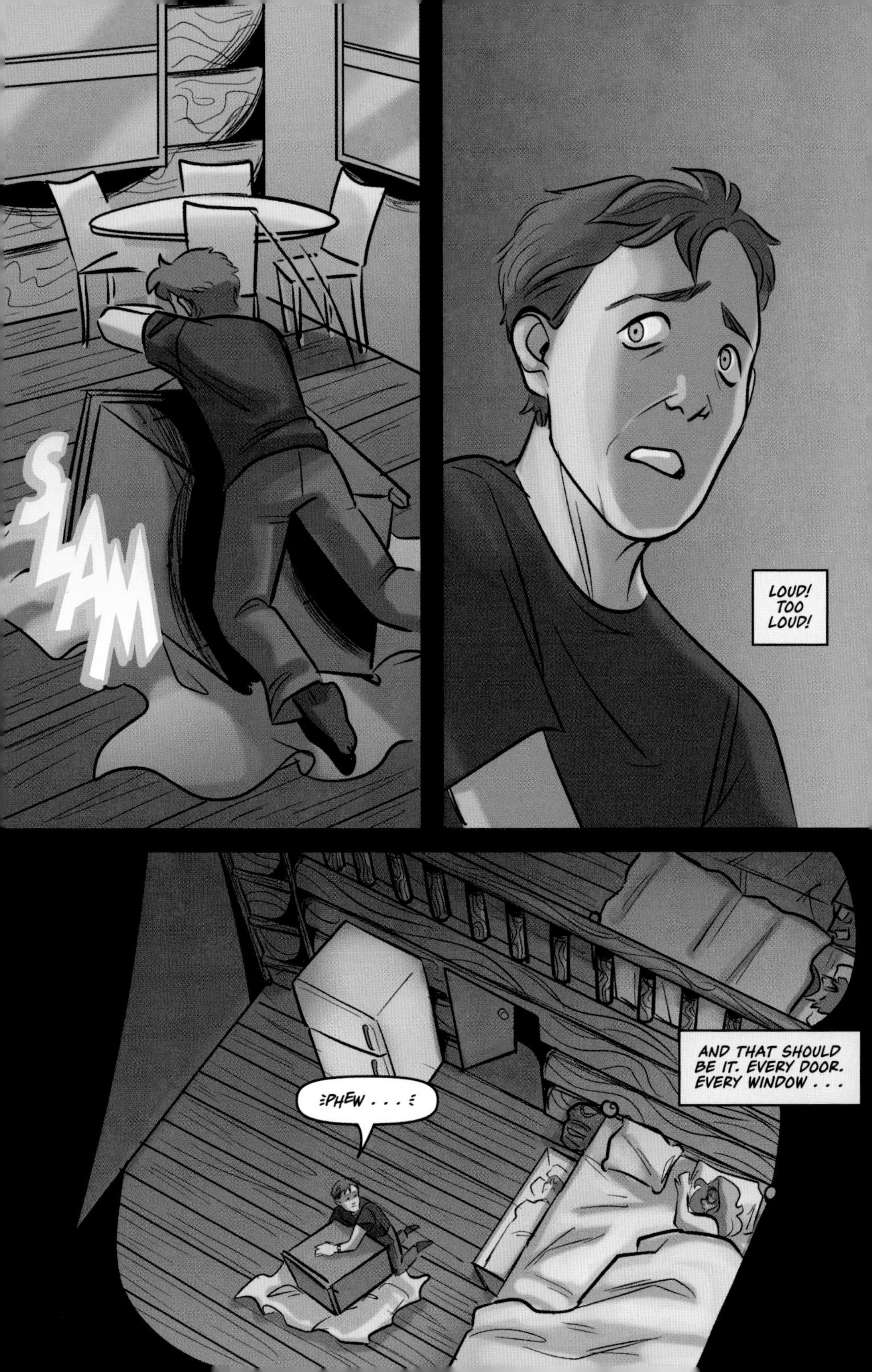
SLAM
LOUD! TOO LOUD!
AND THAT SHOULD BE IT. EVERY DOOR. EVERY WINDOW . . .
PHEW . . .

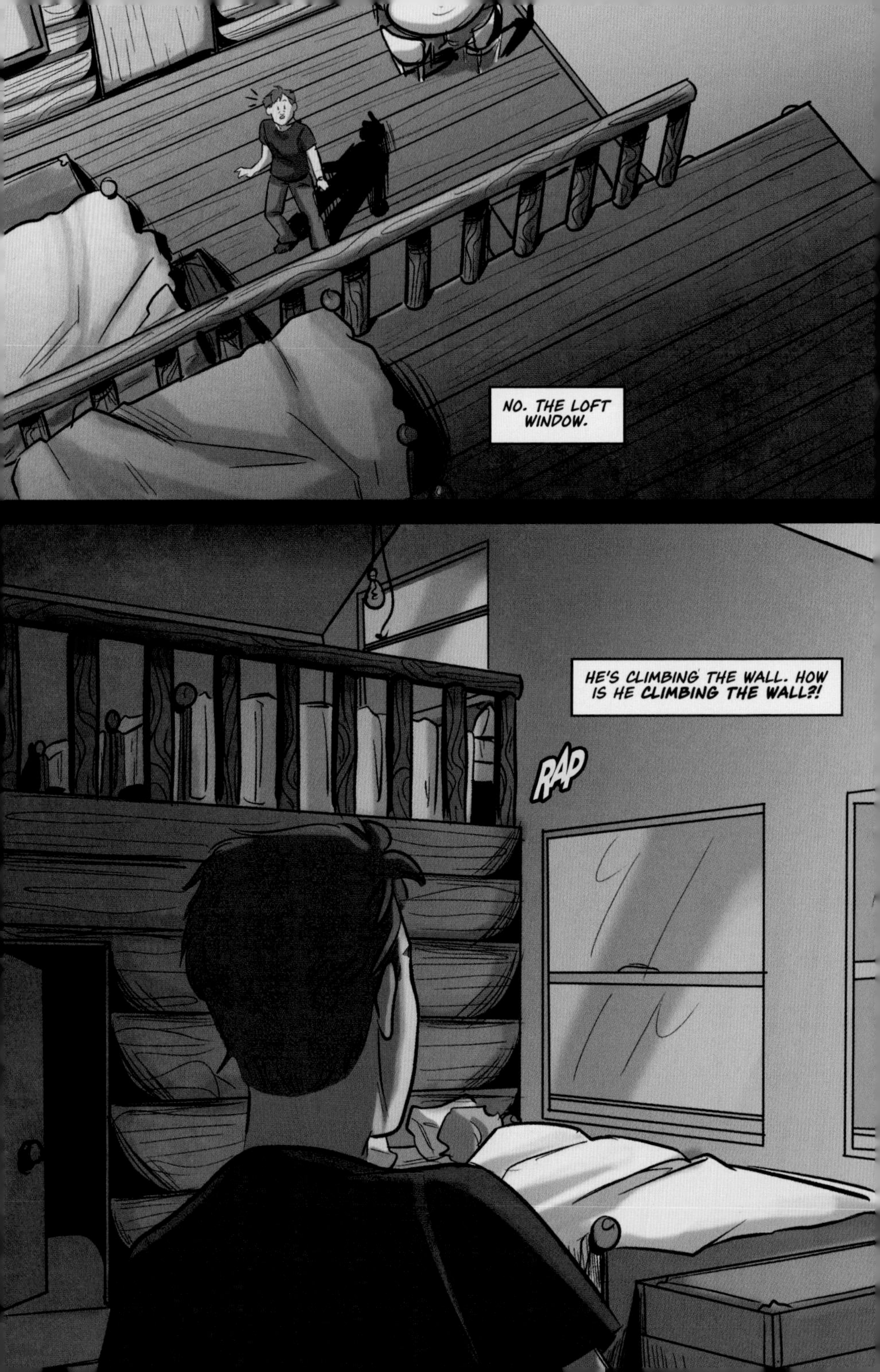
NO. THE LOFT WINDOW.
HE'S CLIMBING THE WALL. HOW IS HE CLIMBING THE WALL?!
RAP

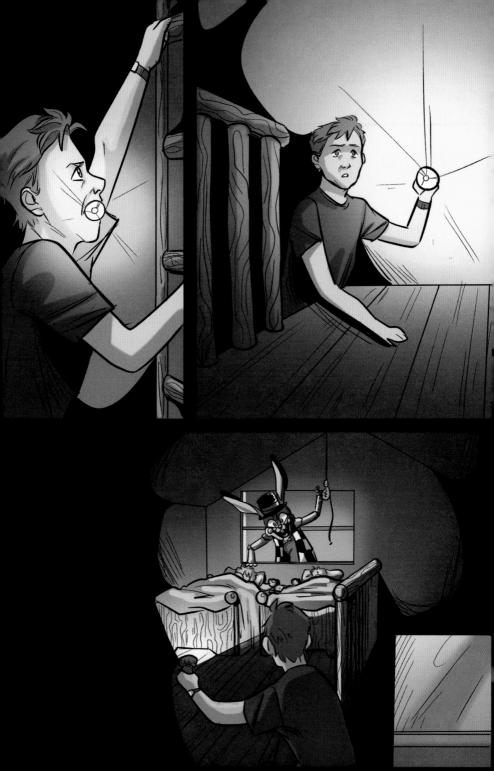

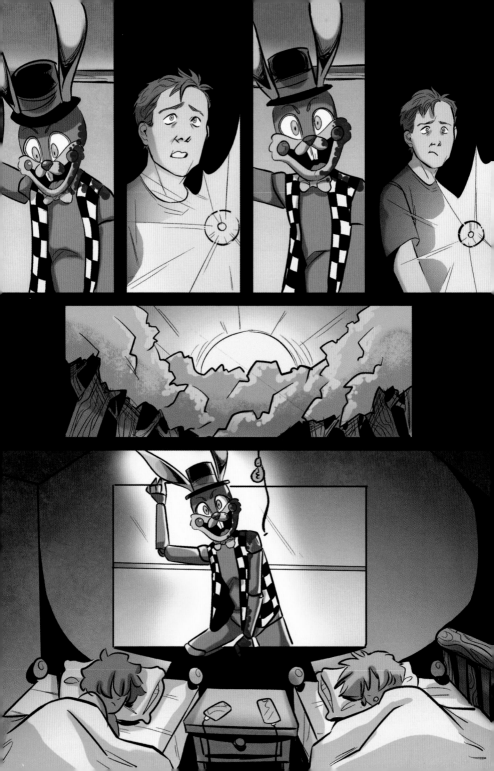

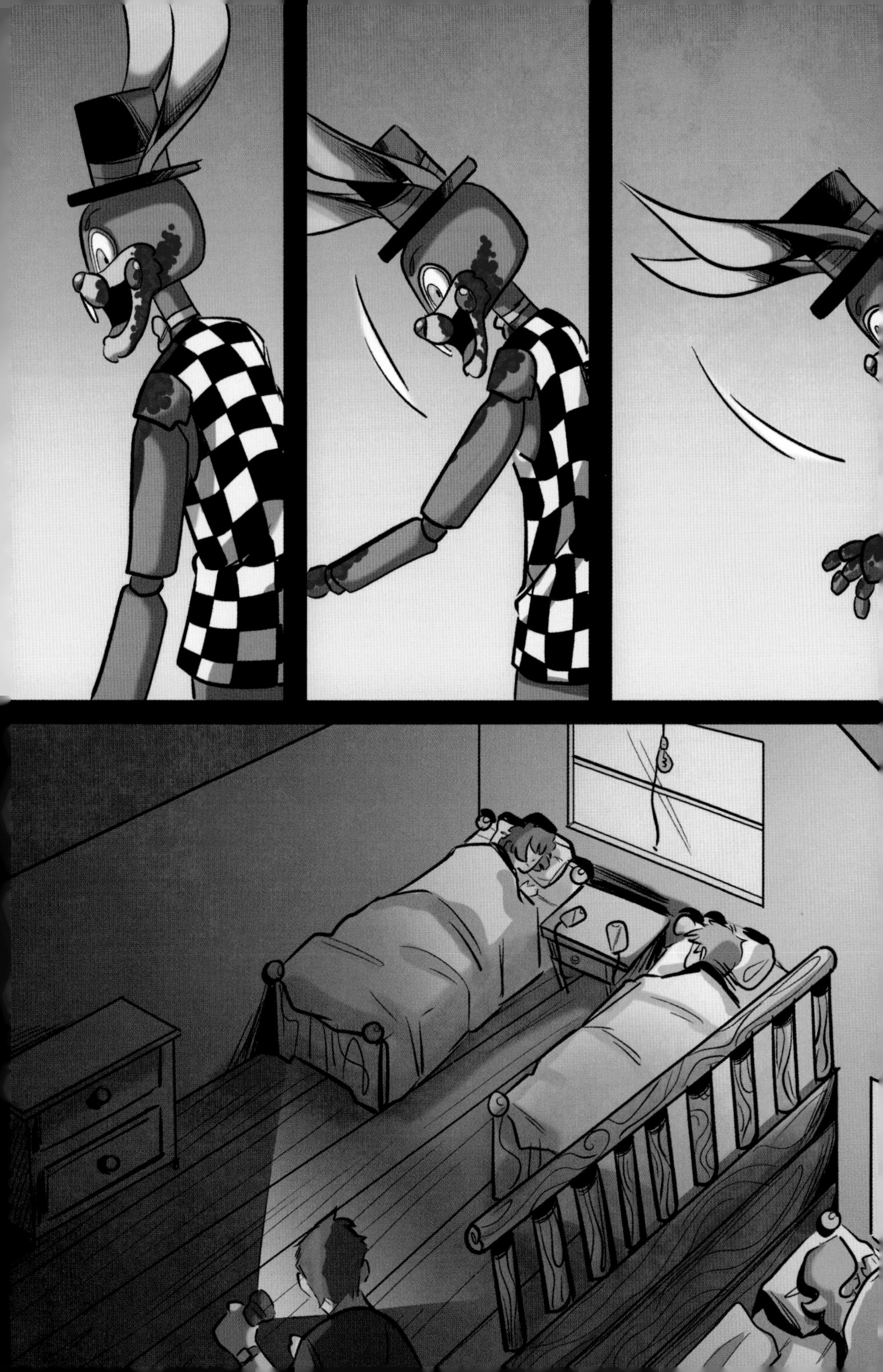

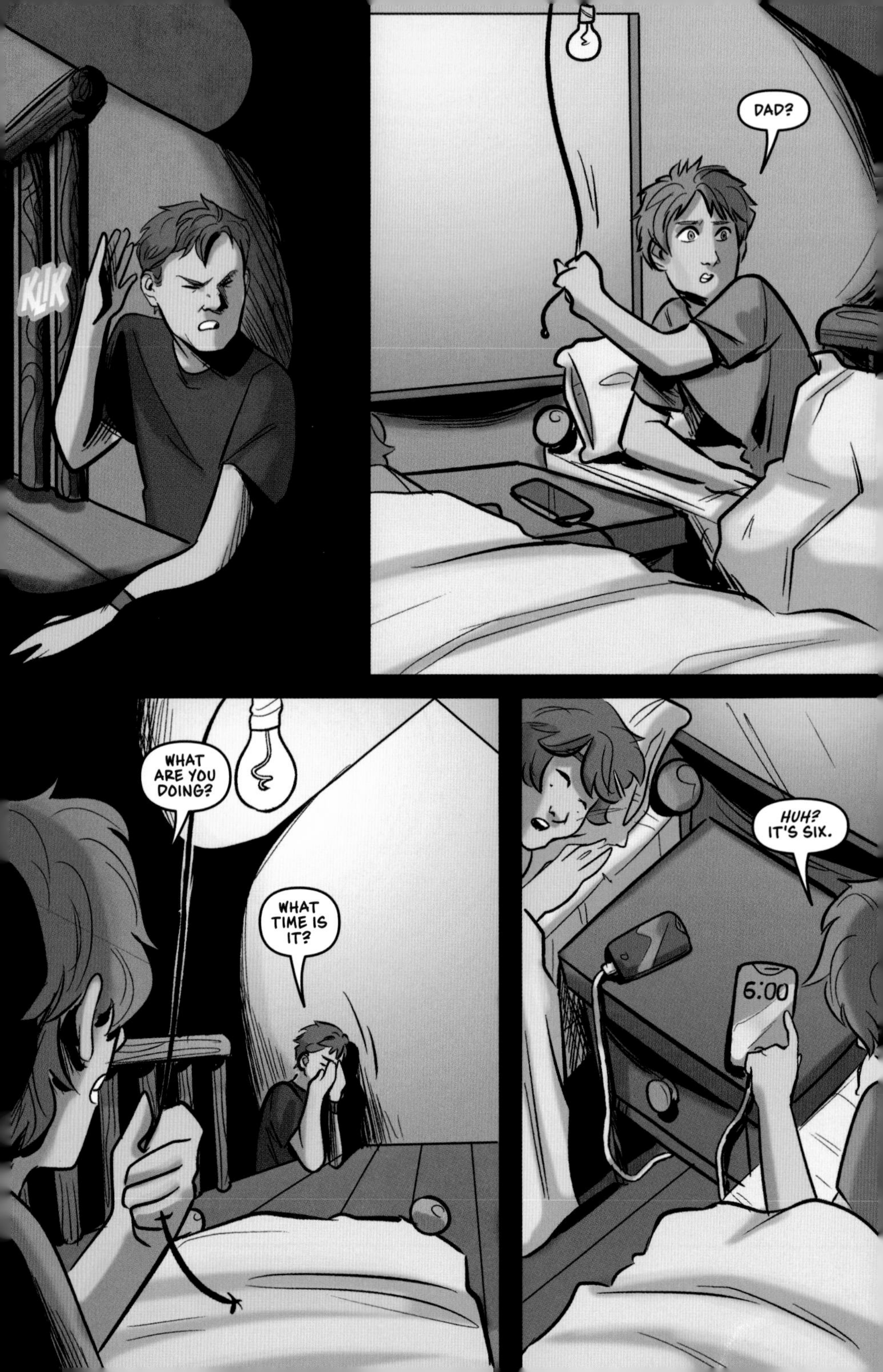
KLIK
DAD?
WHAT ARE YOU DOING?
WHAT TIME IS IT?
HUH? IT'S SIX.
6:00

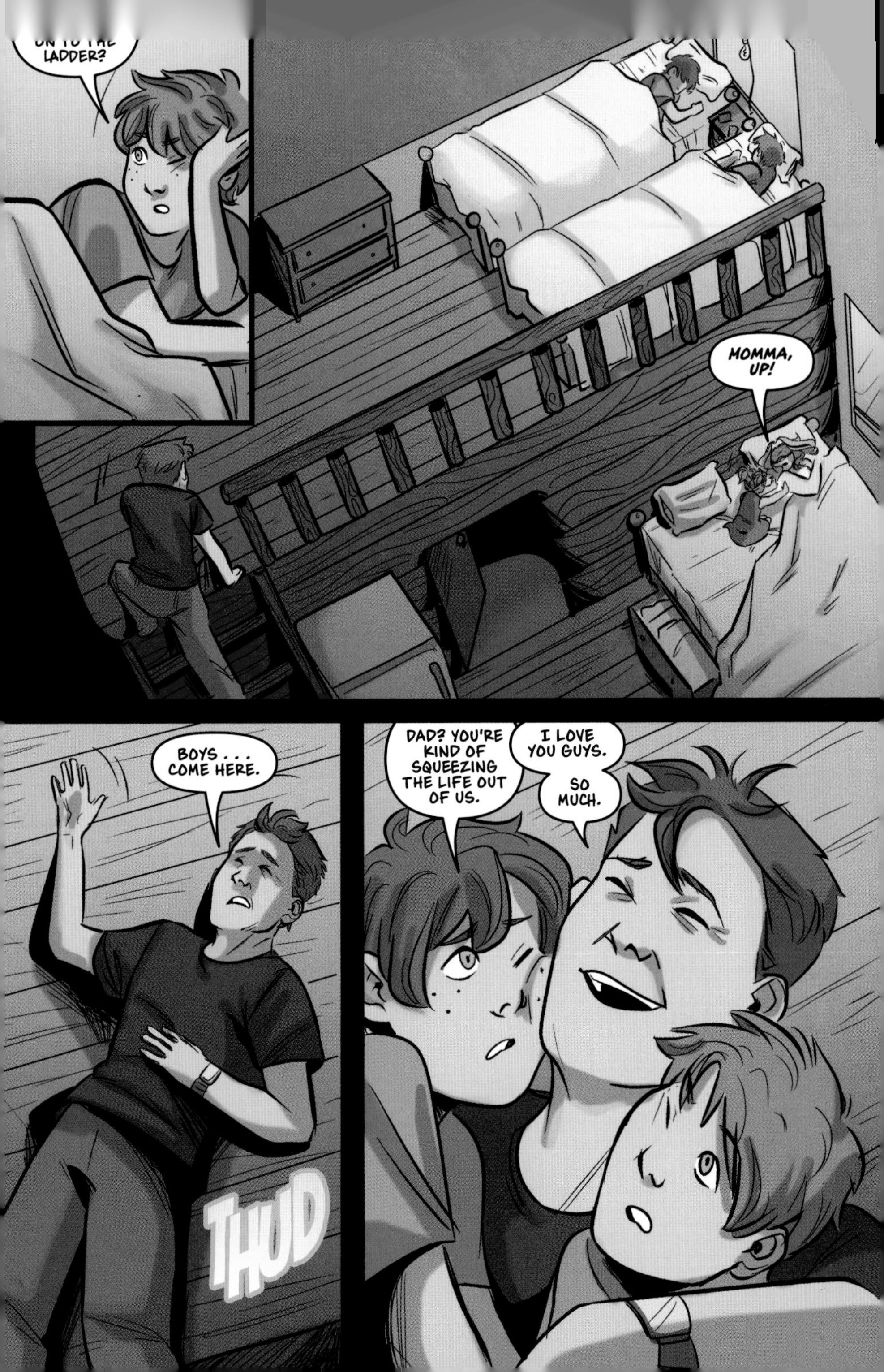
LADDER?
MOMMA, UP!
BOYS . . . COME HERE.
THUD
DAD? YOU'RE KIND OF SQUEEZING THE LIFE OUT OF US.
I LOVE YOU GUYS.
SO MUCH.

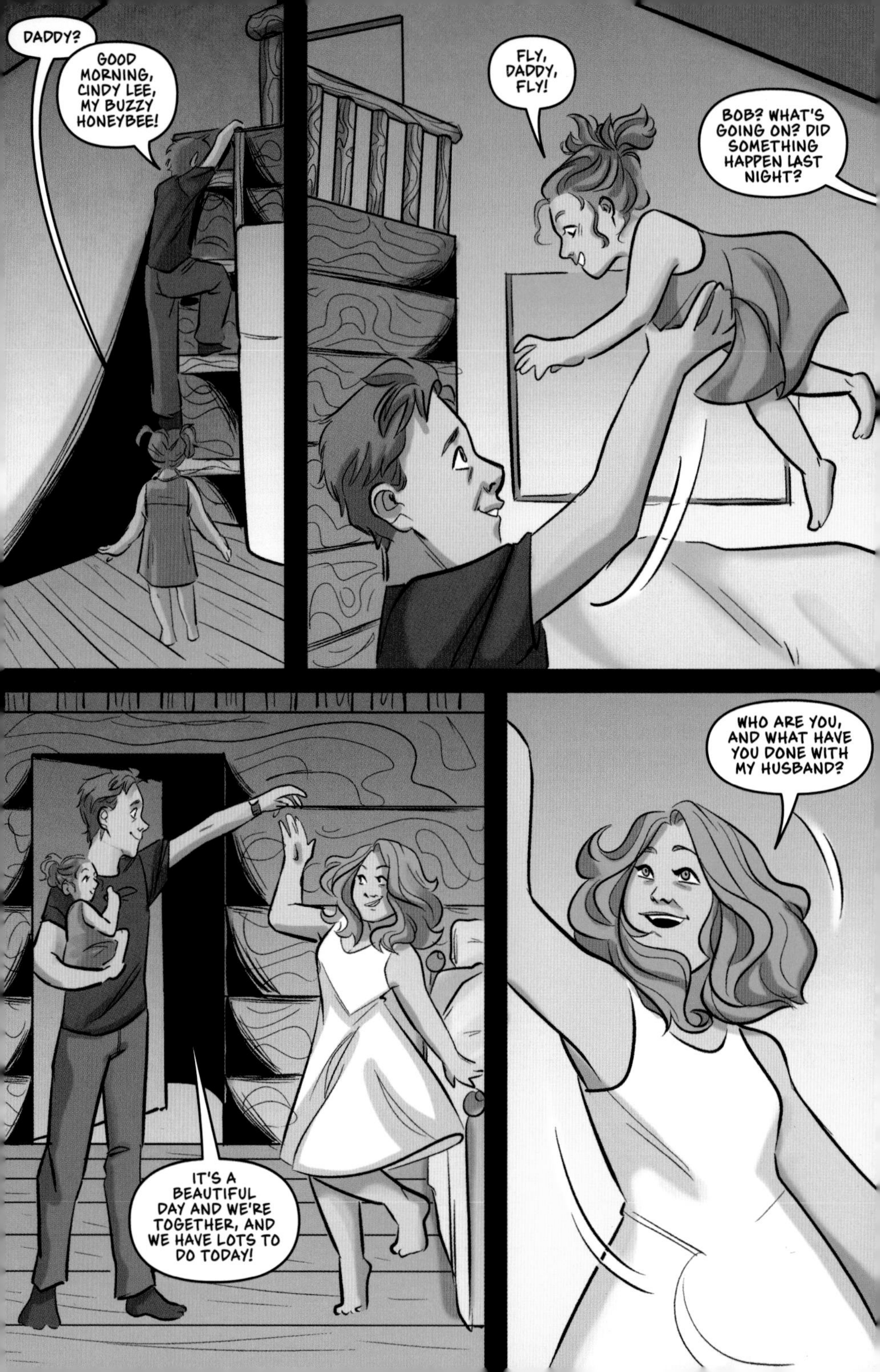
DADDY?
GOOD MORNING, CINDY LEE, MY BUZZY HONEYBEE!
FLY, DADDY, FLY!
BOB? WHAT'S GOING ON? DID SOMETHING HAPPEN LAST NIGHT?
IT'S A BEAUTIFUL DAY AND WE'RE TOGETHER, AND WE HAVE LOTS TO DO TODAY!
WHO ARE YOU, AND WHAT HAVE YOU DONE WITH MY HUSBAND?

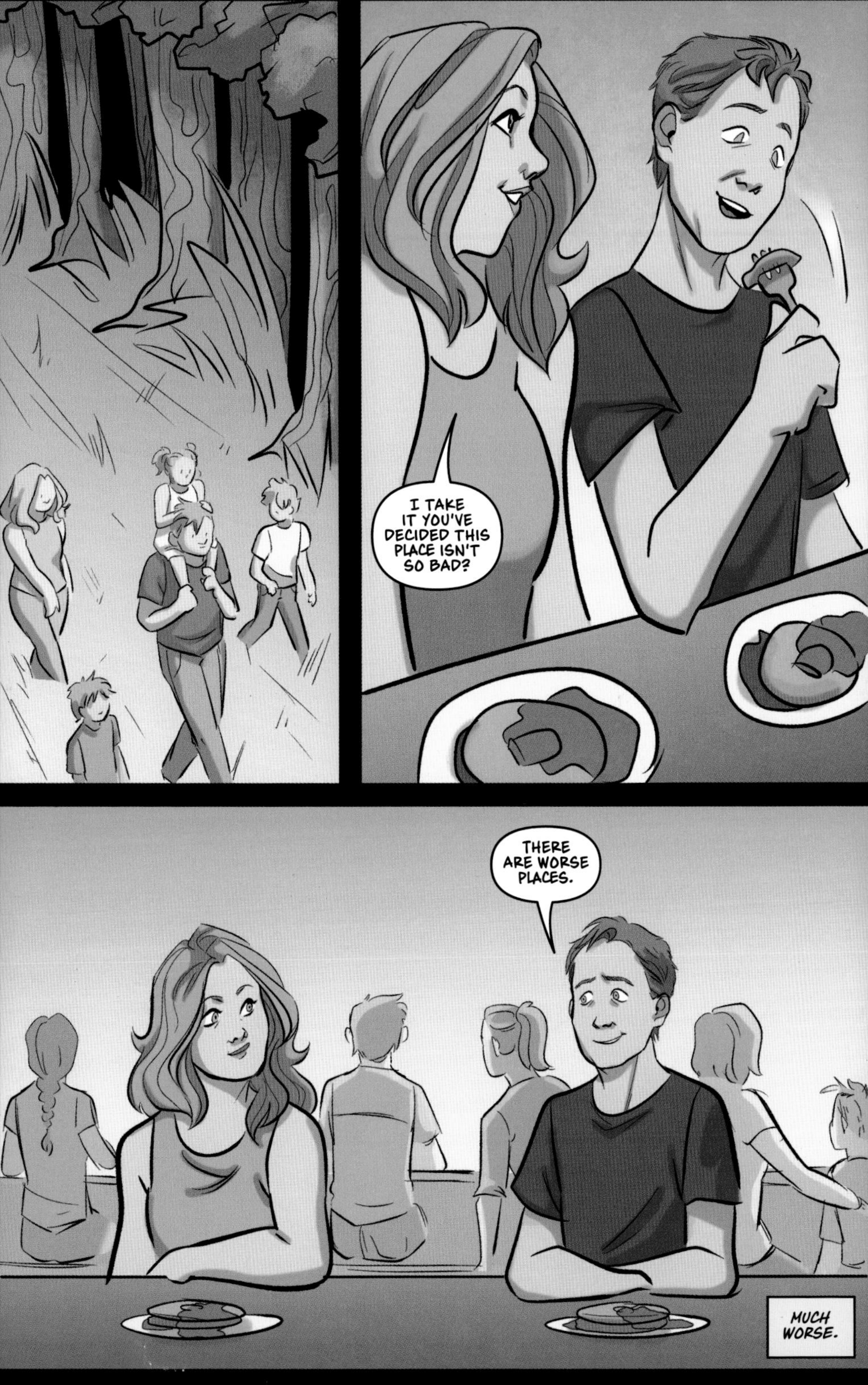
I TAKE IT YOU'VE DECIDED THIS PLACE ISN'T SO BAD?
THERE ARE WORSE PLACES.
MUCH WORSE.

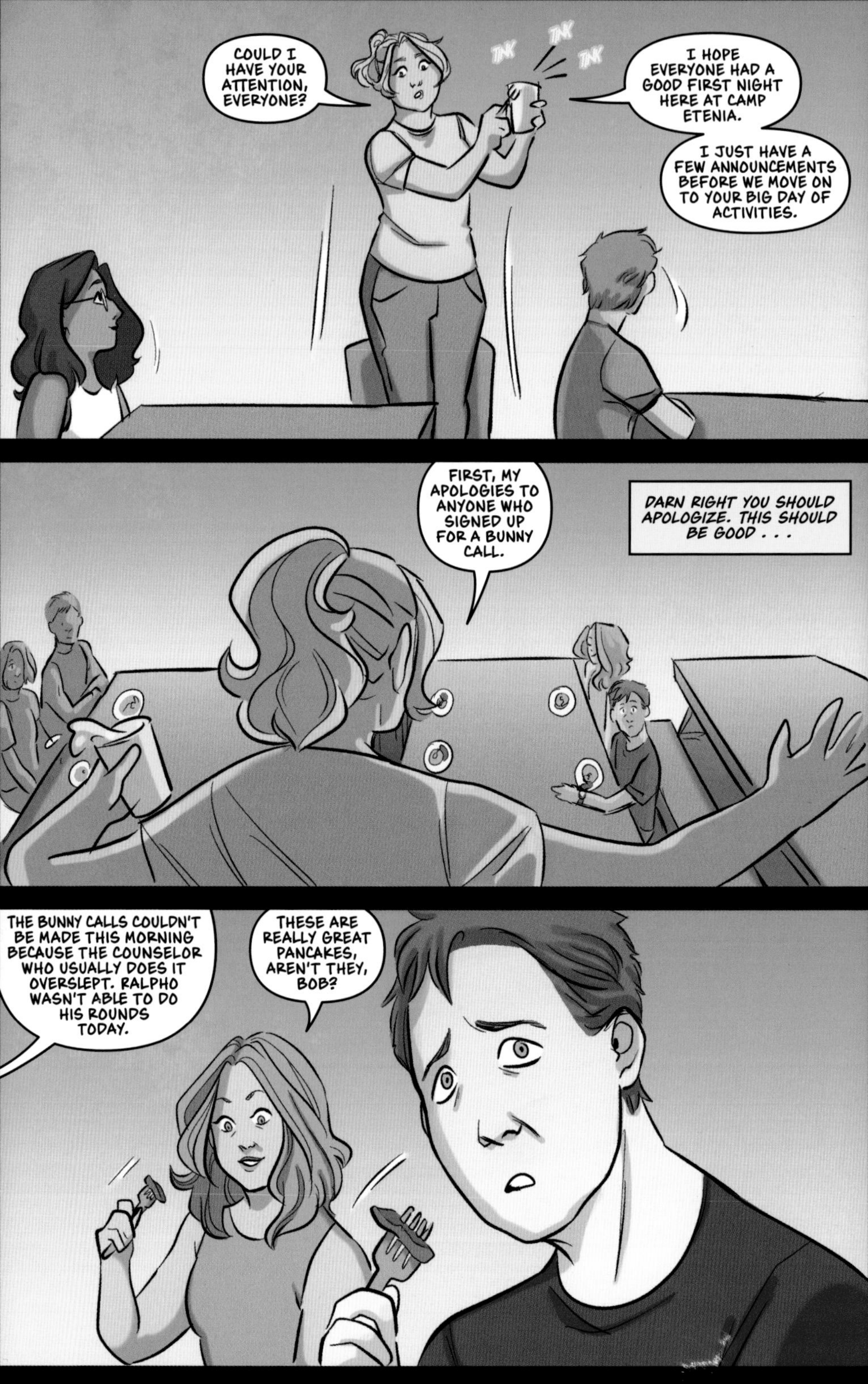
COULD I HAVE YOUR ATTENTION, EVERYONE?
TINK TINK TINK
I HOPE EVERYONE HAD A GOOD FIRST NIGHT HERE AT CAMP ETENIA.
I JUST HAVE A FEW ANNOUNCEMENTS BEFORE WE MOVE ON TO YOUR BIG DAY OF ACTIVITIES.
FIRST, MY APOLOGIES TO ANYONE WHO SIGNED UP FOR A BUNNY CALL.
DARN RIGHT YOU SHOULD APOLOGIZE. THIS SHOULD BE GOOD . . .
THE BUNNY CALLS COULDN'T BE MADE THIS MORNING BECAUSE THE COUNSELOR WHO USUALLY DOES IT OVERSLEPT. RALPHO WASN'T ABLE TO DO HIS ROUNDS TODAY.
THESE ARE REALLY GREAT PANCAKES, AREN'T THEY, BOB?

HIDE-AND-SEEK

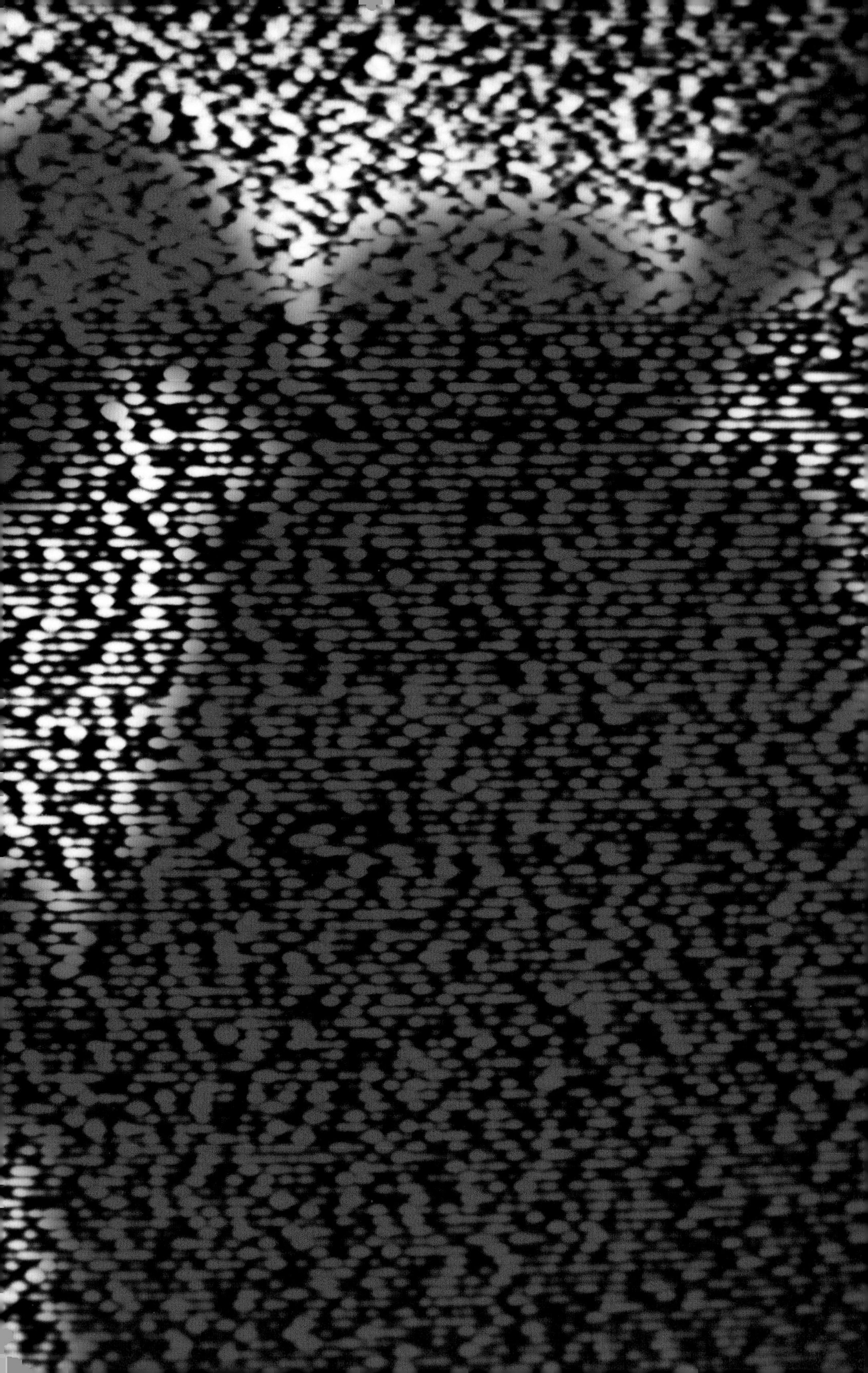

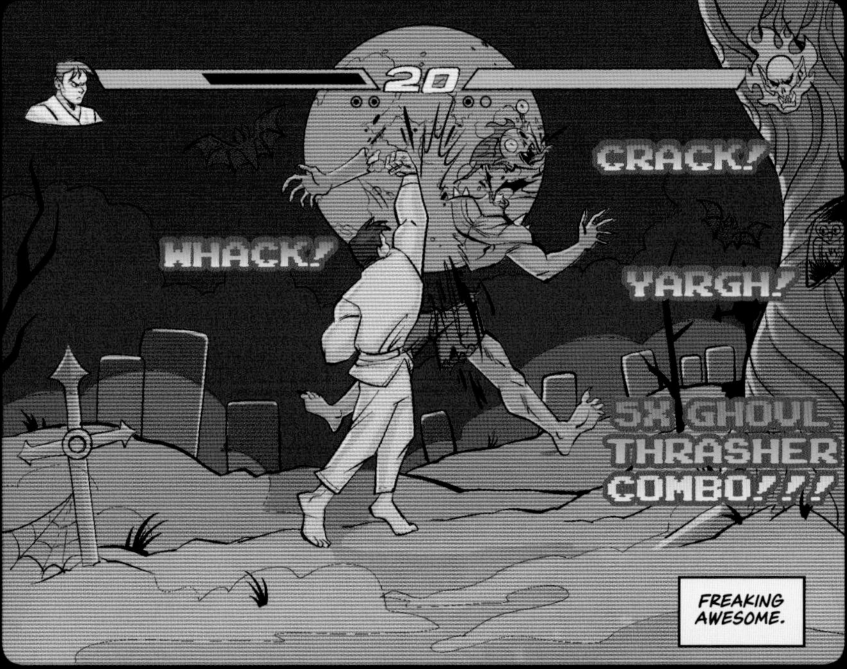
20
CRACK!
WHACK!
YARGH!
5X GHOUL THRASHER COMBO!!!
FREAKING AWESOME.

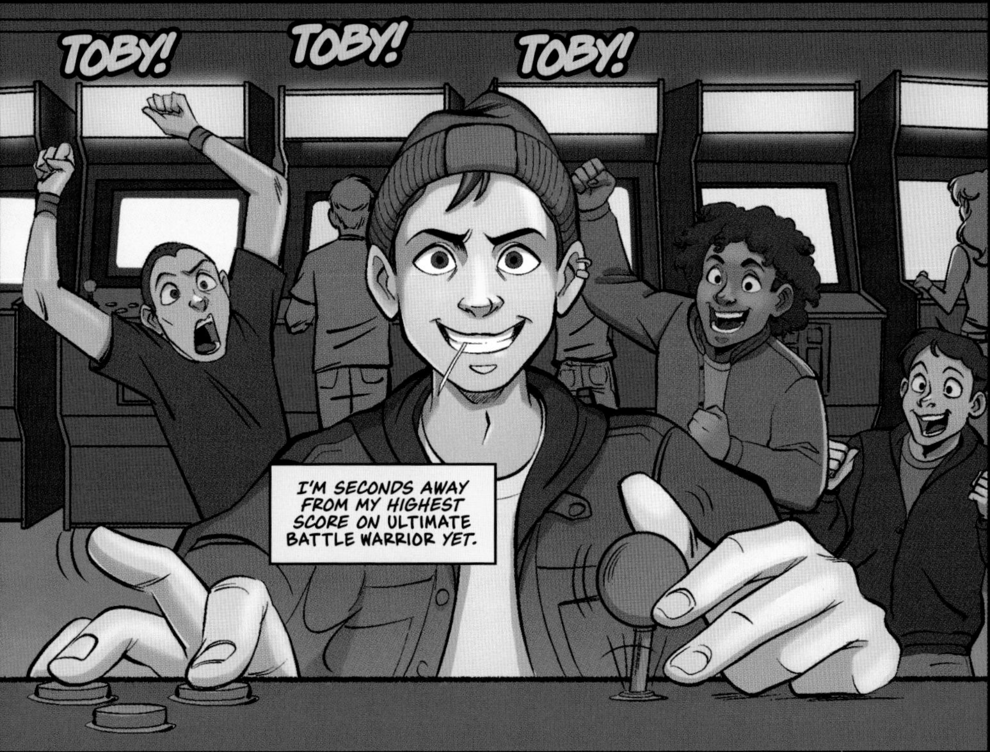
TOBY!
TOBY!
TOBY!
I'M SECONDS AWAY FROM MY HIGHEST SCORE ON ULTIMATE BATTLE WARRIOR YET.

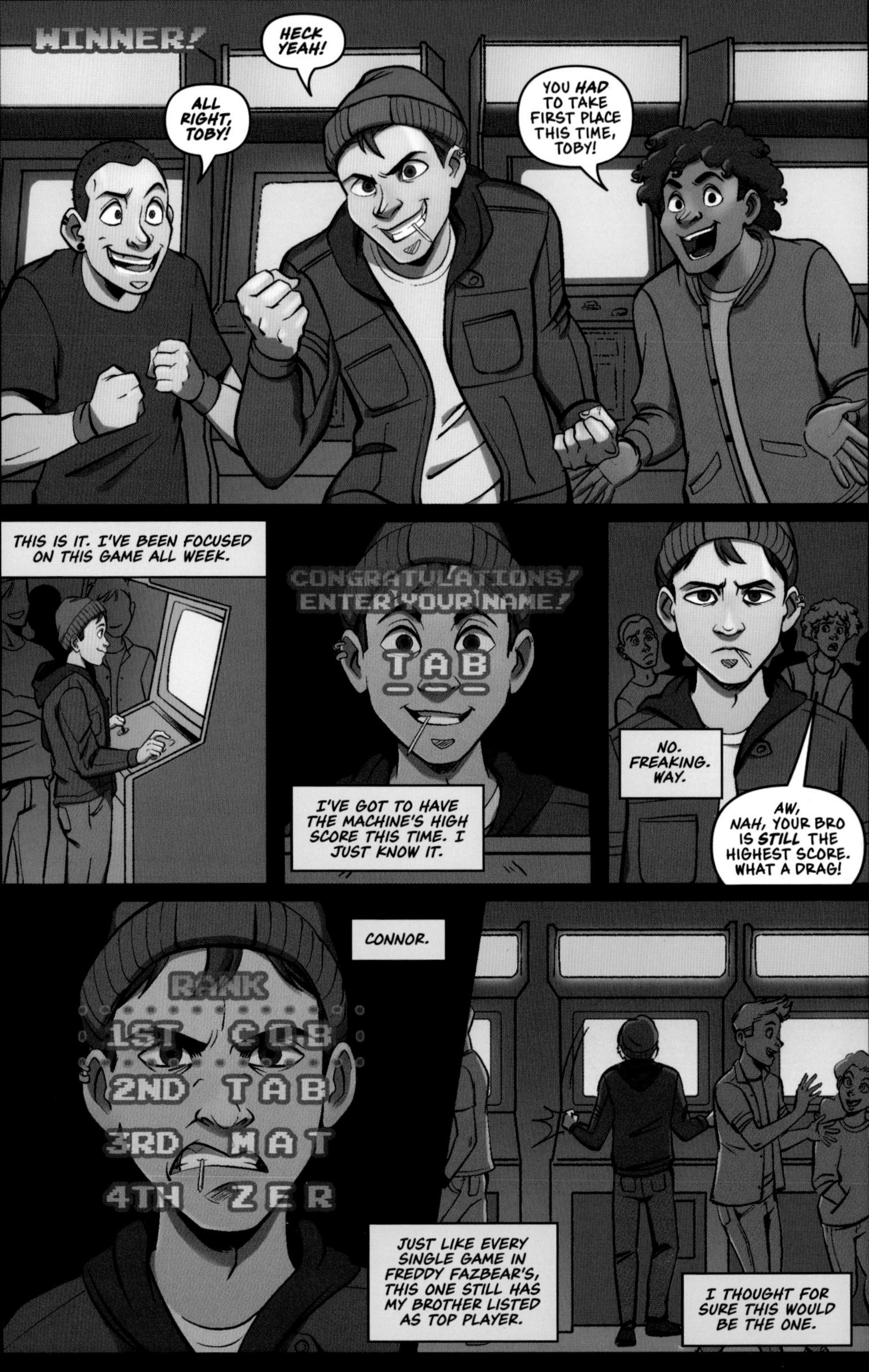
WINNER!
HECK YEAH!
ALL RIGHT, TOBY!
YOU HAD TO TAKE FIRST PLACE THIS TIME, TOBY!
THIS IS IT. I'VE BEEN FOCUSED ON THIS GAME ALL WEEK.
CONGRATULATIONS! ENTER YOUR NAME!
TAB
I'VE GOT TO HAVE THE MACHINE'S HIGH SCORE THIS TIME. I JUST KNOW IT.
NO. FREAKING. WAY.
AW, NAH, YOUR BRO IS STILL THE HIGHEST SCORE. WHAT A DRAG!
RANK
1ST COB
2ND TAB
3RD MAT
4TH ZER
CONNOR.
JUST LIKE EVERY SINGLE GAME IN FREDDY FAZBEAR'S, THIS ONE STILL HAS MY BROTHER LISTED AS TOP PLAYER.
I THOUGHT FOR SURE THIS WOULD BE THE ONE.

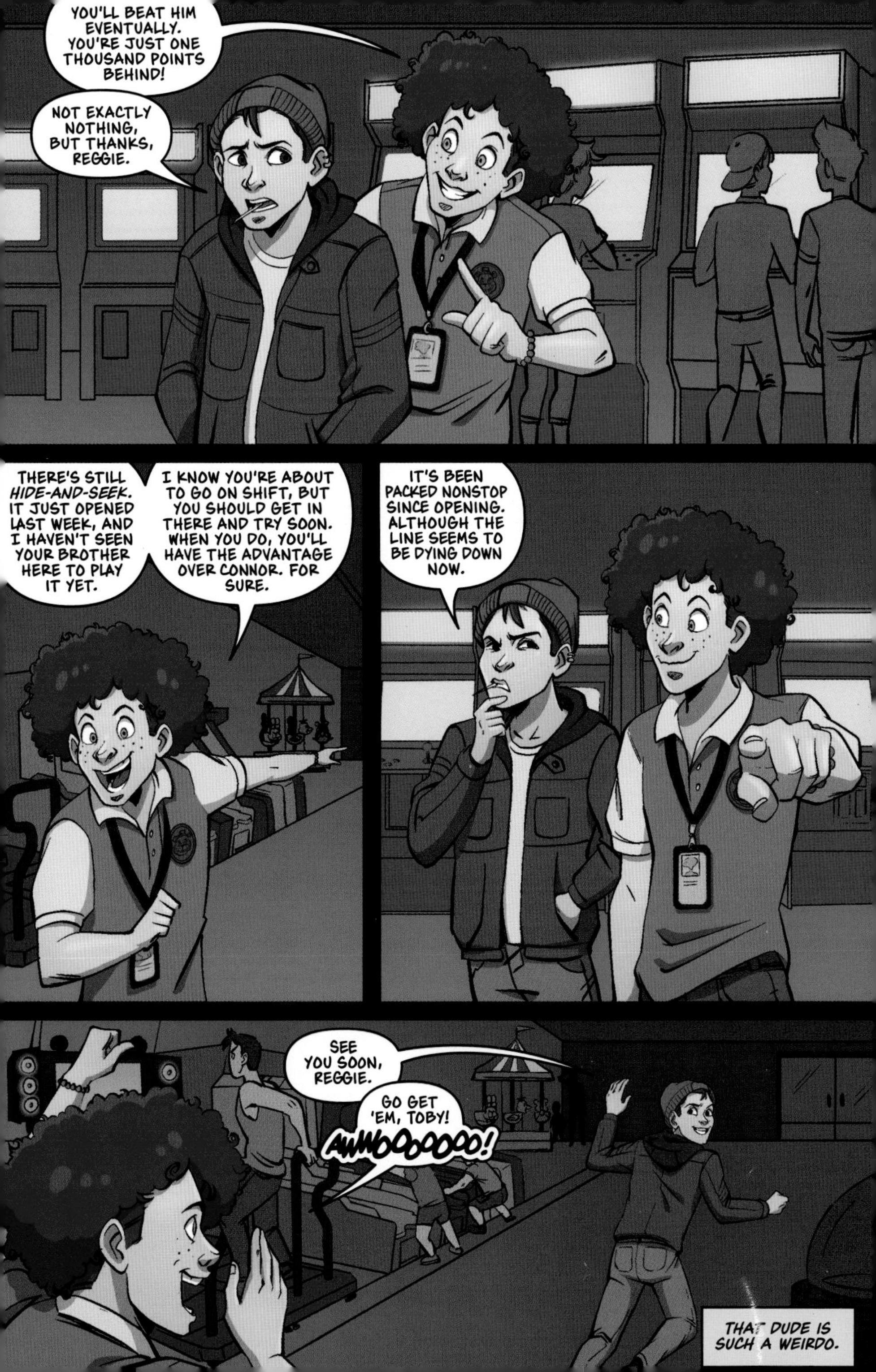
YOU'LL BEAT HIM EVENTUALLY. YOU'RE JUST ONE THOUSAND POINTS BEHIND!
NOT EXACTLY NOTHING, BUT THANKS, REGGIE.
THERE'S STILL *HIDE-AND-SEEK*. IT JUST OPENED LAST WEEK, AND I HAVEN'T SEEN YOUR BROTHER HERE TO PLAY IT YET.
I KNOW YOU'RE ABOUT TO GO ON SHIFT, BUT YOU SHOULD GET IN THERE AND TRY SOON. WHEN YOU DO, YOU'LL HAVE THE ADVANTAGE OVER CONNOR. FOR SURE.
IT'S BEEN PACKED NONSTOP SINCE OPENING. ALTHOUGH THE LINE SEEMS TO BE DYING DOWN NOW.
SEE YOU SOON, REGGIE.
GO GET 'EM, TOBY!
AWWOOOOOOO!
THAT DUDE IS SUCH A WEIRDO.

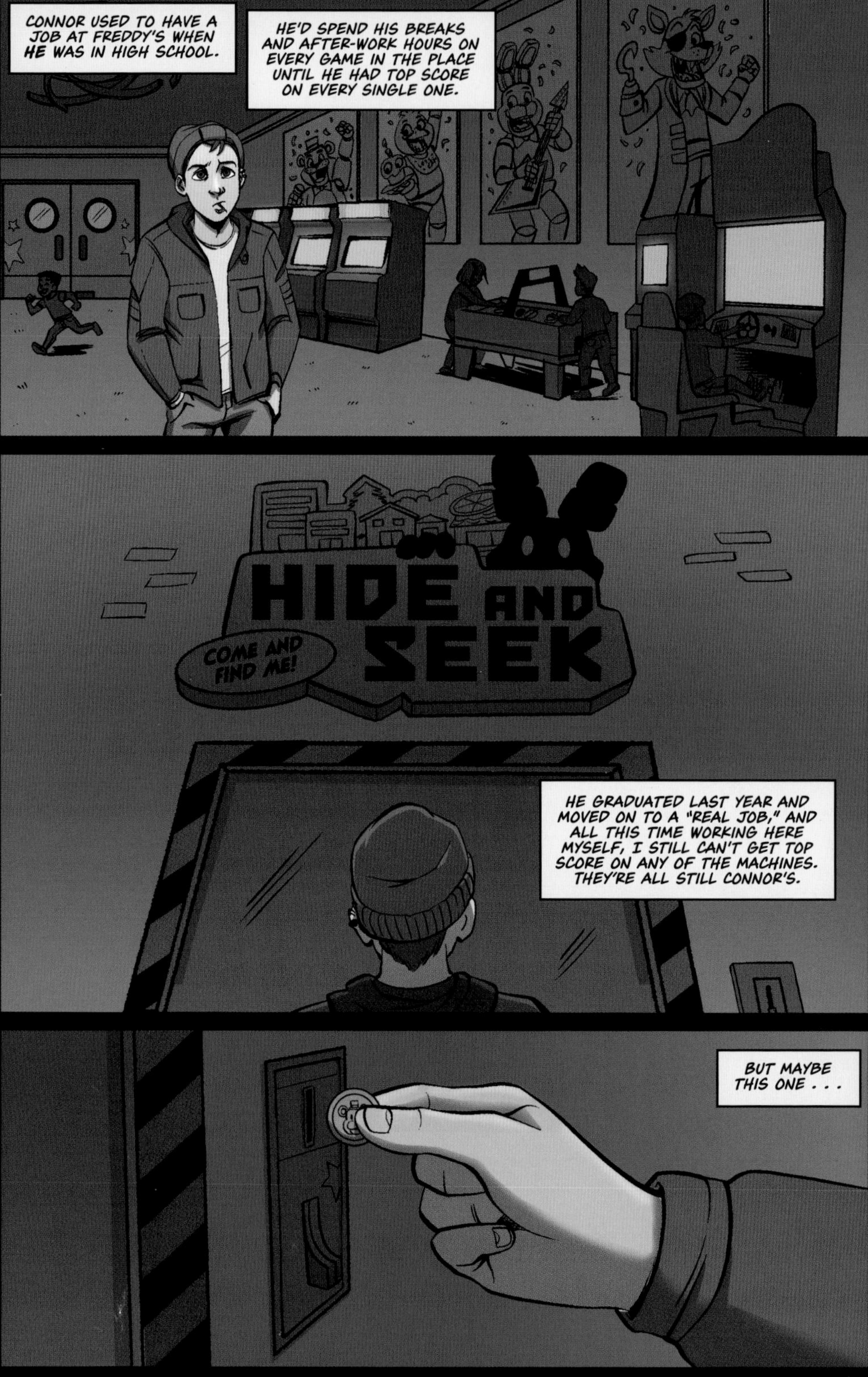
CONNOR USED TO HAVE A JOB AT FREDDY'S WHEN HE WAS IN HIGH SCHOOL.
HE'D SPEND HIS BREAKS AND AFTER-WORK HOURS ON EVERY GAME IN THE PLACE UNTIL HE HAD TOP SCORE ON EVERY SINGLE ONE.
HIDE AND SEEK
COME AND FIND ME!
HE GRADUATED LAST YEAR AND MOVED ON TO A "REAL JOB," AND ALL THIS TIME WORKING HERE MYSELF, I STILL CAN'T GET TOP SCORE ON ANY OF THE MACHINES. THEY'RE ALL STILL CONNOR'S.
BUT MAYBE THIS ONE . . .

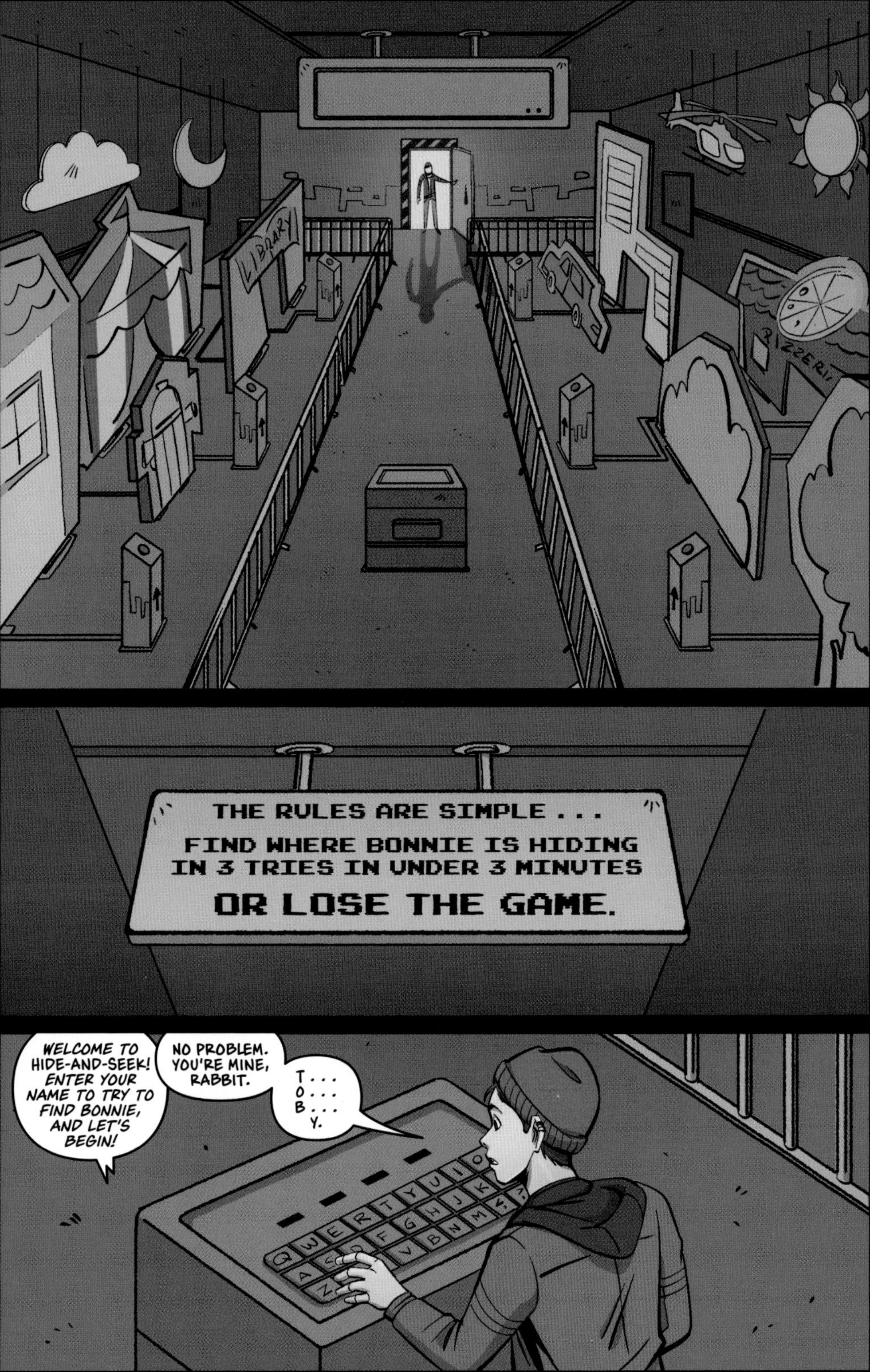
LIBRARY
PIZZERIA
THE RULES ARE SIMPLE . . .
FIND WHERE BONNIE IS HIDING IN 3 TRIES IN UNDER 3 MINUTES
OR LOSE THE GAME.
WELCOME TO HIDE-AND-SEEK! ENTER YOUR NAME TO TRY TO FIND BONNIE, AND LET'S BEGIN!
NO PROBLEM. YOU'RE MINE, RABBIT.
T . . . O . . . B . . . Y.

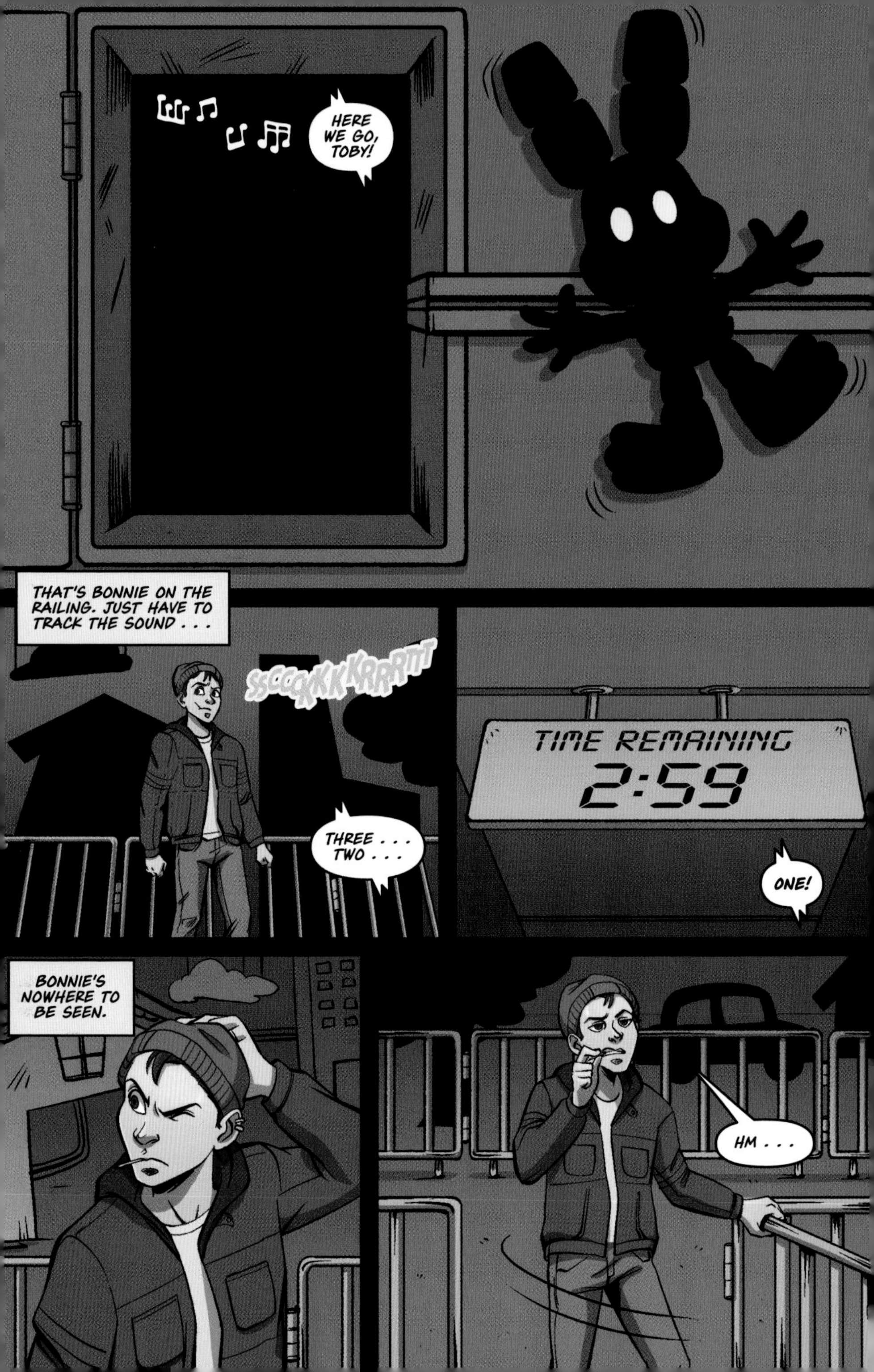
HERE WE GO, TOBY!
THAT'S BONNIE ON THE RAILING. JUST HAVE TO TRACK THE SOUND . . .
SSCCCCKKKKRRRRTTT
THREE . . . TWO . . .
TIME REMAINING
2:59
ONE!
BONNIE'S NOWHERE TO BE SEEN.
HM . . .

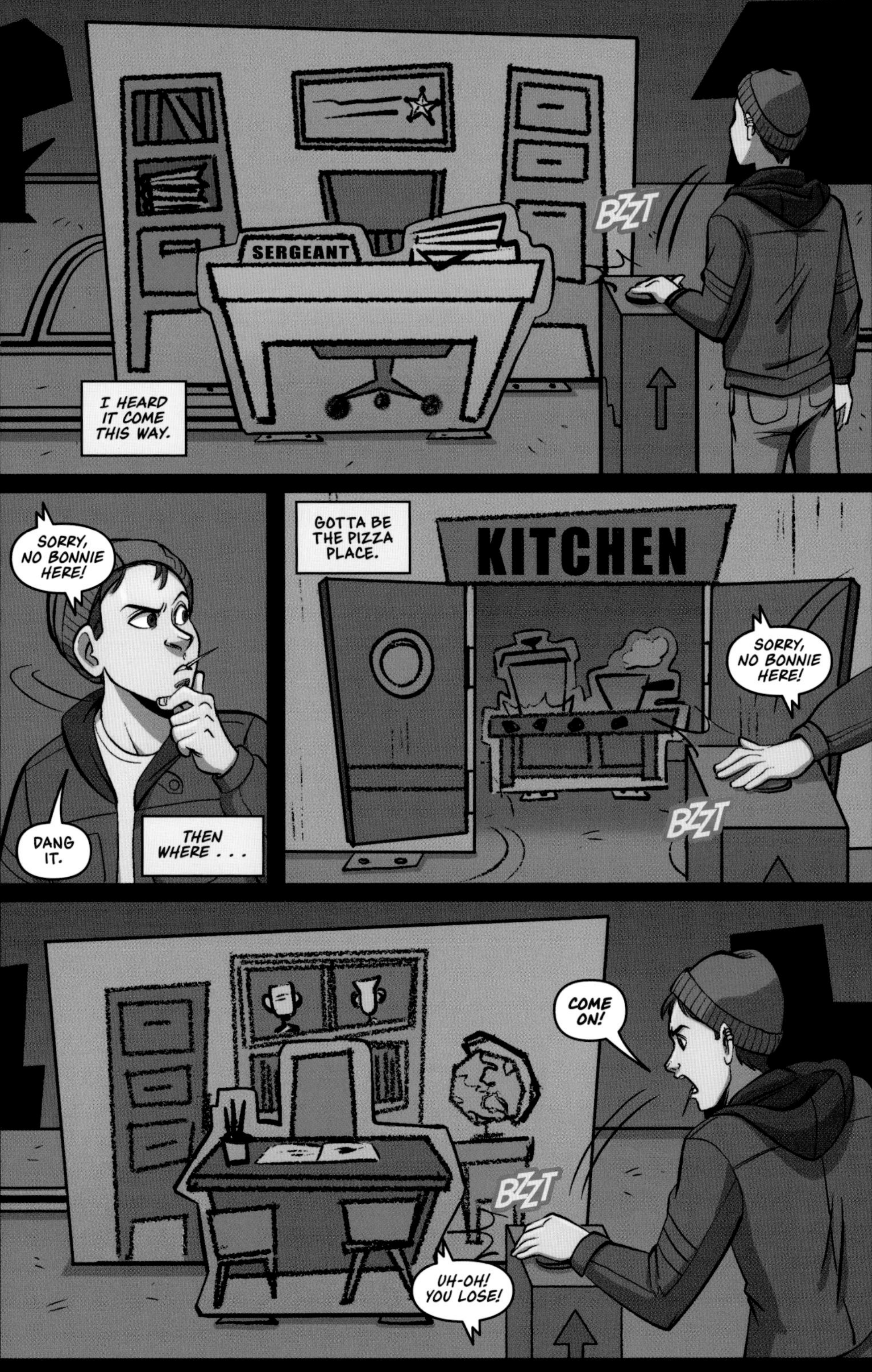
SERGEANT
BZZT
I HEARD IT COME THIS WAY.
SORRY, NO BONNIE HERE!
DANG IT.
THEN WHERE . . .
GOTTA BE THE PIZZA PLACE.
KITCHEN
SORRY, NO BONNIE HERE!
BZZT
COME ON!
BZZT
UH-OH! YOU LOSE!

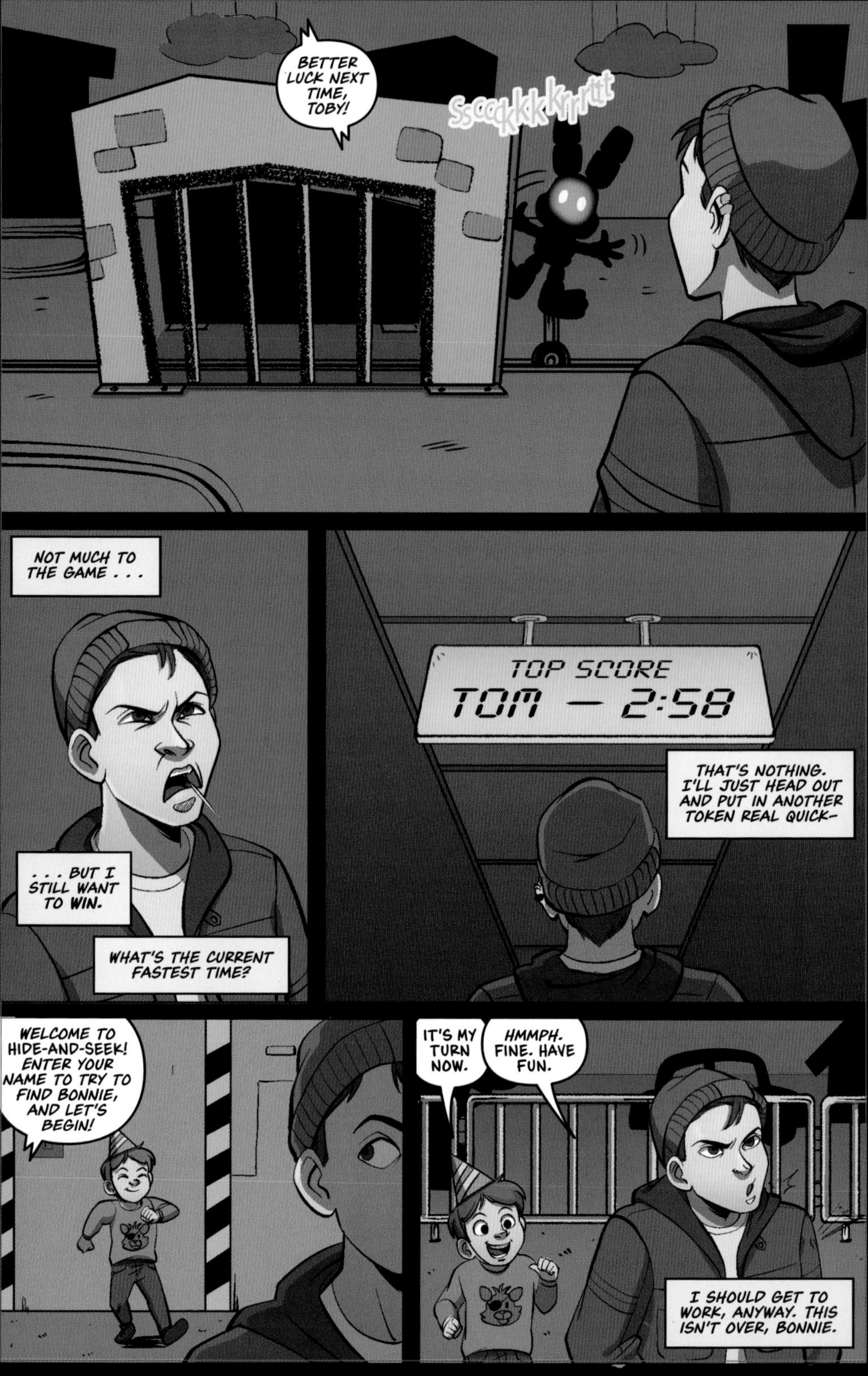

BETTER LUCK NEXT TIME, TOBY!
SSCCCKKKRRRTTT
NOT MUCH TO THE GAME . . .
. . . BUT I STILL WANT TO WIN.
WHAT'S THE CURRENT FASTEST TIME?
TOP SCORE
TOM – 2:58
THAT'S NOTHING. I'LL JUST HEAD OUT AND PUT IN ANOTHER TOKEN REAL QUICK–
WELCOME TO HIDE-AND-SEEK! ENTER YOUR NAME TO TRY TO FIND BONNIE, AND LET'S BEGIN!
IT'S MY TURN NOW.
HMMPH. FINE. HAVE FUN.
I SHOULD GET TO WORK, ANYWAY. THIS ISN'T OVER, BONNIE.

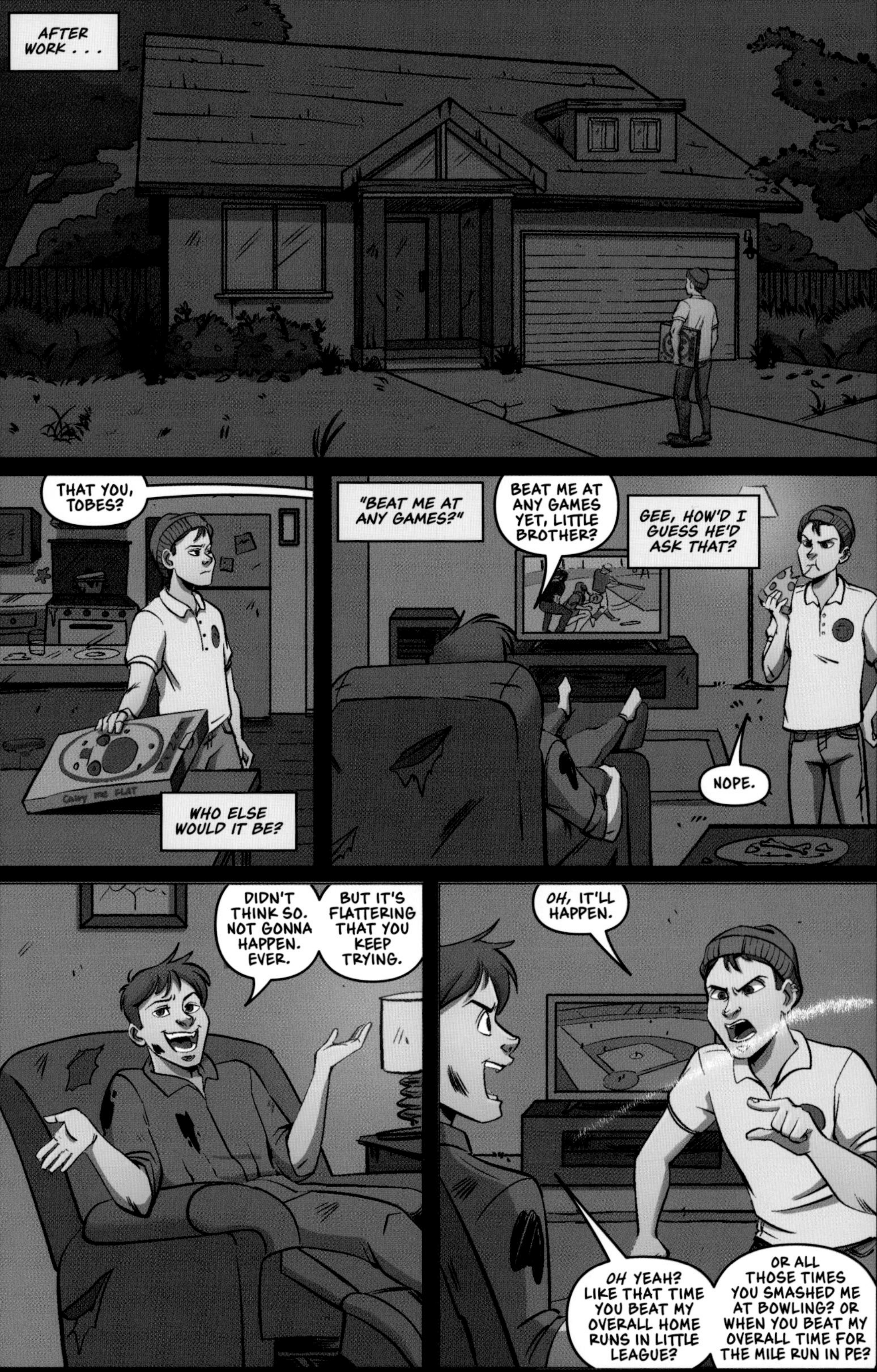
AFTER WORK . . .
THAT YOU, TOBES?
WHO ELSE WOULD IT BE?
"BEAT ME AT ANY GAMES?"
BEAT ME AT ANY GAMES YET, LITTLE BROTHER?
GEE, HOW'D I GUESS HE'D ASK THAT?
NOPE.
DIDN'T THINK SO. NOT GONNA HAPPEN. EVER.
BUT IT'S FLATTERING THAT YOU KEEP TRYING.
OH, IT'LL HAPPEN.
OH YEAH? LIKE THAT TIME YOU BEAT MY OVERALL HOME RUNS IN LITTLE LEAGUE?
OR ALL THOSE TIMES YOU SMASHED ME AT BOWLING? OR WHEN YOU BEAT MY OVERALL TIME FOR THE MILE RUN IN PE?

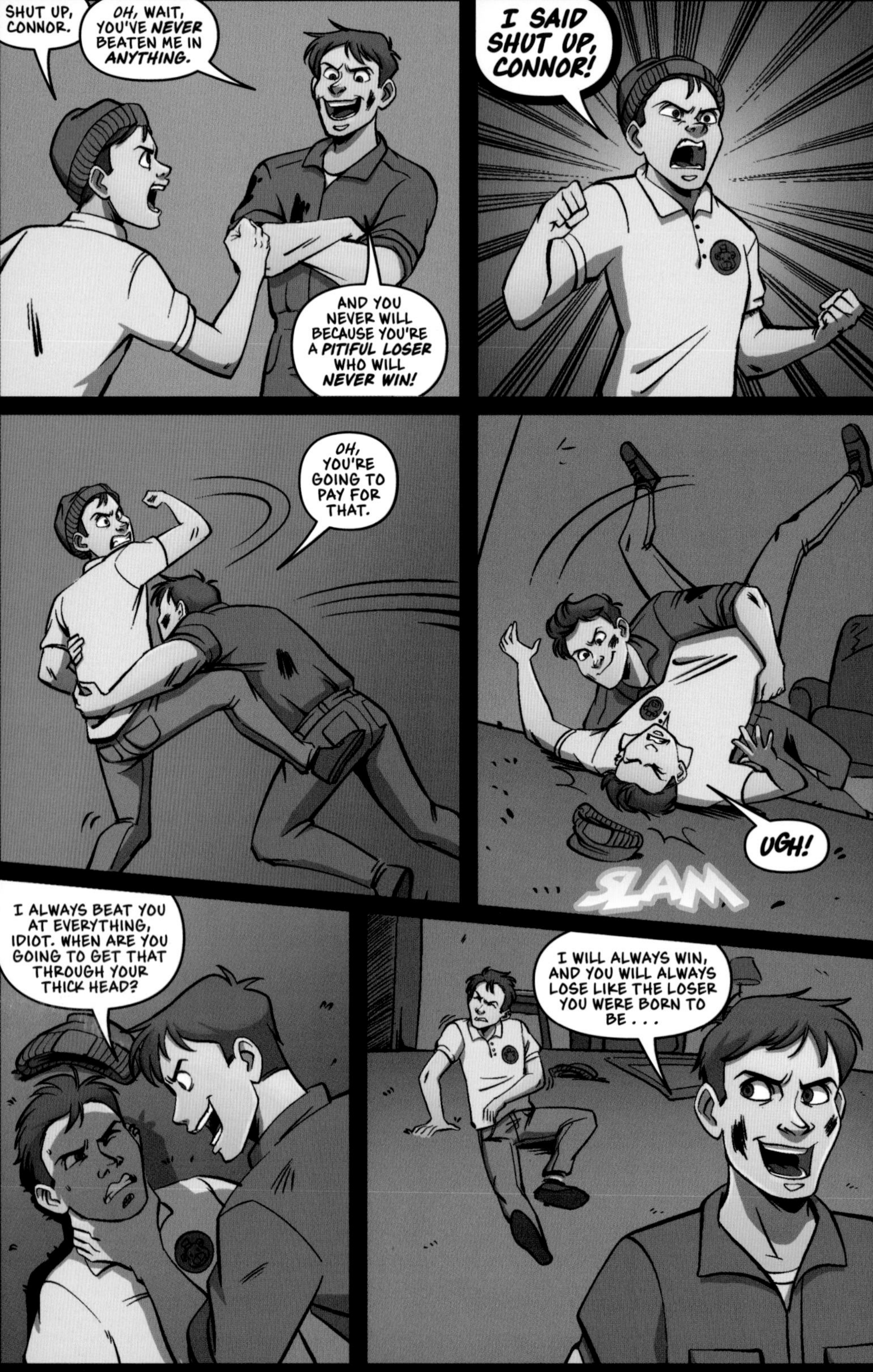
SHUT UP, CONNOR.
OH, WAIT, YOU'VE NEVER BEATEN ME IN ANYTHING.
AND YOU NEVER WILL BECAUSE YOU'RE A PITIFUL LOSER WHO WILL NEVER WIN!
I SAID SHUT UP, CONNOR!
OH, YOU'RE GOING TO PAY FOR THAT.
UGH!
SLAM
I ALWAYS BEAT YOU AT EVERYTHING, IDIOT. WHEN ARE YOU GOING TO GET THAT THROUGH YOUR THICK HEAD?
I WILL ALWAYS WIN, AND YOU WILL ALWAYS LOSE LIKE THE LOSER YOU WERE BORN TO BE . . .

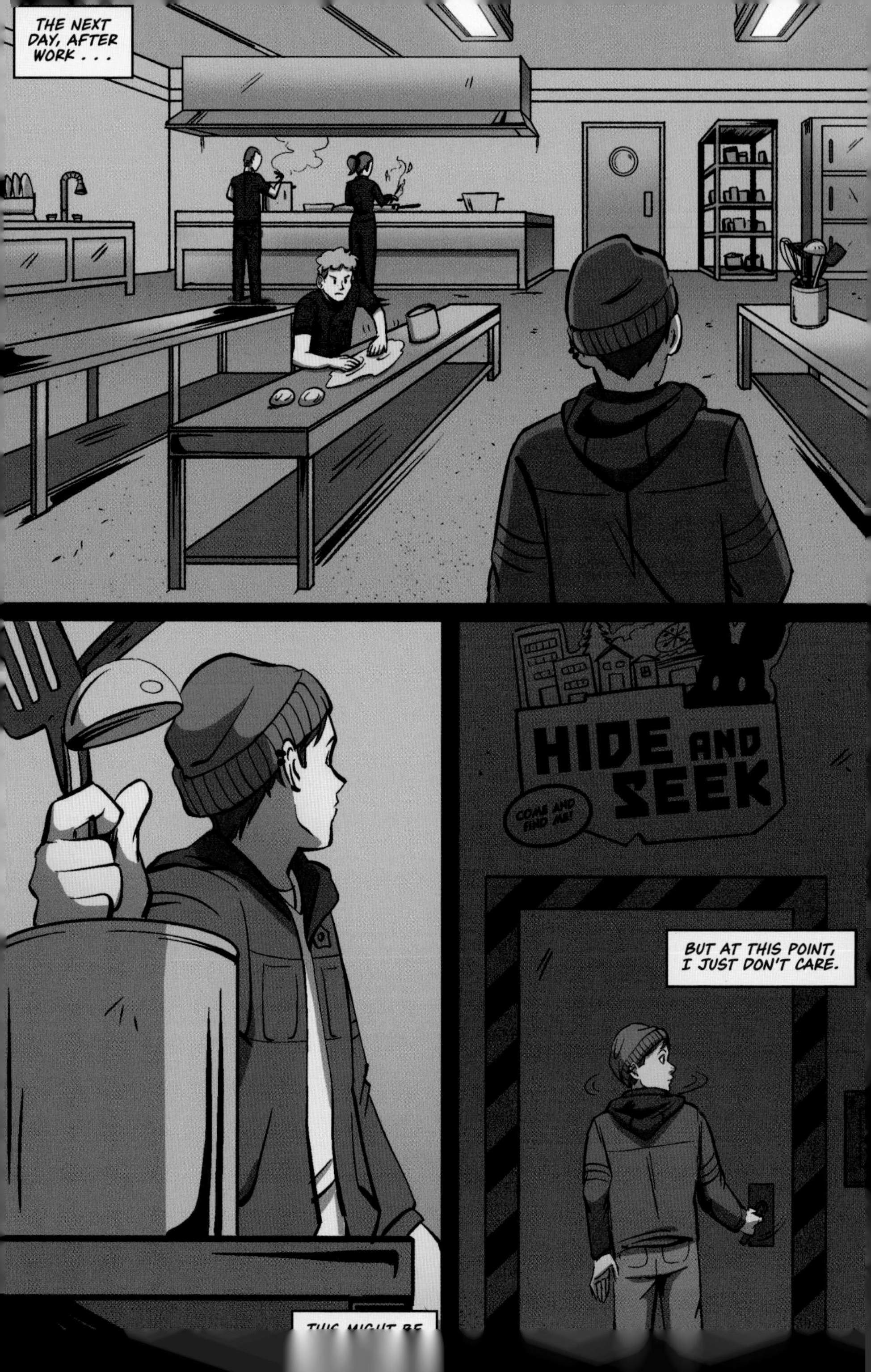
THE NEXT DAY, AFTER WORK . . .
HIDE AND SEEK
COME AND FIND ME!
BUT AT THIS POINT, I JUST DON'T CARE.

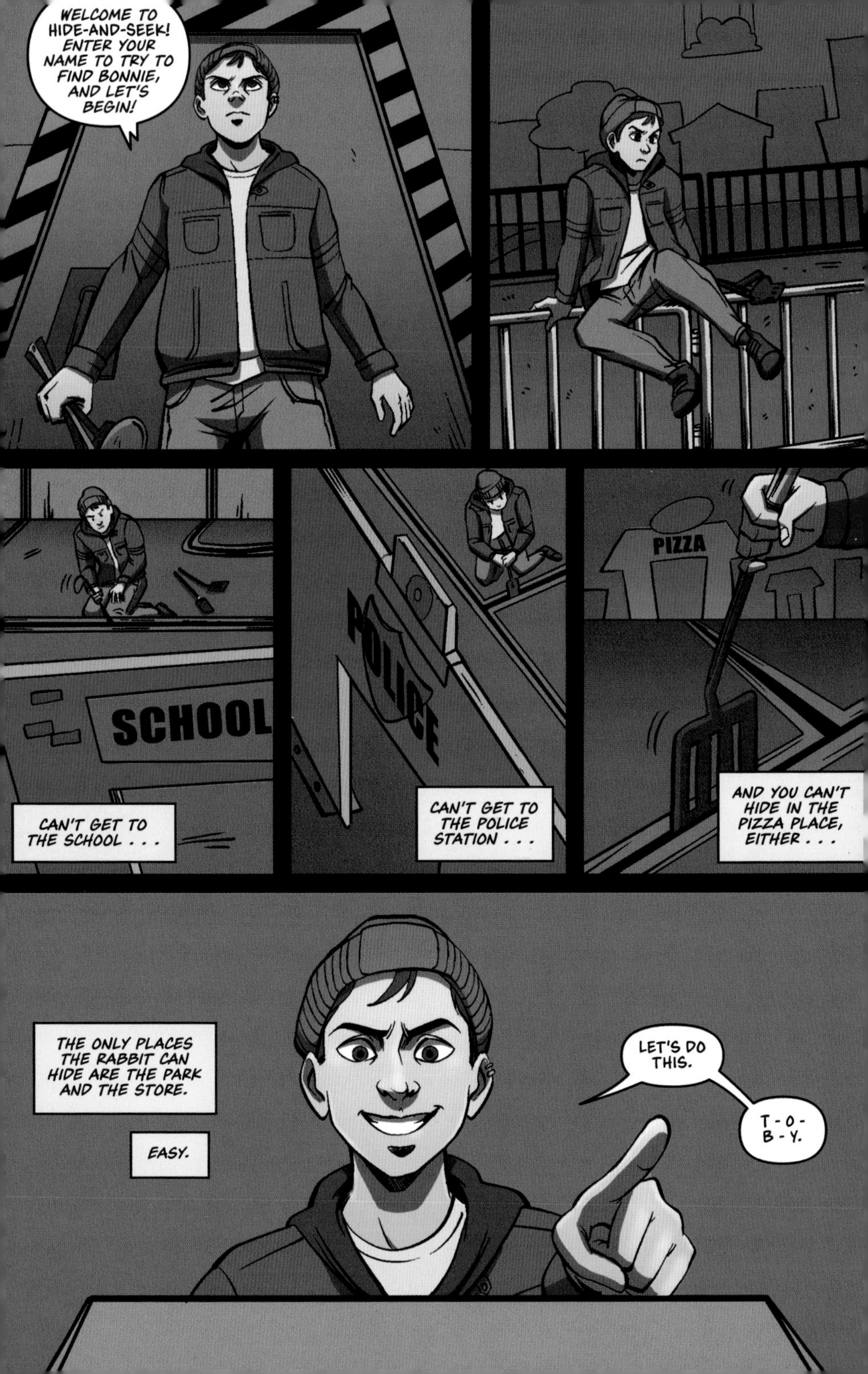
WELCOME TO HIDE-AND-SEEK! ENTER YOUR NAME TO TRY TO FIND BONNIE, AND LET'S BEGIN!
SCHOOL
CAN'T GET TO THE SCHOOL . . .
POLICE
CAN'T GET TO THE POLICE STATION . . .
PIZZA
AND YOU CAN'T HIDE IN THE PIZZA PLACE, EITHER . . .
THE ONLY PLACES THE RABBIT CAN HIDE ARE THE PARK AND THE STORE.
EASY.
LET'S DO THIS.
T-O-B-Y.

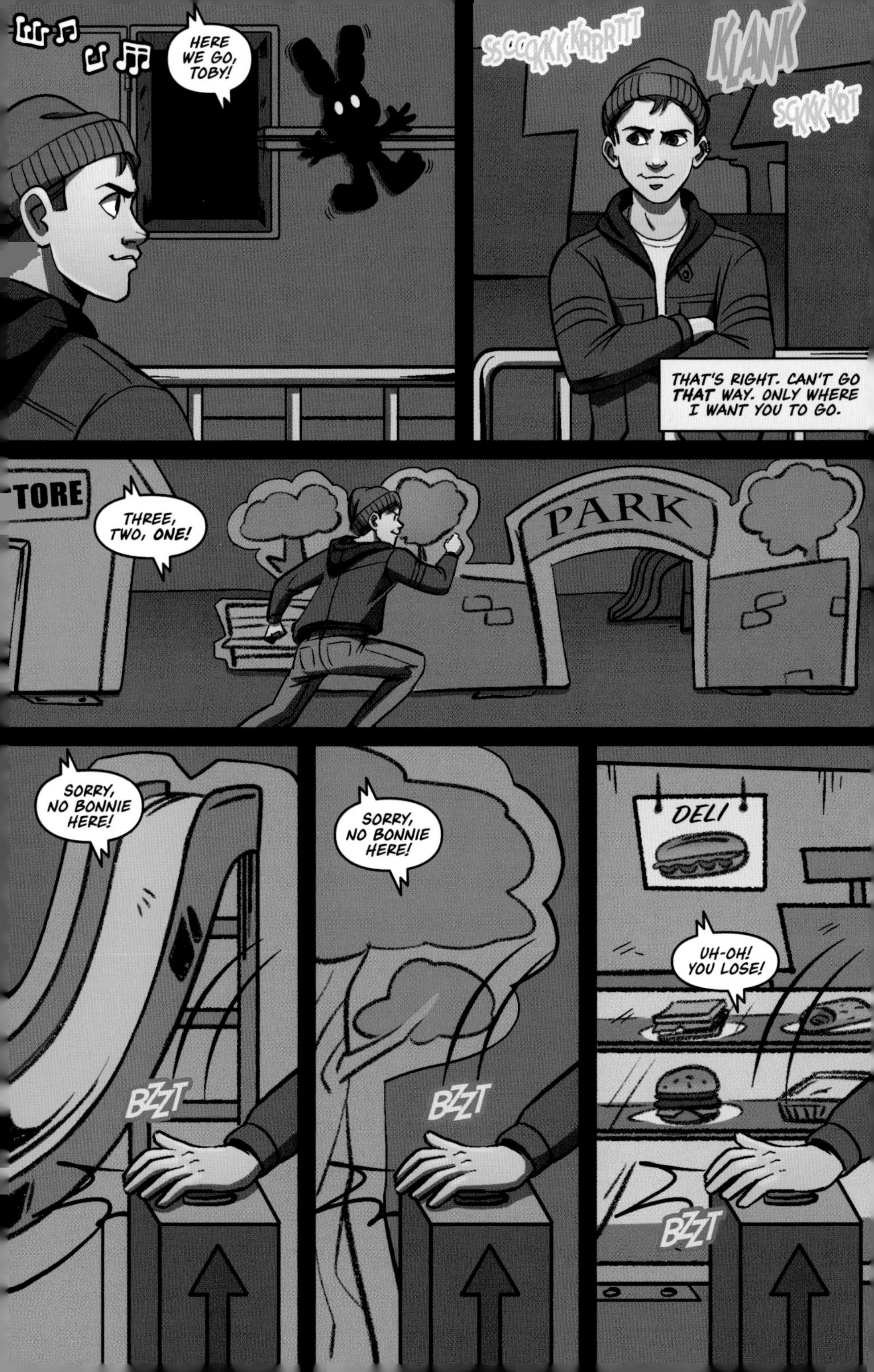
HERE WE GO, TOBY!
SSCCCKKKKRRRRTTT
KLANK
SCKKKRT
THAT'S RIGHT. CAN'T GO THAT WAY. ONLY WHERE I WANT YOU TO GO.
TORE
THREE, TWO, ONE!
PARK
SORRY, NO BONNIE HERE!
BZZT
SORRY, NO BONNIE HERE!
BZZT
DELI
UH-OH! YOU LOSE!
BZZT

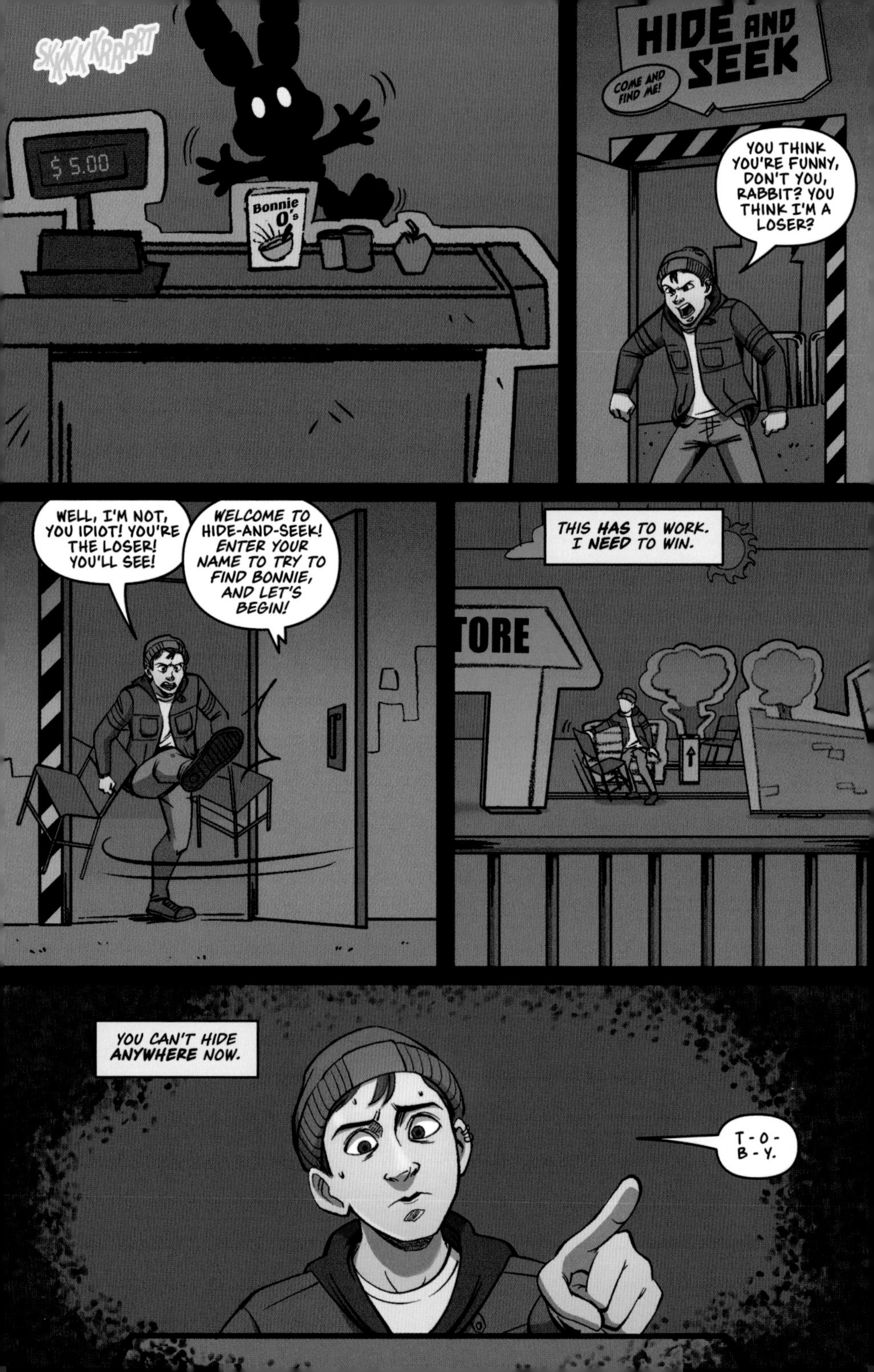
SKKKKRRRRRT
$ 5.00
Bonnie O's
HIDE AND SEEK
COME AND FIND ME!
YOU THINK YOU'RE FUNNY, DON'T YOU, RABBIT? YOU THINK I'M A LOSER?
WELL, I'M NOT, YOU IDIOT! YOU'RE THE LOSER! YOU'LL SEE!
WELCOME TO HIDE-AND-SEEK! ENTER YOUR NAME TO TRY TO FIND BONNIE, AND LET'S BEGIN!
THIS HAS TO WORK. I NEED TO WIN.
TORE
YOU CAN'T HIDE ANYWHERE NOW.
T - O - B - Y.

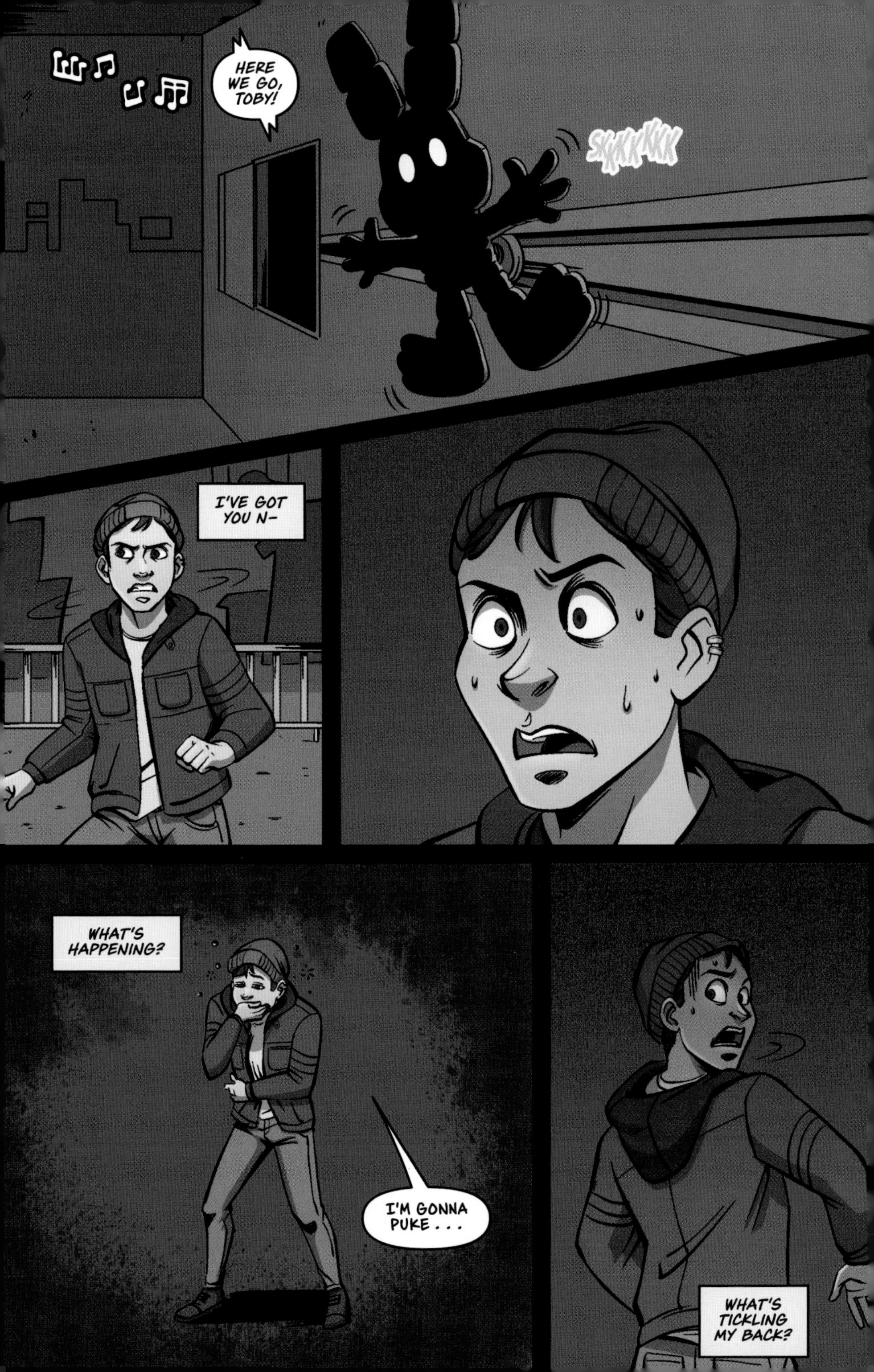
HERE WE GO, TOBY!
SKKKKKK
I'VE GOT YOU N-
WHAT'S HAPPENING?
I'M GONNA PUKE . . .
WHAT'S TICKLING MY BACK?

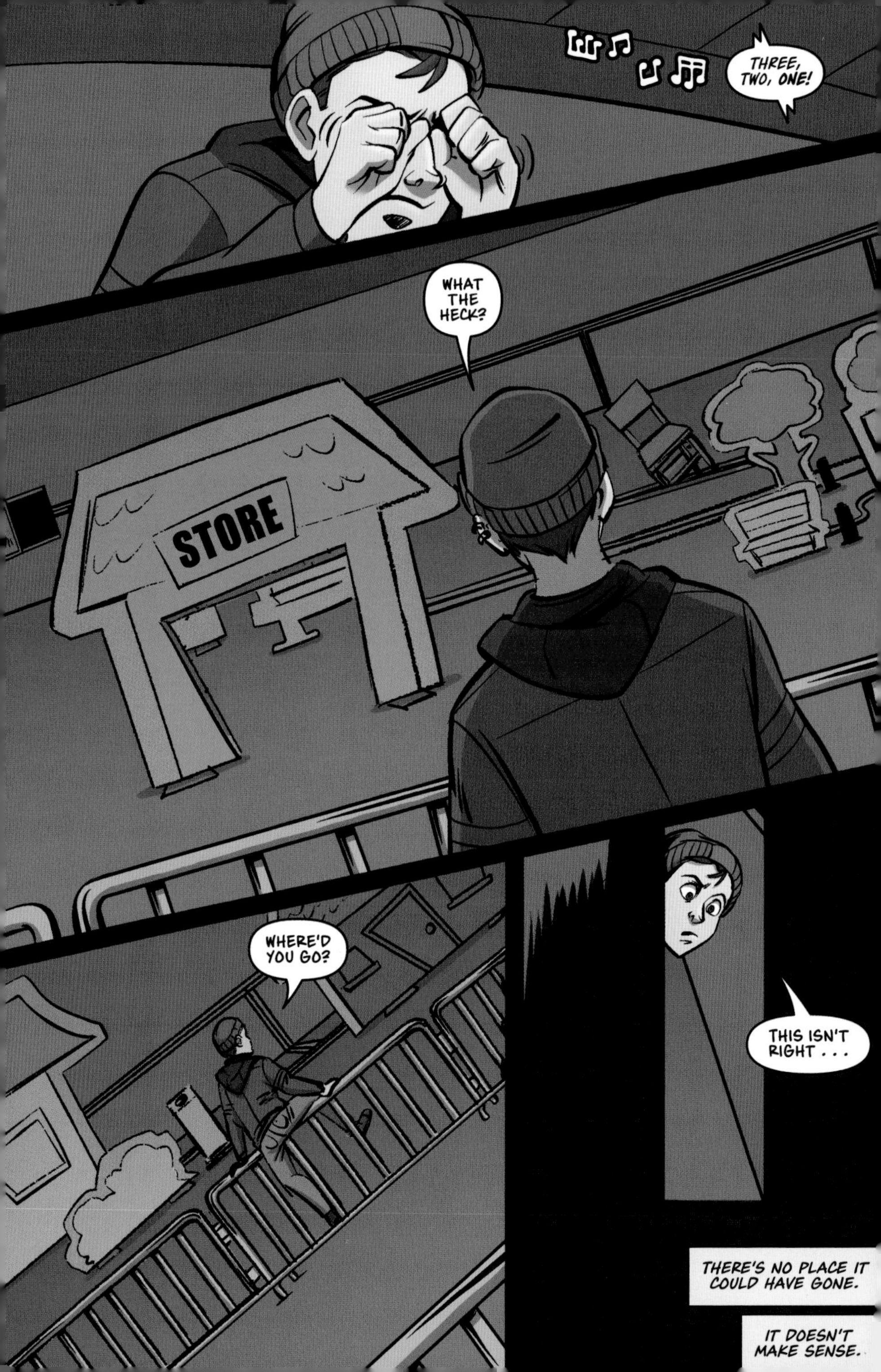
THREE, TWO, ONE!
WHAT THE HECK?
STORE
WHERE'D YOU GO?
THIS ISN'T RIGHT . . .
THERE'S NO PLACE IT COULD HAVE GONE.
IT DOESN'T MAKE SENSE.

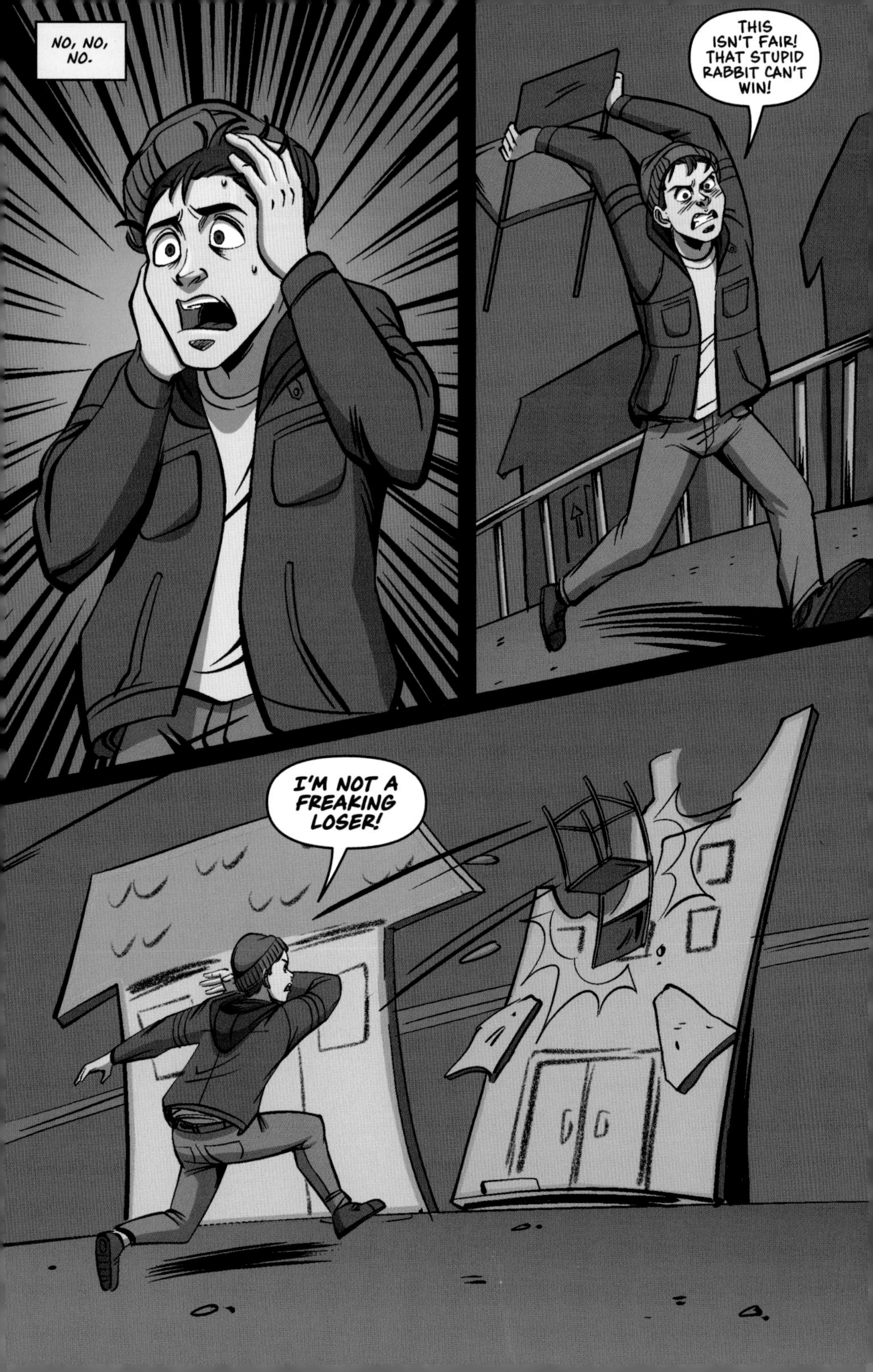
NO, NO, NO.
THIS ISN'T FAIR! THAT STUPID RABBIT CAN'T WIN!
I'M NOT A FREAKING LOSER!

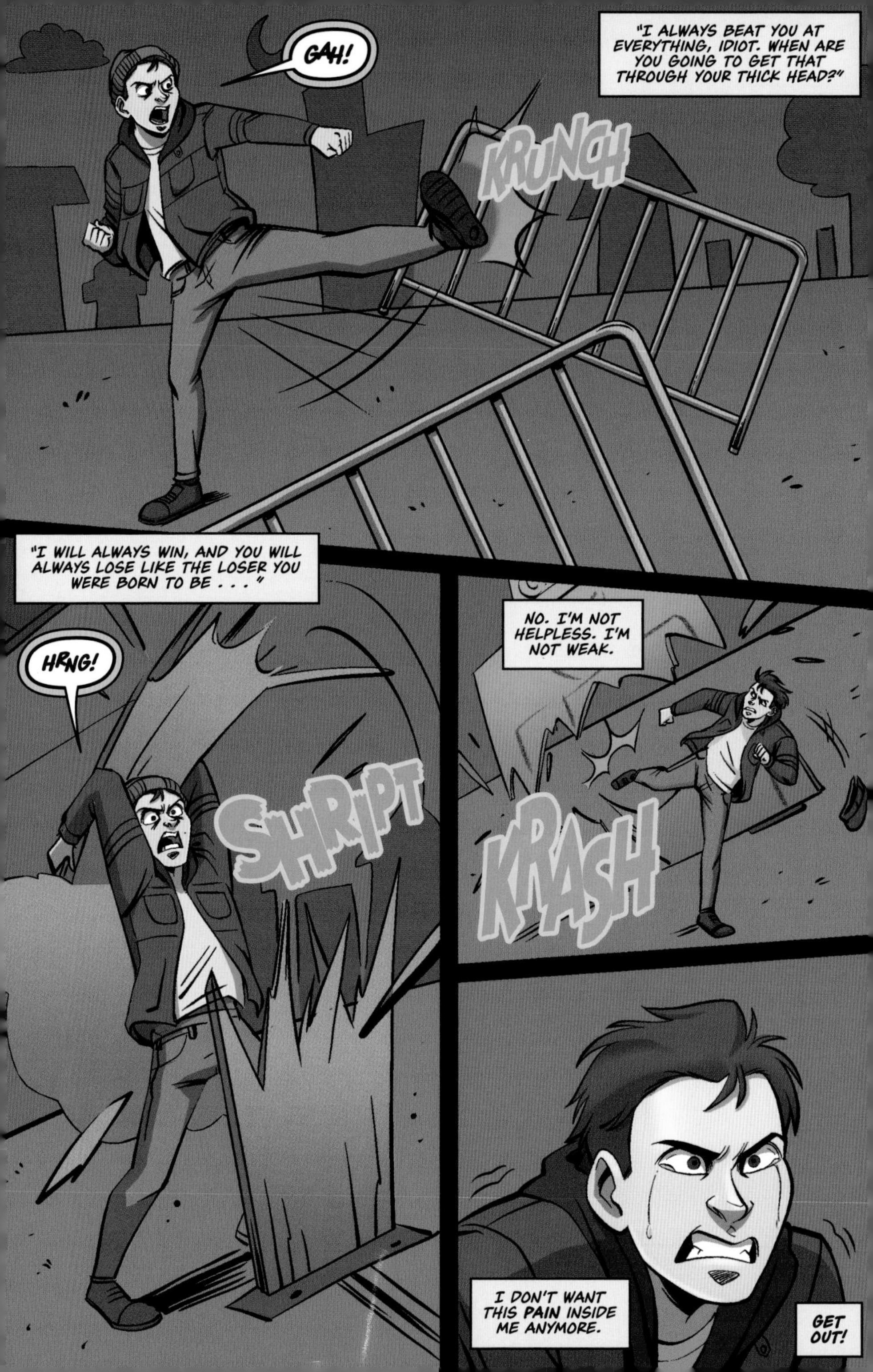
GAH!
"I ALWAYS BEAT YOU AT EVERYTHING, IDIOT. WHEN ARE YOU GOING TO GET THAT THROUGH YOUR THICK HEAD?"
KRUNCH
"I WILL ALWAYS WIN, AND YOU WILL ALWAYS LOSE LIKE THE LOSER YOU WERE BORN TO BE . . ."
HRNG!
SHRIPT
NO. I'M NOT HELPLESS. I'M NOT WEAK.
KRASH
I DON'T WANT THIS PAIN INSIDE ME ANYMORE.
GET OUT!

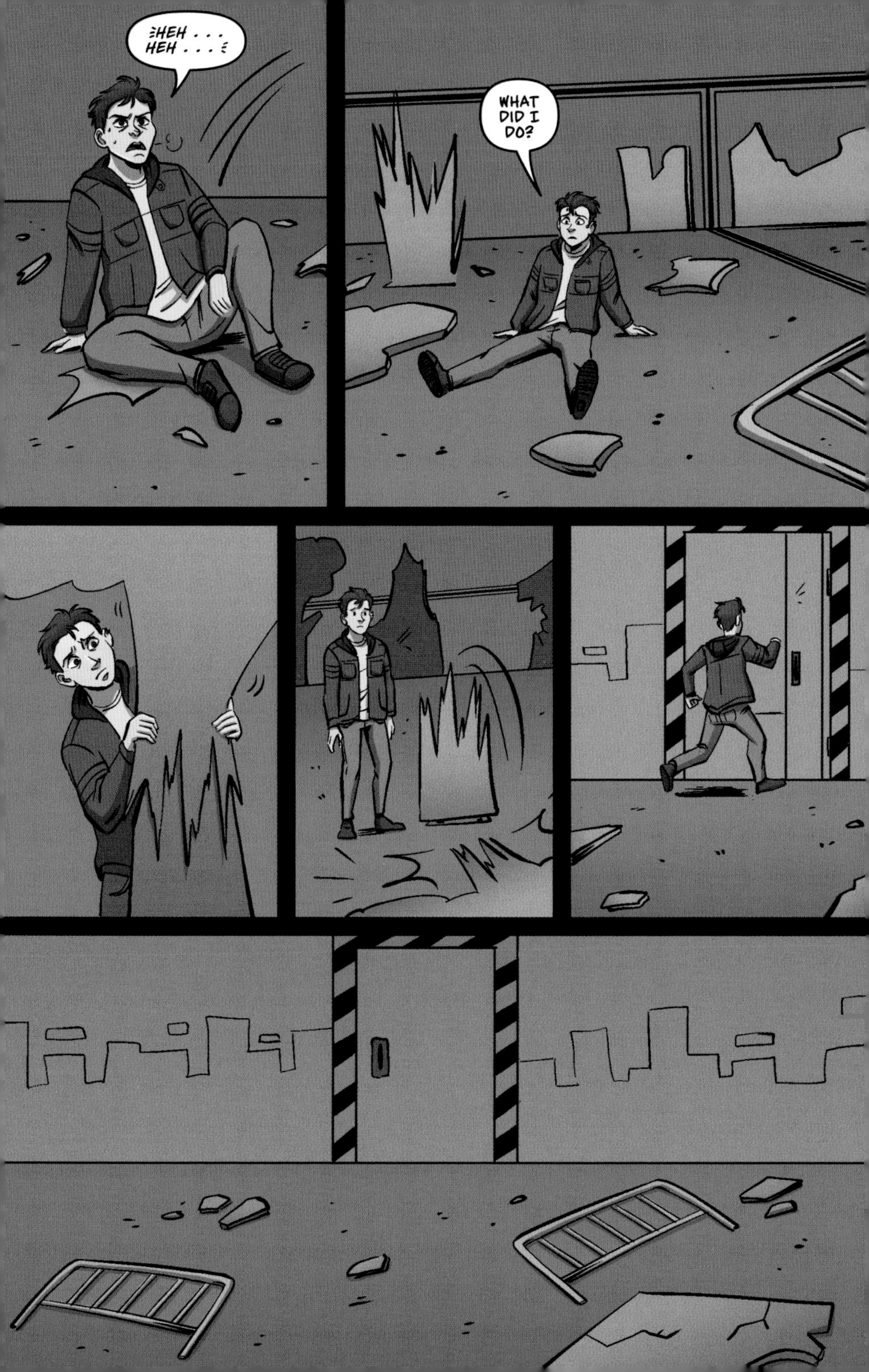
HEH . . .
HEH . . .
WHAT DID I DO?

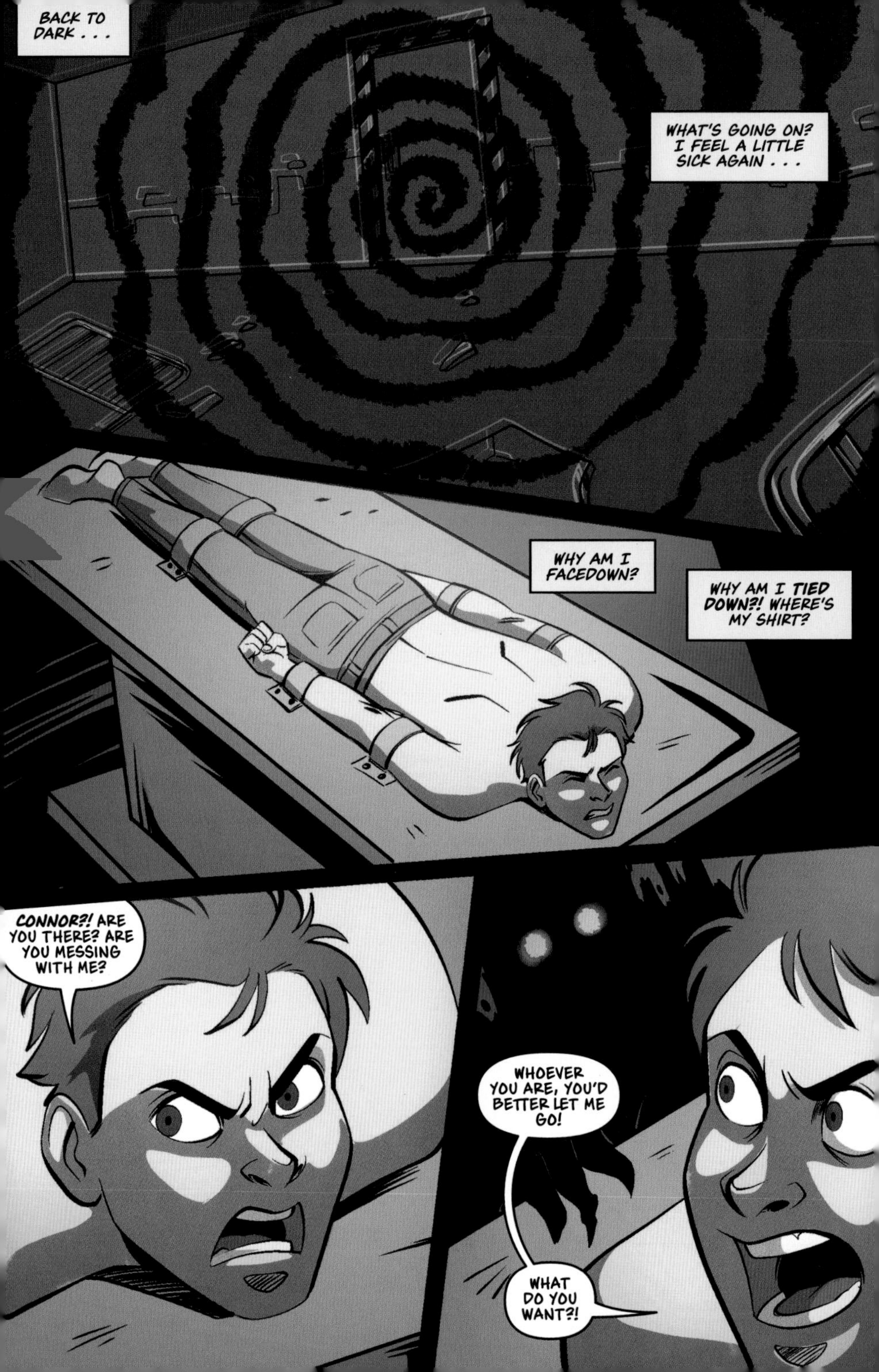
BACK TO DARK . . .
WHAT'S GOING ON? I FEEL A LITTLE SICK AGAIN . . .
WHY AM I FACEDOWN?
WHY AM I TIED DOWN?! WHERE'S MY SHIRT?
CONNOR?! ARE YOU THERE? ARE YOU MESSING WITH ME?
WHOEVER YOU ARE, YOU'D BETTER LET ME GO!
WHAT DO YOU WANT?!

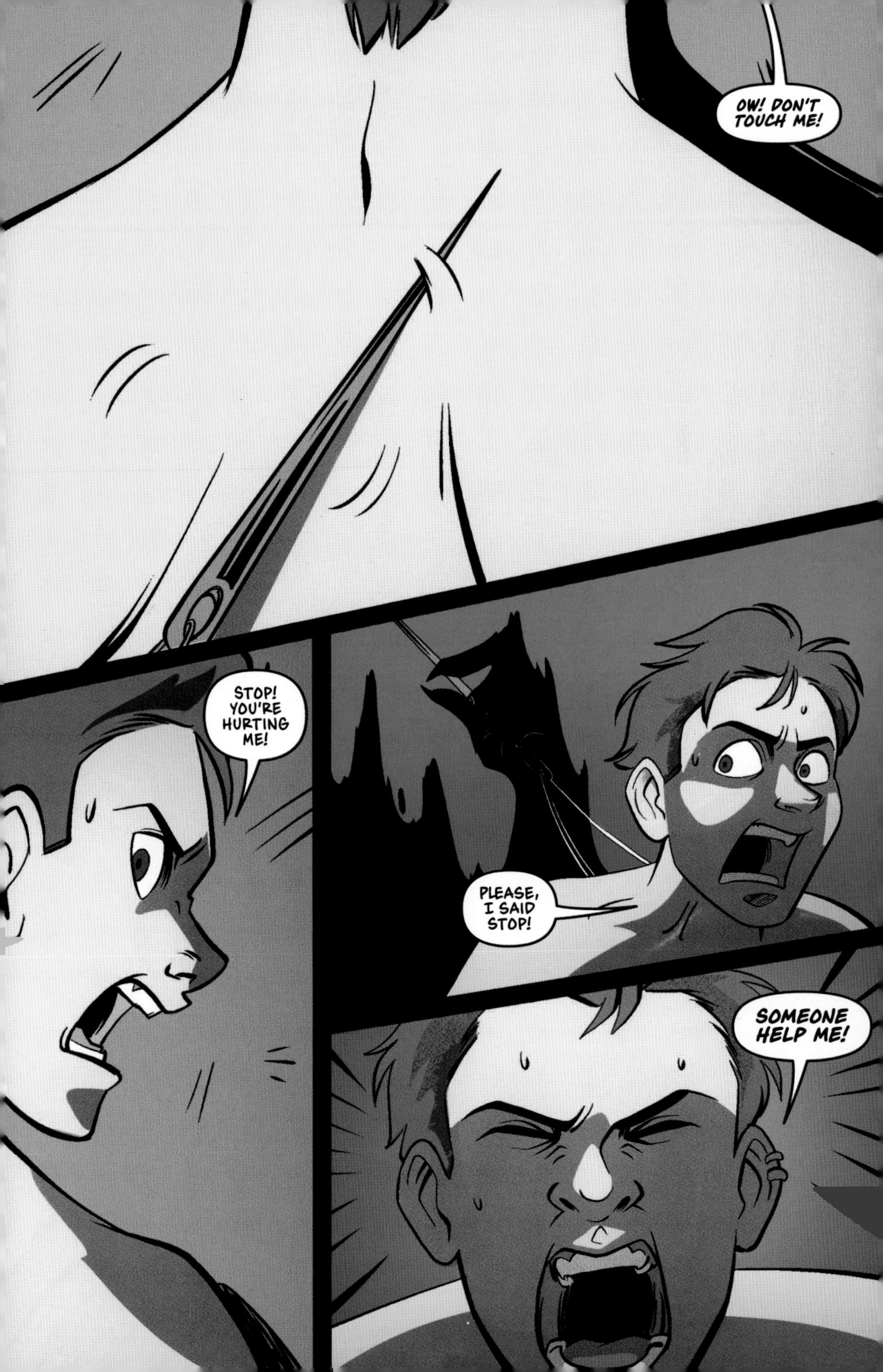
OW! DON'T TOUCH ME!
STOP! YOU'RE HURTING ME!
PLEASE, I SAID STOP!
SOMEONE HELP ME!

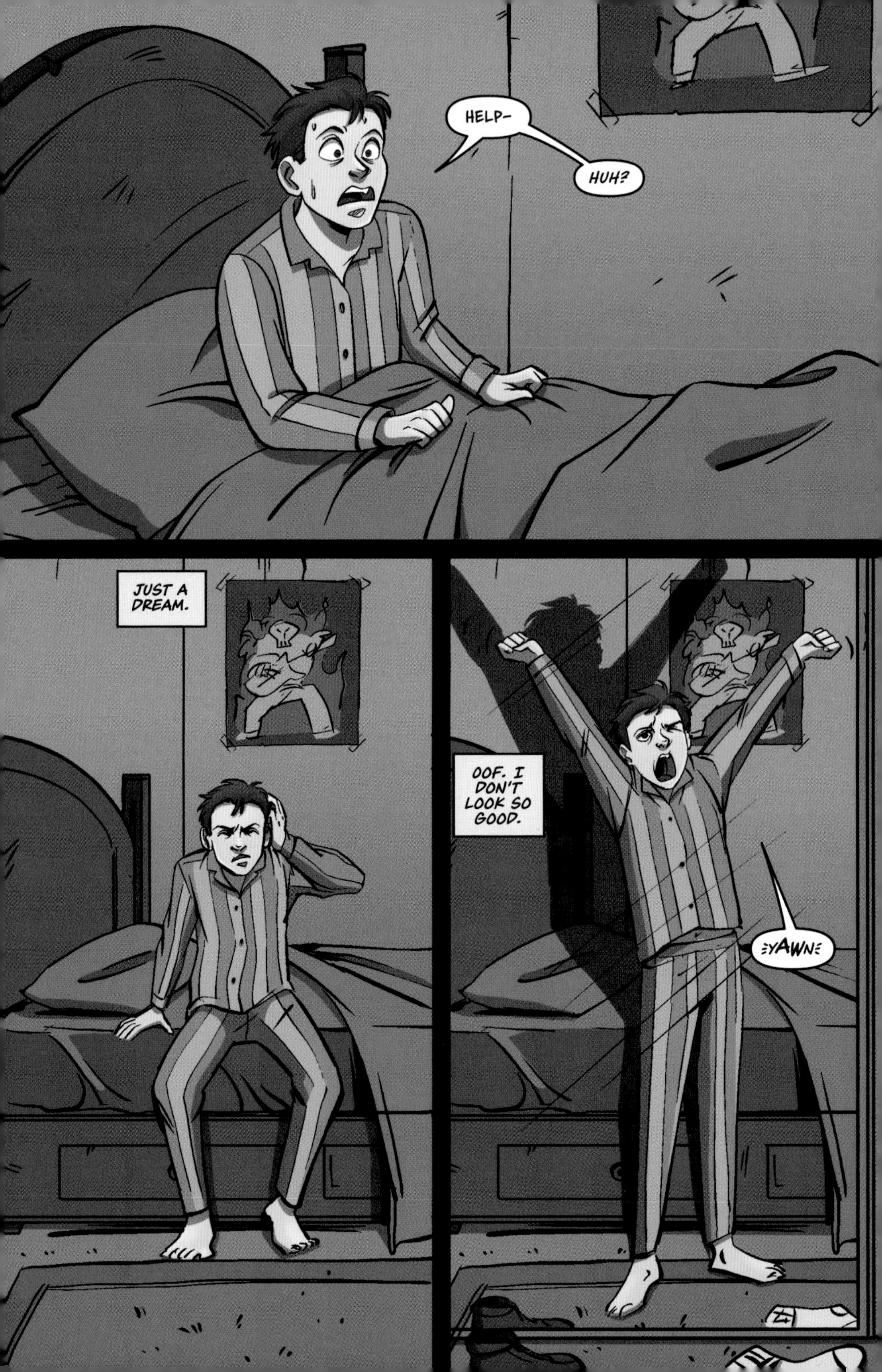
HELP-
HUH?
JUST A DREAM.
OOF. I DON'T LOOK SO GOOD.
YAWN

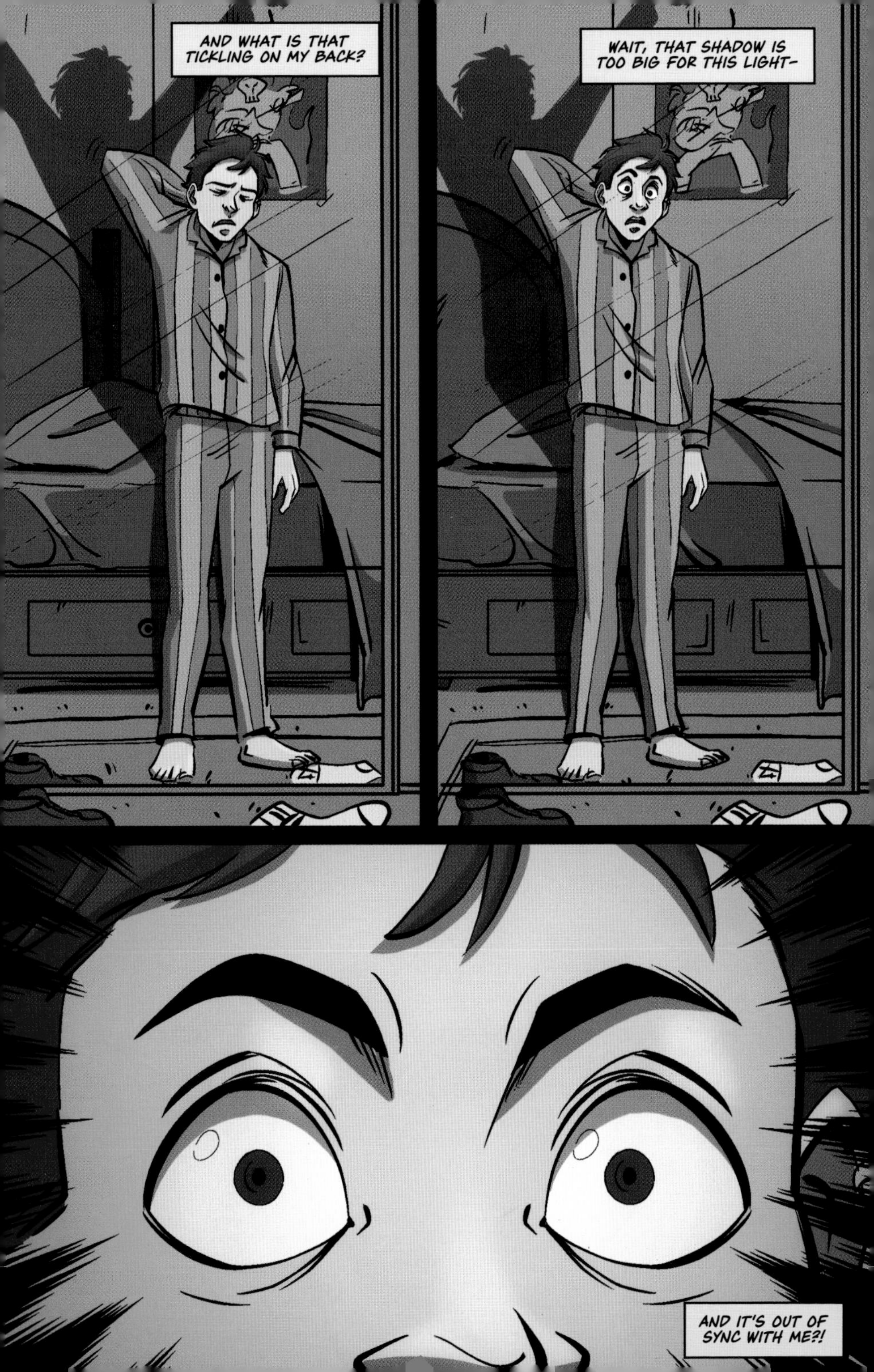
AND WHAT IS THAT TICKLING ON MY BACK?
WAIT, THAT SHADOW IS TOO BIG FOR THIS LIGHT-
AND IT'S OUT OF SYNC WITH ME?!

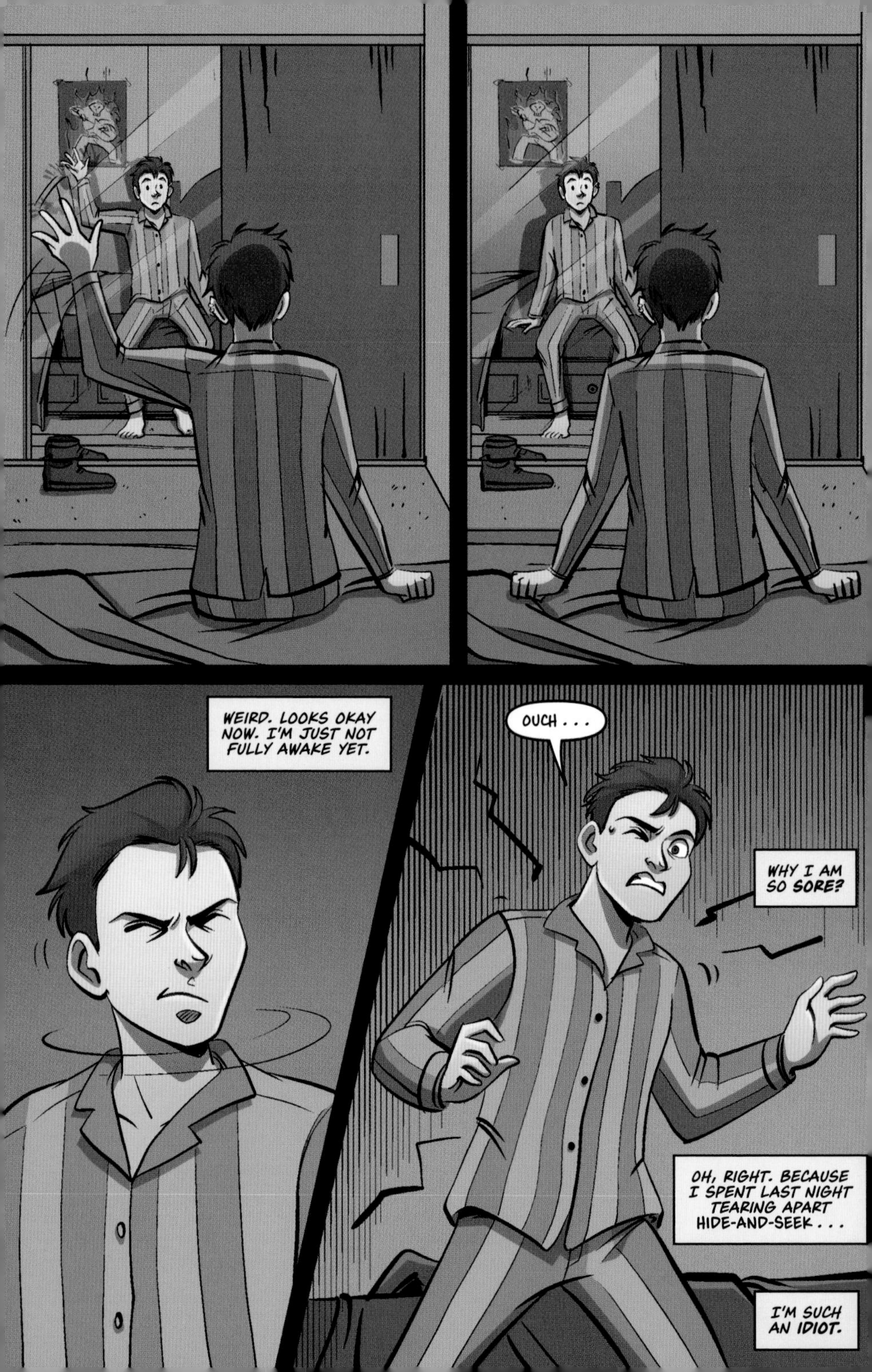
WEIRD. LOOKS OKAY NOW. I'M JUST NOT FULLY AWAKE YET.
OUCH . . .
WHY I AM SO SORE?
OH, RIGHT. BECAUSE I SPENT LAST NIGHT TEARING APART HIDE-AND-SEEK . . .
I'M SUCH AN IDIOT.

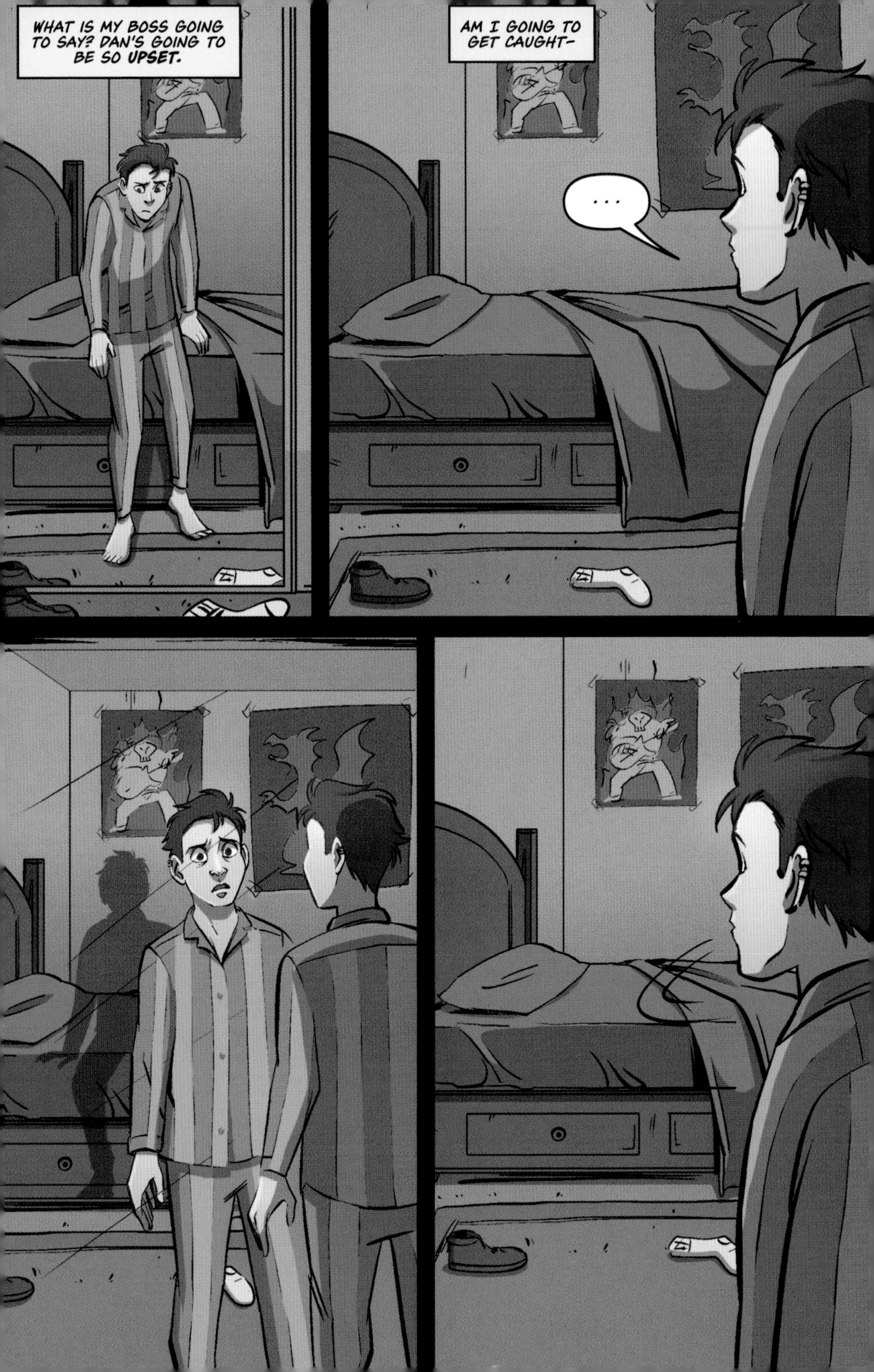
WHAT IS MY BOSS GOING TO SAY? DAN'S GOING TO BE SO **UPSET.**
AM I GOING TO GET CAUGHT-
...

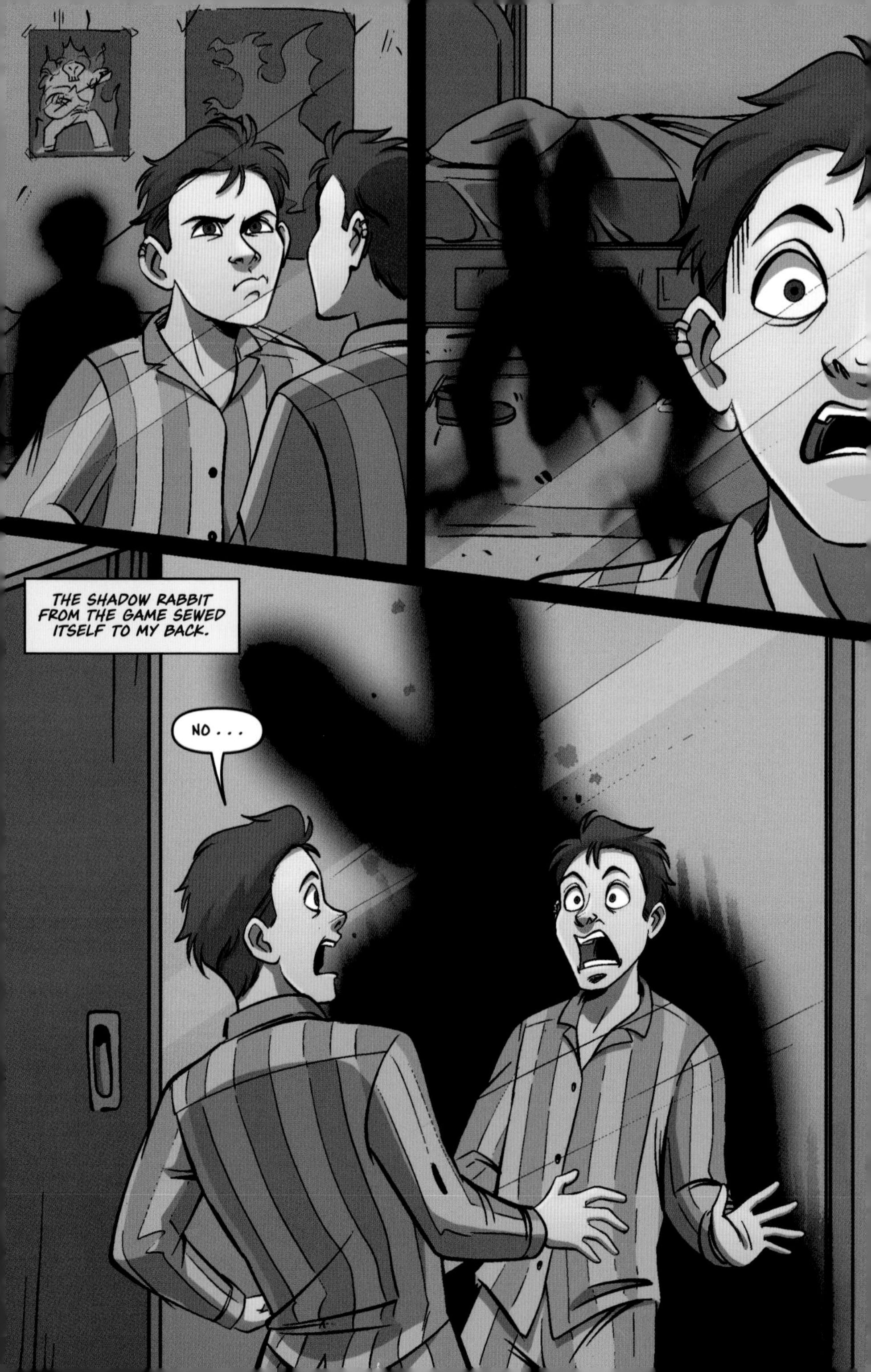
THE SHADOW RABBIT FROM THE GAME SEWED ITSELF TO MY BACK.
NO . . .

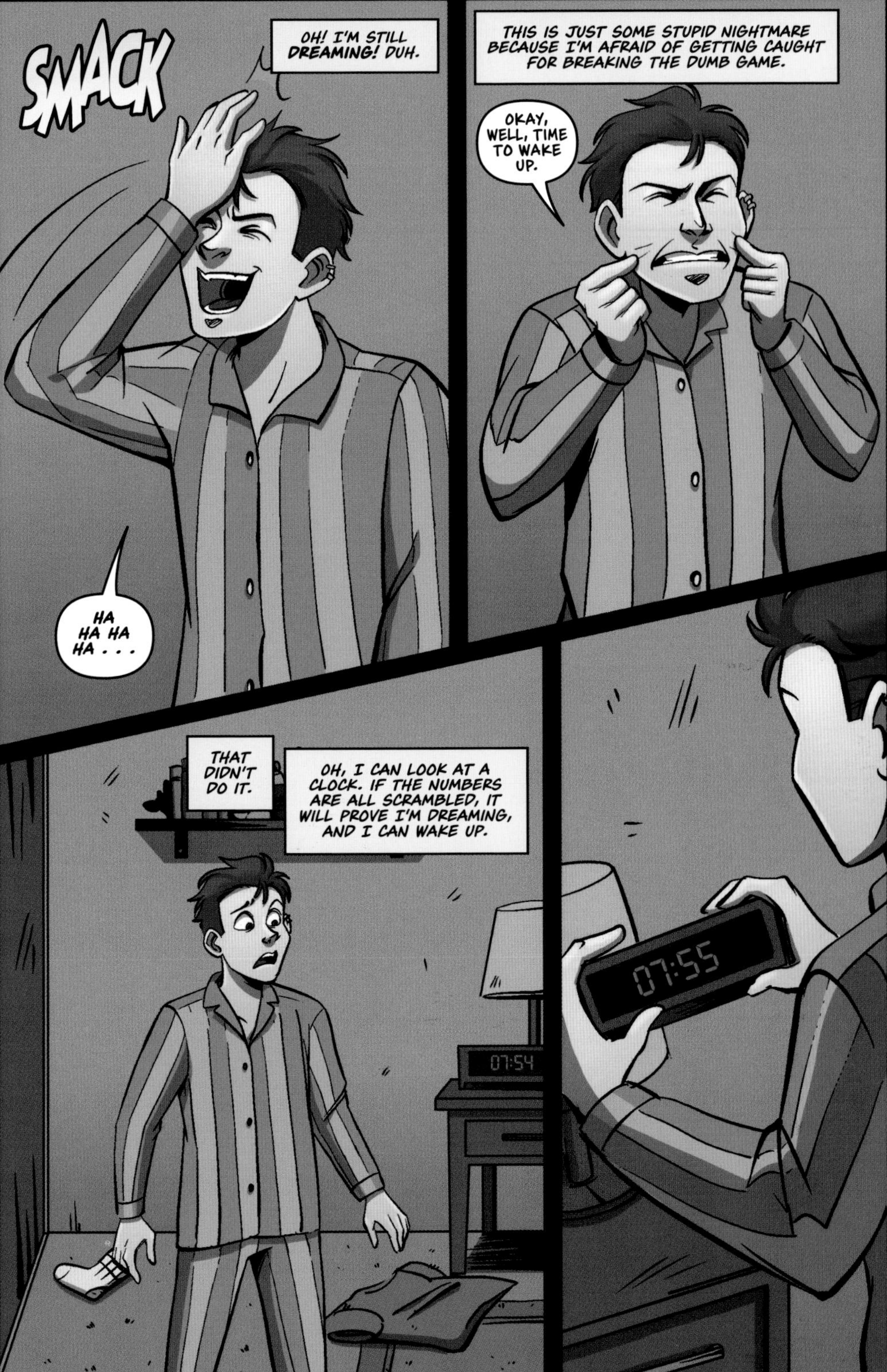
SMACK
OH! I'M STILL DREAMING! DUH.
HA HA HA HA . . .
THIS IS JUST SOME STUPID NIGHTMARE BECAUSE I'M AFRAID OF GETTING CAUGHT FOR BREAKING THE DUMB GAME.
OKAY, WELL, TIME TO WAKE UP.
THAT DIDN'T DO IT.
OH, I CAN LOOK AT A CLOCK. IF THE NUMBERS ARE ALL SCRAMBLED, IT WILL PROVE I'M DREAMING, AND I CAN WAKE UP.
07:54
07:55

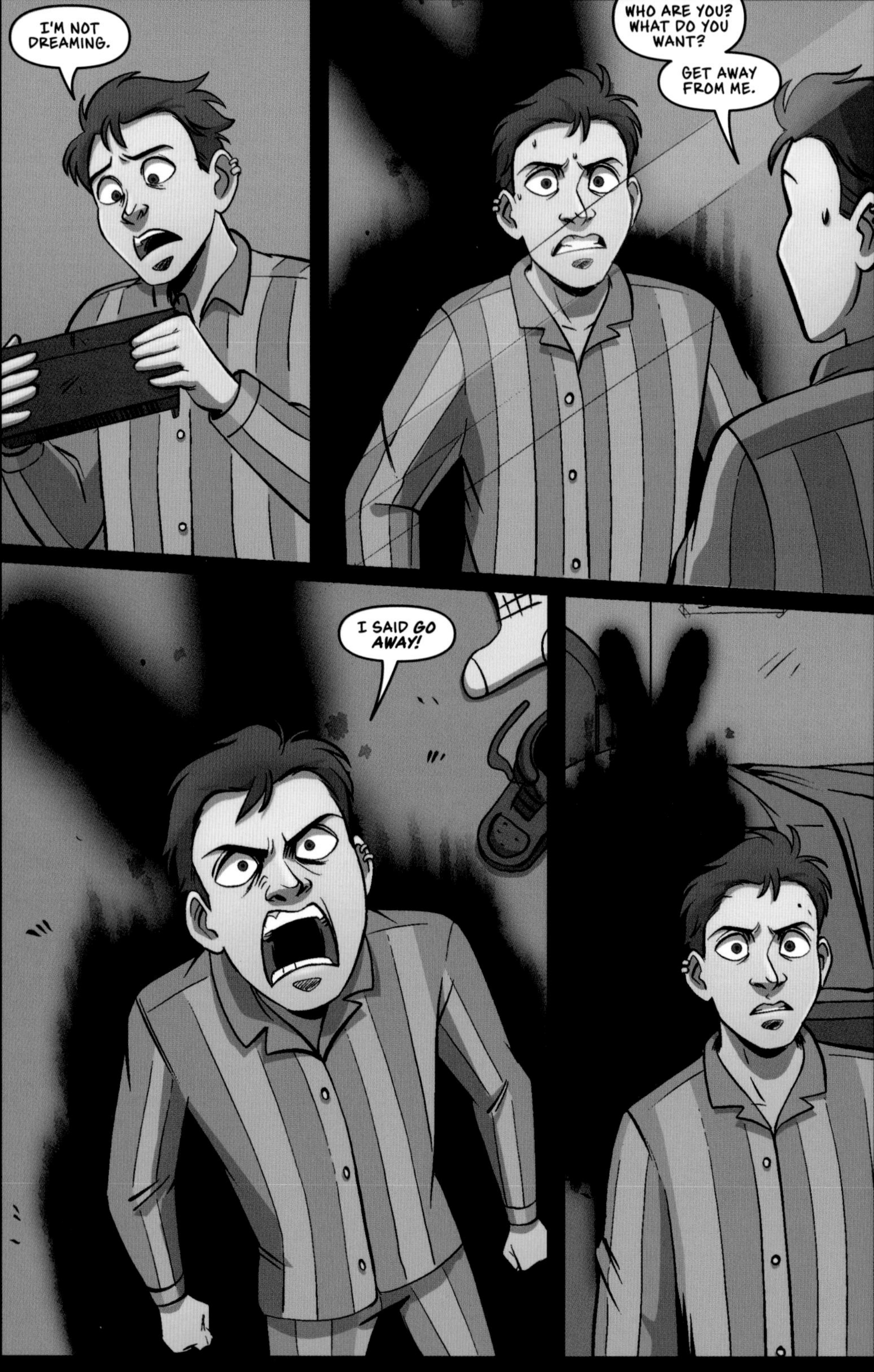

I'M NOT DREAMING.
WHO ARE YOU? WHAT DO YOU WANT?
GET AWAY FROM ME.
I SAID GO AWAY!

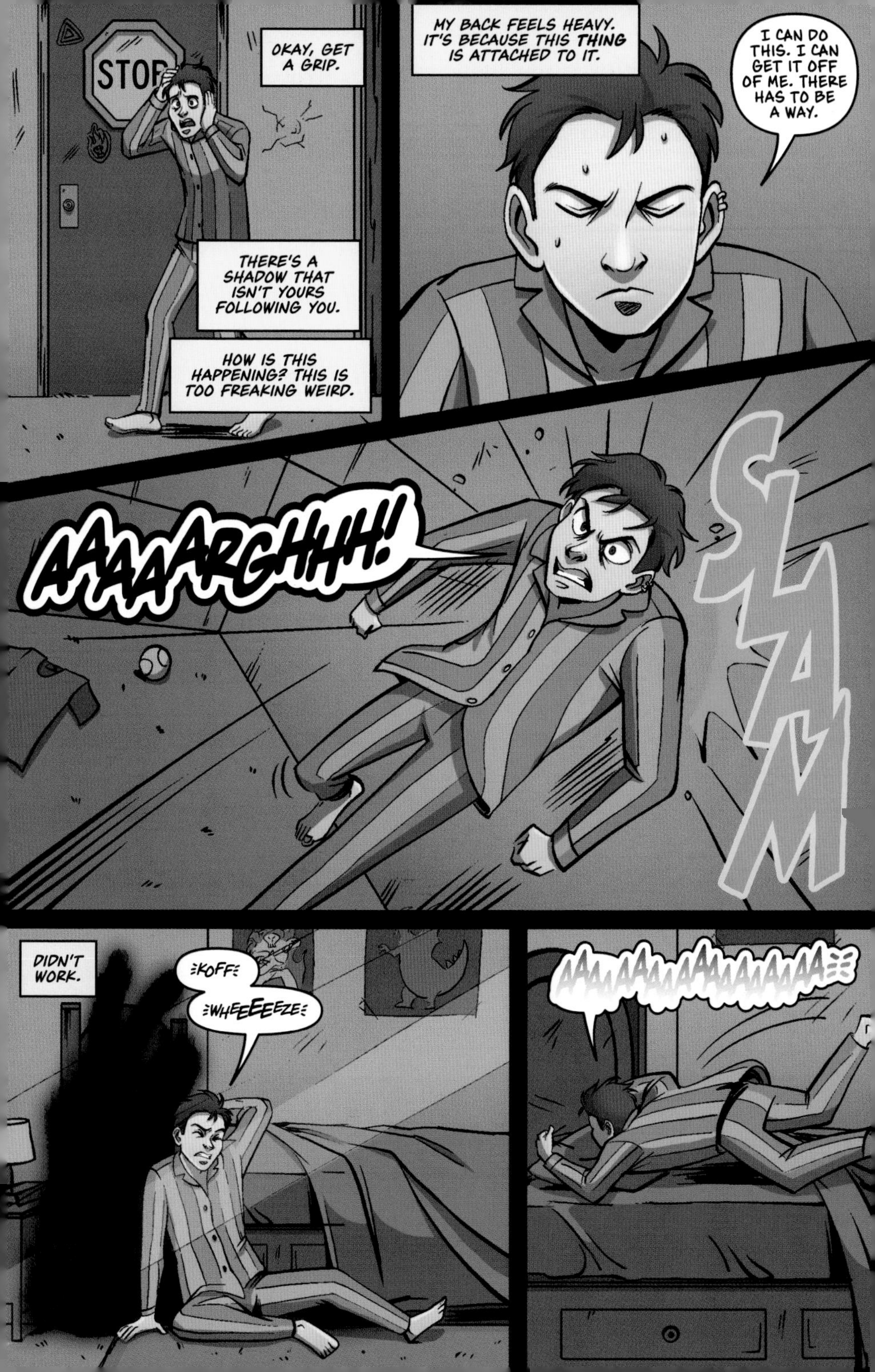
STOP
OKAY, GET A GRIP.
THERE'S A SHADOW THAT ISN'T YOURS FOLLOWING YOU.
HOW IS THIS HAPPENING? THIS IS TOO FREAKING WEIRD.
MY BACK FEELS HEAVY. IT'S BECAUSE THIS THING IS ATTACHED TO IT.
I CAN DO THIS. I CAN GET IT OFF OF ME. THERE HAS TO BE A WAY.
AAAAARGHHH!
SLAM
DIDN'T WORK.
KOFF
WHEEEEEZE
AAAAAAAAAAAAAAAAAAAA

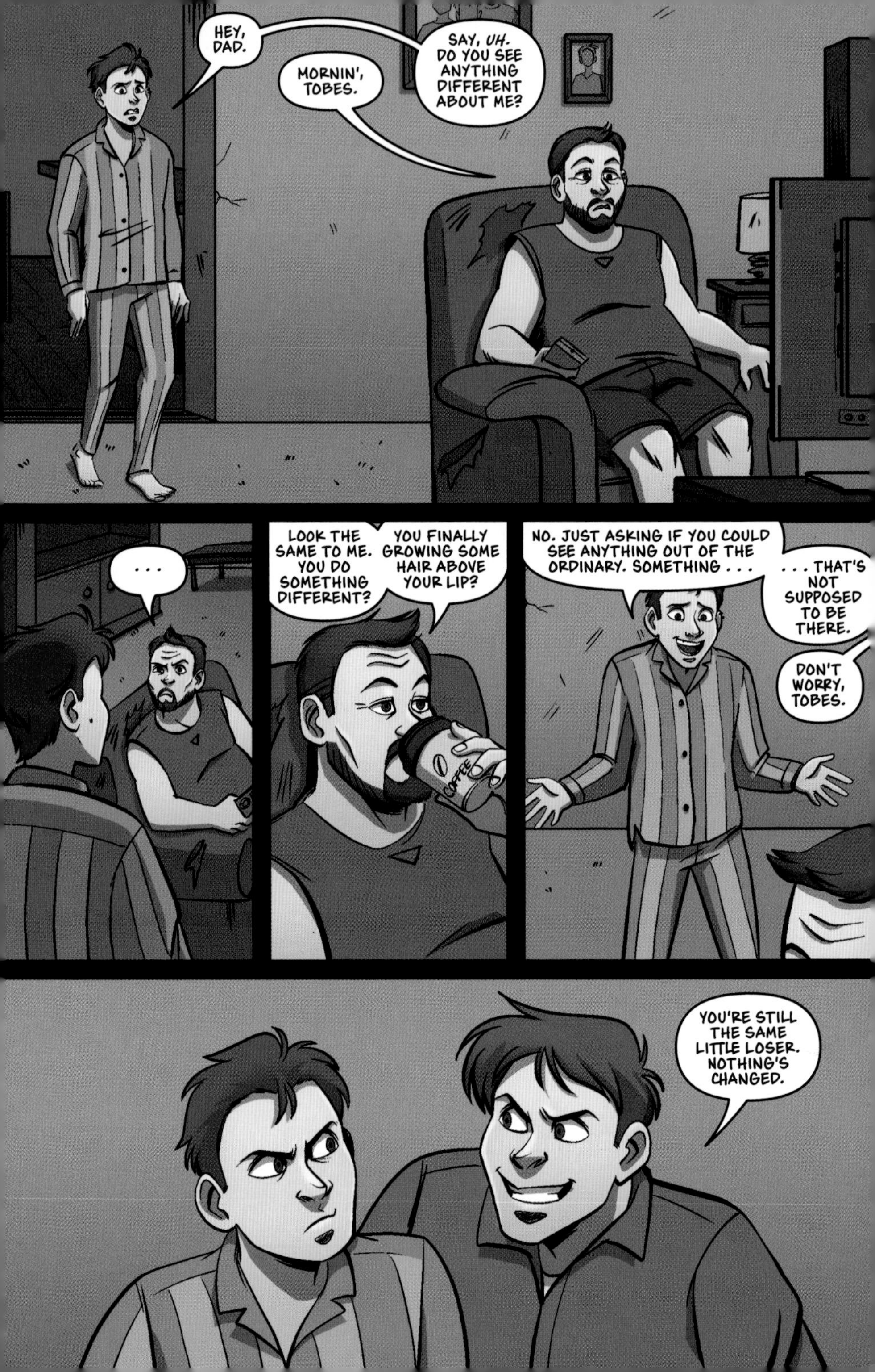
HEY, DAD.
MORNIN', TOBES.
SAY, UH. DO YOU SEE ANYTHING DIFFERENT ABOUT ME?
. . .
LOOK THE SAME TO ME. YOU DO SOMETHING DIFFERENT?
YOU FINALLY GROWING SOME HAIR ABOVE YOUR LIP?
COFFEE
NO. JUST ASKING IF YOU COULD SEE ANYTHING OUT OF THE ORDINARY. SOMETHING . . .
. . . THAT'S NOT SUPPOSED TO BE THERE.
DON'T WORRY, TOBES.
YOU'RE STILL THE SAME LITTLE LOSER. NOTHING'S CHANGED.

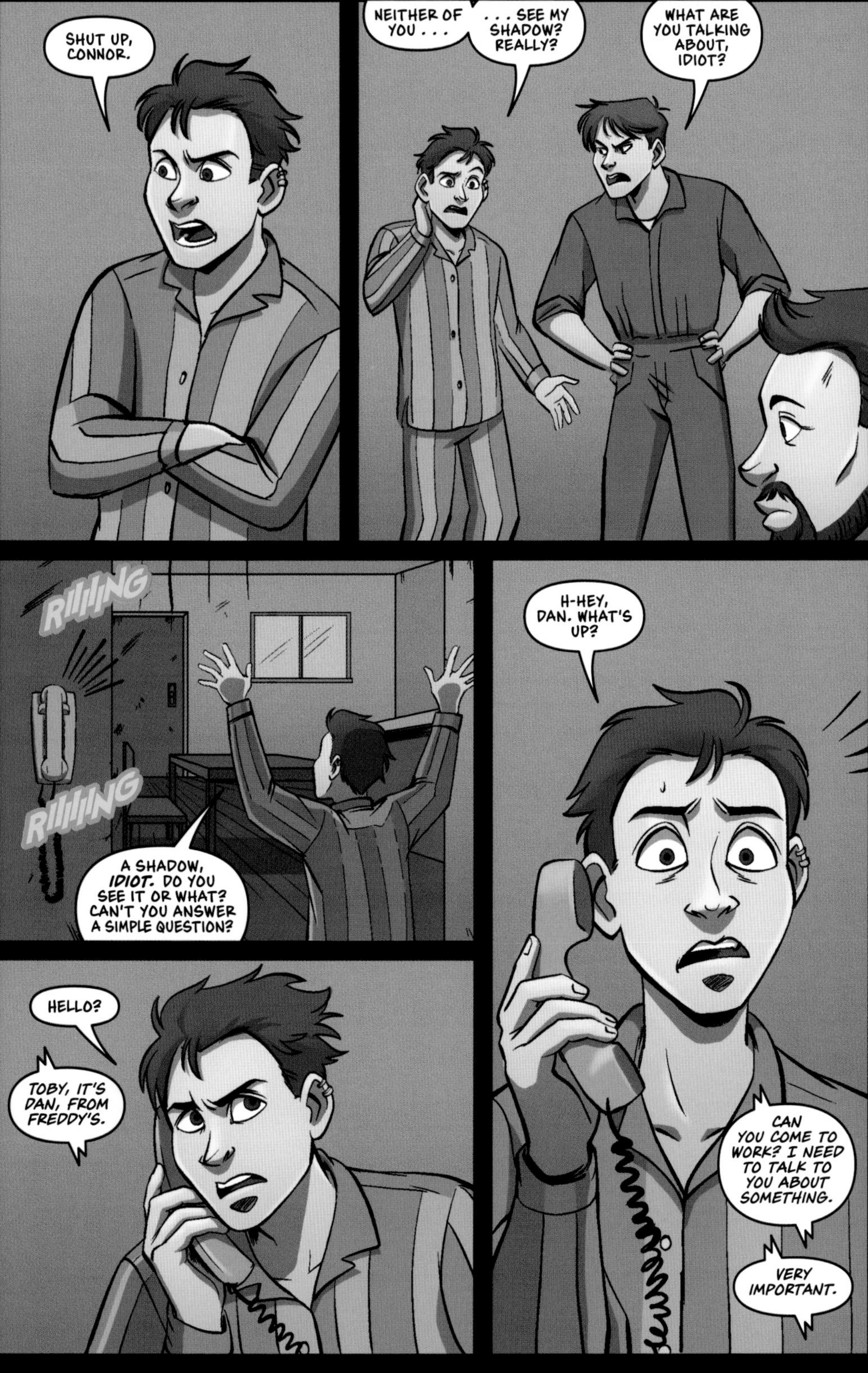
SHUT UP, CONNOR.
NEITHER OF YOU . . .
. . . SEE MY SHADOW? REALLY?
WHAT ARE YOU TALKING ABOUT, IDIOT?
RIIIIING
RIIIIING
A SHADOW, *IDIOT.* DO YOU SEE IT OR WHAT? CAN'T YOU ANSWER A SIMPLE QUESTION?
HELLO?
TOBY, IT'S DAN, FROM FREDDY'S.
H-HEY, DAN. WHAT'S UP?
CAN YOU COME TO WORK? I NEED TO TALK TO YOU ABOUT SOMETHING.
VERY IMPORTANT.

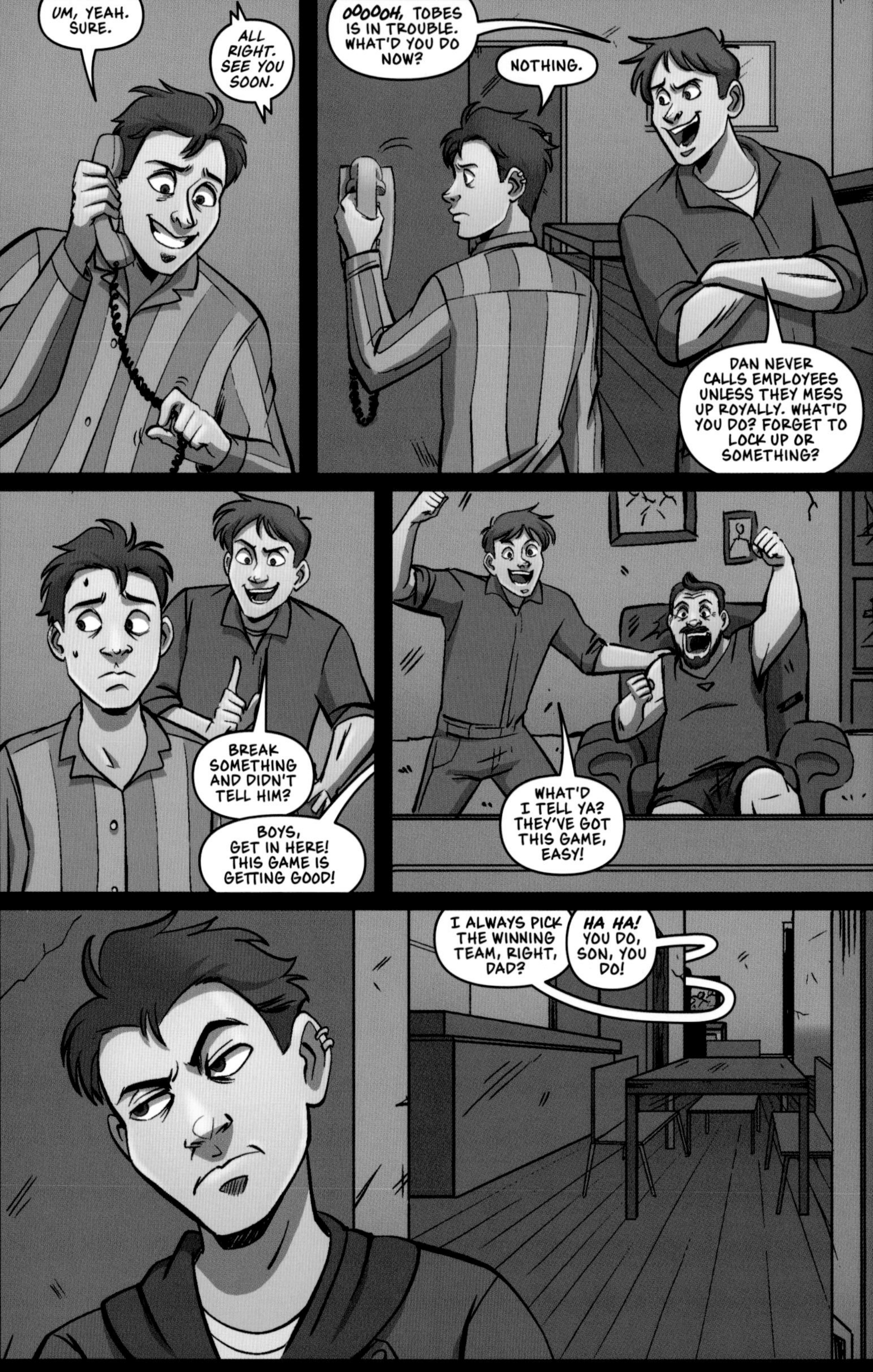
UM, YEAH. SURE.
ALL RIGHT. SEE YOU SOON.
OOOOOH, TOBES IS IN TROUBLE. WHAT'D YOU DO NOW?
NOTHING.
DAN NEVER CALLS EMPLOYEES UNLESS THEY MESS UP ROYALLY. WHAT'D YOU DO? FORGET TO LOCK UP OR SOMETHING?
BREAK SOMETHING AND DIDN'T TELL HIM?
BOYS, GET IN HERE! THIS GAME IS GETTING GOOD!
WHAT'D I TELL YA? THEY'VE GOT THIS GAME, EASY!
I ALWAYS PICK THE WINNING TEAM, RIGHT, DAD?
HA HA! YOU DO, SON, YOU DO!

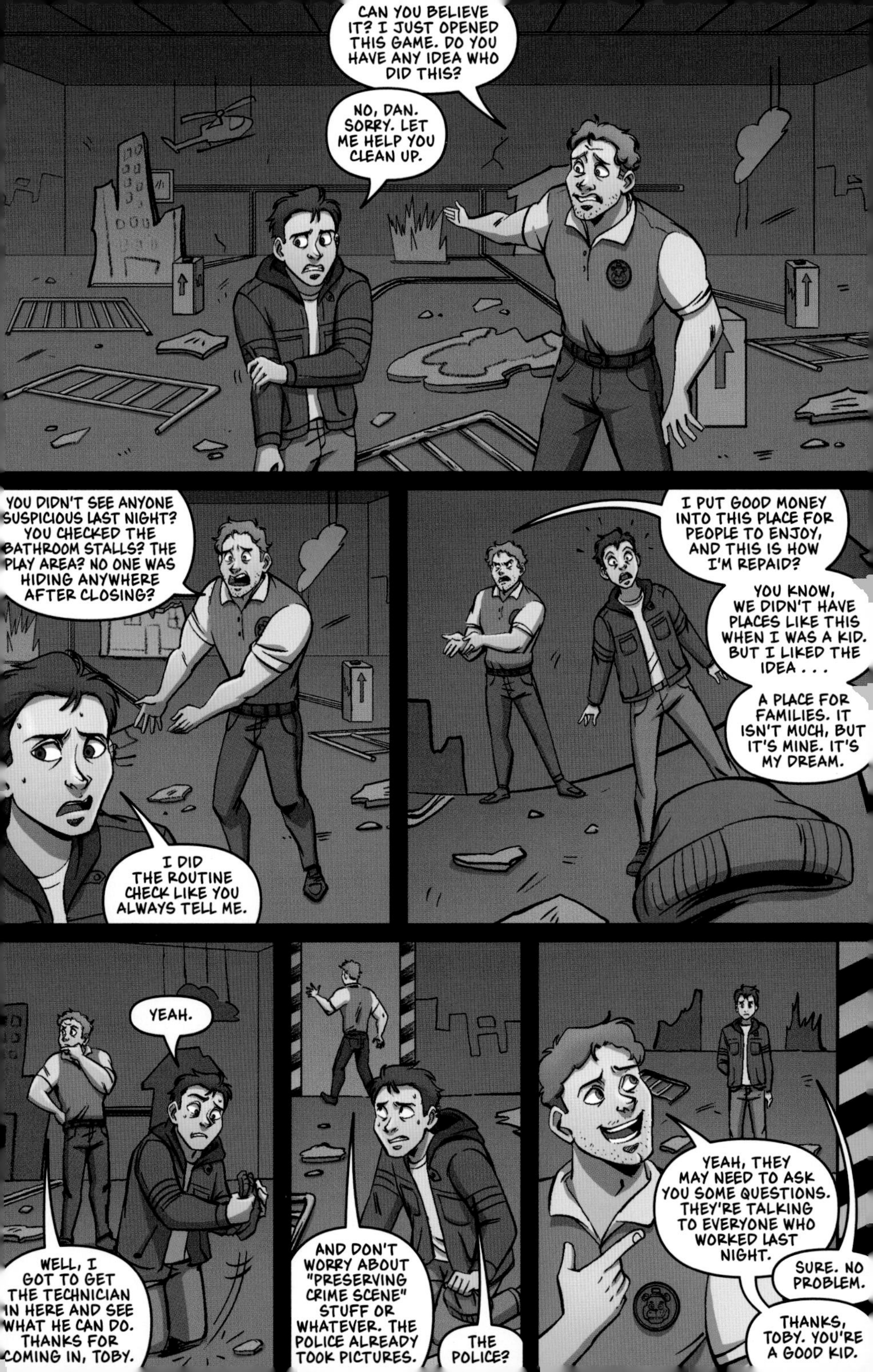
CAN YOU BELIEVE IT? I JUST OPENED THIS GAME. DO YOU HAVE ANY IDEA WHO DID THIS?
NO, DAN. SORRY. LET ME HELP YOU CLEAN UP.
YOU DIDN'T SEE ANYONE SUSPICIOUS LAST NIGHT? YOU CHECKED THE BATHROOM STALLS? THE PLAY AREA? NO ONE WAS HIDING ANYWHERE AFTER CLOSING?
I DID THE ROUTINE CHECK LIKE YOU ALWAYS TELL ME.
I PUT GOOD MONEY INTO THIS PLACE FOR PEOPLE TO ENJOY, AND THIS IS HOW I'M REPAID?
YOU KNOW, WE DIDN'T HAVE PLACES LIKE THIS WHEN I WAS A KID. BUT I LIKED THE IDEA . . .
A PLACE FOR FAMILIES. IT ISN'T MUCH, BUT IT'S MINE. IT'S MY DREAM.
YEAH.
WELL, I GOT TO GET THE TECHNICIAN IN HERE AND SEE WHAT HE CAN DO. THANKS FOR COMING IN, TOBY.
AND DON'T WORRY ABOUT "PRESERVING CRIME SCENE" STUFF OR WHATEVER. THE POLICE ALREADY TOOK PICTURES.
THE POLICE?
YEAH, THEY MAY NEED TO ASK YOU SOME QUESTIONS. THEY'RE TALKING TO EVERYONE WHO WORKED LAST NIGHT.
SURE. NO PROBLEM.
THANKS, TOBY. YOU'RE A GOOD KID.

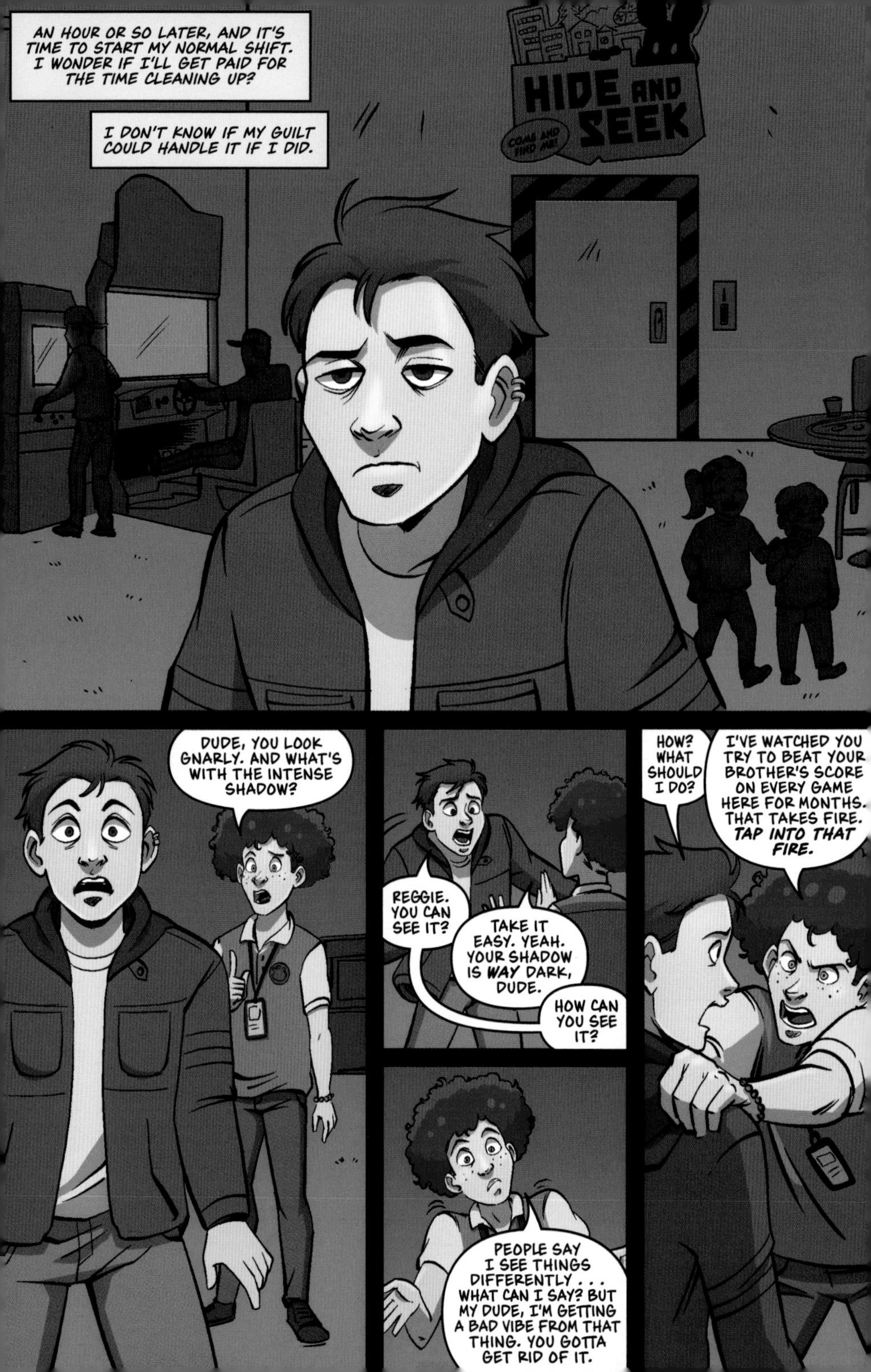
AN HOUR OR SO LATER, AND IT'S TIME TO START MY NORMAL SHIFT. I WONDER IF I'LL GET PAID FOR THE TIME CLEANING UP?
I DON'T KNOW IF MY GUILT COULD HANDLE IT IF I DID.
HIDE AND SEEK
COME AND FIND ME!
DUDE, YOU LOOK GNARLY. AND WHAT'S WITH THE INTENSE SHADOW?
REGGIE. YOU CAN SEE IT?
TAKE IT EASY. YEAH. YOUR SHADOW IS WAY DARK, DUDE.
HOW CAN YOU SEE IT?
PEOPLE SAY I SEE THINGS DIFFERENTLY . . . WHAT CAN I SAY? BUT MY DUDE, I'M GETTING A BAD VIBE FROM THAT THING. YOU GOTTA GET RID OF IT.
HOW? WHAT SHOULD I DO?
I'VE WATCHED YOU TRY TO BEAT YOUR BROTHER'S SCORE ON EVERY GAME HERE FOR MONTHS. THAT TAKES FIRE. TAP INTO THAT FIRE.

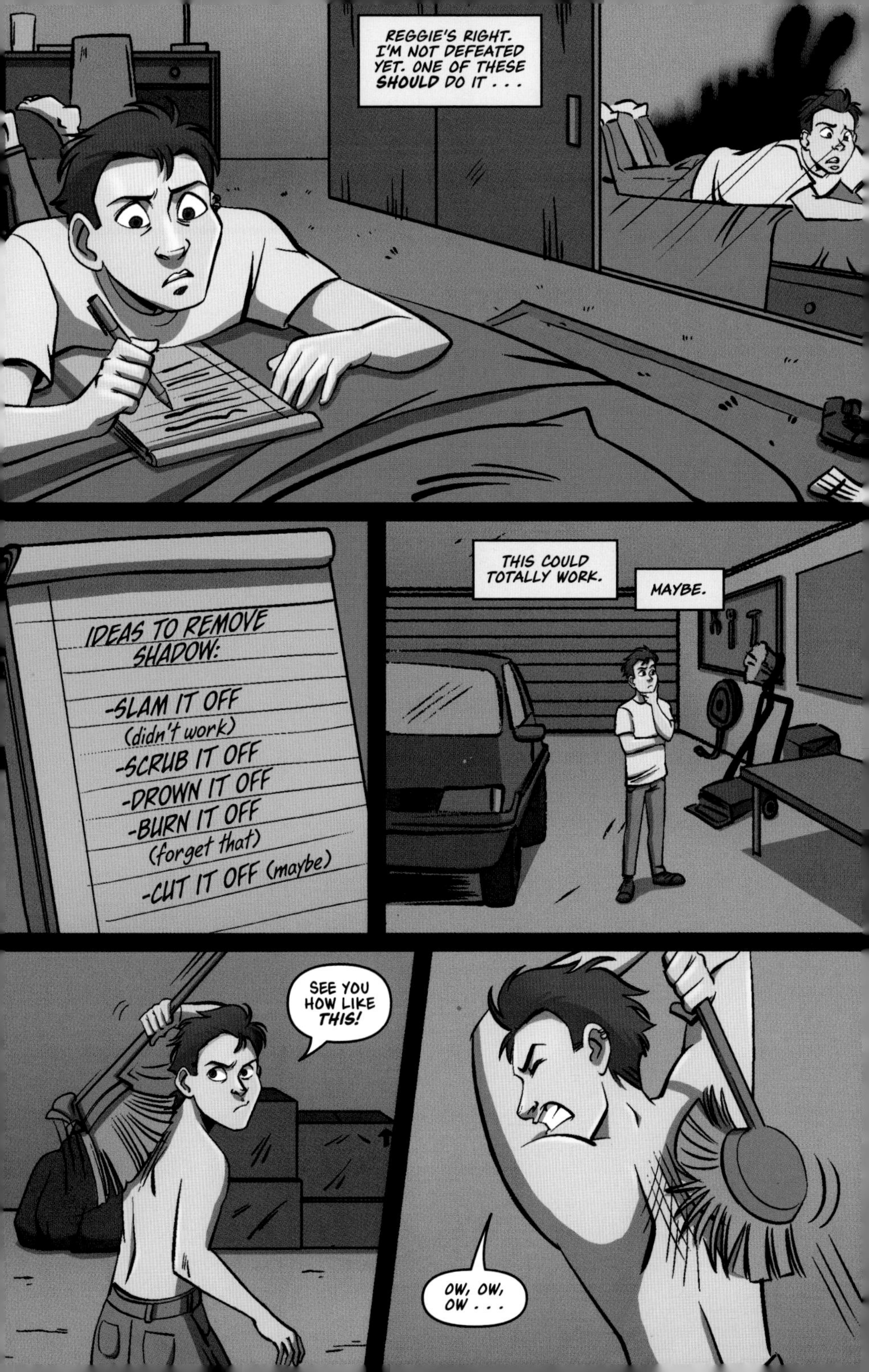
REGGIE'S RIGHT. I'M NOT DEFEATED YET. ONE OF THESE SHOULD DO IT . . .
IDEAS TO REMOVE SHADOW:
-SLAM IT OFF (didn't work)
-SCRUB IT OFF
-DROWN IT OFF
-BURN IT OFF (forget that)
-CUT IT OFF (maybe)
THIS COULD TOTALLY WORK.
MAYBE.
SEE YOU HOW LIKE THIS!
OW, OW, OW . . .

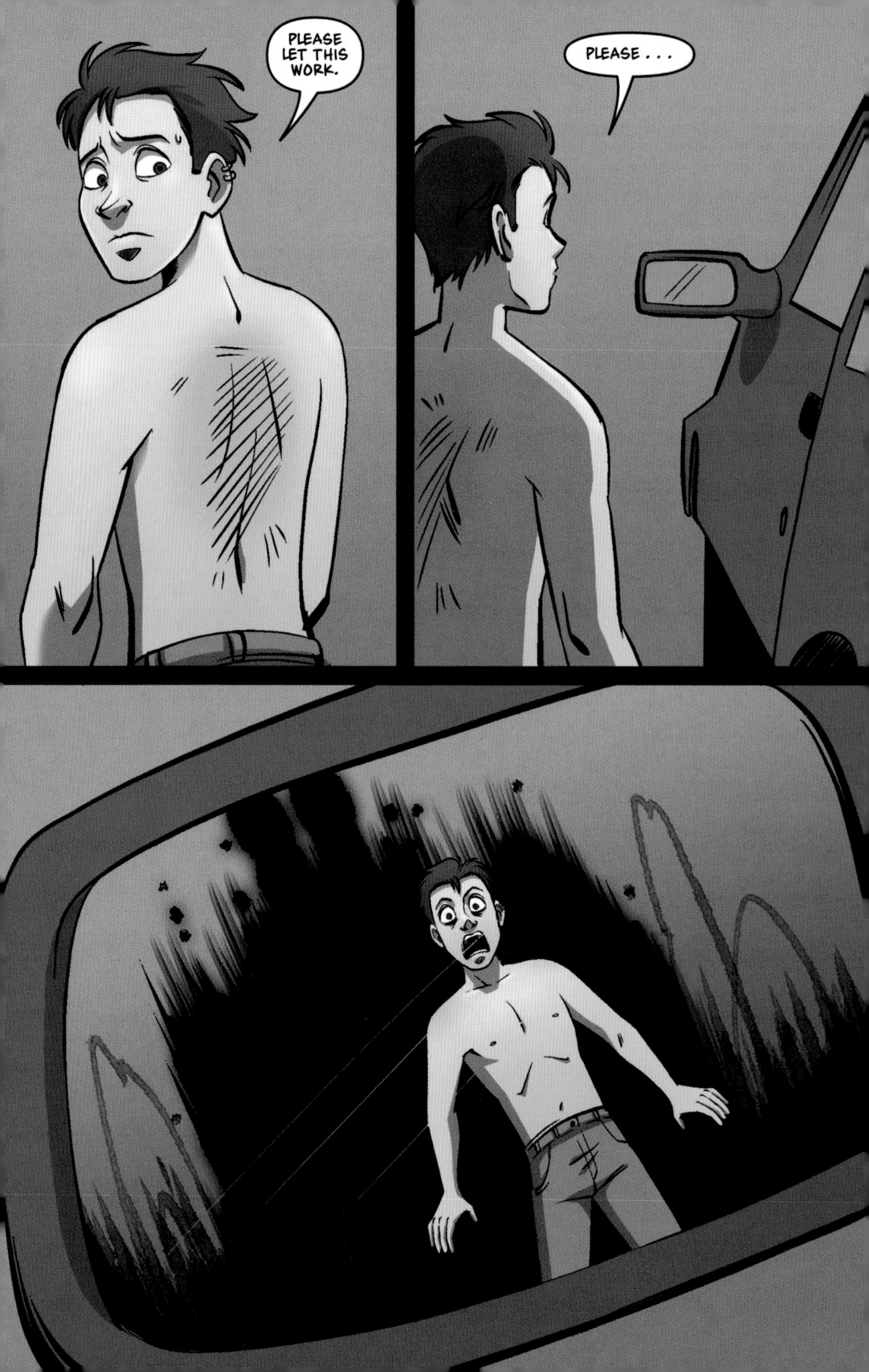
PLEASE LET THIS WORK.
PLEASE . . .

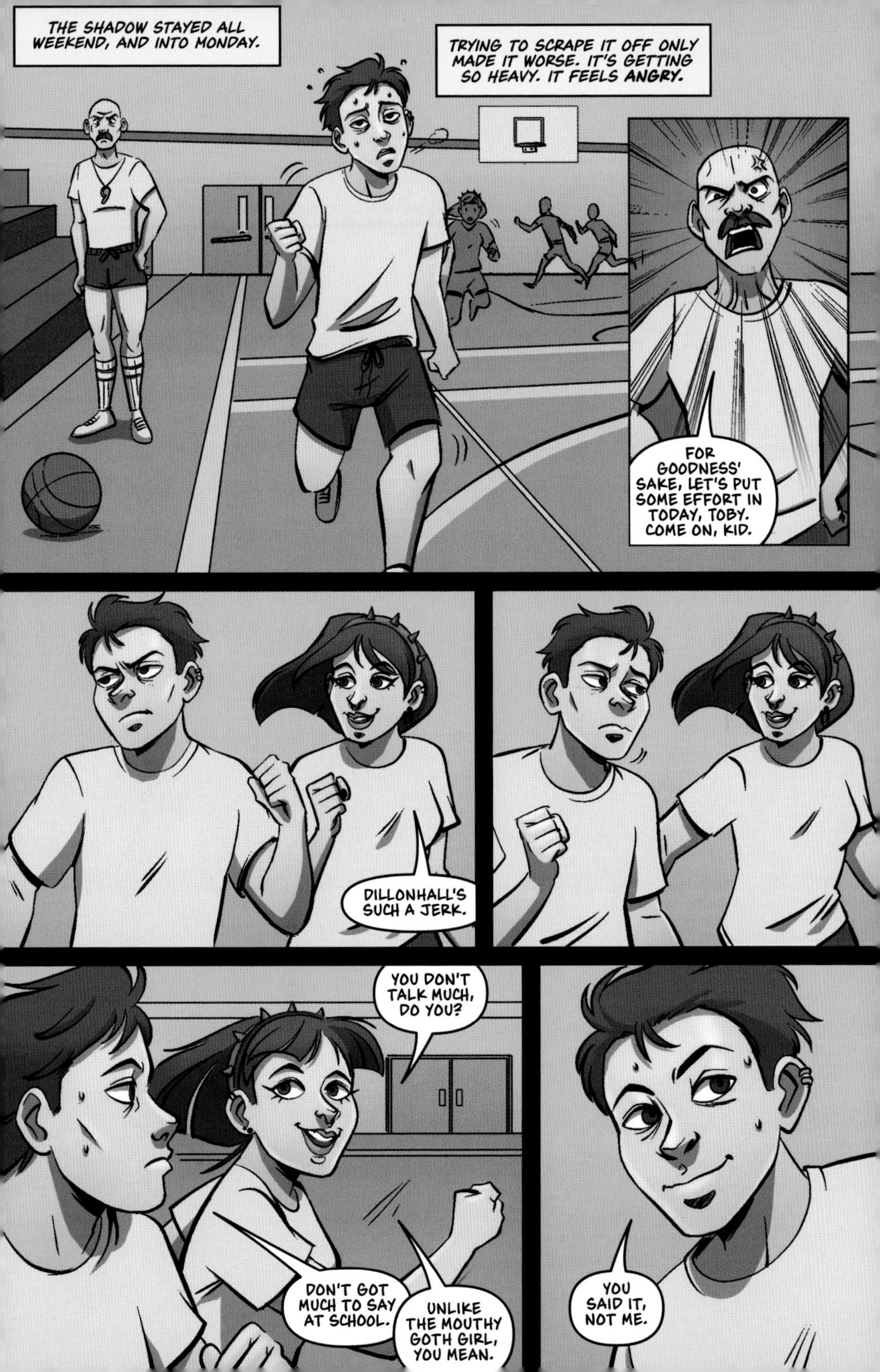
THE SHADOW STAYED ALL WEEKEND, AND INTO MONDAY.
TRYING TO SCRAPE IT OFF ONLY MADE IT WORSE. IT'S GETTING SO HEAVY. IT FEELS ANGRY.
FOR GOODNESS' SAKE, LET'S PUT SOME EFFORT IN TODAY, TOBY. COME ON, KID.
DILLONHALL'S SUCH A JERK.
YOU DON'T TALK MUCH, DO YOU?
DON'T GOT MUCH TO SAY AT SCHOOL.
UNLIKE THE MOUTHY GOTH GIRL, YOU MEAN.
YOU SAID IT, NOT ME.

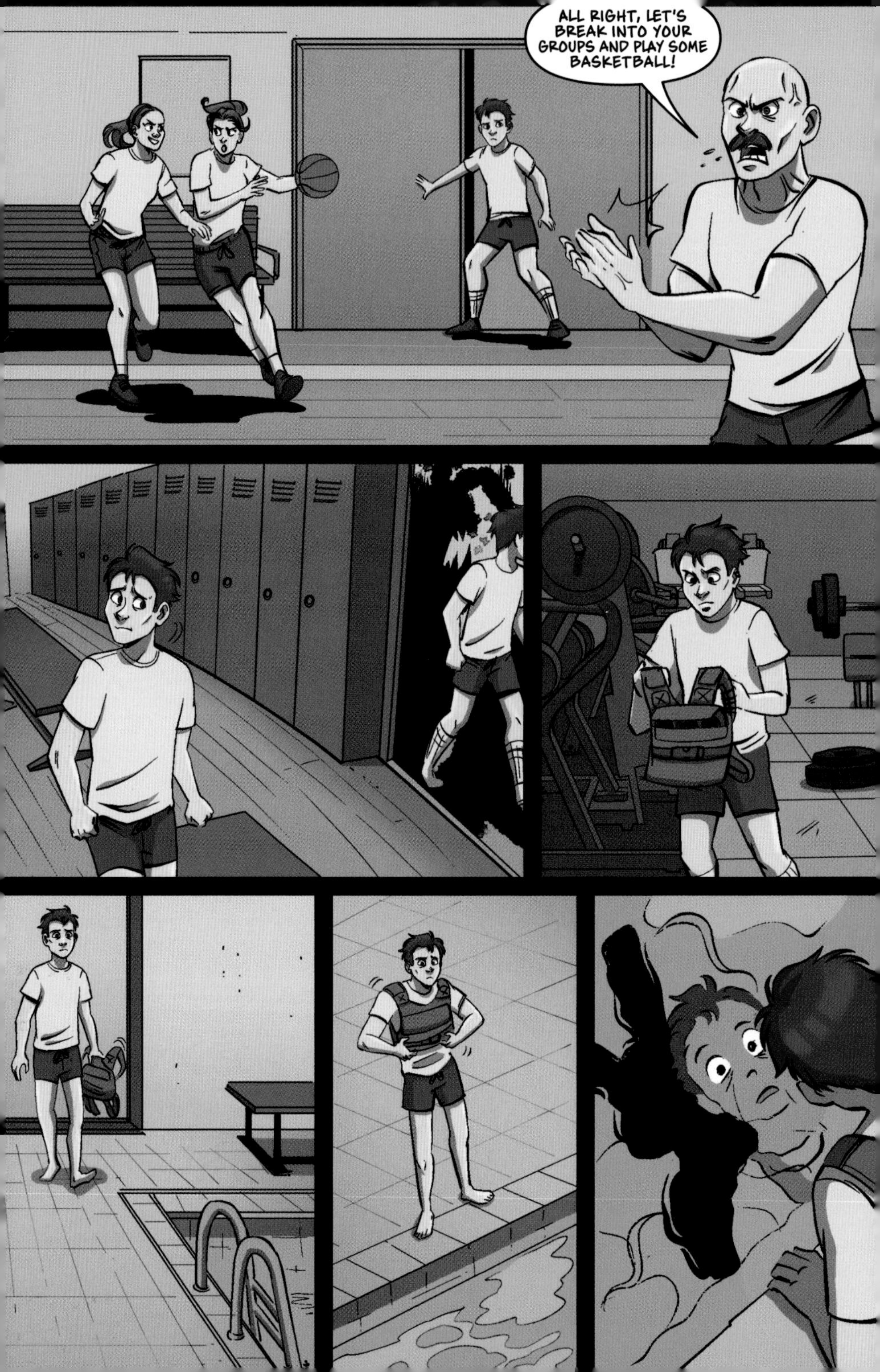
ALL RIGHT, LET'S BREAK INTO YOUR GROUPS AND PLAY SOME BASKETBALL!

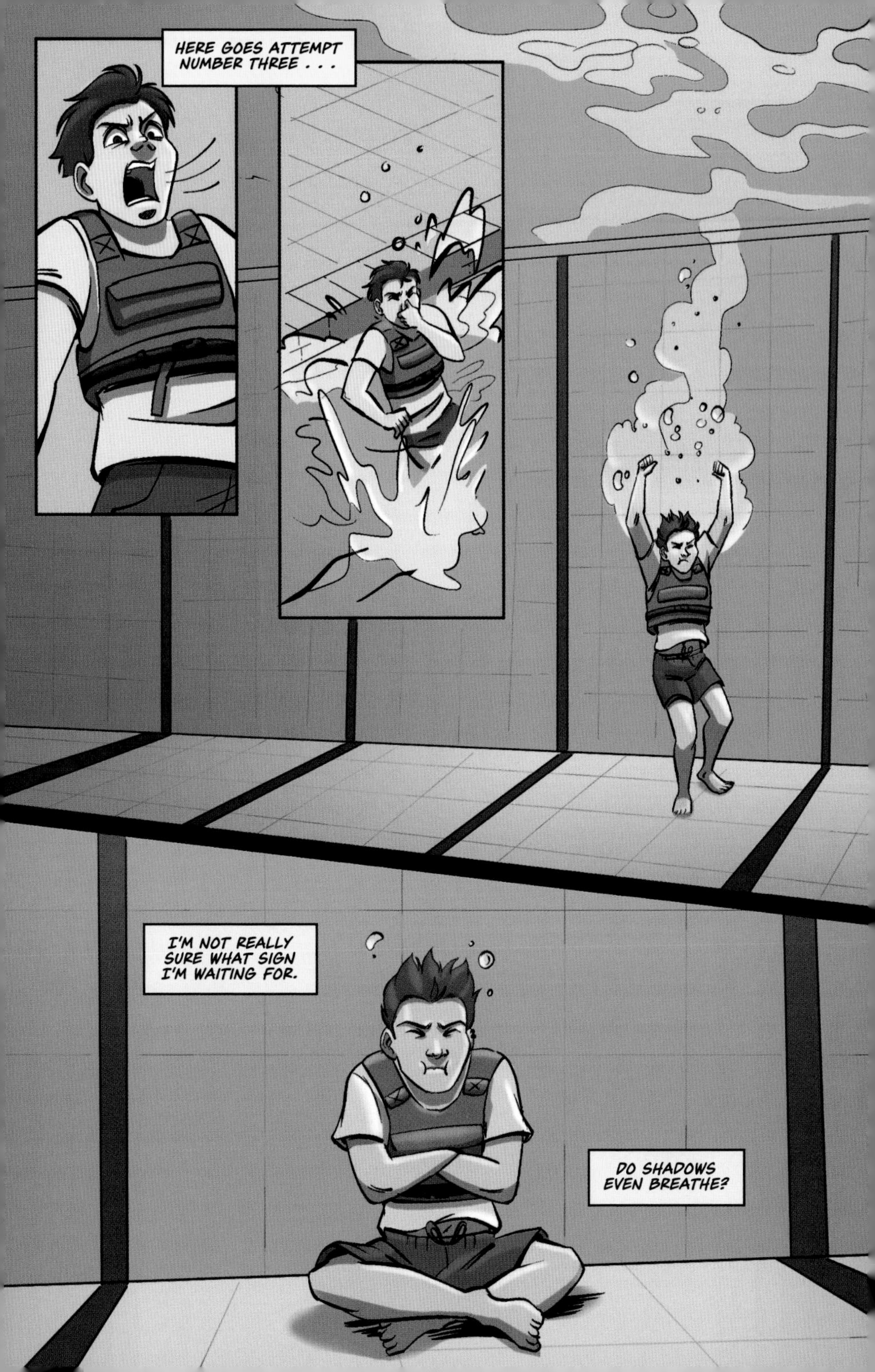
HERE GOES ATTEMPT NUMBER THREE . . .
I'M NOT REALLY SURE WHAT SIGN I'M WAITING FOR.
DO SHADOWS EVEN BREATHE?

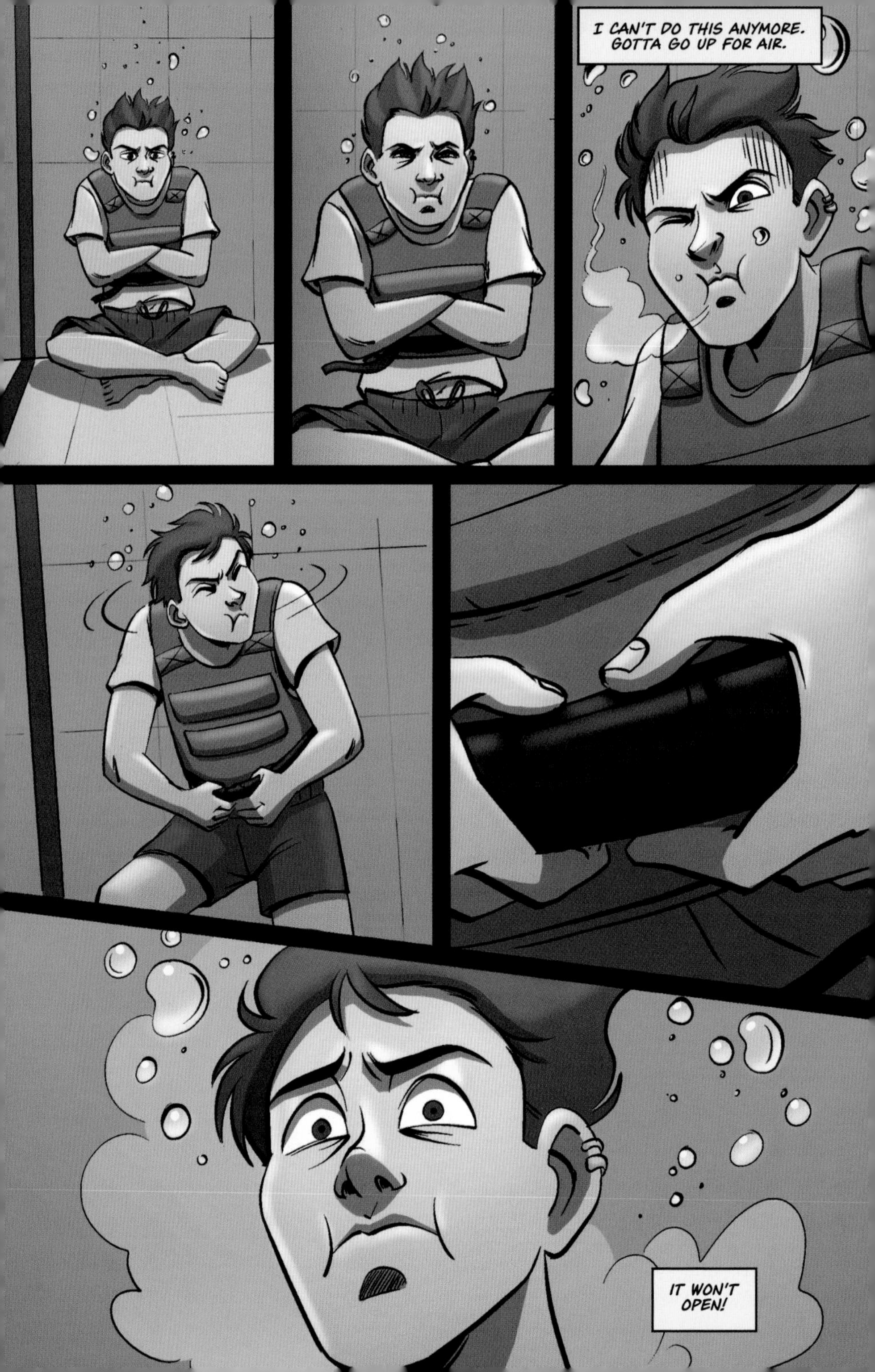
I CAN'T DO THIS ANYMORE. GOTTA GO UP FOR AIR.
IT WON'T OPEN!

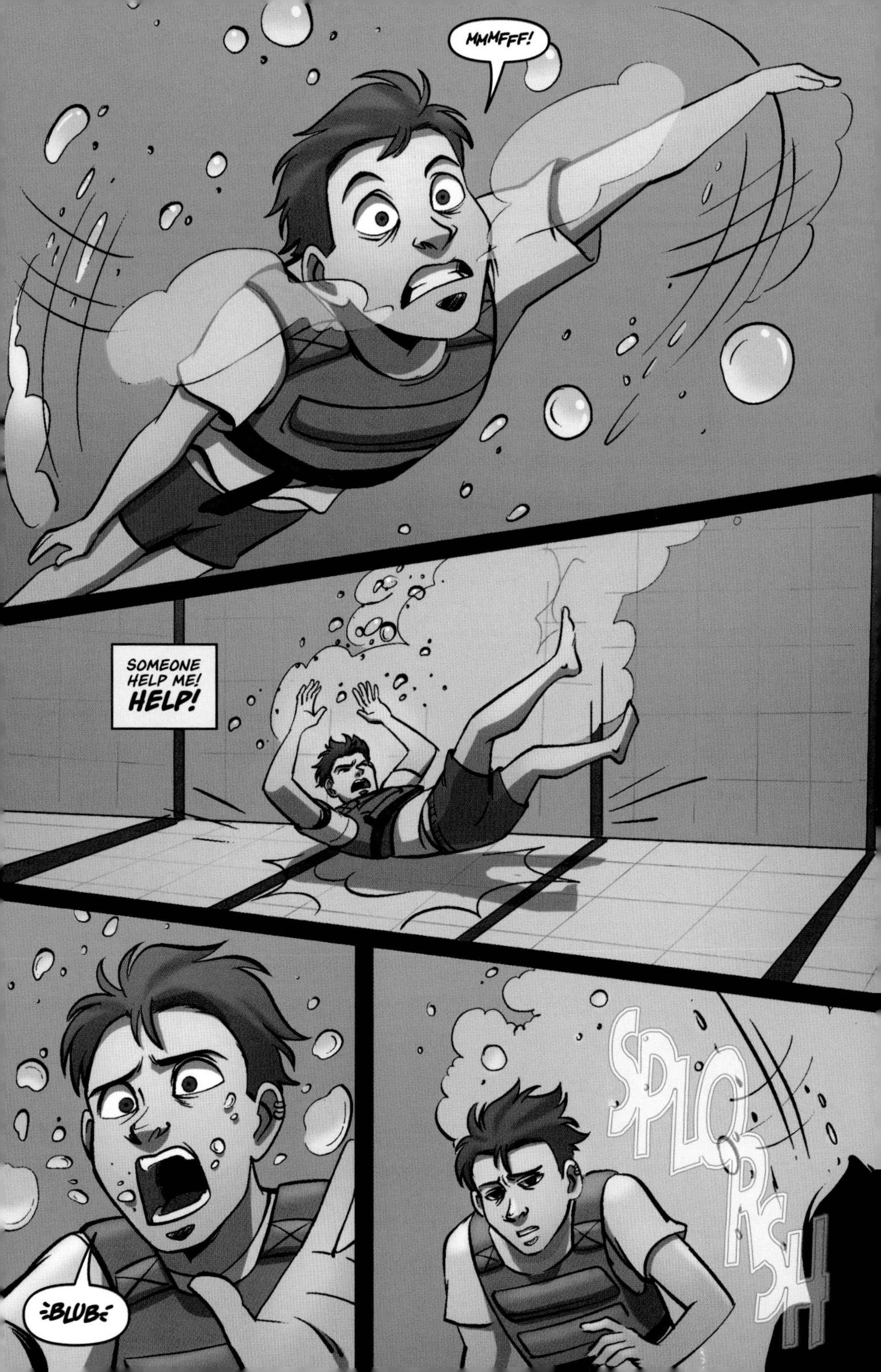
MMMFFF!
SOMEONE HELP ME! HELP!
BLUB
SPLORSH

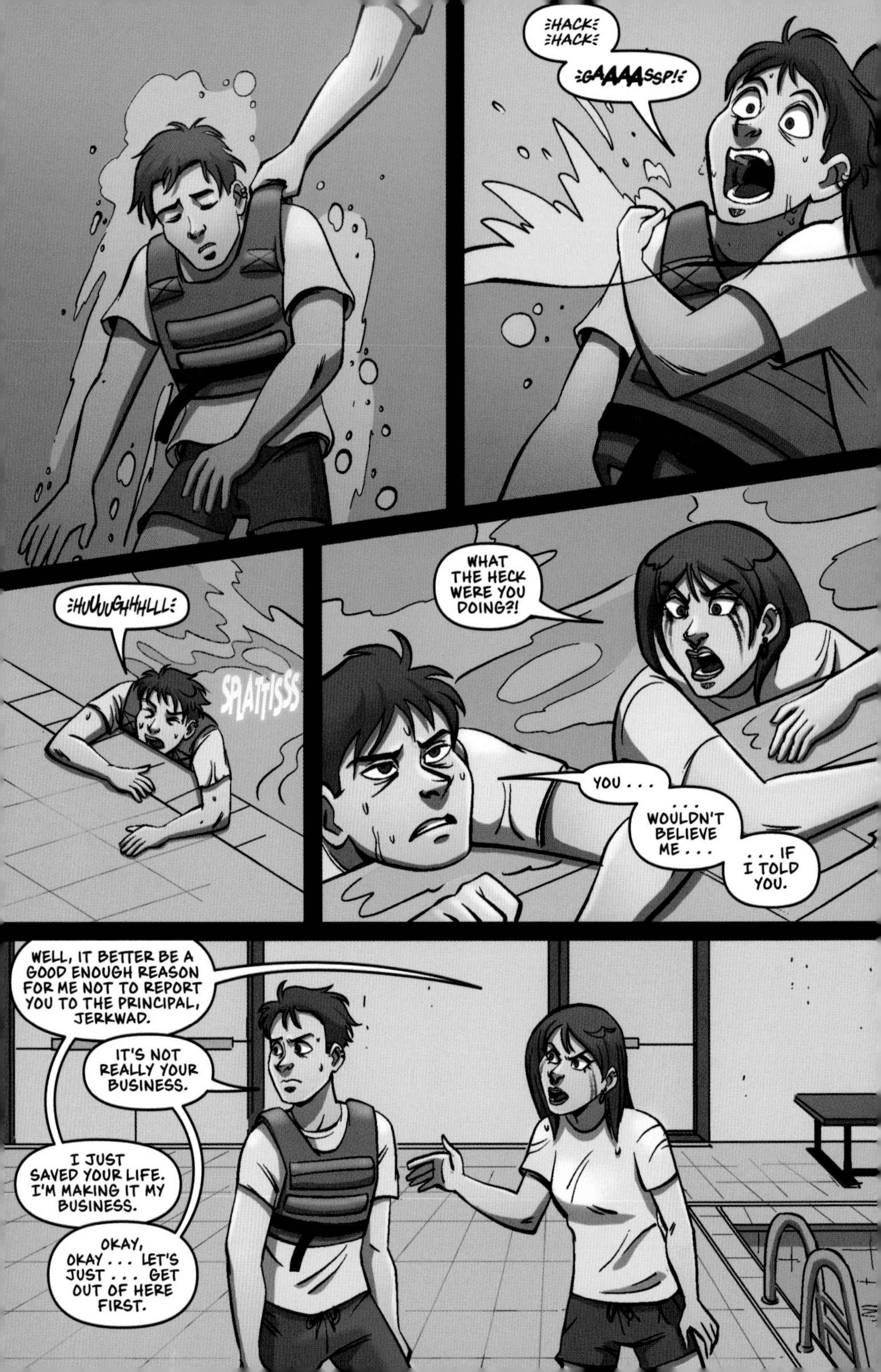
HACK
HACK
GAAAASSP!
HUUUGHHLLL
SPLATTISSS
WHAT THE HECK WERE YOU DOING?!
YOU . . .
. . . WOULDN'T BELIEVE ME . . .
. . . IF I TOLD YOU.
WELL, IT BETTER BE A GOOD ENOUGH REASON FOR ME NOT TO REPORT YOU TO THE PRINCIPAL, JERKWAD.
IT'S NOT REALLY YOUR BUSINESS.
I JUST SAVED YOUR LIFE. I'M MAKING IT MY BUSINESS.
OKAY, OKAY . . . LET'S JUST . . . GET OUT OF HERE FIRST.

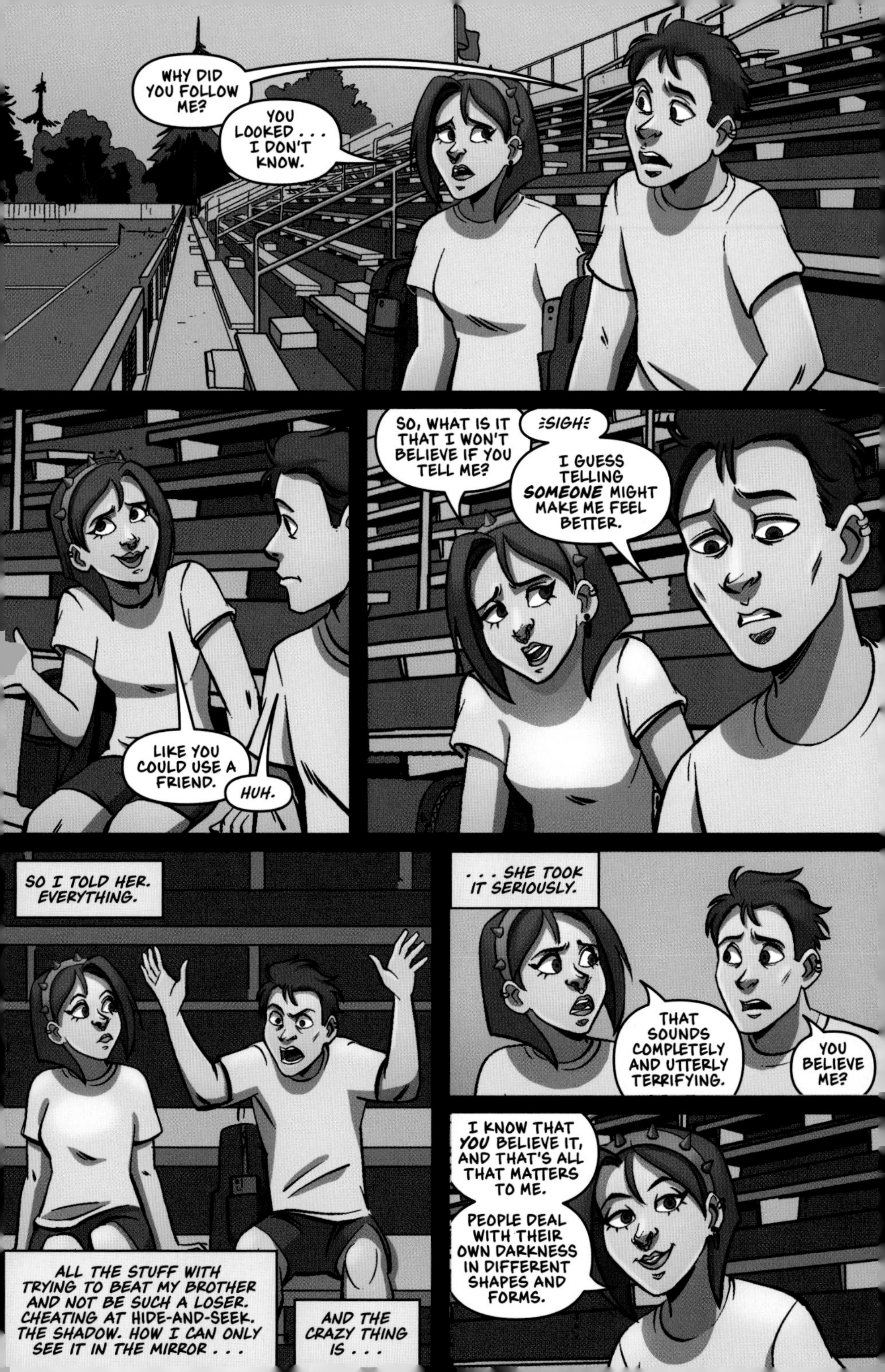
WHY DID YOU FOLLOW ME?
YOU LOOKED . . . I DON'T KNOW.
LIKE YOU COULD USE A FRIEND.
HUH.
SO, WHAT IS IT THAT I WON'T BELIEVE IF YOU TELL ME?
SIGH
I GUESS TELLING *SOMEONE* MIGHT MAKE ME FEEL BETTER.
SO I TOLD HER. EVERYTHING.
ALL THE STUFF WITH TRYING TO BEAT MY BROTHER AND NOT BE SUCH A LOSER. CHEATING AT HIDE-AND-SEEK. THE SHADOW. HOW I CAN ONLY SEE IT IN THE MIRROR . . .
AND THE CRAZY THING IS . . .
. . . SHE TOOK IT SERIOUSLY.
THAT SOUNDS COMPLETELY AND UTTERLY TERRIFYING.
YOU BELIEVE ME?
I KNOW THAT *YOU* BELIEVE IT, AND THAT'S ALL THAT MATTERS TO ME.
PEOPLE DEAL WITH THEIR OWN DARKNESS IN DIFFERENT SHAPES AND FORMS.

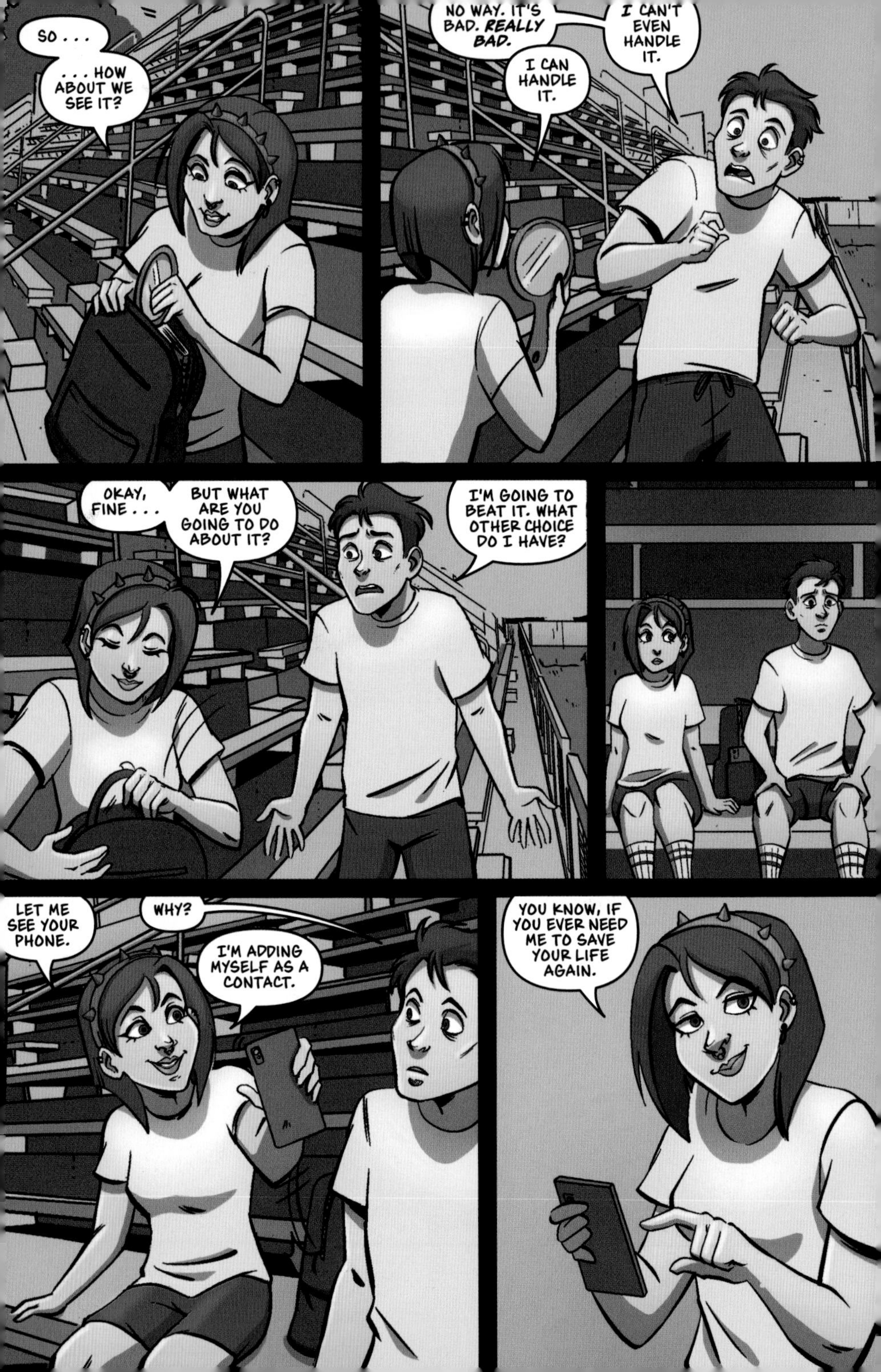
SO . . .
. . . HOW ABOUT WE SEE IT?
NO WAY. IT'S BAD. *REALLY BAD.*
I CAN HANDLE IT.
I CAN'T EVEN HANDLE IT.
OKAY, FINE . . .
BUT WHAT ARE YOU GOING TO DO ABOUT IT?
I'M GOING TO BEAT IT. WHAT OTHER CHOICE DO I HAVE?
LET ME SEE YOUR PHONE.
WHY?
I'M ADDING MYSELF AS A CONTACT.
YOU KNOW, IF YOU EVER NEED ME TO SAVE YOUR LIFE AGAIN.

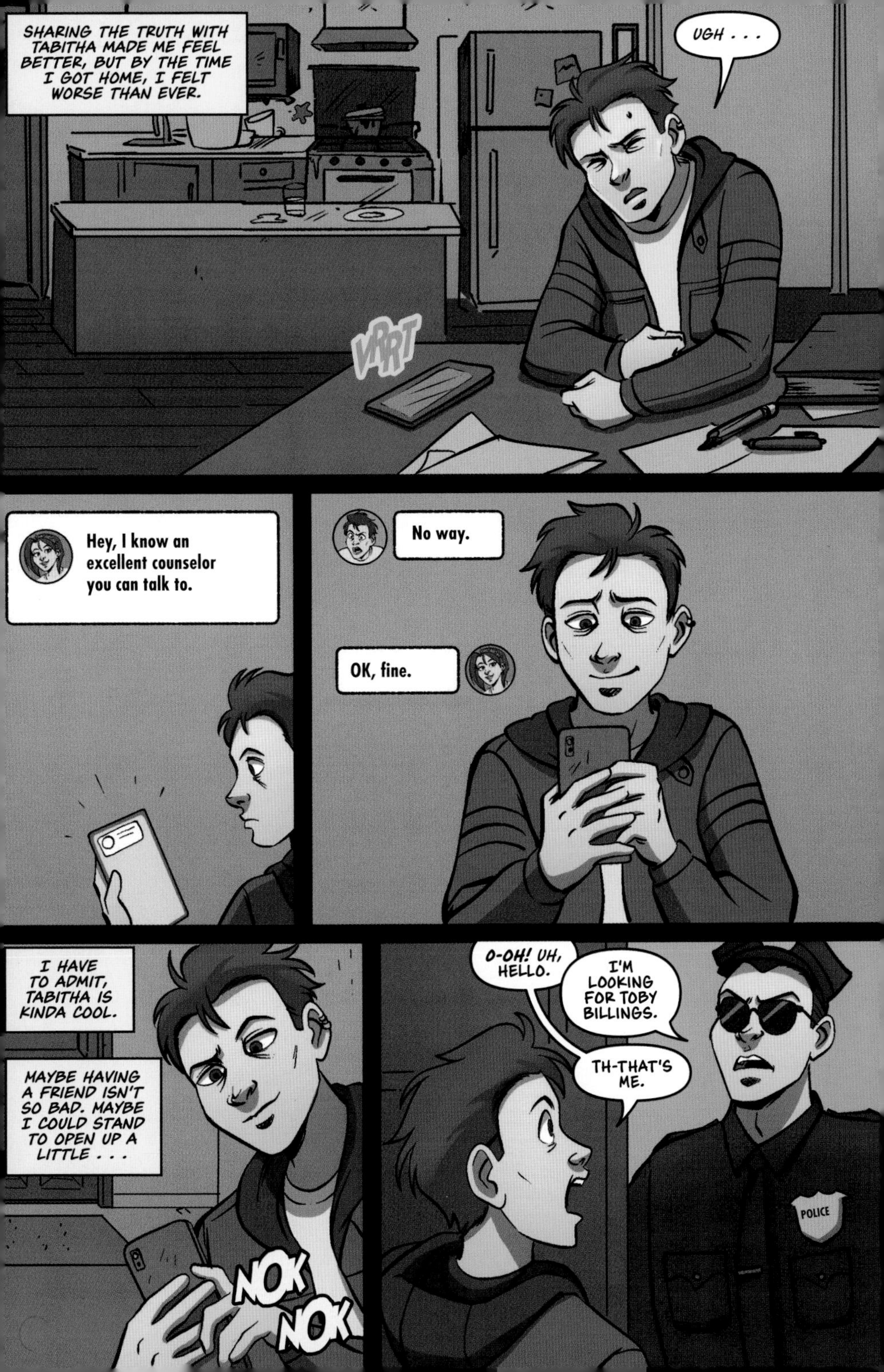
SHARING THE TRUTH WITH TABITHA MADE ME FEEL BETTER, BUT BY THE TIME I GOT HOME, I FELT WORSE THAN EVER.
UGH . . .
VRRT
Hey, I know an excellent counselor you can talk to.
No way.
OK, fine.
I HAVE TO ADMIT, TABITHA IS KINDA COOL.
MAYBE HAVING A FRIEND ISN'T SO BAD. MAYBE I COULD STAND TO OPEN UP A LITTLE . . .
NOK
NOK
O-OH! UH, HELLO.
I'M LOOKING FOR TOBY BILLINGS.
TH-THAT'S ME.
POLICE

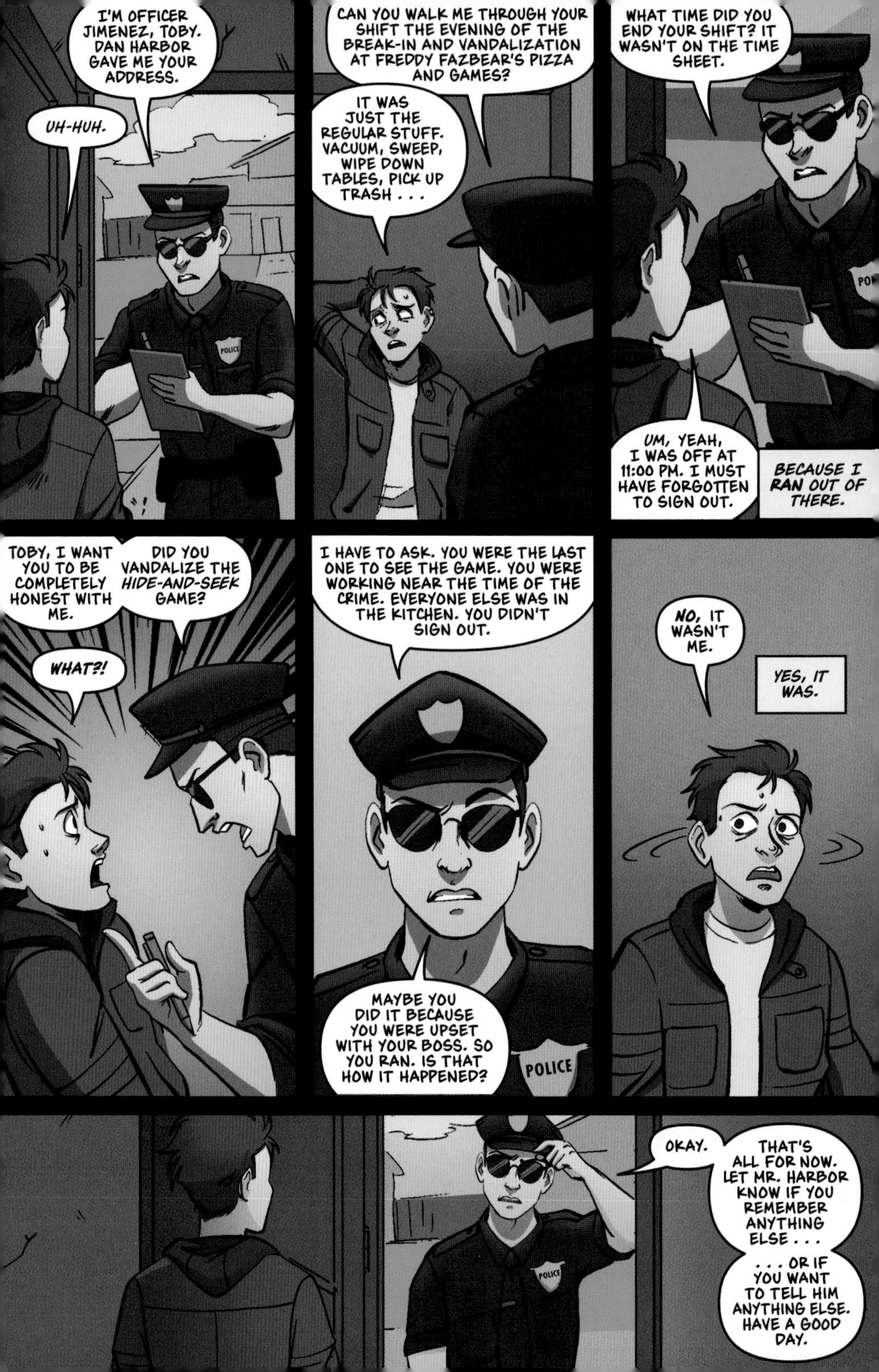

I'M OFFICER JIMENEZ, TOBY. DAN HARBOR GAVE ME YOUR ADDRESS.
UH-HUH.
CAN YOU WALK ME THROUGH YOUR SHIFT THE EVENING OF THE BREAK-IN AND VANDALIZATION AT FREDDY FAZBEAR'S PIZZA AND GAMES?
IT WAS JUST THE REGULAR STUFF. VACUUM, SWEEP, WIPE DOWN TABLES, PICK UP TRASH . . .
WHAT TIME DID YOU END YOUR SHIFT? IT WASN'T ON THE TIME SHEET.
UM, YEAH, I WAS OFF AT 11:00 PM. I MUST HAVE FORGOTTEN TO SIGN OUT.
BECAUSE I *RAN* OUT OF THERE.
TOBY, I WANT YOU TO BE COMPLETELY HONEST WITH ME.
DID YOU VANDALIZE THE *HIDE-AND-SEEK* GAME?
WHAT?!
I HAVE TO ASK. YOU WERE THE LAST ONE TO SEE THE GAME. YOU WERE WORKING NEAR THE TIME OF THE CRIME. EVERYONE ELSE WAS IN THE KITCHEN. YOU DIDN'T SIGN OUT.
MAYBE YOU DID IT BECAUSE YOU WERE UPSET WITH YOUR BOSS. SO YOU RAN. IS THAT HOW IT HAPPENED?
POLICE
NO, IT WASN'T ME.
YES, IT WAS.
OKAY.
THAT'S ALL FOR NOW. LET MR. HARBOR KNOW IF YOU REMEMBER ANYTHING ELSE . . .
. . . OR IF YOU WANT TO TELL HIM ANYTHING ELSE. HAVE A GOOD DAY.

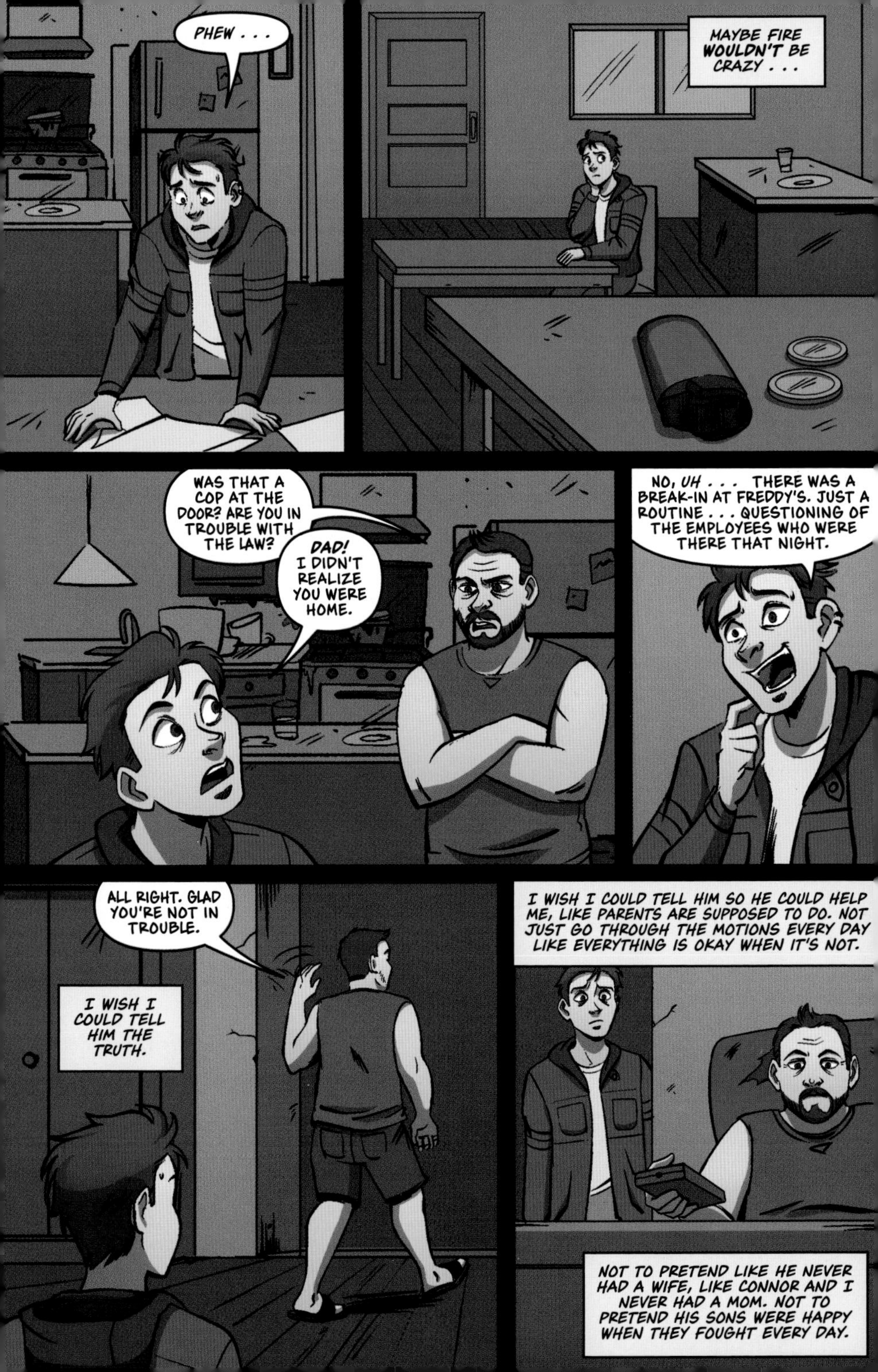
PHEW . . .
MAYBE FIRE WOULDN'T BE CRAZY . . .
WAS THAT A COP AT THE DOOR? ARE YOU IN TROUBLE WITH THE LAW?
DAD! I DIDN'T REALIZE YOU WERE HOME.
NO, UH . . . THERE WAS A BREAK-IN AT FREDDY'S. JUST A ROUTINE . . . QUESTIONING OF THE EMPLOYEES WHO WERE THERE THAT NIGHT.
ALL RIGHT. GLAD YOU'RE NOT IN TROUBLE.
I WISH I COULD TELL HIM THE TRUTH.
I WISH I COULD TELL HIM SO HE COULD HELP ME, LIKE PARENTS ARE SUPPOSED TO DO. NOT JUST GO THROUGH THE MOTIONS EVERY DAY LIKE EVERYTHING IS OKAY WHEN IT'S NOT.
NOT TO PRETEND LIKE HE NEVER HAD A WIFE, LIKE CONNOR AND I NEVER HAD A MOM. NOT TO PRETEND HIS SONS WERE HAPPY WHEN THEY FOUGHT EVERY DAY.

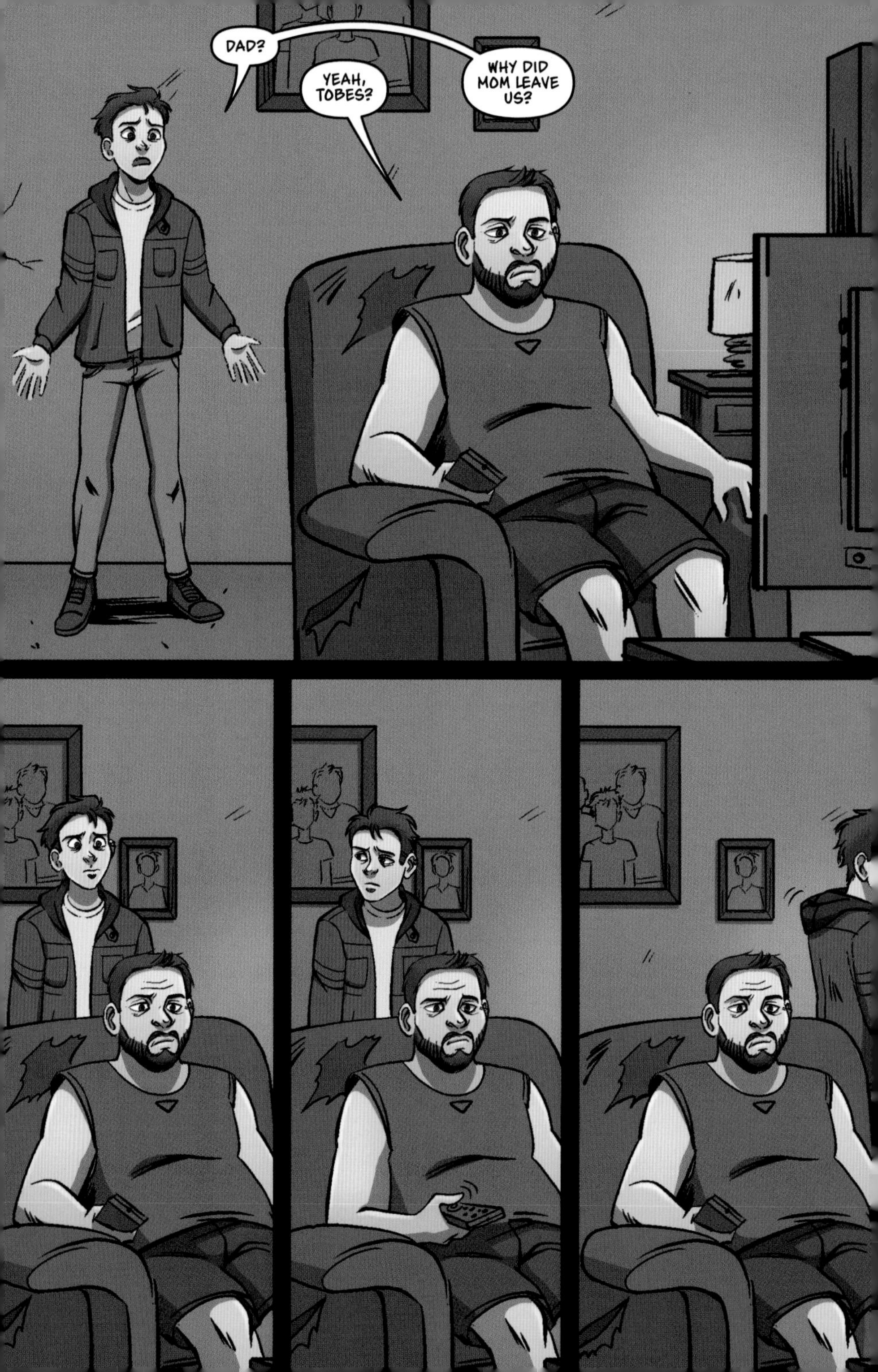
DAD?
YEAH, TOBES?
WHY DID MOM LEAVE US?

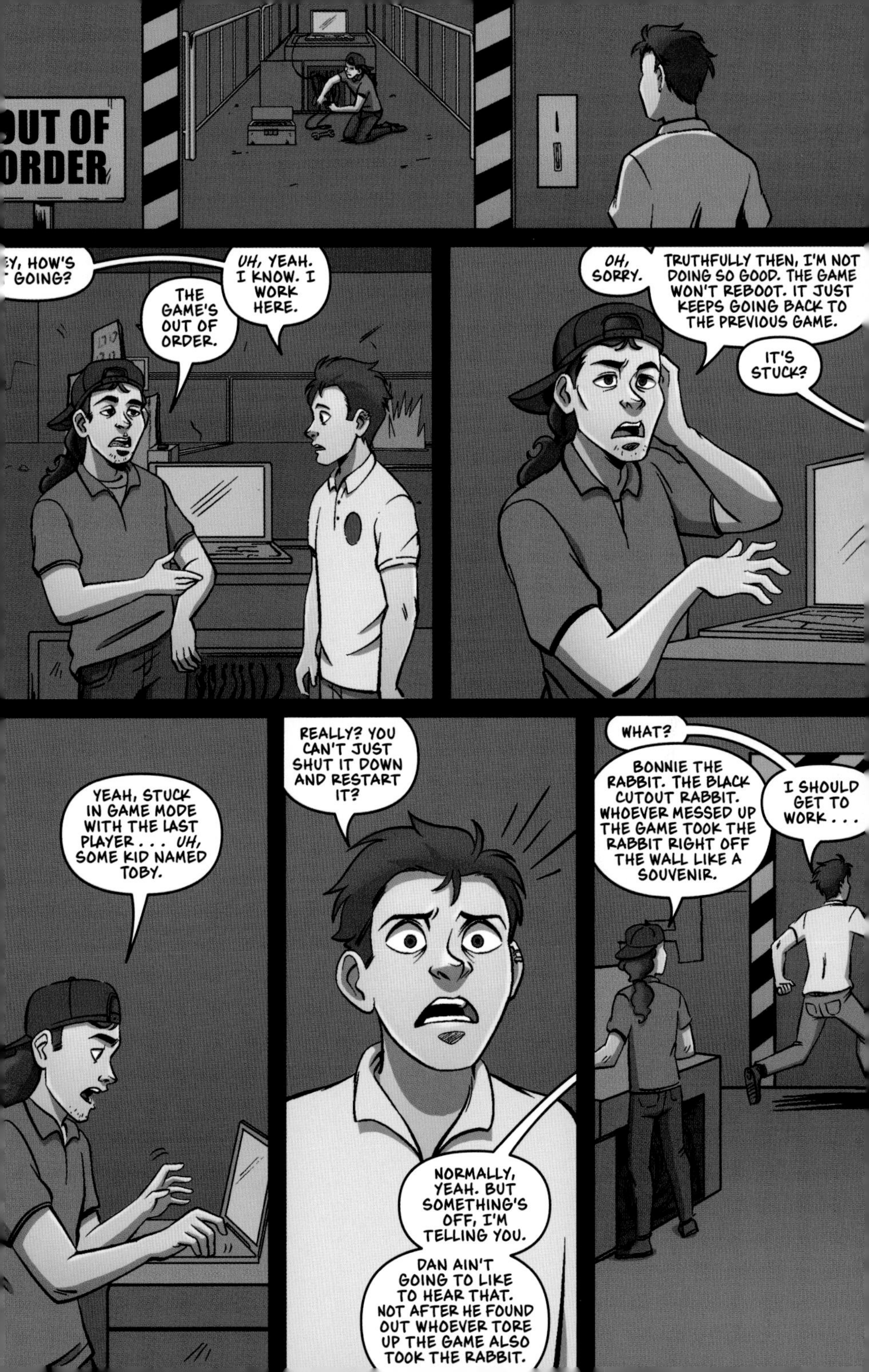
OUT OF ORDER
EY, HOW'S IT GOING?
THE GAME'S OUT OF ORDER.
UH, YEAH. I KNOW. I WORK HERE.
OH, SORRY.
TRUTHFULLY THEN, I'M NOT DOING SO GOOD. THE GAME WON'T REBOOT. IT JUST KEEPS GOING BACK TO THE PREVIOUS GAME.
IT'S STUCK?
YEAH, STUCK IN GAME MODE WITH THE LAST PLAYER . . . UH, SOME KID NAMED TOBY.
REALLY? YOU CAN'T JUST SHUT IT DOWN AND RESTART IT?
NORMALLY, YEAH. BUT SOMETHING'S OFF, I'M TELLING YOU.
DAN AIN'T GOING TO LIKE TO HEAR THAT. NOT AFTER HE FOUND OUT WHOEVER TORE UP THE GAME ALSO TOOK THE RABBIT.
WHAT?
BONNIE THE RABBIT. THE BLACK CUTOUT RABBIT. WHOEVER MESSED UP THE GAME TOOK THE RABBIT RIGHT OFF THE WALL LIKE A SOUVENIR.
I SHOULD GET TO WORK . . .

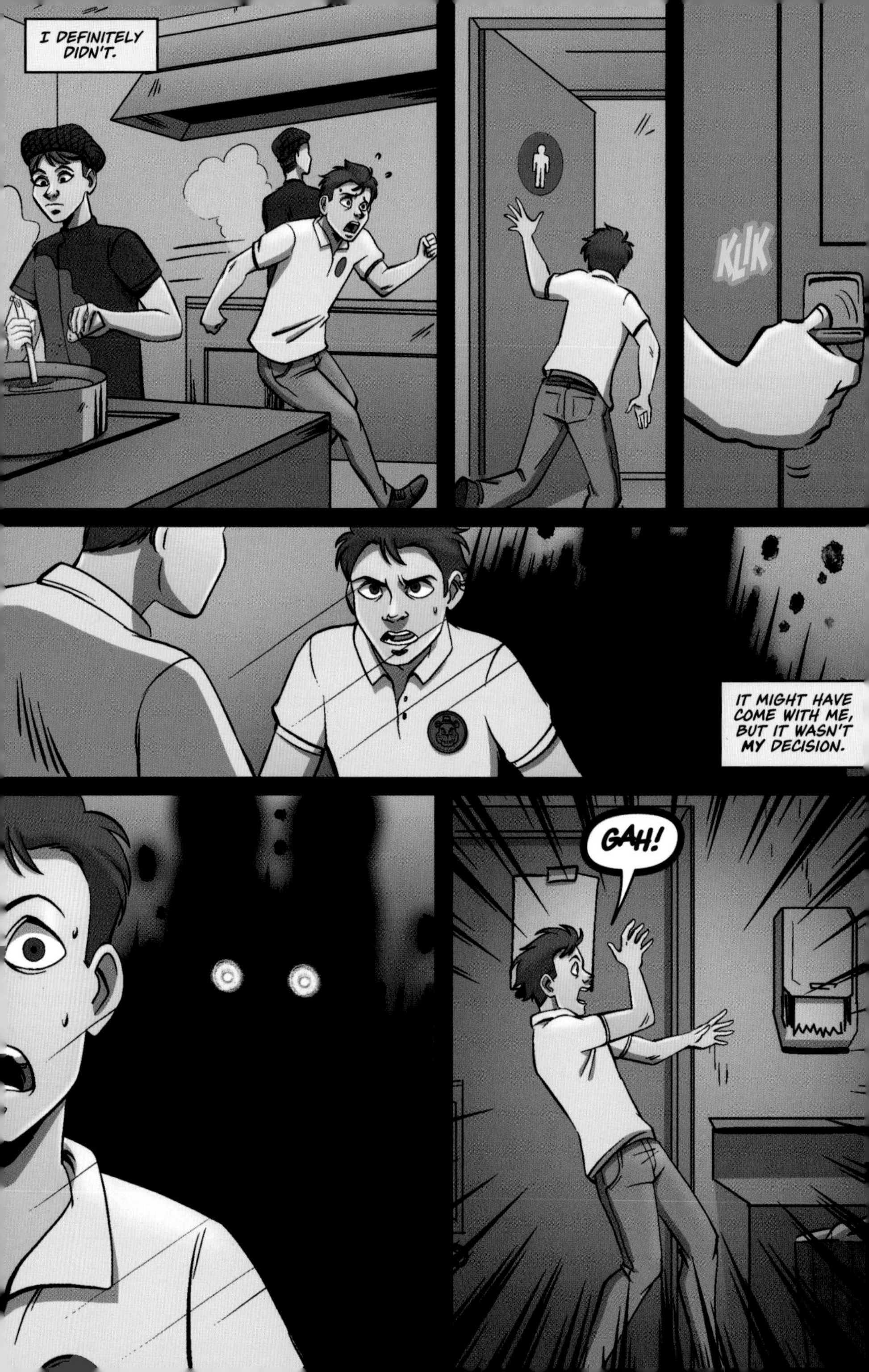
I DEFINITELY DIDN'T.
KLIK
IT MIGHT HAVE COME WITH ME, BUT IT WASN'T MY DECISION.
GAH!

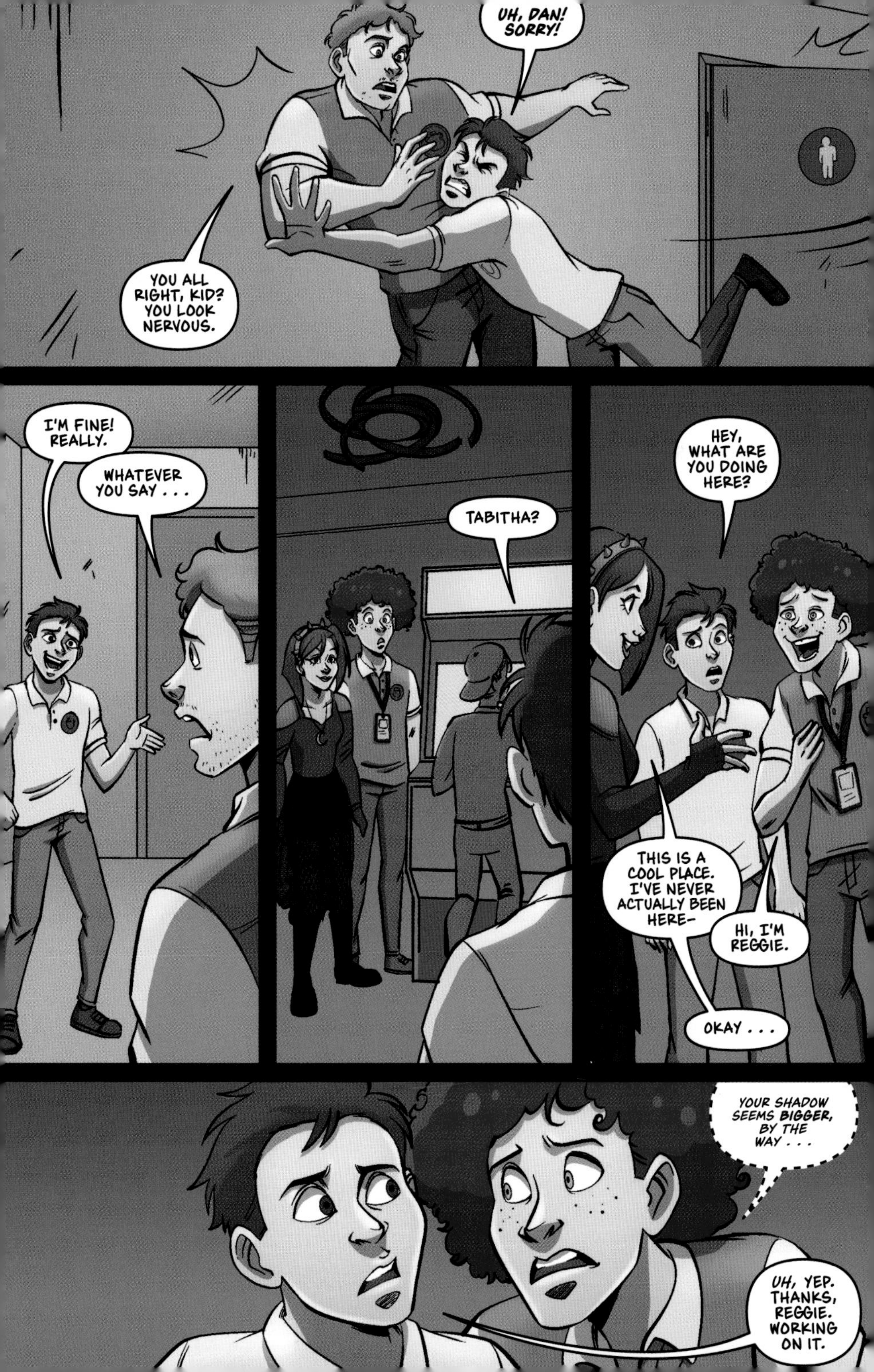
UH, DAN! SORRY!
YOU ALL RIGHT, KID? YOU LOOK NERVOUS.
I'M FINE! REALLY.
WHATEVER YOU SAY . . .
TABITHA?
HEY, WHAT ARE YOU DOING HERE?
THIS IS A COOL PLACE. I'VE NEVER ACTUALLY BEEN HERE-
HI, I'M REGGIE.
OKAY . . .
YOUR SHADOW SEEMS BIGGER, BY THE WAY . . .
UH, YEP. THANKS, REGGIE. WORKING ON IT.

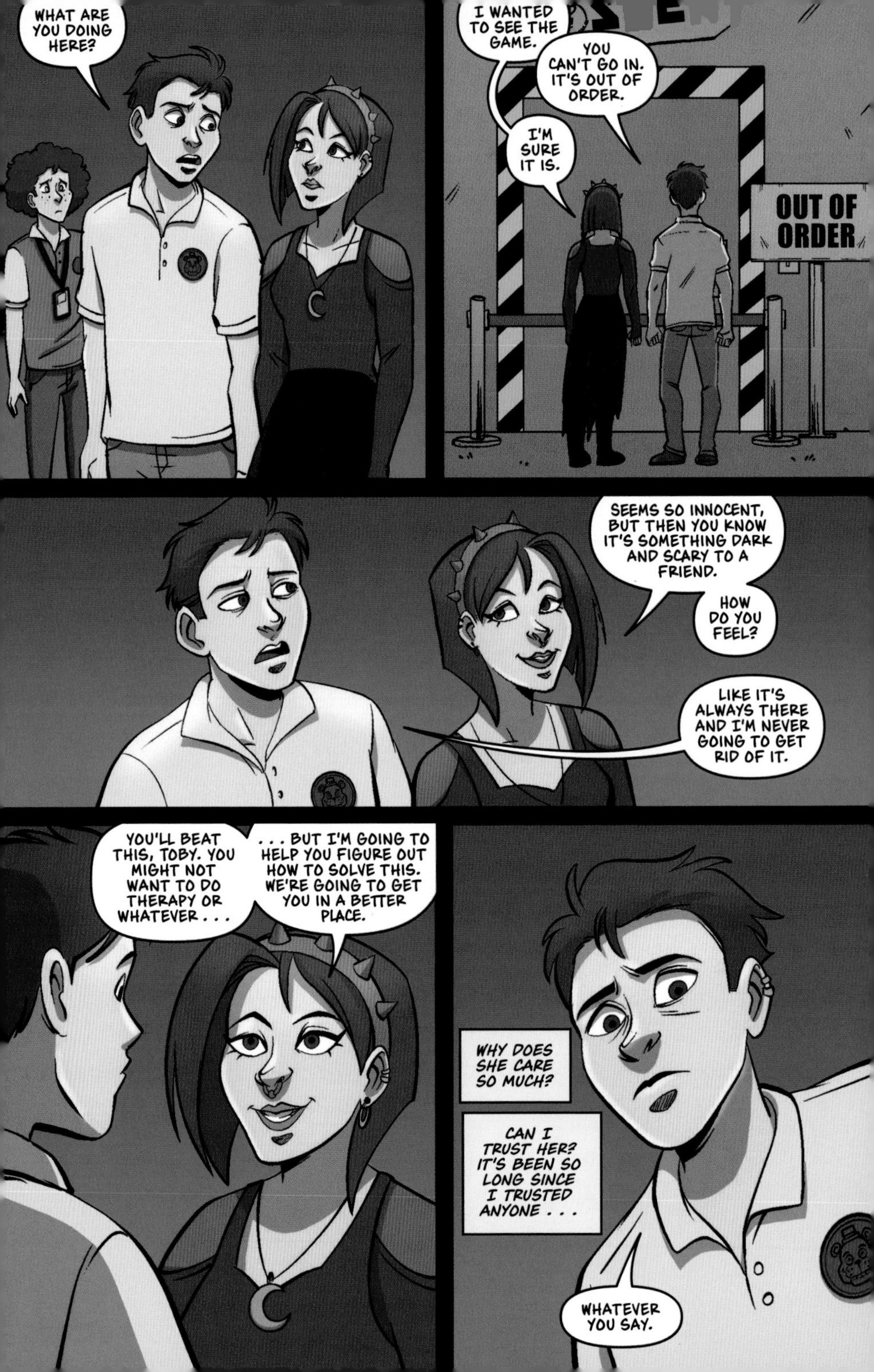
WHAT ARE YOU DOING HERE?
I WANTED TO SEE THE GAME.
YOU CAN'T GO IN. IT'S OUT OF ORDER.
I'M SURE IT IS.
OUT OF ORDER
SEEMS SO INNOCENT, BUT THEN YOU KNOW IT'S SOMETHING DARK AND SCARY TO A FRIEND.
HOW DO YOU FEEL?
LIKE IT'S ALWAYS THERE AND I'M NEVER GOING TO GET RID OF IT.
YOU'LL BEAT THIS, TOBY. YOU MIGHT NOT WANT TO DO THERAPY OR WHATEVER . . .
. . . BUT I'M GOING TO HELP YOU FIGURE OUT HOW TO SOLVE THIS. WE'RE GOING TO GET YOU IN A BETTER PLACE.
WHY DOES SHE CARE SO MUCH?
CAN I TRUST HER? IT'S BEEN SO LONG SINCE I TRUSTED ANYONE . . .
WHATEVER YOU SAY.

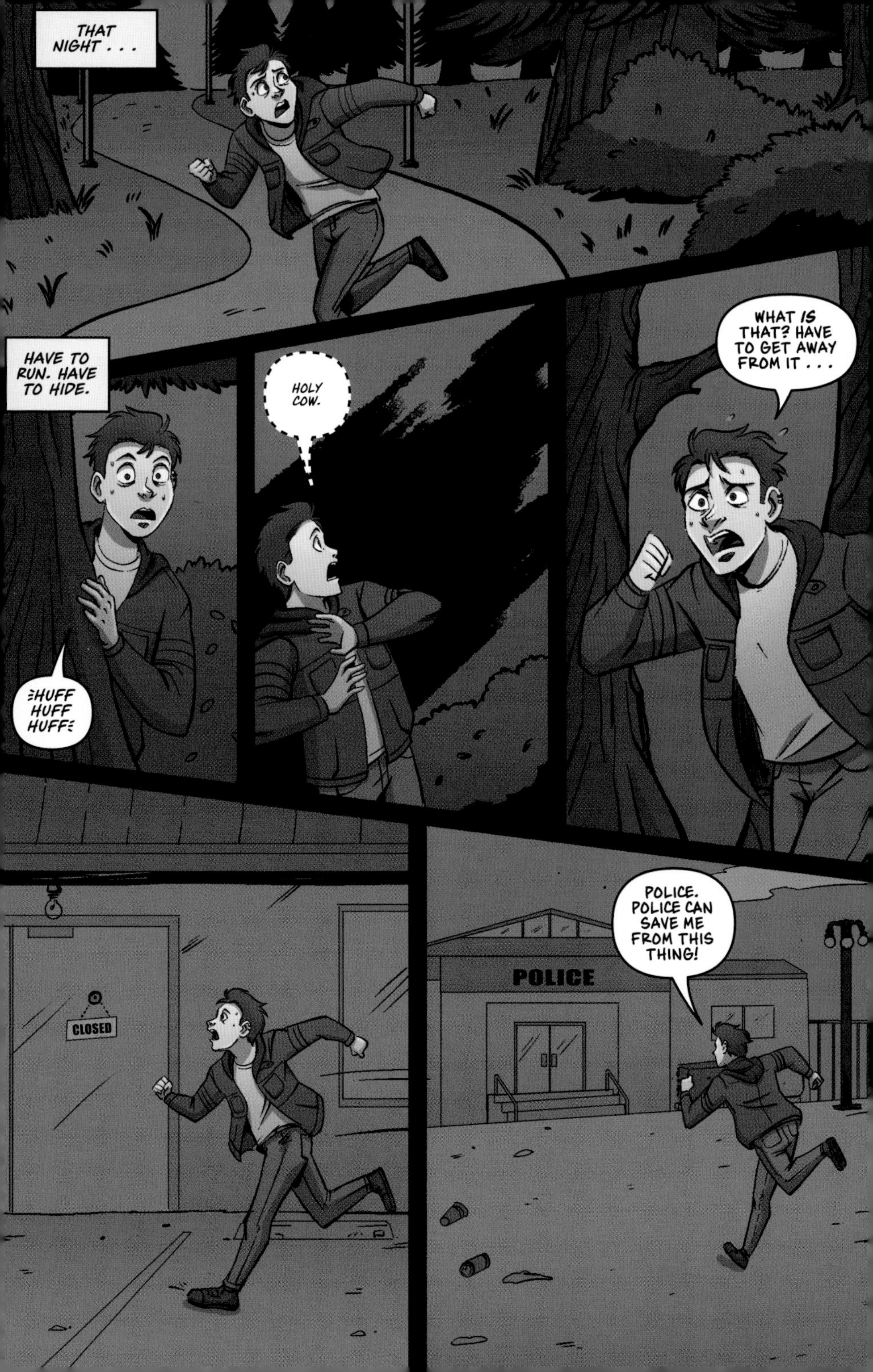
THAT NIGHT . . .
HAVE TO RUN. HAVE TO HIDE.
HUFF HUFF HUFF
HOLY COW.
WHAT IS THAT? HAVE TO GET AWAY FROM IT . . .
CLOSED
POLICE
POLICE. POLICE CAN SAVE ME FROM THIS THING!

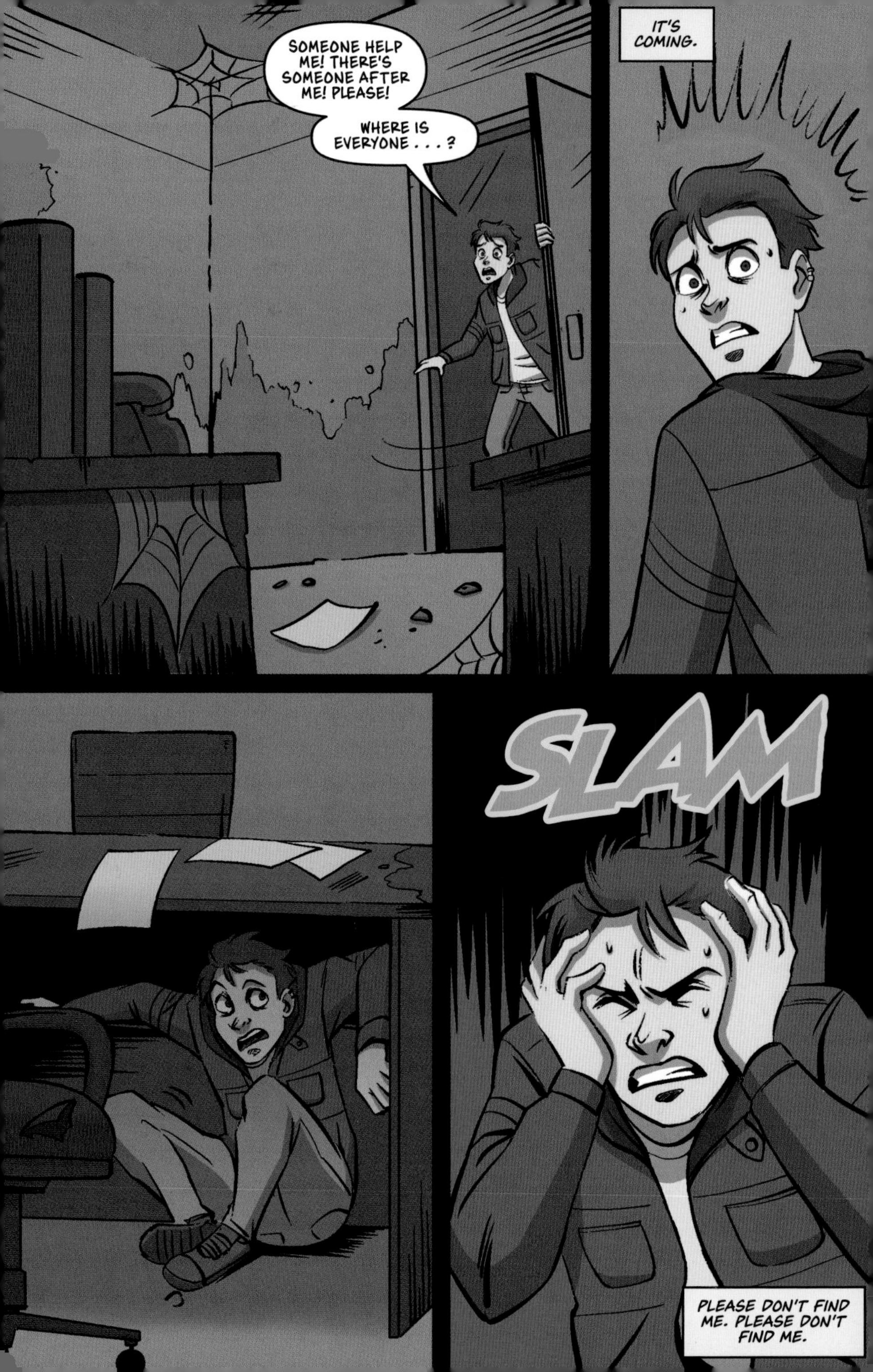
SOMEONE HELP ME! THERE'S SOMEONE AFTER ME! PLEASE!
WHERE IS EVERYONE . . . ?
IT'S COMING.
SLAM
PLEASE DON'T FIND ME. PLEASE DON'T FIND ME.

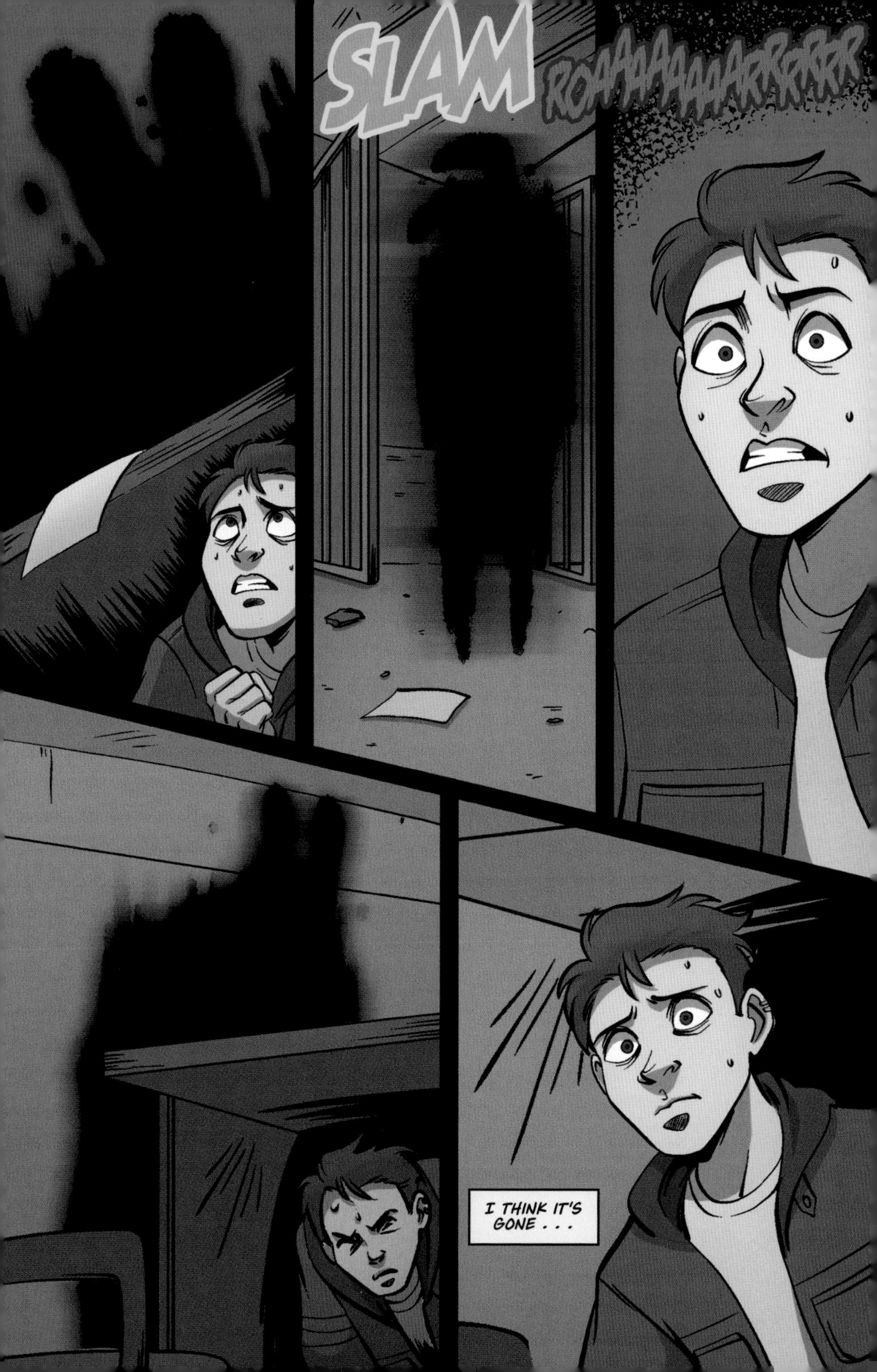
SLAM
ROAAAAAAARRRRR
I THINK IT'S GONE . . .

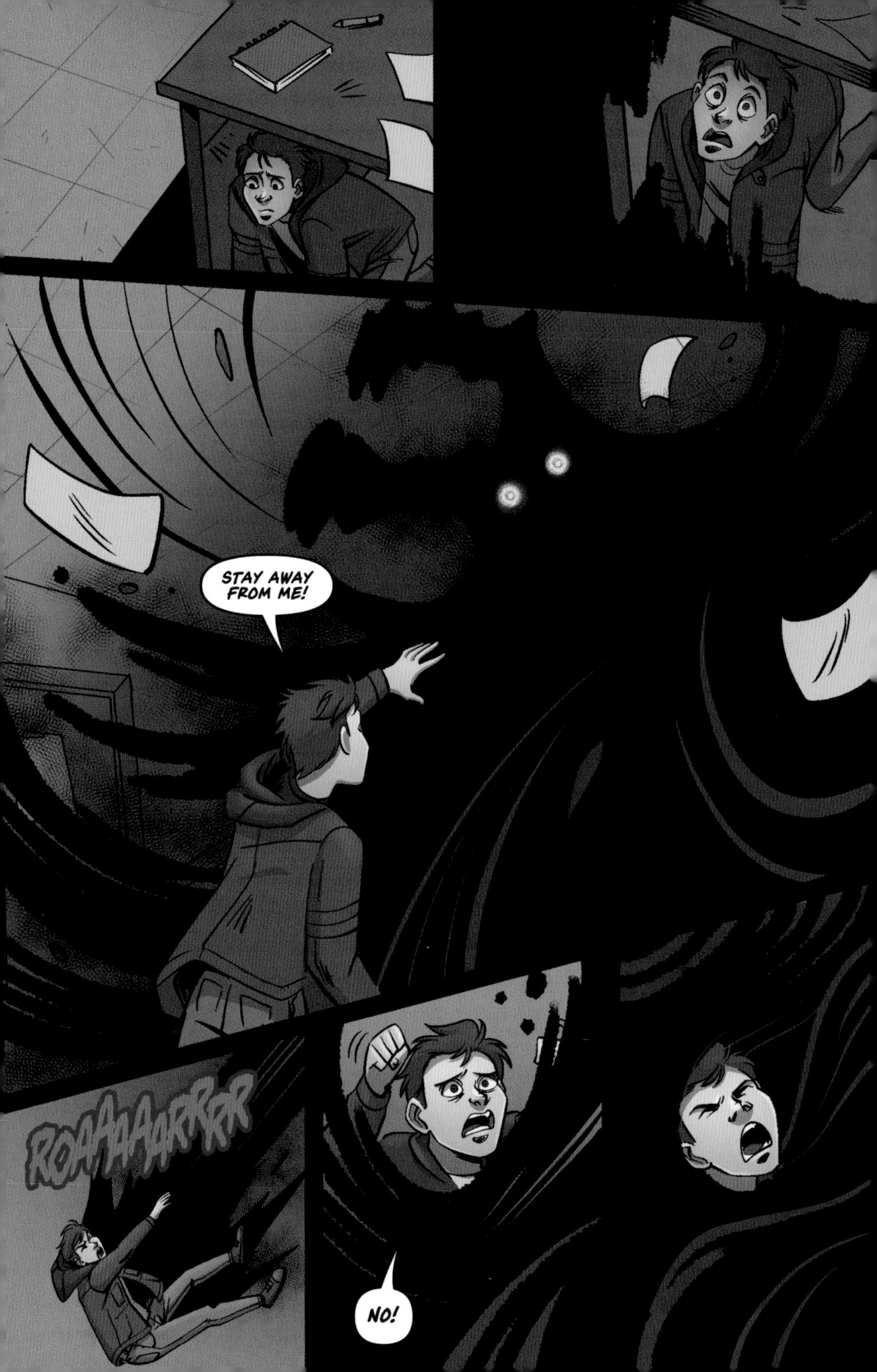
STAY AWAY FROM ME!
ROAAAAARRRR
NO!

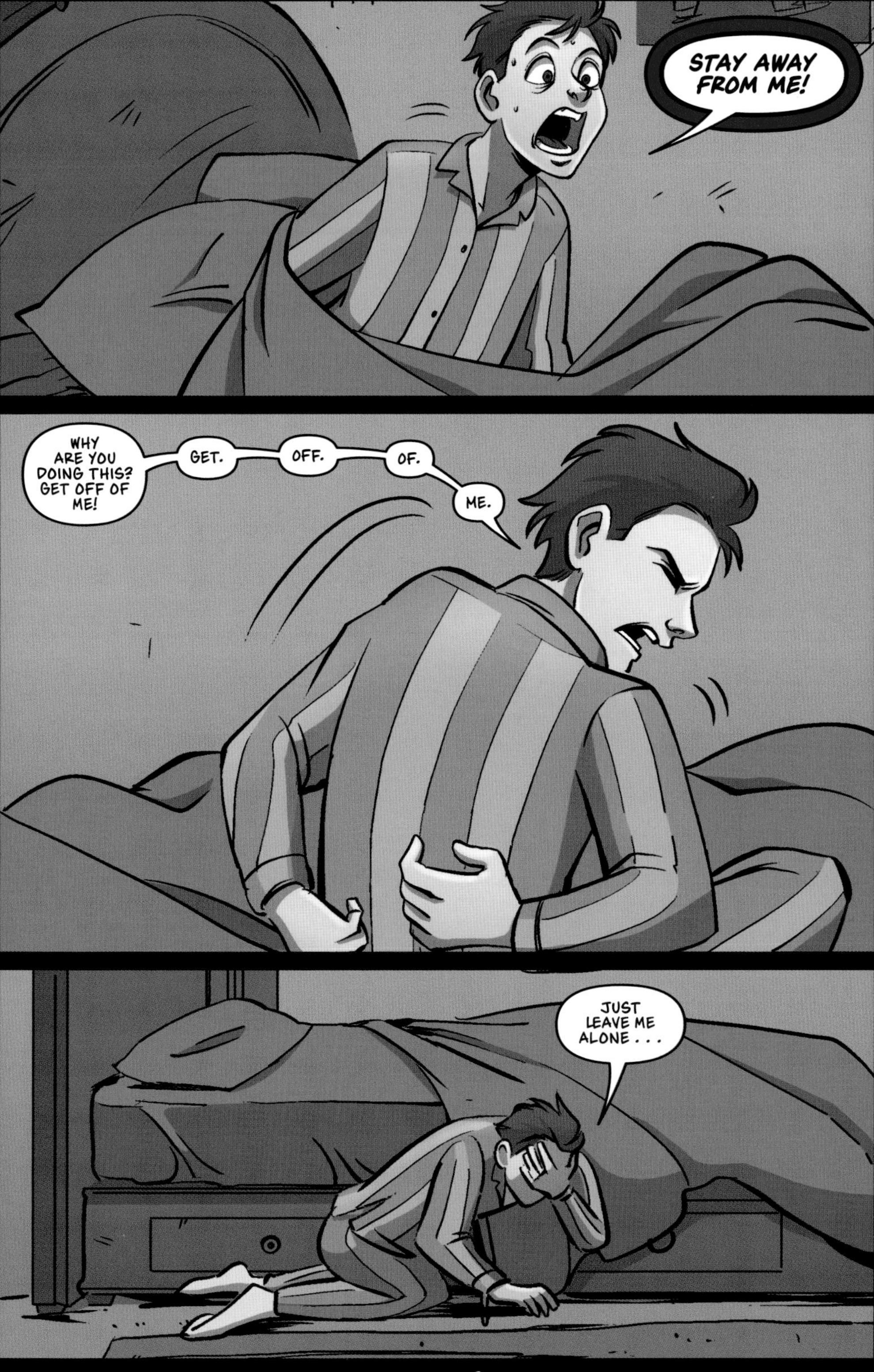
STAY AWAY FROM ME!
WHY ARE YOU DOING THIS? GET OFF OF ME!
GET.
OFF.
OF.
ME.
JUST LEAVE ME ALONE . . .

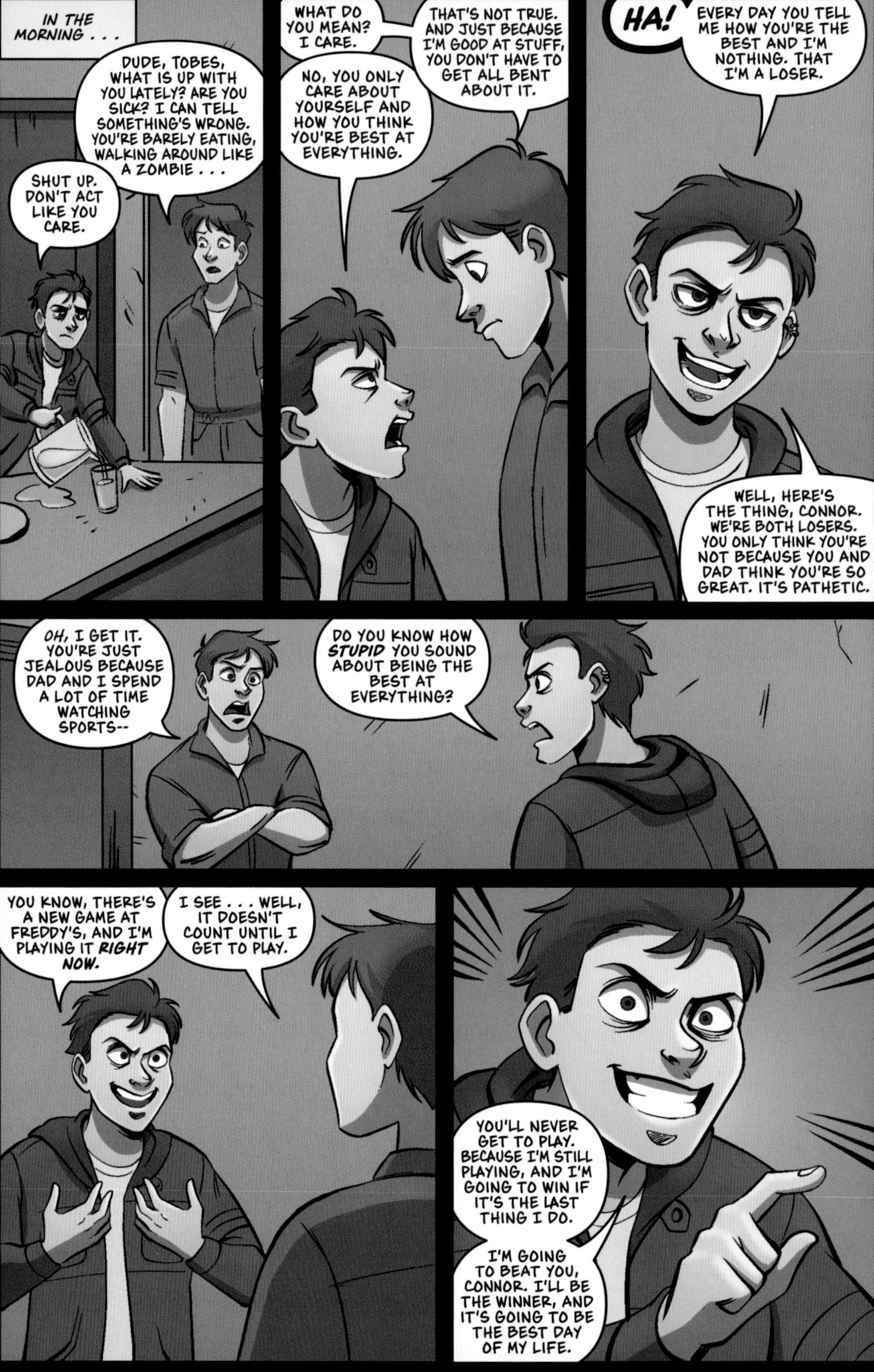
IN THE MORNING . . .
DUDE, TOBES, WHAT IS UP WITH YOU LATELY? ARE YOU SICK? I CAN TELL SOMETHING'S WRONG. YOU'RE BARELY EATING, WALKING AROUND LIKE A ZOMBIE . . .
SHUT UP. DON'T ACT LIKE YOU CARE.
WHAT DO YOU MEAN? I CARE.
NO, YOU ONLY CARE ABOUT YOURSELF AND HOW YOU THINK YOU'RE BEST AT EVERYTHING.
THAT'S NOT TRUE. AND JUST BECAUSE I'M GOOD AT STUFF, YOU DON'T HAVE TO GET ALL BENT ABOUT IT.
HA!
EVERY DAY YOU TELL ME HOW YOU'RE THE BEST AND I'M NOTHING. THAT I'M A LOSER.
WELL, HERE'S THE THING, CONNOR. WE'RE BOTH LOSERS. YOU ONLY THINK YOU'RE NOT BECAUSE YOU AND DAD THINK YOU'RE SO GREAT. IT'S PATHETIC.
OH, I GET IT. YOU'RE JUST JEALOUS BECAUSE DAD AND I SPEND A LOT OF TIME WATCHING SPORTS--
DO YOU KNOW HOW *STUPID* YOU SOUND ABOUT BEING THE BEST AT EVERYTHING?
YOU KNOW, THERE'S A NEW GAME AT FREDDY'S, AND I'M PLAYING IT *RIGHT NOW.*
I SEE . . . WELL, IT DOESN'T COUNT UNTIL I GET TO PLAY.
YOU'LL NEVER GET TO PLAY. BECAUSE I'M STILL PLAYING, AND I'M GOING TO WIN IF IT'S THE LAST THING I DO.
I'M GOING TO BEAT YOU, CONNOR. I'LL BE THE WINNER, AND IT'S GOING TO BE THE BEST DAY OF MY LIFE.

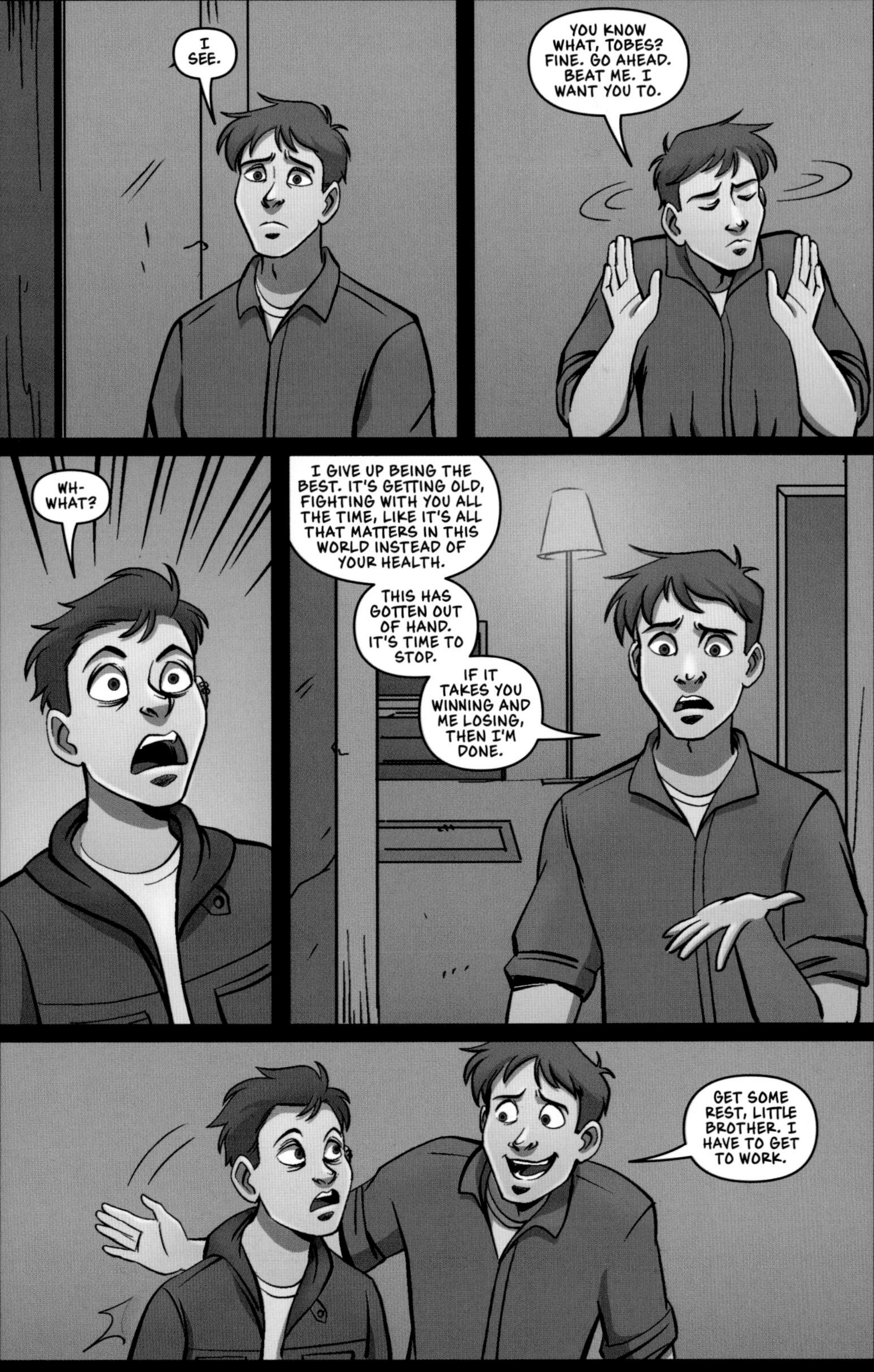
I SEE.
YOU KNOW WHAT, TOBES? FINE. GO AHEAD. BEAT ME. I WANT YOU TO.
WH-WHAT?
I GIVE UP BEING THE BEST. IT'S GETTING OLD, FIGHTING WITH YOU ALL THE TIME, LIKE IT'S ALL THAT MATTERS IN THIS WORLD INSTEAD OF YOUR HEALTH.
THIS HAS GOTTEN OUT OF HAND. IT'S TIME TO STOP.
IF IT TAKES YOU WINNING AND ME LOSING, THEN I'M DONE.
GET SOME REST, LITTLE BROTHER. I HAVE TO GET TO WORK.

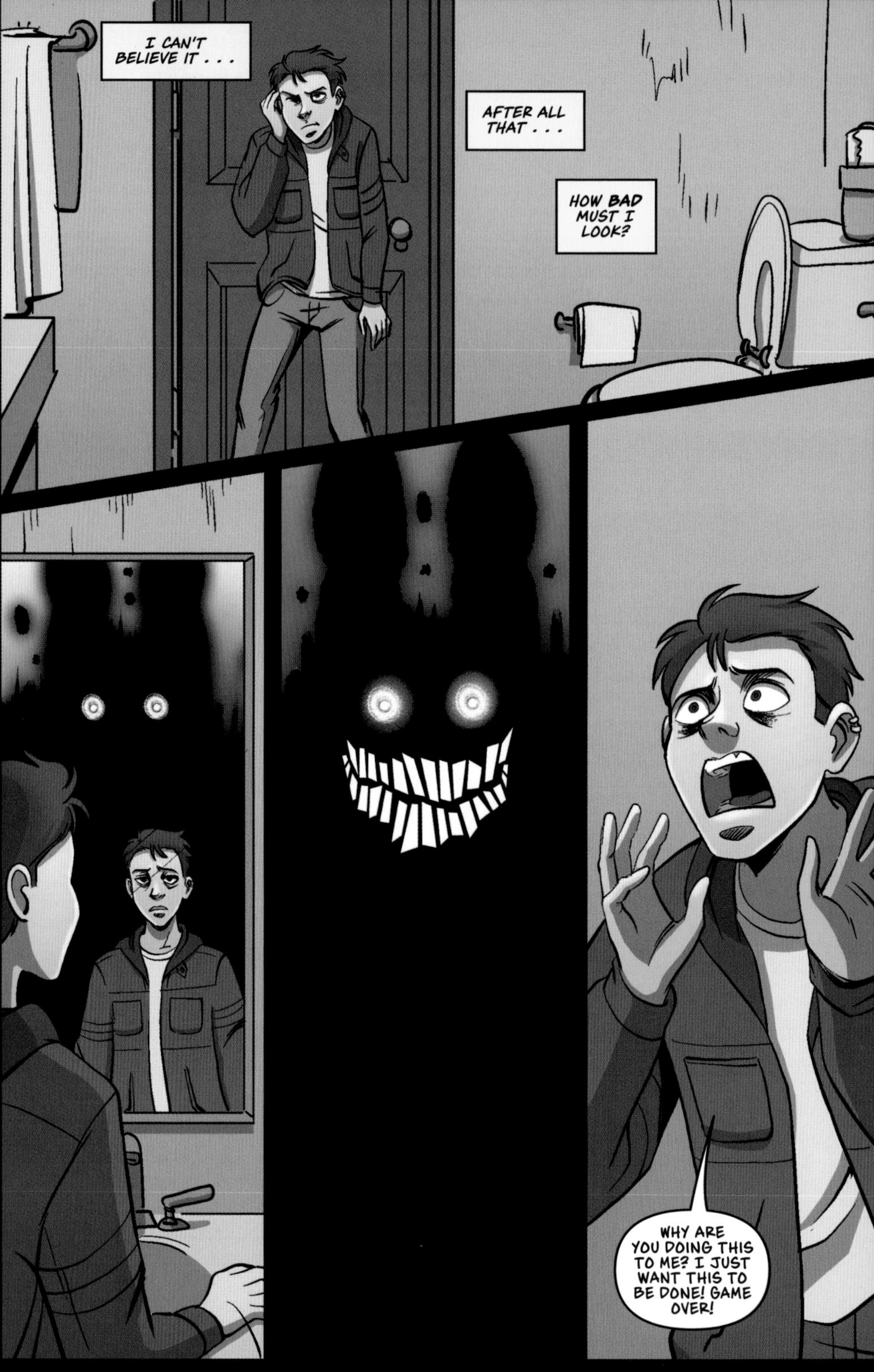
I CAN'T BELIEVE IT . . .
AFTER ALL THAT . . .
HOW BAD MUST I LOOK?
WHY ARE YOU DOING THIS TO ME? I JUST WANT THIS TO BE DONE! GAME OVER!

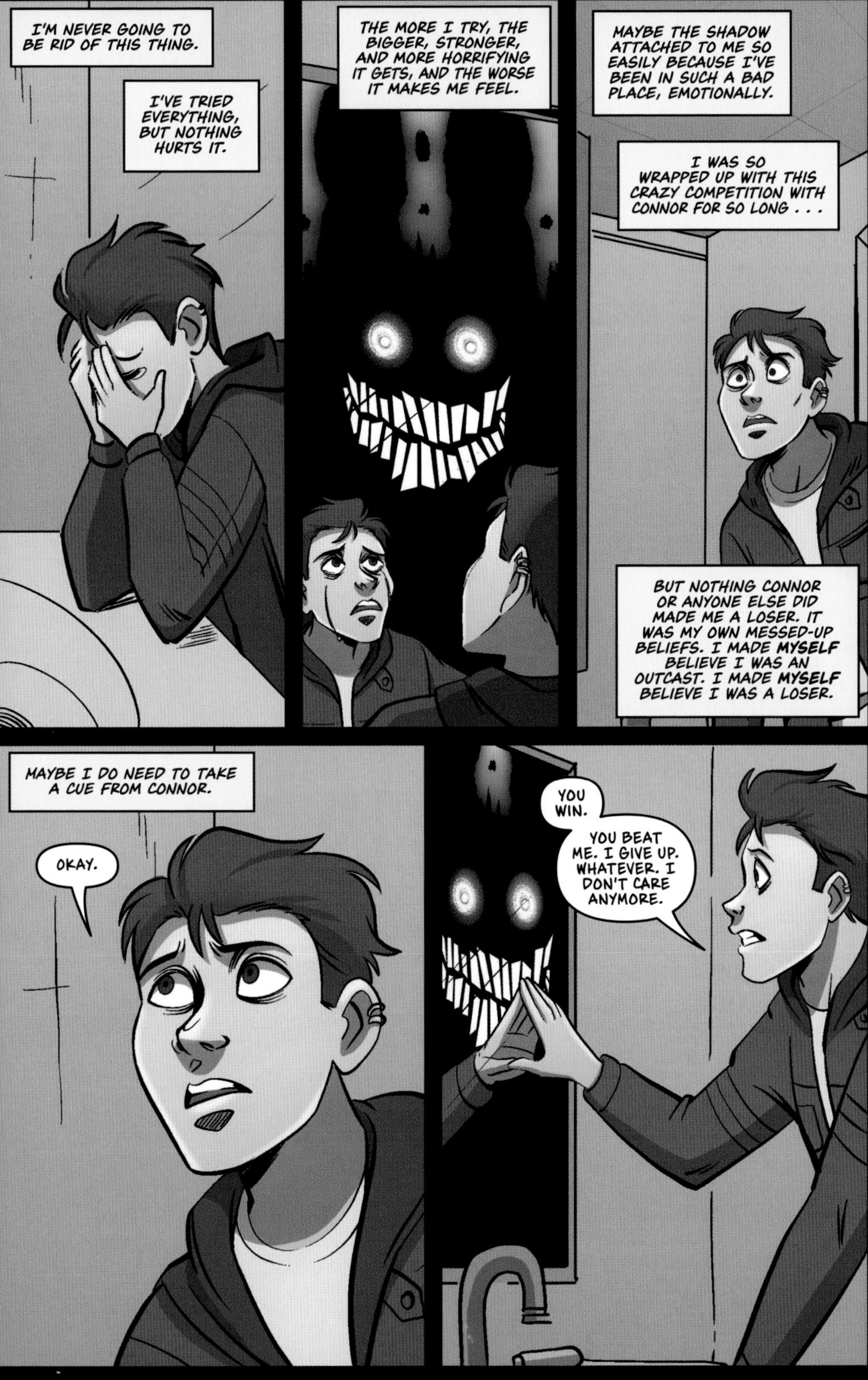
I'M NEVER GOING TO BE RID OF THIS THING.
I'VE TRIED EVERYTHING, BUT NOTHING HURTS IT.
THE MORE I TRY, THE BIGGER, STRONGER, AND MORE HORRIFYING IT GETS, AND THE WORSE IT MAKES ME FEEL.
MAYBE THE SHADOW ATTACHED TO ME SO EASILY BECAUSE I'VE BEEN IN SUCH A BAD PLACE, EMOTIONALLY.
I WAS SO WRAPPED UP WITH THIS CRAZY COMPETITION WITH CONNOR FOR SO LONG . . .
BUT NOTHING CONNOR OR ANYONE ELSE DID MADE ME A LOSER. IT WAS MY OWN MESSED-UP BELIEFS. I MADE **MYSELF** BELIEVE I WAS AN OUTCAST. I MADE **MYSELF** BELIEVE I WAS A LOSER.
MAYBE I DO NEED TO TAKE A CUE FROM CONNOR.
OKAY.
YOU WIN.
YOU BEAT ME. I GIVE UP. WHATEVER. I DON'T CARE ANYMORE.

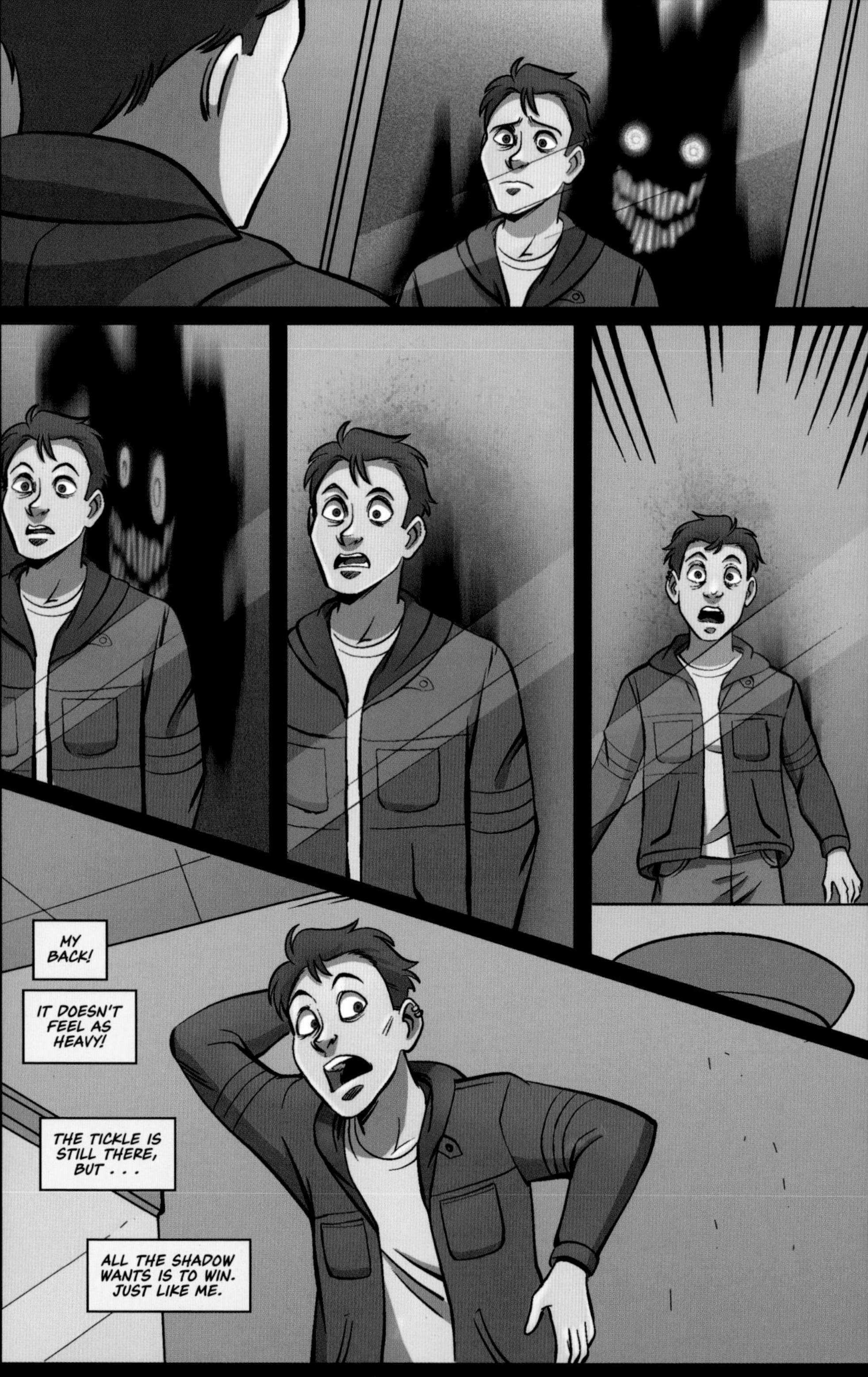
MY BACK!
IT DOESN'T FEEL AS HEAVY!
THE TICKLE IS STILL THERE, BUT . . .
ALL THE SHADOW WANTS IS TO WIN. JUST LIKE ME.

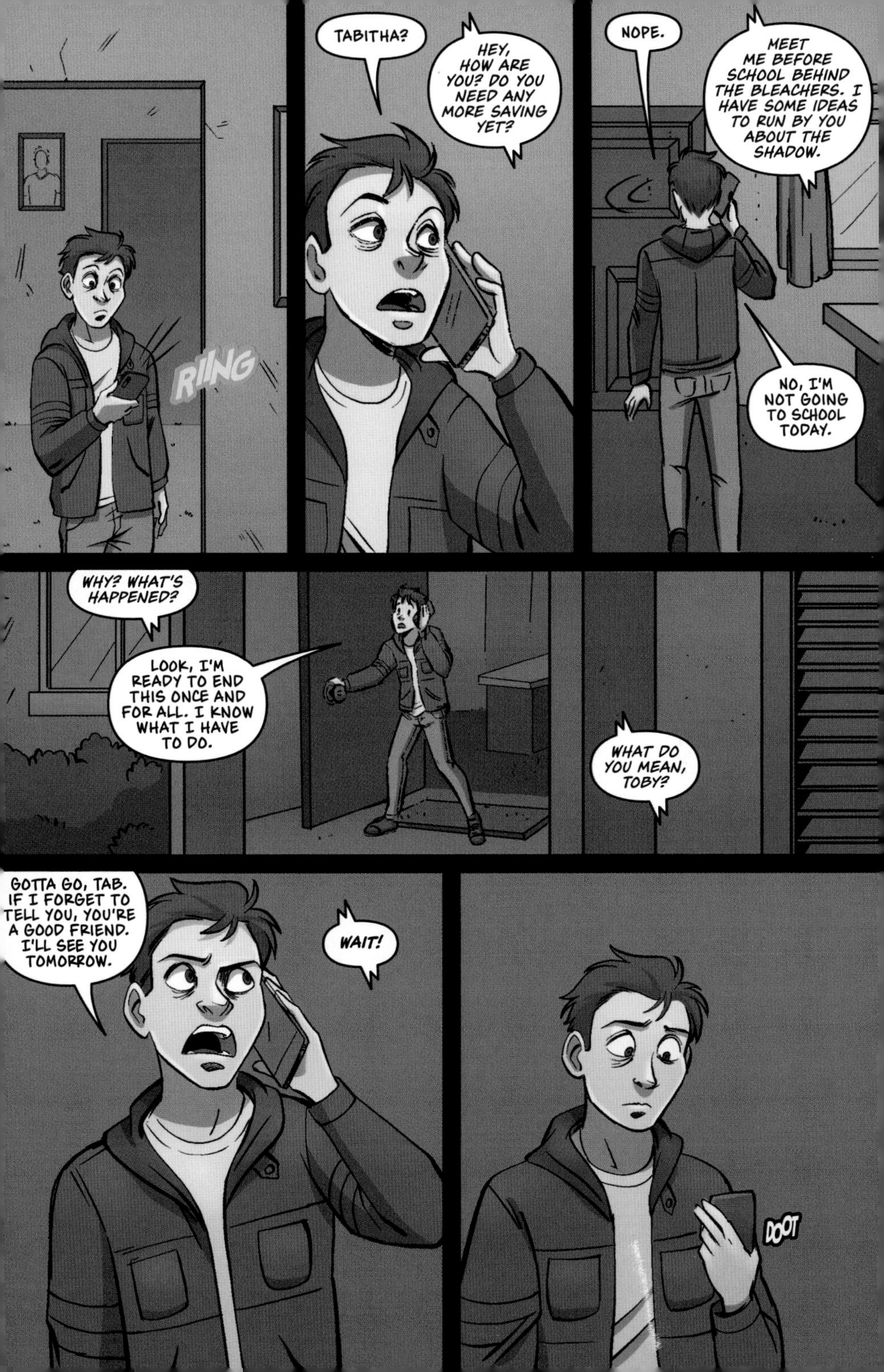
RIING
TABITHA?
HEY, HOW ARE YOU? DO YOU NEED ANY MORE SAVING YET?
NOPE.
MEET ME BEFORE SCHOOL BEHIND THE BLEACHERS. I HAVE SOME IDEAS TO RUN BY YOU ABOUT THE SHADOW.
NO, I'M NOT GOING TO SCHOOL TODAY.
WHY? WHAT'S HAPPENED?
LOOK, I'M READY TO END THIS ONCE AND FOR ALL. I KNOW WHAT I HAVE TO DO.
WHAT DO YOU MEAN, TOBY?
GOTTA GO, TAB. IF I FORGET TO TELL YOU, YOU'RE A GOOD FRIEND. I'LL SEE YOU TOMORROW.
WAIT!
DOOT

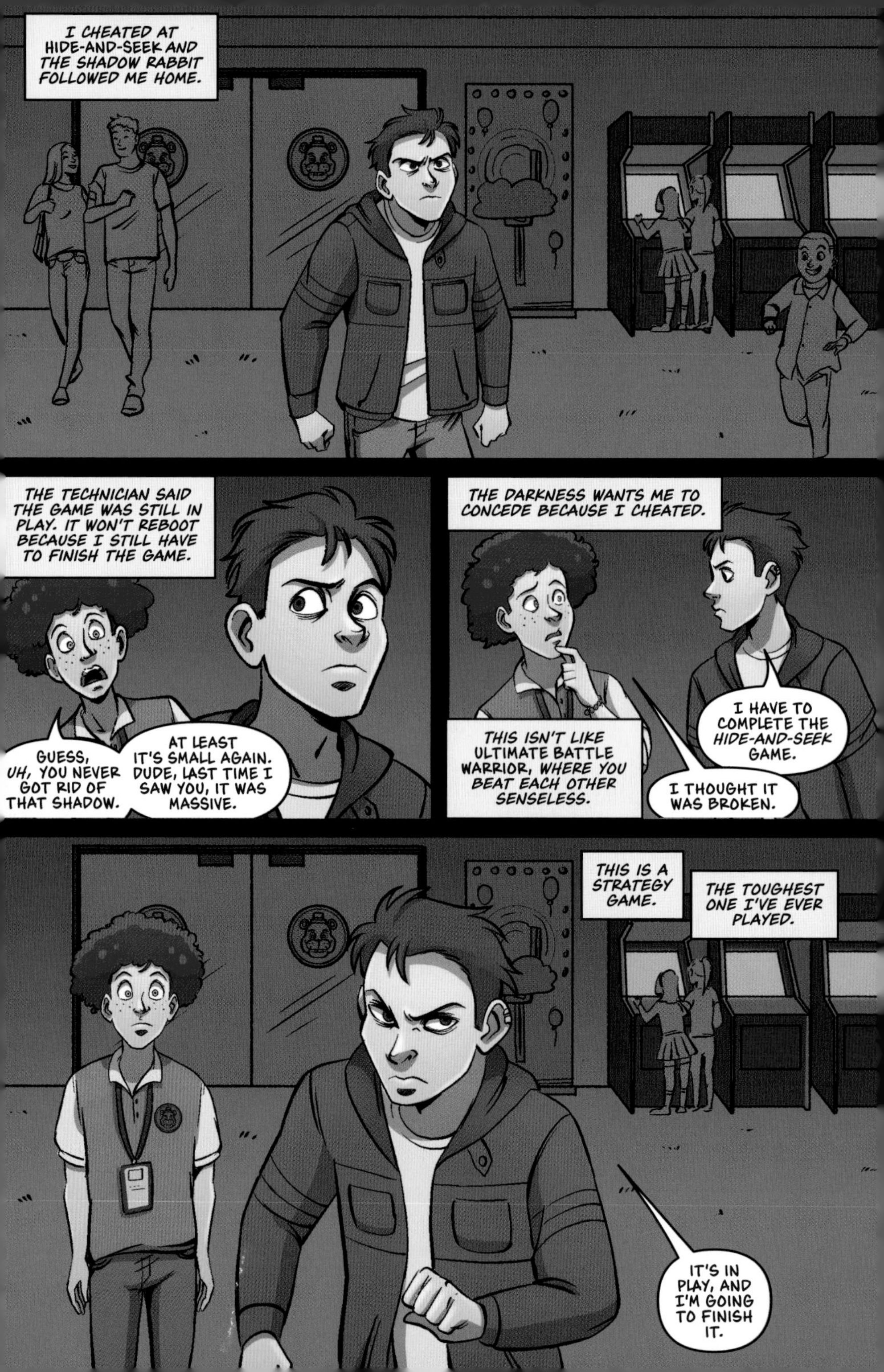
I CHEATED AT HIDE-AND-SEEK AND THE SHADOW RABBIT FOLLOWED ME HOME.
THE TECHNICIAN SAID THE GAME WAS STILL IN PLAY. IT WON'T REBOOT BECAUSE I STILL HAVE TO FINISH THE GAME.
GUESS, UH, YOU NEVER GOT RID OF THAT SHADOW.
AT LEAST IT'S SMALL AGAIN. DUDE, LAST TIME I SAW YOU, IT WAS MASSIVE.
THE DARKNESS WANTS ME TO CONCEDE BECAUSE I CHEATED.
I HAVE TO COMPLETE THE HIDE-AND-SEEK GAME.
THIS ISN'T LIKE ULTIMATE BATTLE WARRIOR, WHERE YOU BEAT EACH OTHER SENSELESS.
I THOUGHT IT WAS BROKEN.
THIS IS A STRATEGY GAME.
THE TOUGHEST ONE I'VE EVER PLAYED.
IT'S IN PLAY, AND I'M GOING TO FINISH IT.

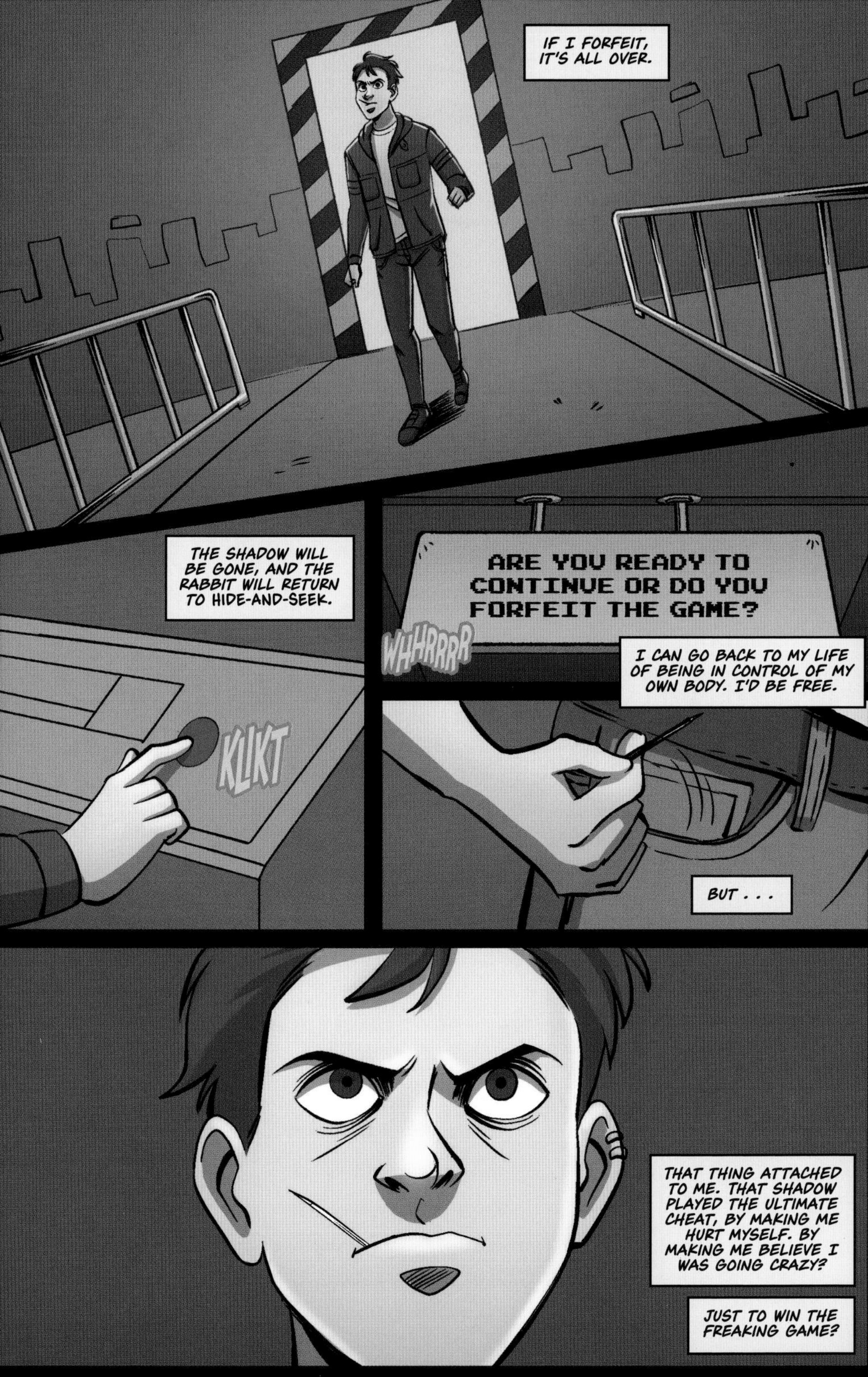
IF I FORFEIT, IT'S ALL OVER.
THE SHADOW WILL BE GONE, AND THE RABBIT WILL RETURN TO HIDE-AND-SEEK.
KLIKT
ARE YOU READY TO CONTINUE OR DO YOU FORFEIT THE GAME?
WHHRRRR
I CAN GO BACK TO MY LIFE OF BEING IN CONTROL OF MY OWN BODY. I'D BE FREE.
BUT . . .
THAT THING ATTACHED TO ME. THAT SHADOW PLAYED THE ULTIMATE CHEAT, BY MAKING ME HURT MYSELF. BY MAKING ME BELIEVE I WAS GOING CRAZY?
JUST TO WIN THE FREAKING GAME?

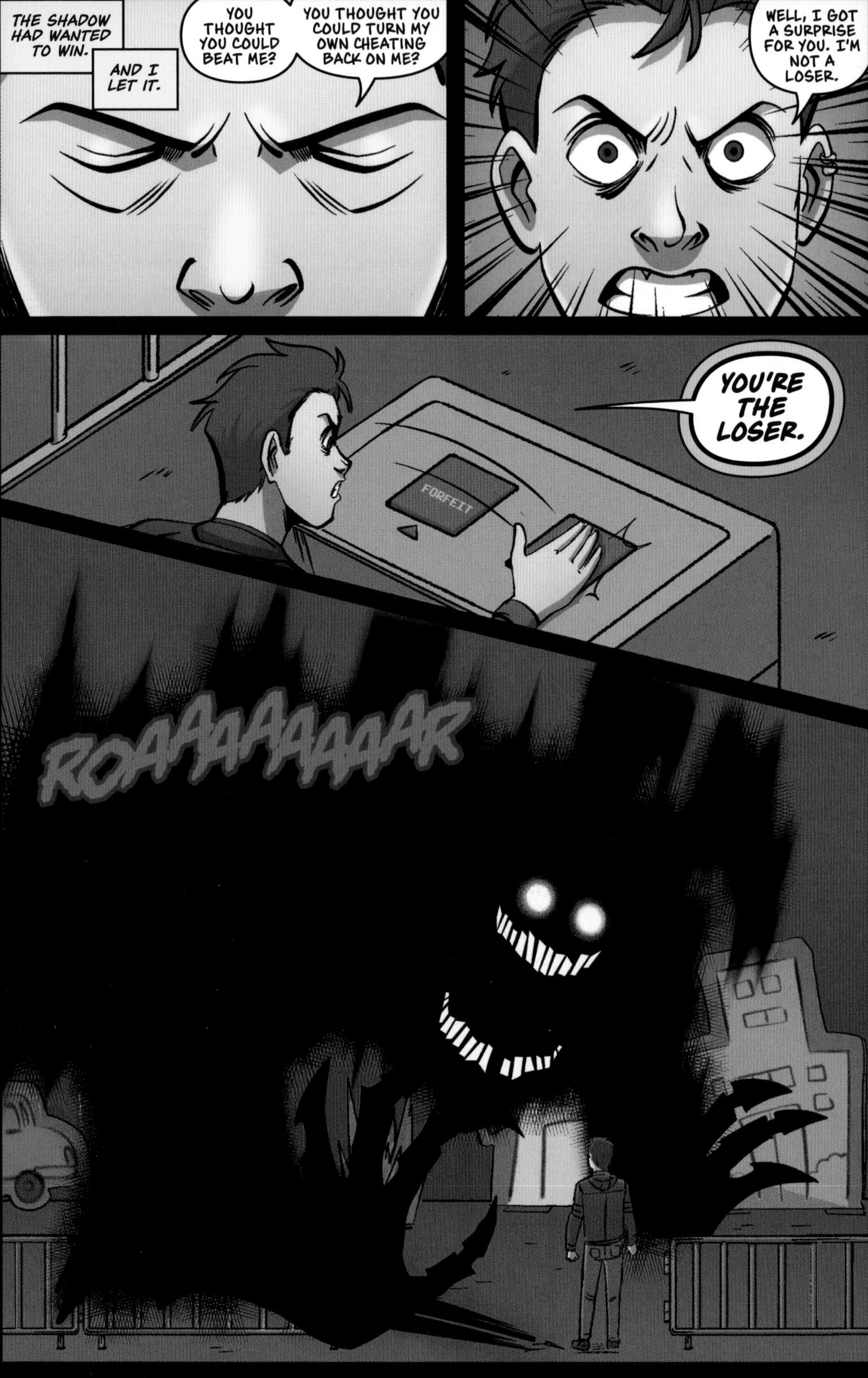
THE SHADOW HAD WANTED TO WIN.
AND I LET IT.
YOU THOUGHT YOU COULD BEAT ME?
YOU THOUGHT YOU COULD TURN MY OWN CHEATING BACK ON ME?
WELL, I GOT A SURPRISE FOR YOU. I'M NOT A LOSER.
YOU'RE THE LOSER.
FORFEIT
ROAAAAAAAAR

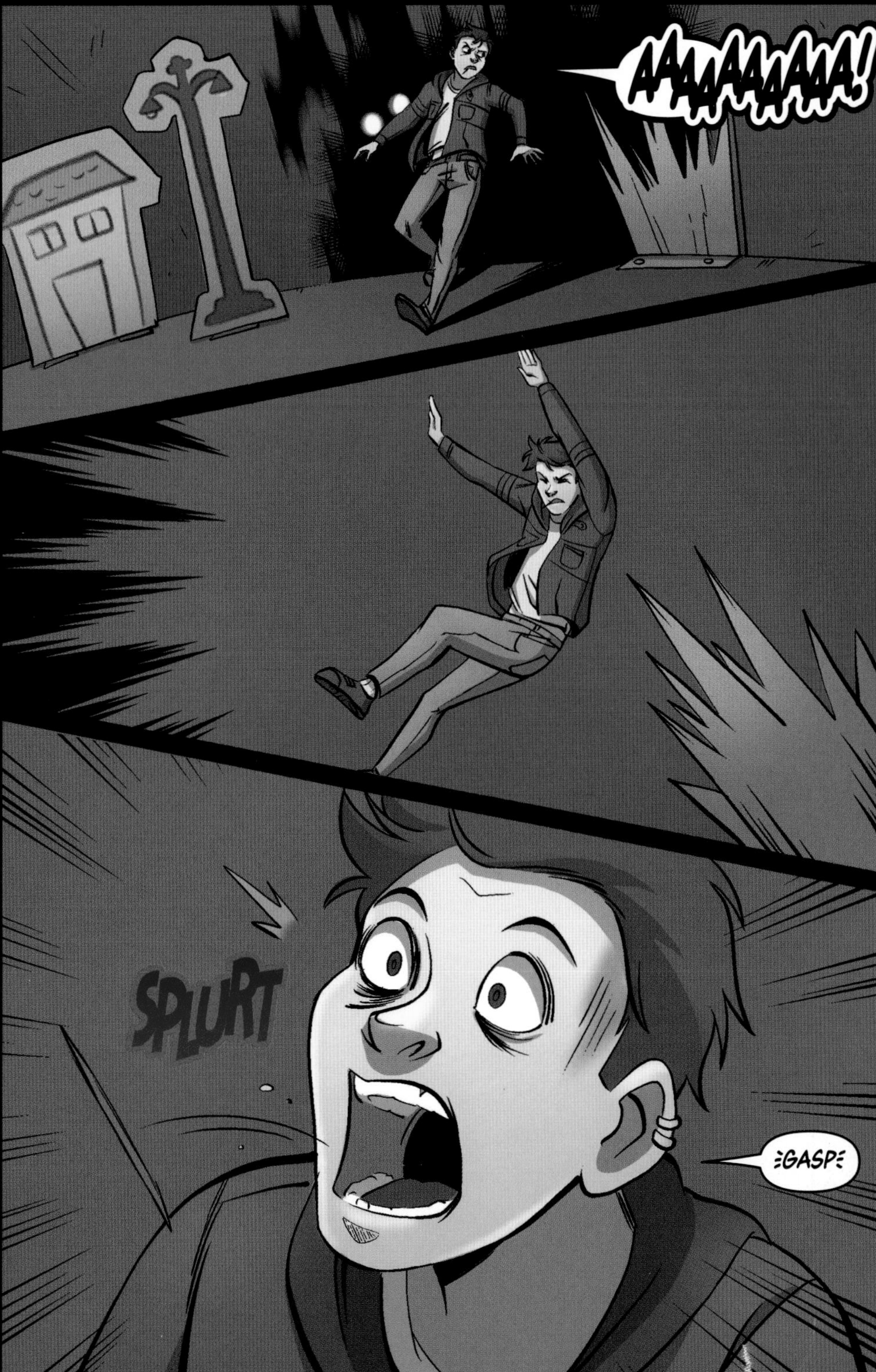
AAAAAAAAAA!
SPLURT
GASP

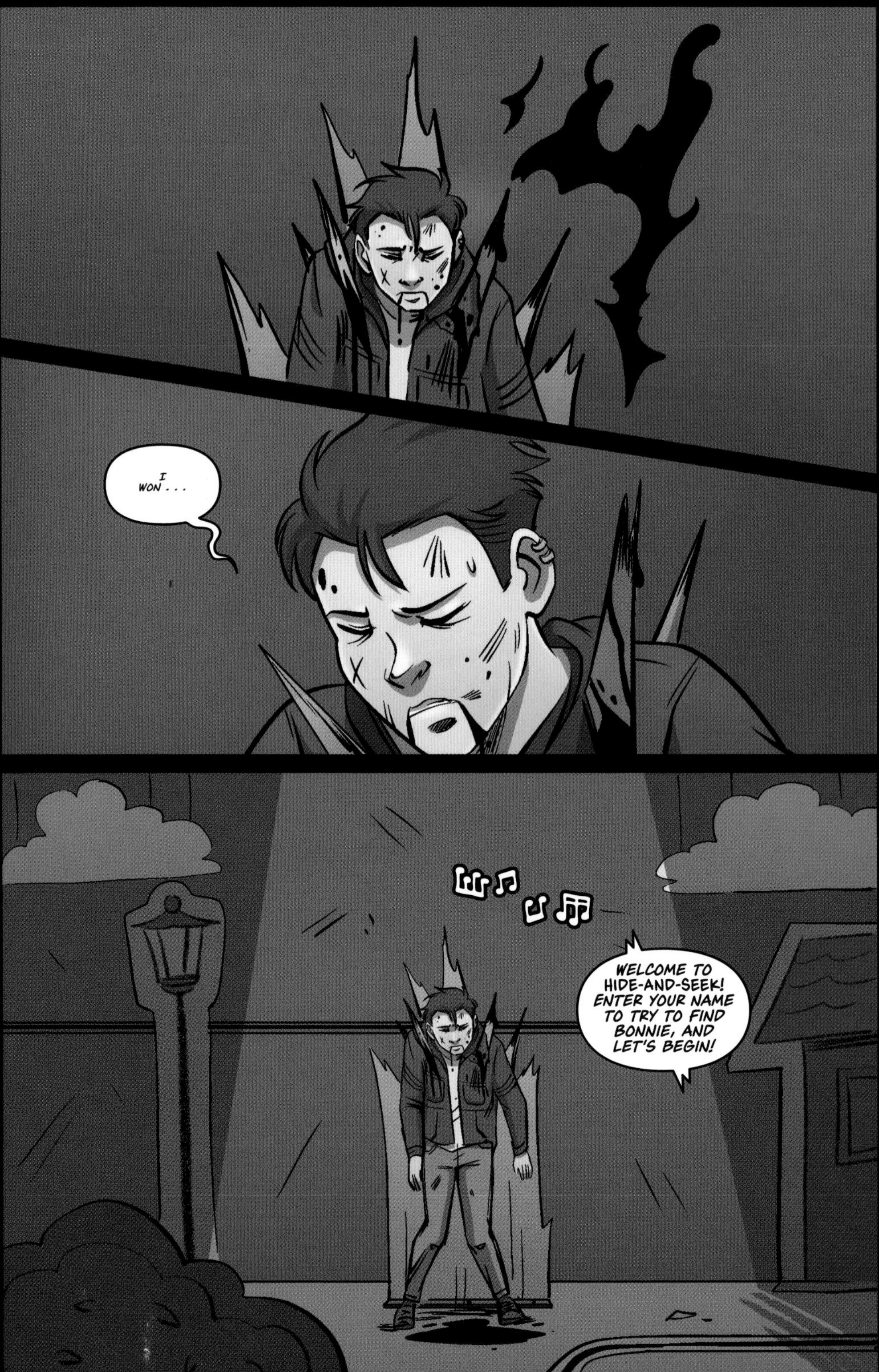
I WON . . .
WELCOME TO HIDE-AND-SEEK! ENTER YOUR NAME TO TRY TO FIND BONNIE, AND LET'S BEGIN!